HIDDEN MICKEY 3 WOLF!

HOW FAR WOULD YOU BE WILLING TO GO TO SAVE YOUR LIFE—AS WELL AS THE POTENTIAL FUTURE OF YOUR BOSS, WALT DISNEY? WOULD YOU PUT YOUR LIFE IN THE HANDS OF A MYSTERIOUS SECURITY GUARD NAMED WOLF WHO SEEMS TO HAVE UNCANNY ABILITIES THAT REACH FAR BEYOND THE REALMS OF LOGIC? WOULD YOU BE WILLING TO BREECH THE VERY FABRIC OF TIME ITSELF TO SAVE WALT'S LEGACY?

WOLF HAS DEDICATED HIS LIFE TO GUARDING HIS BOSS WALT DISNEY. LITTLE DID HE KNOW HOW FAR-REACHING THAT DEDICATION WOULD EXTEND.

DR. CLAUDE HOUSER, A DOCTOR AND SCIENTIST EMPLOYED BY WALT DISNEY, FINDS HIS LIFE AND WALT'S FUTURE THREATENED BY AN UNKNOWN BLACKMAILER. RELOCATING THE DOCTOR WHERE HE CAN'T BE HARMED WOLF TIRELESSLY SEEKS TO FIND AND STOP THIS MALICIOUS VILLAIN. ONLY THEN WILL HE CONSIDER BRINGING THE DOCTOR BACK TO CONTINUE HIS VITAL WORK.

WOLF SENDS DISNEYLAND CAST MEMBER WALS DAVIS TO AID THE DOCTOR AND A DAMSEL IN DISTRESS. WALS NOW FINDS HIMSELF IN A BIZARRE—YET STRANGELY FAMILIAR— SETTING WHERE TIME MOVES DIFFERENTLY AND THINGS THAT OCCUR IN THE PRESENT SEEM TO HAVE A PROFOUND EFFECT ON THINGS THAT HAPPEN IN THE PAST.

IT WILL TAKE ALL OF WOLF'S CUNNING TO BRING THREE VASTLY DIFFERENT PEOPLE BACK THROUGH THE SWIRLING VORTEX OF TIME.

THE LEGEND OF TOM SAWYER'S ISLAND

HIDDEN MICKEY 3

WOLF! ★

THE LEGEND OF TOM SAWYER'S ISLAND

BY

Nancy Temple Rodrigue

NANCY TEMPLE RODRIGUE

2011
DOUBLE-R BOOKS

DOUBLE-R BOOKS ARE PUBLISHED BY
RODRIGUE & SONS COMPANY
244 FIFTH AVENUE, SUITE 1457
NEW YORK, NY 10001
WWW.DOUBLE-RBOOKS.COM

COPYRIGHT © 2011 BY NANCY RODRIGUE
LIBRARY OF CONGRESS NUMBER 1542317321
WWW.HIDDENMICKEYBOOK.COM

HIDDEN MICKEY 3 WOLF!
THE LEGEND OF TOM SAWYER'S ISLAND
VOLUME 3, 1ST EDITION - 2011
THIRD BOOK IN THE HIDDEN MICKEY SERIES

PAPERBACK ISBN 13: 978-0-9749026-4-7
PAPERBACK ISBN: 0-9749026-4-0
EBOOK ISBN 13: 978-0-9749026-7-8
EBOOK ISBN: 0-9749026-7-5

COVER DESIGN BY JEREMY BARTIC
 WWW.JEREMYBARTIC.DAPORTFOLIO.COM
HIDDEN MICKEY PENDANT DESIGN
COPYRIGHT © 2010 BY NANCY RODRIGUE
LIBRARY OF CONGRESS NUMBER 1557245293
WWW.AWESOMEGEMS.COM

PRINTED IN THE UNITED STATES OF AMERICA

*Dedicated to Kyla & Silas,
and especially my husband,
Russ Rodrigue.
Thank you for all your support
and encouragement.
This book would not have been
possible without you.*
Nancy Temple Rodrigue

Disclaimer

Dear Readers,

I am pleased to present to you the third book in the Hidden Mickey Series: *Hidden Mickey 3 Wolf!: The Legend of Tom Sawyer's Island.*

There has been a lot of interest in my new character Wolf who was introduced in *Hidden Mickey 2: It All Started…* He is a very mysterious man and I felt he deserved to have his story told.

I have also introduced a new element into the series— fantasy! You will still find the rollicking adventure you have come to expect in the Hidden Mickey series, but I think you will enjoy the new places to which you will be taken.

You might notice how I used the words "River" and "Island" throughout the novel. While the correct rendering would not involve capital letters, I want you to think of the River and the Island as their own entities, a vital part of the story and the lives of the people therein.

You probably saw my writing partner David W. Smith is not present with this novel. He is working on his own novel, *Hidden Mickey 5: Chasing New Frontiers*, scheduled for release later this year! Then I have Wolf's continuation *Hidden Mickey 4 Wolf!: Happily Ever After?*

Your lingering questions from *Hidden Mickey 2: It All Started…* will be answered in this novel. And, as you have come to expect from Hidden Mickey, a few more questions will be raised in Wolf! I can't make it too easy for you!

So, settle back in a comfortable chair, and "hang on to yer hats 'cause this here's going to be a wild ride!"

Best Wishes,
Nancy Temple Rodrigue

PROLOGUE

Disneyland – Walt's Apartment – 1966

The Blond-Haired Man sat quietly on the red brocade sofa. The two men he was observing were intent on their discussion of cryogenics. Since this particular aspect of their ongoing discussion was not in his field, he sat back and enjoyed the banter as the two debated back and forth. His part was done—for now. He knew there would be a far greater role for him to fill that would come later, hopefully much, much later—that of continuing Walt's work and guarding his legacy. When another hacking cough brought the good-natured debate to a halt, he wondered if it would begin sooner than they all would want.

His friend, Dr. Claude Houser, paused in the explanation he was about to give as the coughing spasm overtook Walt and he tried to catch his breath. Quietly pulling a stethoscope out of his non-descript briefcase, he listened to his boss's breath-ing, a frown crossing his face. "You really need to quit smoking, Walt," he softly admonished as he draped the stethoscope over his shoulders.

Instead of the disagreement both the men expected, Walt gave a sigh and nodded. "Yeah, I know. But, it takes the edge off."

Neither man had to ask what was encompassed in that alleged edge. With another expansion at Disneyland going on, a secret expedition to Florida looking for property, a major animated feature, a few live-action movies thrown in, and their own secretive work, they knew how thinly their boss was spread. Still, his smoking wasn't helping matters.

When Walt didn't get his expected argument, he smiled to himself and brought the discussion back to where he wanted it. "So, am I going to be dreaming the whole time I am…I am… What the heck am I going to be?" he laughed, looking over at his Number One Man. "Gone? Sleeping?"

The Blond-Haired Man gave a small smile. Nobody ever used the "D" word. "Sleeping is a good word." He looked over at Dr. Houser, who simply shrugged and nodded. "We aren't sure, of course. With our cutting-edge technology, it could be as pleasant as a really good night's sleep. I would guess, though, that it would be more like a loss of consciousness."

Walt was quiet, thoughtful, as he wandered out on the patio and stared unseeingly through the wide, open latticework at the backside of the Jungle Cruise. His fingers pulled a couple of leaves off the vine that had been recently planted that would eventually fill in the spaces and give Walt more privacy. Across the wide walkway that ran behind Main Street, though, on the other side of those tall trees, would be the native village. As he stood there, he could hear two shots being fired from a Jungle Cruise skipper as his boat was "attacked by an angry hippo."

When the other two men wondered what Walt was doing out there and followed him as far as the open doorway, their boss seemed to be talking to himself when they heard him say, "A good night's sleep. Yeah, that would be nice...." He broke off when a falling branch caught his attention. Eyes coming back into focus, he spotted a man high up in one of the tall trees on the Jungle Cruise's berm, saw in hand, watching him. Walt gave a friendly wave. Startled, the worker gave a hesitant wave back and nervously began hacking away at another branch that had been damaged by the severe Santa Ana winds that had roared through Orange County the previous night.

Dr. Houser, not as used to Walt's moods as his friend was, looked at the Blond-Haired Man and gave a 'what do we do now?' gesture.

"You have any other questions, Walt? Do you want to look at the schematics again?"

Walt gave a light laugh, his pensive mood broken. "Oh, I'll always have more questions!" he replied as he turned away from the Jungle Cruise and the three friends went back inside. As Claude grabbed a handful of peanuts out of a small crystal dish on the kitchen counter, Walt's eyes kept going above the doctor's head to one of the cabinets behind him. "While you both are here, I would again like to go over the work we have already done in the cavern," he stated, his eyes now looking directly at Dr. Houser. "Do you have time right now?"

"Of course," came the expected answer. "I can

go over the equipment and the calculations once more." He carefully packed his stethoscope back into his briefcase—his medical bag had been prohibited on the property by Walt. Wouldn't look good to see the boss being followed around by a doctor.

Walt looked him over and smiled. "Are you sure you are really twenty-eight? I'd swear you look just like those fresh-faced teenagers we have working here on the rides!"

"Good genes, I guess," was the doctor's standard reply. Sandy haired and boyishly good looking, he was used to being challenged about his age and qualifications. He came to expect that when he graduated high school at fourteen, college at seventeen, then eight years of med school and post-graduate work specializing in cryogenics.

Walt slapped him on the shoulder. "No offense, of course!"

Good-natured, Claude could honestly say, "None taken. Shall we go?" He needed to get back to the laboratory for a shipment he was expecting.

Walt seemed preoccupied again. "Hmm? Oh, you two go ahead to New Orleans Square. I'll meet you in the cavern in five minutes, ten tops."

When the front door quietly clicked shut behind the two departing men, Walt walked over to the kitchenette. He opened the second bi-fold louvered door that had concealed the remaining half of the serving area. Opening the far left cabinet, he moved an unneeded stack of dishes and coffee cups out of the way. Reaching in, way in the back, his fingers closed over a velvet box. Pulling out the black box, he frowned at the dust coating the underside. As he brushed it off, wiping the stains on his trousers, he gave a chuckle. "I guess I can't complain to housekeeping. Would ruin my hiding place!"

Looking around for the best spot to open his prize, he again returned to the patio and the bright sunlight pouring in through the latticework. Opening the box, he once again marveled at the brilliant display of fireworks that exploded off the brilliant red diamond settled within the velvet confines of the container. The gold setting, even though its surface appeared to have been dulled over the ages by the sheen of patina, still glowed in the bright light, and its three familiar circles seemed to greet Walt. "Hello, Mickey. I'd love to hear your story, how you came to be," he murmured as he turned the boxed pendant this way and that in the sun. "Even though I don't know the why and the how, you are still pretty nifty. Maybe now you can give me some assurance of what I am about to do."

Walt reached towards the heart-shaped red diamond, knowing the touch of his fingers would somehow activate this mysterious stone. He was hoping it would once again show him what he so desperately wanted to see—his future. Or, what he thought would be his future....

"Walt? You in here?" came a sudden voice, calling in from the front door. Walt immediately recognized it was one of his Imagineers.

Snapping the lid to the velvet box shut, Walt put the box behind his back as he came back into his apartment, pulling the door shut behind him. "Yeah, I'm here. Supposed to meet some workers in New Orleans Square, though. What's up?"

"It's Mr. Lincoln," he explained, referring to the animatronic figure of Abraham Lincoln over in the ornate Opera House on the opposite side of Main

Street. "During the Gettysburg Address, he tried something different. Thought you would like to see it."

Walt could see the amused smile on the man's face and knew it wasn't something tragic. Relaxed now, he nodded. "Give me a minute and I'll follow you over."

As the Imagineer—a term Walt used for those specialists who designed and built basically everything he needed—turned for the door, Walt hurriedly replaced the box in the back of the cabinet, leaving the door slightly ajar. He didn't have time to reposition the stack of dishes just as they had been, but no one else was expected to come into the apartment.

Walt caught up to the man waiting on the stairs. "So, what did Abe do? Start speaking in Latin?"

"Nope. He bent over backwards from the knees! Scared the bejeebers out of some of the guests who still thought he was real!"

Walt chuckled. It had been a technological wonder to get Abraham Lincoln to rise from his chair to deliver the historic speech. He knew there was always an on-going debate as to whether he was a real man or a robot. This little trick might cool the debate for a little while, but only until the next roomful of guests saw the show.

"Well, let me take a look, and then fix him! I don't want the show closed for days on end. You have until tomorrow."

"You got it, boss."

Tom Bolte, a General Maintenance man, sat

still in his high perch in the tree, stunned. He stared at the empty patio that he had already known led into Mr. Disney's private apartment atop the Fire House. It wasn't seeing The Man himself that had stunned Tom. That was pretty much a regular occurrence around Disneyland these days. No, it was that…that brilliant *thing* Walt had had in his hands moments ago. Even from his high perch about forty feet away, the sparkle, the light, the *fire* had been amazing.

What was it, though? It was certainly red. He could see that very clearly. But, what was red like that? A garnet? A ruby? *Did rubies sparkle like that?*, he wondered to himself. *How the heck would I know with the lousy pay they give me….*

Tom felt his heart start pounding. His discontent with the positions he was assigned in the Park was always forefront in his mind, never far from his hot temper. He had to learn to control his mouth, especially after that first warning he had received from his supervisor. *Supervisor*, he spat. *The man is an idiot. He dropped out of high school and I majored in engineering. They make him a supervisor and me a lousy fix-it guy. They can't even decide what department to stick me in. One day I'm painting some stupid railing, the next day I am changing light bulbs. Today I am stuck up a tree.*

Silently hacking away at a few more tree limbs, he kept looking over at the patio—the off-limits patio, he reminded himself. And who were those other guys, especially that one with the stethoscope? He had to be a doctor. Walt must really trust them to have them in his private quarters. But, Walt hadn't taken out that beautiful gemstone—it had to be a gemstone—until the two of them had left the apartment. Maybe no one else knew it was there....

The saw in his hand quit moving as Tom continued going over and over the scene he had just witnessed, his mind whirling. *I could use a nice ruby like that*, he thought. *Take some guitar lessons. Join a band. Buy a nice house. Get a fancy car. Quit this lousy job.... I just need a plan.*

Tired of straddling the tree branch, Tom was ready to climb down when he had another, sudden thought. *How could I ever fence that ruby? Uncle Charles?* Tom grimaced. Too many questions. The ruby was probably insured and more than likely it would be well-known by those in the know. *Bad idea*, he thought. *Cash is better. Cash is always better.*

I'll bet Walt would give a lot of money to get the ruby back. That sudden thought stopped Tom in his tracks. If he stole the ruby, he could hold it for ransom! Brilliant!

Tom had seen the two men who left first head through the walkway behind Main Street towards Adventureland. It had to be Adventureland, or else they would have used Main Street itself. Or they could be going to Frontierland. Or maybe they had headed to that new land they were still working on, New Orleans Square. He shook his head. It didn't matter. They were gone now and that's all that mattered. Walt had gone across Town Square to the Opera House. That meant the apartment was empty. A slow smile crossed his lips.

A few days later, a stunned Walt was pacing in

front of the sitting area of his apartment, a piece of paper held tightly in his hand. The Blond-Haired Man and Walt's favorite security guard, Mani Wolford, more commonly known as Wolf, were there with him.

"Tell me again the last time you saw the pendant, Walt," Wolf repeated. "I want to make sure you didn't leave out anything."

Walt knew not to get angry with the request. He hadn't left anything out, but Wolf was, well, Wolf. He was thorough, among other more mysterious things. Walt pointed at the Blond-Haired Man and said to him, "You and Dr. Houser were here, going over the final plans for the chamber. I told you to go ahead to New Orleans Square and then, as soon as you had left, I got the pendant down from my hiding place. I was looking at it out on the patio when I was interrupted. I quickly put the box back on the shelf in that cabinet and I left. It took just a few minutes to sort out the Lincoln problem, and as soon as I was finished, I met with you and Dr. Houser under the Pirates of the Caribbean construction."

"You didn't come back here at all that night?"

"No, I got too busy, and then I went home. You know how it is. I was at the Studio for the next few days." He shook his head, thinking back. "This is the first time I have been back since then. And I found this note where the pendant should have been. That was when I called both of you."

"You notice anyone suspicious recently?"

His boss shrugged, bothered. "I don't know everyone any more. It's all too big now. I can't say I have seen anyone suspicious and I can't say I haven't."

Wolf looked at the Blond-Haired Man. "I assume it is safe to say that you, Walt and I are the only three people who know about the pendant? Well," he amended, sourly, "Four people, including the culprit, I guess. Dr. Houser never saw it, right?"

The other two men nodded. "No sign of forced entry," Wolf observed, looking around. "Nothing else out of place. The person who left the note apparently knew where your hiding place for the diamond was. You must have been watched, Walt." He walked over to his boss to read the note again, catching a faint hint of eucalyptus as he walked over the plush floral carpet.

*"I have your ruby. It means nothing to me, but I know it means a great deal to you, Walt. I suggest a trade—your ruby for $100,000 cash. No tricks, no trying to follow me. Have your doctor make the drop. I'll be watching to make sure he isn't followed and he goes exactly where I tell him. Here is the first place I want him to go. It's a clue, so pay attention. **I found the bubbling pots of mud refreshing**. When he figures this out, I will give him more instructions once he arrives there. You have one week to get the money or the ruby will be cut into much more manageable sizes. And if you try any tricks, the doctor will pay with his life."*

"Do you think he touched the stone?" the Blond-Haired Man wondered, looking at Wolf.

Frowning as he thought, Wolf gave a one-shouldered shrug. "Personally, I don't think so. The note would have been worded much differently or else there wouldn't be a note at all. He would have just kept it."

"We can't risk Dr. Houser." Walt's words were low, almost unheard.

"What did you say, Walt?"

He turned to face his companions, pale. "I said the doctor cannot be risked. Not to mention his own personal safety, I have too much riding on all this for him to be possibly hurt. My whole future is at stake." It wasn't a lack of compassion. It was an honest appraisal of the truth.

"We know, Walt," his right-hand man said softly. "We don't want to endanger either one of you. Claude doesn't even know about all this yet. Are you going to tell him, or do you want me to?"

"This Dr. Houser...does he have any family? Wife? Kids?" Wolf wanted to know.

The Blond-Haired Man shook his head. "Nope, it's always been just him. I don't know what happened to his parents, but they have been gone a long time."

"Why? What does that matter? What are you thinking, Wolf?"

Wolf went to the patio door, looking over towards Frontierland, unseen through the trees of the Jungle Cruise. He took his time to answer. "I agree with Walt. We can't risk the doctor. There is nobody else with his expertise in cryogenics. Even though he doesn't have all the answers now, he will. This situation puts him in real danger, and, if he is in danger, as I think he is, he needs to be protected. Do you agree?"

Slowly, both men nodded, even though they weren't sure which one of them Wolf was asking. "Do you have an idea? This embezzler will be expecting the doctor to follow his plan."

"Yes, I have an idea. I will follow the trail. I don't look much like him, but I think I can pull it off by wearing his hat and coat."

"If I have been watched, it stands to reason

that Dr. Houser has been watched, as well," Walt reasoned with the scowling security guard.

"I seriously doubt this thief has ever seen the doctor face to face, Walt, and I think this will work."

"But...but...if he did see the doctor, and then he sees you instead at the bubbling pots...this still puts the doctor in real danger. This lunatic said he would kill him," Walt paused here and let that sink in. Frowning, unable to come up with any solution of his own, he then continued, "So, what do you propose to do to protect him?"

Wolf paused. He didn't like having to resort to this. There were too many variables. But...it would do for the time being. "I can move him," he explained quietly.

The other two men remained silent, their lips compressed. It was what they were afraid Wolf would say. The thought made their blood run cold. "You sure that's the only way, Wolf?"

"Well, according to the note, we are running out of time. I can deliver the doctor to a safe place and he can stay there until such time as the pendant is returned and this man is caught. As long as he is at large, I agree that the doctor is at risk."

"No other options, Wolf?" Walt asked.

"I can't think of any." Wolf looked at the Blond-Haired Man. "You?"

"He won't be injured? You'll be able to bring him back?"

Wolf looked out of one of the windows at the lowering sun. "It has to be tonight. No, he will be fine...startled, but fine." *Coming back is the tricky part,* he mumbled under his breath. Turning back to his two bosses, Wolf asked, "Can you get the money by tomorrow? I already know where to go for the first clue."

In spite of his nervousness, Walt managed a smile. "Yeah, that part was pretty obvious. Where else but Nature's Wonderland in Frontierland? Maybe this guy isn't as dangerous as we think he is. That wasn't very well thought out."

"Sometimes the less intelligent ones are the most dangerous. They take risks that aren't thought through. The money?" he repeated.

"Tomorrow morning," Walt promised. He sighed and looked at his companions. "Well, we'd better call Dr. Houser. I have a feeling he won't like this very well."

Wolf looked at the Blond-Haired Man. "Could you have the River shut down for the night? I'm going to need it."

Repressing a shudder, he nodded and picked up Walt's phone. He had a couple of calls to make.

The Island – 1786

Smoke from the cooking fire curled slowly up-wards. The gray-headed Cooking Woman stirred the massive black pot suspended over the low flames. A stack of broken firewood sat nearby, a small child waiting patiently to feed the fire. A tall woman, dressed in fringed deerskin pounded white and beaded at the neckline, approached, her hand resting easily on her protruding stomach. Out of re-spect due the wife of the Shaman, the Cooking Woman bowed her head and waited for the other to speak.

This amused Tacha. "You helped raise me, Cooking Woman. You needn't stand on ceremony like that."

A smile flitted across the otherwise serious face and quickly faded. "Oh, I know. It is to teach the young ones respect. How are you feeling today? Any kicking?"

As the hand on her stomach moved in a circle, a pleased, maternal smile transformed her already lovely face into a radiantly beautiful face. "He is quiet today. His brother Mato gave me no peace when I carried him. It is a pleasant change."

"Perhaps this one will be a great thinker." The Cooking Woman motioned for the child to add another couple of sticks to the fire. "The Shaman and the men will be back from their hunt soon. Do you think they will find your wolf?"

The reference made Tacha shudder. Her peaceful life had been disrupted by the appearance of a huge, dark wolf lurking on the outskirts of their village. It had never ventured into the camp, but seemed to be watching only her. When she went out with the women to gather, its presence could be felt by her alone, watching, waiting. She would turn suddenly and see the huge head slowly withdraw behind a tree or a boulder. After she told her husband, the braves had been unable to track the wolf. It seemed to sense their thoughts and intentions and they could never find even a trail of him. Its cunning was…unnatural.

Tacha could almost pinpoint the date when the wolf first appeared. It was right when she discovered she was expecting another child. Since then, the joy had been overshadowed by this unwelcome presence lurking outside the encampment.

"I hope they find it," Tacha hissed with an angry flash in her eyes. "I can always use another fur to warm our bed."

Five-year old Mato was standing out on the log protruding over the River, his white shaggy dog Suka next to him. Both of them were peering into the dark green water, watching the fishing line Mato had tied to a branch and jammed into the log to hold it upright. A flicker of movement in the dense trees caught Mato's eye. Peering into the darkness he thought he saw another dog crouching down, his bushy tail up and waving. Ignoring the warning bark of his smaller dog, the huge one playfully jumped up and nodded his head at the little boy. Turning, the dog ran a little deeper into the trees. Looking back over its shoulder as it ran, the dog seemed to be waiting for the boy. Delighted with the idea of another pet, Mato commanded his upset pet to stay and watch for a fish. Without a backwards glance, he took off running in the direction of this new dog.

Tacha was approaching the fishing log when she saw her son signal for Suka to stay and then run into the forest. Used to the energetic youth, she smiled and held back from calling him in to his lessons. Her smile faded when she peered through the trees and spotted the object of her son's interest. Without another thought, she broke into a run and plunged into the darkness after the boy.

Hearing the pursuit of two humans now, the wolf slowed and circled back toward the sounds of the woman. He smiled to himself as the boy stopped in confusion, not knowing where the animal had gone. He didn't want the boy. He wanted the woman. He had been impatiently waiting for her for months now.

Tacha refrained from screaming for Mato. She hoped he would become wary as he had been trained to do and return to their home. Screaming wouldn't help anyone. Her blood turned cold when she heard a branch snap behind her. *How did that happen?* she frantically thought to herself. She slowly drew the knife out of her boot and turned.

It was too late. The crash of a body colliding with hers knocked her sideways. She cradled her stomach and curled to protect the baby. The feeling of fangs puncturing her arm was her last remembrance before the world turned black and she fainted.

The softness of rabbit skins. The smell of fish broth. Cool hands touching. Fire raging over her skin. Moist cloth washing over her face. Soft words murmured in the distance. A kicking sensation deep within her body. Darkness, always darkness. Mato crying over her.

It was only those sensations that Tacha could grasp as reality. The wolf's bite had infected her and she had not regained consciousness in weeks. The women came in and cared for her and tried to comfort both the dismayed Mato and the distraught Shaman. He wouldn't leave her side. The oldest brave took over the needs of the encampment.

"The wolf still lurks outside the village," the brave told the Shaman one day. "He is getting bolder. He is letting himself be seen."

"Is he getting reckless?" the Shaman wanted to know.

The older brave thought before answering. "No. He seems to be waiting, watching. We want to know if you want us to go after him."

"You will not go without me," he commanded. "And I cannot leave."

The brave didn't like being ordered into inaction. He wanted to revenge the woman and protect the camp. But, respect for their leader made him acquiesce. With a silent nod, he backed out of the tipi.

A painful groan came from his wife, her back arching against the pain. "Call the women!" he ordered. "I think it is her time."

The women quickly arrived and, against custom, physically pushed him out of the tent. The hide flap was lowered in his face when he tried to protest. The watching braves surrounding him knew to keep their faces straight.

The sounds of a painful childbirth came from the Shaman's tent. When it seemed he couldn't take it any longer and made an attempt to rush in, the sounds within were replaced by the high-pitch cry of a newborn. The strain of worry was eased by a self-satisfied, silly grin on his lined face.

"She calls for you," the Medicine Woman told him as she stuck her head out of the flap, motioning for him to hurry. "She is very weak. I don't think she…." She broke off, unable to complete the sentence, her eyes filled with tears.

Alarmed now, the Shaman pushed past her, and kneeled at his wife's side. A small dark-headed bundle, wrapped in rabbit skins, was at her side. He touched the baby's soft red face just as the baby opened his eyes. His filmy eyes were a beautiful bright sapphire blue. He lifted his gaze from his child. "Tacha," he whispered gently, caressing his wife's ashen face.

Her eyes briefly opened and she managed a small smile. "You have another son," she managed to say before becoming exhausted.

The Shaman tried to hold down his terror. She was so pale, her breathing almost non-existent. "You rest, O Lyokipi."

She didn't seem to hear him or the use of his pet name for her. "Our son." The words seem to float from her rather than being spoken. There wasn't much time left.

"He will be a strong warrior. You must get better so we can name him when the time comes." *Please let that time come.*

"His name is Sumanitu Taka."

The Shaman's mouth fell open in surprise. "Wolf?"

"Yes." The sound was faint as the last breath left her body. The hand he was holding went limp.

The rogue wolf was pacing at the edge of the forest, and at just that moment the entire encampment heard him let out a loud, triumphant howl as he disappeared into the darkness. It was done.

At the sudden, abrupt noise—the reminder of what had caused this tragedy—the Shaman quickly rose from his wife's bedside. The women, surprised by his movement, jumped back. Grabbing up his bow and arrows that were leaning against the side of the tent, he rushed out into the center of the village.

"Come with me!" he commanded to his men, raising the bow high above his head.

There was a flurry of activity as the men rushed to their dwellings for their arms and they quickly followed the Shaman. "Where?" he demanded.

The oldest brave pointed to the north.

Without another word, he plunged into the forest, following a faint trail of bent leaves and displaced pine needles. The wolf would not make this easy. He tried to lose them by taking to the water where the River bent so he wouldn't be seen. His ability to leap over boulders showed an agility not normally seen in wolves. He doubled back on his own nearly-invisible tracks and hid in a cave until the war party had passed. Emerging, he followed their footsteps back towards the direction of the encampment. When the sound of their pursuit again reached his sharp ears, his tongue lolled out of his head as if he was laughing at them. They would be getting tired by now.

He plunged into the River again and easily swam across the green waters. Once on the other side, he sat and waited until the braves emerged from the forest. He wanted to make sure he was seen, and when the men took to the water, he loped slowly past the waterfall. Cocky, he sat to let the men imagine they were catching up to him. Not paying attention to the sounds that were being muffled by the thundering water cascading behind him, the wolf had misjudged and didn't hear the men until they were almost upon him. An arrow flew past his head, missing by mere inches.

Jumping to his feet, the huge animal took off in a run, his head thrown back, a loud, lingering howl coming from his throat.

A fog suddenly seemed to seep from the river, swirling with low, misty fingers. Ignored by the braves, the fog became thicker as they ran after the fleeing wolf. By the time they reached the Beaver Dam, they could no longer see across the river, had they cared to look. A sudden wind picked up, gusting past them in a swirl of leaves and dust.

A flash of lightning and instantaneous thunder sounded around them. The wolf, seeing that he was rapidly approaching the unsteady Beaver Dam, quickly surmised that it was too new and rickety to run across. Swimming the beaver pond would expose him. He had forgotten that. He glanced at the lightning flashing around him and turned, snarling at the slowly approaching men.

A bow was raised, but the Shaman gave a sharp command. "This one is mine!" As he raised his own bow, he quickly notched his longest arrow.

The men were startled when a bolt struck the water and traveled straight towards them, a swirling vortex of black water appearing before it. The wolf snarled at them once more and bunched his legs to leap.

The arrow was loosed at the same moment the wolf leaped towards the angry agitated water. It struck the wolf directly through the heart and, twisting at the pain, he soundlessly fell on the riverbank.

The lightning, the thunder, and the yawning blackness all vanished when the wolf fell. And just as suddenly, the wind settled as if it had never been.

Unseeing and unmindful of the mysterious force of nature he had just witnessed, the Shaman had only one object in his mind. His knife in hand, he slowly approached the fallen, unmoving wolf. He could see the huge sides of the animal barely rise as it tried to catch its breath. Keeping a safe distance from the deadly claws and being mindful of the sharp canine teeth, the Shaman held the knife steady.

As he neared the head, the eyes opened suddenly. In that flash, the Shaman saw the same piercing sapphire blue eyes he had seen in his infant son. Those eyes momentarily narrowed with cunning. "Doksa ake waunkte," the wolf managed to whisper before his brilliant blue eyes rolled back into his head and the Shaman knew it was dead.

Without a word to his wary men, he plunged in the knife and got to work skinning the huge animal, the words echoing through his mind: *I will see you again later.*

As the years passed, the boy Sumanitu Taka grew as all boys do. He showed signs of early strength and agility. His father, proud of his tall dark son, watched from beneath the wolf headdress and skin robe he always wore in honor and remembrance of his wife. Sumanitu Taka took the teasing of the other children over his bright blue eyes stoically and figured he must have them for a reason. He knew the story of his birth and the subsequent death of his mother. He also knew the story of the wolf skin robe his father wore. When he became taller and faster than the other boys, the teasing stopped. Except for his brother Mato. Named after the bear, Mato had strength of his own. But Wolf could still outrun him.

One day, when the men were gone on a hunting foray into the forest, the boys were playing near the River. They had gathered near Bear Country, a favorite fishing hole for the forest animals. The boys were displaying their own talents as only boys can do. They would prance and preen as their name-sake animal would, playfully challenging their play-mates with their respective cries.

Wolf easily leaped to the top of the nearest boulder and howled at his surrounding cousins. They called back at him and laughingly threw rocks that he easily dodged. At his next howl, however, the entire group of boys was startled to see an in-stant change in the weather. As a thick mist started to roll in, they could hear the sounds of a storm that was rapidly approaching, causing the boys to be-came silent and wary. None of them had ever seen storms come upon them like this. The season was not right.

The storm came in more rapidly than they thought it should and the River quickly turned ugly and threatening. They backed away in fear as a swirling dark mass of water opened in front of them.

Eyes wide, Wolf walked slowly towards the void, gazing into the blackness as if he was drawn to it. Rushing forward, Mato threw his arms around his brother, holding him tight and not letting him continue. Wolf struggled against his brother's re-straint, having an almost uncontrollable urge to throw himself into the water and allow it to envelope him completely.

In a matter of moments, the swirling water seemed to fall in upon itself and recede. The wind buffeting against the boys died down and soon all was back to normal. Only then was Wolf able to relax in his brother's arms. Without a word, Bear released him, eyes frowning, as they all hurried back to their camp.

In a private conversation with their father, Bear

tried to explain exactly what had happened back there at Bear Country. His face half concealed by the wolf headdress, Bear could still see the expression on his face, as he went pale at the news.

As Bear went to sleep that night, his father just sat staring into the dying fire. Both he and his son were sure of one fact: if that strange phenomenon were ever to appear again, Wolf would go through it.

CHAPTER ONE

Disneyland – 1966

"Tell me, Doctor, do you speak French?"

Dr. Houser's eyebrows went up in surprise. That wasn't what he was expecting. Actually, he had no idea what to expect when he had been summoned back to Disneyland, but his knowledge of languages certainly wouldn't have been at the top of his list. "Yes, fluently, as a matter of fact. Why?" He looked over to Walt and then back to his friend, the Blond-Haired Man. They, too, seemed to be waiting for Wolf to continue. Getting no response from them, he turned back to the black-haired security guard who had asked him the odd question.

It was dark out now, late in the evening. The white lights outlining the buildings on Main Street could be seen through the front window of Walt's apartment, casting a festive glow on the somewhat somber men gathered inside. The doctor had been the last person to join the group when they reassembled in that private room. He had been confused as well as concerned by the late call from the Blond-Haired Man who asked him to come right over, bring his medical bag, and—for some unknown reason—to dress in the oldest dark suit he owned. He had never before met this particular security guard and stood uneasily as the mysterious, silent man circled him after he had first arrived, apparently looking over his choice of clothing.

There was a tension in the air that he could feel, and it was the doctor who broke the uneasy silence. "What's going on? I was asked to bring my bag. I thought I was never supposed to do that. Are you ill, Walt?" he asked, turning to his boss and choosing to ignore the scrutiny he was receiving.

Walt gave a sigh and looked away for a moment. How does one explain something like this? Walt always believed in being direct, so he figured he might as well follow that principle now. "Please take a seat, Claude. No, I'm fine. Well, I'm as fine as I can be right now. Actually, this has more to do with you right now than me. There was something stolen from me the last day you were here. Something very important to me." He held up a hand to stop the protest that he could see forming on the doctor's face and gave a small smile. "No, no, I don't mean to say that you took it. Not that at all. Just a second, here." He opened a drawer in his desk and pulled out a sheet of paper. "I was left this ransom note from the person who did take it. He demands a certain amount of money, which I am, well, not happy to give him, but will do so just to bring all of this to an end. You are involved because he demands that *you* personally make the exchange. He gave specific instructions on what was to be done and said to make sure that you weren't being followed."

The doctor's frown deepened as he sat back in his chair, thinking this over. "That's odd. Why would he pick me? I'm not exactly well known here at the Park."

Shaking his head, Walt shrugged and made a wide gesture that took in the many windows on the walls. "We can only figure he has somehow been watching this room and has seen you come and go. Perhaps he has seen us go to the chamber. We don't know. I hope not," he mumbled more to himself, knowing what would happen if that hidden chamber and its contents were discovered. "What bothers me most is that he threatened you," Walt stressed, waving the note.

"I'm not afraid for myself," Dr. Houser asserted, unconsciously forming a fist.

"We are," stated his long-time friend, spreading his hands out in front of him. "We are dealing with an unknown here, Claude. We don't know what he is capable of. We are very concerned for you and feel that you need Wolf's protection. That is why Mr. Wolford is here."

Turning in his chair to face the security guard he thought was still standing behind him, Claude was startled to find Wolf now standing over by the patio window. Seeing him stare out the window, arms folded, Claude thought he gave off the air of being either detached or disinterested in the ongoing discussion. Nor had he spoken since his odd opening question to the doctor. Claude wasn't sure why the man was even here with his friends and colleagues and wanted no dealings with him. "No disrespect, Mr. Wolford, but I don't need a body-guard. We are probably just dealing with an unhappy employee who saw what he thought was a chance to make a quick buck."

Aware of the doctor's veiled animosity towards him—his voice inflection and body language spoke that loud and clear—Wolf turned from his scrutiny of the patio. *This has to be the place the blackmailer used*, he was thinking. *But, who?* His contemplations interrupted, he turned his full attention to the room. He had heard every word. He just knew his participation hadn't been needed until now. "We can't take that chance, Doctor. Not with you. Not with Walt. There is a lot at stake here. And," he added, his gaze steady on Doctor Houser, "I'm not here to guard you. I'm here to take you to a safe place."

"Oh." The doctor relaxed from his tense posture. That wasn't what he expected to hear. He had been braced for a fight. "I assumed you meant you were going to follow me around or something. So, if I am taken somewhere safe, who, then, will make the drop?"

"I will," Wolf stated. "I'll use your overcoat and hat." Knowing better than the others that they needed to get on with it, that time was quickly running out, he looked at Walt. "Do you want to tell him, or do you want me to?"

"Tell me what?" The wary stance was back.

"Where you are going."

Three sets of eyes immediately turned to Walt. He took a deep breath. "I'll tell him, from what I understand of the process. Claude, here's the tricky part," Walt started, coming over to the man and putting a concerned hand on his shoulder. "Since we don't know who we are dealing with and what they are capable of doing, you need to be put in a place where they can't possibly reach you. If they know you well enough to name you here, they could also know where you live and, more importantly, where you work. If they *do* know where you work and the nature of your specialty—and how it relates to me...." He paused a moment to let that sink in before continuing. "Wolf can put you in a place where even the FBI couldn't find you if they tried. He assures me you will be perfectly safe. You just need an open mind...." Walt broke off, unsure of what exactly his mysterious security guard had in mind and what all was involved. He gave a pat on the doctor's shoulder and began a nervous pacing of the room. "Wolf?"

"Have you ever been to New Orleans, Doctor?"

That, also, was unexpected. "Uh, no. Never got that far south. Is that where you intend on taking me?"

"Yes," Wolf replied slowly. "And no. Hopefully, with you being a scientific man, you can appreciate what I am about to tell you and see it as a possible adventure."

"Go on." Claude sincerely doubted it, but would at least hear him out.

"I have a...unique ability to move in a different way. We three have talked it over at length and feel it would be best if you could go to New Orleans until such time as I solve this mystery and know for a fact that both you and Walt are again safe."

"What do you mean by move in a different way?" he asked, his eyes narrowed. "Do you have a side job with Global Van Lines?" He tried to make it sound humorous, but there was no amusement in his eyes.

Wolf didn't give the doctor the satisfaction of a

self-deprecating smile that indicated he realized how odd it all sounded so far. He simply ignored the last comment. "You will be going to New Orleans…only when you arrive you will find it will be around the year 1815 or 1816."

The expected stunned silence greeted them as Claude tried to work his mind around this preposterous statement from Wolf.

"And we have to go tonight," Wolf continued after a few silent seconds ticked by, glancing out of the window again. "I'm pretty sure the portal will be open tonight. The fog is already gathering over the River." He didn't mention how he felt the electricity along the back of his neck and the change forming deep inside his body.

"And you expect me to both believe you and actually go…somewhere…with you?" He looked unbelievingly at the other two men in the room. There were limits to being considered good-natured. This was preposterous.

Walt came back to the doctor and put a calming hand on his shoulder. "I know this is a lot to take in all of a sudden, Claude. But, we really feel, at this point, that you just need to trust us in this. I sure as heck don't understand all of it, but I have seen evidence that Wolf has done this many times over the decades. I've known him for many years myself and I trust him implicitly. I'd like to try it myself, but he won't let me!"

Claude looked over at his silent friend. "And you? You believe this?"

The blond head nodded slowly. "Our friend Wolf is a unique man. I trust him with my life. And yours. And Walt's." He paused and added, "You need to do this, Claude. We think it is the only way to assure your safety, as well as Walt's future. You know what all's at risk."

The doctor's brown eyes turned to scrutinize Wolf, to see some flaw, something they must have overlooked to believe this wild assertion he had just made. Wolf's unblinking blue eyes met his steadily. There was no deception in them. He believed every word he said.

His heart pounding, Dr. Houser shook his head, unable to believe what he was about to ask. "Let's just say, for the moment, that I agree to this…this…. What can I expect? What will happen to me?"

The other two men again deferred to Wolf. There wasn't any way they could answer those questions. In his quiet manner, Wolf replied, "I have already called for the portal to open." He paused momentarily as the doctor frowned and looked at Walt's white cradle telephone sitting on a side table. Letting that part of the explanation slide, he simply added, "I don't know exactly how or why it works, but it just comes. There will be lightning and some-times thunder and a strange bright light. The waters of the River will become very agitated. In the cen-ter of the water will be a sort of whirlpool. We need to go through that. You will not be harmed. You will be soaked, but not hurt. There will be a little disori-entation. But, hopefully, that will clear up quickly."

"Hopefully?" There was a note of panic in the back of the doctor's voice that he was trying des-perately to conceal.

Wolf gave a one-shoulder shrug. "I can't tell you more. You haven't made the transition before. There isn't any way I could know how it will affect you personally. And, I will be there…in one form or another," he mumbled with a covering cough, "so don't worry. You won't be going alone."

"Just for the sake of argument, how do you know we will end up in New Orleans at the time period you state?"

"The location of the portal here determines the arrival point there. The projected date is just based on the years I have been there in the past. You will need these coins," Wolf added, pulling out numerous gold and silver pieces from the pocket of his uniform. "They are from both Walt's collection and my personal one. Your paper money, of course, would be worthless. And any coins you might have with the current date stamped on them would be awfully hard to explain. You might want Walt to hang onto your wallet, as well. You won't be needing your driver's license."

Claude stared at the various sizes of the coins in his hand. Some of them looked more like silver doubloons than silver dollars. "You are really serious about all this."

"When we come out on the other side, I want you to head for the steamship dock," Wolf continued, ignoring the last remark. "That is the side of the River you will need to be on."

"What's on the other side?"

"Fort Wilderness."

"Of course it is," the doctor mumbled, rubbing his forehead. He was getting a pounding headache.

Wolf went out on the patio and looked through the lattice paneling. The fog had already obscured Frontierland and was drifting towards them over the Jungle Cruise. Coming back inside, he told the doctor, "We *really* need to go."

Standing alone with the doctor at the edge of the River near the canoe dock, Wolf gave him a minute to watch the water as it foamed and turned in on itself. He wasn't unsympathetic towards the doctor—he could smell the barely-concealed fear emanating from him—but now was the time for action. When the lightning streaked across the sky and began hitting the water, Wolf gave him a few last words of warning, and, hopefully, encouragement. "Keep a tight grip on your medical bag. As a doctor, you will fit into any situation. Remember to go to the French Quarter. I can find you there. Can you paddle a canoe?"

Nodding mutely, the doctor, unable to tear his eyes away from the turmoil in front of him, still not believing what he was about to do, blindly grabbed the paddle held out to him and climbed to the forward seat.

"Aim for the center of the River! Hold the bag and the top of the paddle together," Wolf shouted over the roar of the wind. "Don't lose your bag! Now, go!"

Wolf pushed off from the dock and aimed the little canoe towards the swirling maelstrom.

Unseen by the two men, a squawking flurry of white and feathers got caught in the vortex and the swan was swept in behind them as a final shower of blinding pink flashes faded from view.

"**T**he lightning stopped," the Blond-Haired Man quietly remarked as he turned away from the latticework.

Walt paled. "Then they made it through."

New Orleans – 1814

Rough hands pulled the doctor up onto the wharf. "Are you all right, sir? How you fall in the water?"

"Maybe he's drunk, Silas," commented the second voice. "Set him down here on the dock."

"Dr. Houser," he was able to mumble, trying to rub the water out of his eyes.

"You be needing a doctor? I don't see no bleeding."

He could feel the two men staring at him. Where was…where was…who was supposed to be here with him? They were supposed to go through together…. He couldn't remember. "No. I am a doctor. French Quarter?" His mind was jumbled. "My bag?"

"Uh, you be holding a bag in your other hand. Is that your doctor bag?" One of the strangers squatted down beside him, a look of concern on his weathered face.

Claude looked down at his left hand. His knuckles were white as they gripped the handle of his soggy briefcase. He had to tell himself mentally to relax his fingers. "I thought I was with someone, but I can't remember…." He broke off when he saw a large white boat tied up to the wharf beside him.

Startled, he tried to get to his feet. Seeing how shaky he was, the other two men assisted him into a standing position. "That's the Mark Twain. I didn't make it?" He looked frantically around, trying to peer into the darkness. The area was illuminated only by flickering torches. He could barely see crates and barrels and some kind of wooden wheelbarrow. "New Orleans Square should be all lit up. Where are all the lights?"

"You musta hit your head pretty good," the dock worker mumbled. "Yeah, this here is the Mark Twain. She's done tied up for the night. Supposed to make a run to Rainbow Ridge tomorrow. Jonah, you ever heard it called New Orleans Square?"

The other man scratched his head. "Nope. Just New Orleans, or N'awlins. There ain't no doctor in the French Quarter. If'n he is who he says he is, they sure could use one. It's kinda late, but y'-think maybe Madam Annette will have a room for him?"

"You think you can walk, Doc?" The hands that had been holding up the doctor eased away. When he didn't fall back into the muddy river, they figured he was good to go.

"What did you say your name was?" Jonah asked as the three men finally got moving down the wooden wharf. "You know, just in case I need a doctor some day."

"Dr. Houser. Dr. Claude Houser." He continued walking between the two men, his confused eyes focused on the distant flickering lights of the city. His name and profession seemed to be the only concrete reality he could grasp as his fingers tightened around the handle of his medical bag. "Dr. Houser," he whispered to himself as the wooden wharf soon gave way to a dirt road and the smells of the River fell behind. The ache in his head lessened as he breathed in the fresher air. His fuzzy memory of the flashing lights and the angry water faded as he neared the busy port city of 20,000 residents.

Behind the doctor, out of sight behind a stack of crates labeled "Fort Wilderness" and completely forgotten, Wolf shook the muddy water off of his body. His eyes were thoughtful. "He seemed to be pretty disoriented already." Wolf swore softly to himself. "Was hoping that wouldn't happen this time. Nothing I can do about it now.... Madam Annette's? That's a good place," he nodded in the darkness. "Now I will know where to find him." He looked up at the moon, partly obscured behind patchy clouds of gray fog. "Need to get back. I have a thief to catch...and I really need to stop talking to myself."

Dr. Houser, Silas, and Jonah stopped suddenly. The howl of a wolf floated over them, carried on the misty air. It lingered for a moment before finally fading from their ears. Without a word to each other, unconsciously huddling their shoulders, their pace quickened as they hurried towards the sleeping city.

Disneyland – 1966

"**B**ubbling pots of mud. Of all the stupid places…." Wolf stared disgustedly at the twelve brightly colored holes that were in Nature's Wonderland, part of the popular Mine Train ride in Frontierland. Built up to look like natural pools of mud, each pot had its own air jet from a hidden compressor that led to a metal plate under the surface that collected the air and finally released it to make a large, visible bubble in the thick colored mud. Behind the pots were the geysers, including the largest, "Old Unfaithful—because you never knew when she might blow!"

He set down the black bag that contained the $100,000 ransom money that Walt had gotten from cashing in some of the treasure he had found on Tobago back in 1960. He had had the Blond-Haired Man use his authority to shut down that area of Frontierland, and now he had approximately thirty minutes left before the Mine Train Ride would start up again.

Wolf walked around each hole, hoping to see some disturbed soil that might indicate something was buried rather than hidden inside the mud. When it became obvious that wasn't the case, he knew he would have to search each one of the holes. Arms folded, he glared at the mud pots. The largest were mostly red, yellow and blue pots. There were also a few green and white ones thrown in for nice effect. Looking for some color out of place on the hard-packed ground, Wolf wanted to find a tell-tale drip that would show which pot he needed to search. Again, he found nothing out of place. Removing the doctor's overcoat, he rolled up the sleeves of the white dress shirt he had worn instead of his tell-tale uniform. He tried the smallest pot, one of the red ones, first.

The mud pots were deceptively deep. He was able to reach the metal shelf that dispersed the bubbles. Not finding anything but rocks and the air jets and a few coins tossed in by passing train riders, he tried the other two red ones since his arms seemed to be stained red with dye now. Again he found nothing unusual. Wiping off as much red residue as he could, he tried the largest blue pot. His fingers touched something smooth and square with a large rock on top of it. Frowning, he pulled out a blue-stained plastic sandwich container. Figuring he was probably being watched by the unknown thief, he tugged the doctor's hat lower on his face and held the container up in the air. "I found it, you dirty…." Hearing the sharp whistle of the Mine Train echo in the approaching tunnel, Wolf scooped up the overcoat and the money bag and hurried behind the colorful layered rocks that lined the railroad tracks. The geysers started spouting as he ducked down out of sight and settled with his back against the red and yellow rocks that looked as if they had been transplanted from Utah's beautiful canyon land.

The bright yellow Mine Train engine came to a stop just short of his hiding place as Old Unfaithful grandly took to the air, sending a fine mist of water over the passengers seated in the open train cars. Once the geyser stopped, the train continued on its way through the Balancing Rocks and disappeared into the waiting tunnel and the lovely Rainbow Caverns.

Wolf pulled open the sandwich container with his now blue fingers. He found the plastic was filled with sand and dirt, obviously to weigh down the container so it would not float to the surface. He glanced at the dirt at his feet and noticed that it wasn't the same as the dirt in the container. Reaching in with his fingers, he found a buried piece of paper. He couldn't help but notice that it was written in the same handwriting as the first note. *"Hello, Doctor, I want you to wait three days. Then leave the money in the 'microwave oven'—like that would really work—and your ruby will be where it tells you to go. If you are not followed, that is."*

"Microwave oven? What the heck is that?" Wolf mumbled to himself as he headed for a nearby access tunnel used for the trains. This tunnel would put him on a road going around most of the Park that the maintenance workers used to remain unseen by the Park's guests. It would also give him time to think. "Why am I smelling eucalyptus again?" he wondered, bringing the container up to his sensitive nose. Glancing around, he saw only pine tree needles and some kind of oak. He put the container out of sight in the pocket of the doctor's overcoat. "Where are there ovens in the Park other than the restaurants? Does he work in one of the restaurants?" Wolf had more questions than answers right now. And, he had only three days to figure out the puzzle and then make the drop. Realizing he was still probably being watched, he headed for Main Street and would leave the Park the same way the guests would so that hopefully his *real* identity would remain undetected. He couldn't very well go back to the Security office. After all, he was supposed to be Dr. Houser.

During the next three days, Wolf was busy visiting the various kitchens of the nicer restaurants in the Park. As he didn't know who the man was that he was seeking, he was careful with his questions. Since his intuition told him his quarry was a man, he decided to only ask the women servers. The women were more than happy to assist the tall, dark mysterious security officer—the same women that he had been eluding for years.

The answer he was receiving was the same everywhere he went. "I have no idea what you are talking about. What is a microwave oven?"

Frustrated, Wolf aggressively started going to some of the restaurants outside of Disneyland. Again, no one could tell him anything that helped him locate this mysterious oven, or anything that helped him identify the mysterious thief. With the days counting down, he figured he might need a little help, so he headed to the home of the Blond-Haired Man in the Fullerton Hills. If Wolf had been seen inside Walt's apartment with the other men, it would not do to be seen with him inside Disneyland. He navigated the curves with ease in his brand new Mustang. It was the only item he owned that he had bought solely for vanity.

Smiling as he drove, he thought back to the day when he had dropped into the McCoy Ford dealership on West Lincoln Avenue in Anaheim. The new '67 models had just come out a few months earlier and there it was…a bright red 1967 Mustang GT, the Fastback model. It had two wide racing stripes running over the hood all the way to the tail end of the car. Hearing the roar of the great-sounding 427 engine, it just spoke to him. He had settled into the black bucket seat and immediately demanded, "Lé mázaska tóna he?" to Richard, the confused salesman. With a silly grin on his face, Wolf didn't even realize he had reverted to his native tongue. "Never mind the price. I'll take it!"

He roared to a stop outside the hilltop mansion. Like all his neighbors, the Blond-Haired Man had heard him coming. "This is a heck of a car, Wolf," he commented as he slowly walked around the machine.

"My father will be pleased to know I still have a Mustang," Wolf kidded. "My brother Mato's mustang isn't nearly this fast."

Knowing Wolf wasn't still talking about cars, his boss smiled to himself. Figuring his friend didn't come by just to show him the new car, he asked, "How is your investigation coming? Any leads yet?"

Wolf's rare levity faded. He grimaced and looked away. "There are a few conflicting elements I am trying working around. I know he has to be a worker within the Park; I am just narrowing down the areas I think he might be in. I do need some help, though," he admitted, pulling out the paper he had found inside the sandwich container. "For the life of me I can't figure out what a microwave oven is! I have asked around in ten different restaurants and no one knows! How can I make the drop if I don't know what it is and where I need to go?"

Arms folded across his chest, his boss gave a broad grin. "I've never seen you flummoxed before, Wolf. This is a historic occasion."

Wolf snorted. "Glad to see you are finding humor in this. I was under the assumption there was a lot at stake here."

The Blond-Haired Man put a friendly hand on Wolf's shoulder. "You're a good man, Wolf," he stated with an understanding grin. "And, yes, you are correct. This isn't a time to be joking around. I am assuming you didn't check out the 'Atoms for Living Kitchen'?"

Wolf gave him a glaring stare and said nothing.

Unfazed by the surly reaction, his boss grinned again. "Monsanto House of the Future. In Tomorrowland?"

He could see recognition settle onto Wolf's face. "That big ugly plastic thing? Oh, of course. But, what is a microwave oven?," the security guard asked, referring to the note again.

"Best not let Walt hear you call it a big ugly plastic thing...," he coughed, and then shrugged. "Best explanation I have heard is that it can cook food in minutes using some kind of rays." He shook his head. "I don't know. Not my area of expertise or interest. Monsanto or somebody else must be working on one for Walt to add it as an appliance in his House of the Future."

Wolf was still unimpressed. "At least now I know where to go. Whatever it is…."

It was already one day passed the prescribed waiting period. Dressed in the same coat and hat as before, Wolf entered the distinctive four-winged plastic house sitting at the entrance of Tomorrowland. He had to wait—somewhat impatiently—as the few guests inside finished their walking tour and left the building. Climbing over the ineffective rope barrier that was deterring guests from going too far into the kitchen, he was relieved to find an envelope waiting inside a futuristic-looking oven that was supposed to cook an entire meal in just minutes. "If they say so," he muttered, shaking his head in disbelief. Looking around quickly to see if there were any new guests entering the building, Wolf stuffed the black bag that held the ransom money inside the oven, locking the door with a small combination lock that had just been dangling on the latch. Not at all interested in the Bathroom of Tomorrow, he went back outside and found an empty bench on which to sit and read the next set of instructions he hoped was inside.

He held up the envelope and held out his other arm, hopefully indicating to the unknown perpetrator that he was alone and not followed. Opening the envelope, he pulled out a single piece of lined paper. "Good work, Doctor Houser. Yes, I know who you are. If all the money is there, the ruby will be waiting for you in another three days. Look for the out-of-place cabbage at Casey Jr. But I am warning you, Doc, if I see anything that makes me feel uneasy after this is all done, I promise you this—you're a dead man."

As Wolf sat there pondering the next three-day wait, a fellow security guard, Michael, rushed up. "Wolf? Is that you? Nice hat. There's an urgent call. The entire force has been out looking for you."

Hoping his cover wasn't blown, Wolf immediately stood and melted into the crowd in Tomorrowland, knowing Michael would follow. "Slow down, Michael. What happened?"

Taking a deep breath did nothing to calm

Michael. Worry and concern were etched on his young face. "It's Walt. He's in the hospital."

Wolf sat quietly in a plastic waiting room chair, just outside the hospital room's door. To occupy his mind, he pondered over who would possibly have had access to the view into Walt's apartment, and thought about the different people to whom he had already spoken. Clues as to the identity of the blackmailer were swirling around in his mind. Not wanting to leave his post outside the door, he hadn't taken the time to see if the red diamond pendant was really buried in Fantasyland. He watched everyone coming and going, making mental notes of anyone not familiar to him.

The Blond-Haired Man exited the room and indicated for Wolf to follow him. He just shook his head slowly when Wolf looked to him for some word of progress. When they were in a private spot, he told Wolf, "He's asking for the pendant. 'One last time' he says. I…I don't know if that's a good idea or not, Wolf. You know what it will probably show…" he broke off, emotion choking his voice.

"Well, I have no problem with it. If he wants it, he should have it. He might see something good, something hopeful." Wolf wasn't sure either. The mysterious diamond had never worked for him. He had never seen his own future, or anything else for that matter, when he touched it. "I think I am closing in on who did this," Wolf told his friend who was lost in his own thoughts.

The blond head shot up. "Really? You know who it is?"

"Well, I think I have narrowed it down to two possible departments he worked, or is still working in. For a while, with the directions to a microwave oven, I was thrown off the trail, thinking he might be a kitchen employee somewhere. But that sand and dirt that filled the first plastic box kept coming back to me, and there were those smells...." He broke off at the look on his friend's face. Sometimes people just don't want to know all the details. "Anyway, I am now convinced that he has to be either a Maintenance man or a Groundskeeper. I'm not sure which, though. Either department would have given him easy access to the places he sent me...and for watching Walt's apartment. Remember, Walt said he was looking at the pendant on the patio that looked out towards the Jungle Cruise. He mentioned someone he saw trimming those eucalyptus trees...."

"I can make some inquiries."

Wolf's eyes narrowed. "No, I want to finish this. And, Walt will have his pendant tomorrow. I'll bring it to your house tonight." Then, remembering it was past the three days when he was supposed to retrieve it, he added, "I just hope this guy followed through with putting it where he said he would."

The Blond-Haired Man opened his mouth to voice his reluctance, but, at the look on Wolf's face, closed it again. He briefly nodded and turned to go back to the hospital room. There was still a lot of work to be done.

"It all started with a moose."

The words were mumbled, faint. It took too

much effort to chuckle at his own private joke, but the corners of his eyes crinkled as a smile passed over his pale lips.

The only other person in the room glanced up from the paperwork in front of him, a wave of sympathy and grief flooded his face before he could say anything to the man lying on the hospital bed. He self-consciously coughed to clear the lump in his throat. *How am I ever going to be able to carry this off?* he thought to himself before speaking. "You say something, Walt?" he managed to ask out loud.

Walt's eyes drifted back to the present and rested on the man peering anxiously at him. He gave a dismissive wave of his hand, a gesture that rose only two inches off his bed. Energy spent, the hand dropped soundlessly to the covers. "Oh, just having some fun reminiscing."

The Blond-Haired Man gave a small smile. *Maybe now is the best time.* "Wolf sent you something, Boss. I think you will be pleased to see it." With a glance out of the window to make sure no one was approaching the room, he pulled a black velvet box out of his pocket.

A spark of pleasure filled Walt's face. "He found it!" he whispered, content for the moment just to look at the fiery presence. "Did he catch the guy? Is Dr. Houser back?" Walt looked over his friend's shoulder as if the doctor should be walking in the room right now to make everything solid.

The green eyes shifted away from Walt's. "Well, he knows who took the pendant, but the guy is still out there somewhere. We aren't sure where he is right now. And, with the last set of instructions Wolf got, he once again threatened to kill Claude if he so much as got a whiff that we were on to him.

So, no, the doctor is still safe in New Orleans."

Some of the eagerness faded from Walt's face.

"It's all right, Walt. We are still on track with what we need to do. You will be safe," was the sure promise.

The weakness showed itself as Walt tried to reach for the pendant. "I want to touch it again. Just this one last time. You'll have to help me." It wasn't a request.

Swallowing his hesitations on what might happen, the pendant was carefully taken from its velvet cocoon. Holding it by its gold link chain, the slowly turning pendant was held out near Walt's hand. As the pendant turned this way and that, the three circles in the back once again revealed Mickey's outline. That sight brought a smile to Walt's face every time he saw it.

He lifted one finger to touch the cold stone. Just as it had first happened in the jungle of Columbia over twenty years earlier, his mind was instantly transported somewhere into the future. *His* future. Only now he saw a red Monorail hovering a foot above the cement track as it raced across the beloved entrance of his Park. He saw himself walking through a turnstile at the entrance and into the tunnel under the steam train. In the Town Square, he watched as he pushed a button and some kind of clear projection of himself popped out and started a speech....

His hand dropped to the cover of the bed once more. Happiness radiated out of his face. The Blond-Haired Man silently put the mysterious pendant back in its box, chastising himself for doubting. Walt was happy. That was all that mattered.

He thought Walt might have drifted off to sleep

and was going to gather the papers spread out in the room. However, he heard a whispered, "Thank you. You're a good friend. And the doctor is safe. Thank Wolf for me, too." Walt gave a contented sigh and seemed to gather himself. "You know where to put it now?" he asked, indicating the velvet box sitting on top of a little black book.

Nodding, his right-hand man reached over and put the box out of sight, deep into his pocket. He indicated the black diary. "You're sure about this?"

Thinking back on what he had just seen, Walt gave a firm, final, "Yes!"

New Orleans – 1815

"**C**ome on, Doc! The show's about to start. You know Paulette won't go on unless y'all are in your seat!"

Doc gave a laugh. "Now, girls. You know the show isn't set to go on for another ten minutes," as he checked his gold pocket watch and carefully tucked it back in his vest pocket. "Master Gracey here was just telling me about the fine mansion he is building on the outskirts of town near the River. If y'all are real nice to him, he might invite you to dinner some evening," he smiled at the girls hanging on his free arm.

Master Gracey took a sip of his drink and gave a dignified snort. "I think my new bride might have something to say about that, Doctor."

"Probably so, sir, probably so! Still, I would enjoy another tour of your plantation. The views of the River are quite appealing."

"Once the problems with the British are solved—here's to Andrew Jackson's success," as he paused to raise his glass in a salute, and then continued, "we can get back to farming our own land and raising our families. Napoleon sold this land as part of the Louisiana Purchase in 1803. That should have ended the entire matter."

Doctor Houser had no interest in either politics or war. He sipped his own drink politely as his companion continued, only half listening. Watching how the candles burning in the red and white globes of the chandelier made the amber liquid in his glass sparkle and shimmer, he was actually relieved when they were interrupted again.

"Doc!" the feminine voices called again, and this time he allowed the serving girls pull him away from the ornate bar and its etched mirrors. As he grabbed the glass of bourbon in front of him, he gave a 'What can I do?' look to Master Gracey—who was suitably unimpressed by the girls' shenanigans. Doctor Houser was tugged along the wooden floor until they reached his curtained-off, secluded box. Clamoring loudly up the wooden steps, the girls, dressed in low-cut, tight-fitting black lace, bumped the oil painting on the back wall. He dropped into the saloon chair next to the scarred oval table in the center of the little opera box, the red velvet privacy curtain falling back into place. He then gave a contented sigh and propped his booted feet on the dark railing that covered the white carved posts curving outward and over the actual wooden stage. All was lit by brass-backed hurricane lamps.

"Doc is in the house! Start the show!" came

the call from the rest of the audience. Hands slapped the tabletops and boots stomped on the floor. Somebody threw a shot glass at the huge red velvet curtain edged with golden tassels that covered the stage. It ineffectively bounced off the fabric and fell noisily to the stage. At the loud racket, the can-can girls, each with a different colored flounced petticoat showing under her shocking knee-length dancing dress, peeked from the wings and smiled over at the private box. Settled on the doctor's lap, his favorite server, Collette, regally waved the girls away, the feather in her hair tickling his unshaven chin.

The piano player pounded out the opening song as the curtain slowly parted and the Irish tenor emerged to a hail of applause and boos. The tenor who wasn't sure which to believe—the clapping or the hissing—was relieved, once again, that Slue Foot Sue didn't allow firearms inside of her Golden Horseshoe Saloon.

CHAPTER TWO

The Island – 1815

On the edge of the forest in a clearing near the riverbank, a wolf sat at ease on the hard dusty ground. He was a magnificent specimen. His silver-tipped black fur concealed the solid muscle of his 120-pound frame, heavier than the ordinary wolf. He measured forty-two inches at the shoulder, taller than the ordinary wolf. His eyes were masked by dark gray that extended down his pointed nose and around his mouth. There was a small patch of white fur on his broad black chest. The vivid white usually drew the attention of the observer, but only for a moment. The attention was always drawn back to the wolf's eyes—eyes that mesmerized and terrorized almost everyone who looked into them—eyes that were alert, watching, soul-searching, and an intense shade of sapphire blue. This was no ordinary wolf.

Seated in a semi-circle in front of the wolf were four braves. They neither acknowledged nor ignored the wolf. He was just there, as silent and attentive as they were. A slow breeze drifted over them as they sat listening. The breeze carried scents familiar and comforting to them—the ever-present River, the pine trees that surrounded their encampment, occasional smoke from the cooking fire, the deer hide being scraped over in the camp. The smells washed over them and so did the words they were hearing. The words were stories of the past, their past—stories they would pass down to their children and their children's children. Victories. Struggles. Changes. How the flute came to their people. The Shaman spoke in his low, deep voice, his face half hidden by the wolf headdress he wore. A strip of cloth woven in a vivid blue edged with orange was draped over his shoulders as the furred fringe of his deerskin tunic moved in the breeze when he gestured as he spoke. Behind him was a three-sided rocky outcrop that sheltered him from most of the wind that was getting stronger as he continued to teach them. Ignoring the chill and the hard ground on which they sat, the wolf and the four braves, wrapped in their colorful blankets, listened in respectful silence.

"Go now," the Shaman finally told them when the stories were finished. "Go to your homes and remember. Tell the tales to the women and your children—even though they were listening as they prepared the meal," he added with a half-smile. He turned away from them and looked out across the River, dismissing them. As his men filed away, his dark eyes were focused on the Island that was located on the other side of the life-giving River. There was a clearing on the Island way in the distance upstream, barely seen from where he now stood. He could see activity going on there and his smile faded as he watched. There was something else weighing heavily on his mind. He didn't acknowledge the wolf when it came and sat beside him.

"Atewaye ki," the wolf said, respectfully dipping his head.

The Shaman gave a short harrumph. "You call me 'My Father', yet you do not obey me."

The wolf's mouth opened, showing his teeth, grinning only as he could. "Does any son?"

"That is true." He allowed a small smile as he paused before speaking again. There was much he wanted to say, but did not know how much would be favorably received. "You stay on with the wiya. You should be here. This is your home." He turned to look at his son. It was an old argument, one he knew he would not win. He saw the silver-tipped fur on the shoulders rise and fall in an inaudible sigh. The sharp, unnatural blue eyes closed once as the large head slowly shook side to side. The Shaman knew his son was counting to ten before answering him. That pleased him greatly.

"The wiya has a name, Father. The woman is Rose, as you know," Wolf answered, ignoring the amusement in the black eyes that were watching him closely. "After you found her in the River, and brought her back to health, you appointed me as her Protector and she still requires my help. As you also know," he added in an undertone.

Wolf looked back across the River where his father's attention was again fixed. Rose, or Mrs. Stephens as she was formally called, could barely be seen working her meager garden in front of the dilapidated log cabin in which she lived. Her brown mare, Sukawaka, stood and watched patiently from behind a worn split-rail fence. Some clothes were drying on a line and were starting to whip around more and more as the impending storm drew closer. She would soon have to take in the clothes as it was beginning to get dark and they were threatening to blow into the nearby River. Hands on her hips, they saw her look around her clearing and into the dense, surrounding forest. Lifting her fingers to her lips in a most unladylike manner, they heard the remnants of her shrill whistle as it faded in the air around them.

The Shaman looked back at Wolf, impatient and irritated. Wolf ignored him and gave a short answering howl. Rose turned in the direction of the sound, but could see nothing in the great distance between them. Satisfied that he was somewhere nearby, she turned with a smile to her laundry that was threatening to come loose from the wooden pins holding it. Not wanting to have to wash it all by hand again, she quickly got to work.

"You have been summoned, Wolf. Inahni."

"There is no need to hurry." Choosing to overlook his father's sarcasm, Wolf brought the discussion around to where *he* wanted it. "You spoke of changes in your story today. You understand there are changes coming to the Island, yet you choose not to see my part in it. I was chosen to protect—both here and in my other time. Even though I do not know exactly when she came to be here—as you choose not to tell me—we both know Rose doesn't belong in this time, and she should go back soon."

The Shaman ignored Wolf's references to the wiya. "There have always been changes. Some for the good. Some for the bad. I have not seen any evidence of the changes of which *you* speak."

"These changes will be dangerous for the wiya," Wolf insisted.

His father would not let it go. "You must let the changes come as they will. Some get swept away. Others get stronger. Let her be and return to your home. Here, with us."

"Taku khoyakipha he?" asked Wolf pointedly.

"What do I fear?" the Shaman repeated, mildly surprised. He paused. He hadn't expected Wolf to question him. He should have known better. He pulled the wolf skin closer around his shoulders against the chill in the air. His mouth tightened before he answered. His voice, when he spoke, was low, hesitant, as if no one else should hear his words spoken aloud and perhaps make them come true. "I fear you will go through the fog to their world one night and never come back," he finally admitted.

Wolf moved over next to his father and leaned against his leg. He felt the Shaman's hand come to rest lightly on top of his head. "It gets more difficult each time I pass through," he admitted. "The confusion, the disorientation…," he broke off and shook his head, remembering all too well the feeling and hating it. "I will always return, Father," he promised, "Just as I have come back to check on the doctor over time, and the man Daniel Crain that I brought through last time."

"That one is evil," his father commented sourly. "Why did you feel you had to bring him here?"

Knowing which man his father meant, Wolf looked in the direction of the Fort and lifted one shoulder in a shrug. "That was where I was when the necessity arose. I had to remove Crain immediately. Luck of the draw, I guess." He would have smiled if his face allowed it.

"Next time draw from a different deck, my son. He has a hatred of your wiya, you know."

Wolf glanced up at the deceptively passive face. "How do you know that?"

"I am the Shaman. I know everything."

Waiting in silence, Wolf just sat there, staring at his father's face.

"And, your brother told me," he finally admitted with a wry smile.

"That's more like it," Wolf muttered. Mato was always good for news from the Fort. "The wiya reminds the soldier of another woman from his own time, only he doesn't remember that. She is a beautiful blond as well…. Speaking of that soldier, that red pendant I gave you when I brought him here. Is it still safe?"

"No, I traded it for that canoe over there." With a tilt of his chin, he indicated the wooden rack of canoes near the water's edge. "Of course it is safe." The twinkle in the dark eyes faded as he thought about the odd piece of jewelry. It had been hanging from Wolf's jaws, clenched tight as the wolf had swum to the clearing and collapsed at his father's feet. "That stone. It has strange powers. You must be aware of that."

Wolf nodded his head. "It doesn't work for me. Did you touch the stone? Did you see anything?"

His father was silent again for a long time. When he spoke, his voice was low. "Yes, I touched the diamond. What I saw…it did not make sense."

Intrigued, Wolf asked, "Can you tell me or would you rather not?"

"I would rather not have touched it," was the dry reply. "But, I did." He stopped talking and Wolf wasn't sure if he would continue. When the Shaman did decide to tell his story, his voice was hushed, confused. "I saw myself, dressed as I am now. It seemed many seasons went by and the leaves changed and changed again. Yet, I was always as I am now, here within this shelter of rocks, telling my stories to my braves over and over again. I never changed. I do not understand the significance."

Wolf dropped his head and sighed. He thought as to how to explain the village of the friendly Pinewoods. "You will be remembered for ages to come. Your words and stories will be heard by many generations."

That seemed to please his father who instinctively realized he should not question it any further. He said simply, "It is good to be remembered." The Shaman looked up at the darkening sky. The sliver of the moon was becoming obscured by fog. He knew the signs as well as his son. "You will go back tonight?"

"Yes, after Rose sleeps."

Knowing any argument would be fruitless, his father nodded. "Take care, my son."

"And you, atewaye ki."

The Shaman watched as the wolf entered the green water of the River and began the long swim towards the Island. The black shape of the wolf disappeared as the darkness overtook him. Soon the sound of Wolf's strokes diminished and he could hear only the River. He turned towards the cluster of tipi and his dinner, his thoughts sad.

"There you are, Wolf! I wondered what happened to you. I heard you howling a lot earlier this evening. It gave me the shivers! At least, I think it was you. It sounded so…so odd. It was like you were calling for someone and it made you very sad. You sounded more like yourself just a minute ago. Oh, you are all wet. You must have been in the River again. I guess you really love fish for dinner. Come by the fire and dry off."

Rose had stopped her sewing when Wolf padded into the isolated cabin. She had already dropped the heavy beam of wood across the entry door to bar it for the night, knowing Wolf would use his hidden access when he was ready to come home. His blue eyes watched her from across the room. Ignoring the welcome warmth of the fire, he dropped down in the small kitchen and put his head on his front paws, feigning tiredness. He hoped that she would take the hint and go to bed. The storm was almost upon them and he had a lot to do. He gave a huge, tooth-filled yawn.

She resumed chatting as the lonely do when someone or something else is in the room with them. "My, you must have had a big day! You seem awfully tired. I didn't see much of you today. But," she sighed, "I did get a lot done. That laundry takes me all day. Looks like a storm might be coming in. What do you think?"

Wolf yawned again, and stretched out on his side, breathing evenly.

The second yawn worked. Rose put a hand over her mouth to cover her own. "Oh, excuse me! Well, perhaps it is getting late. My eyes are pretty tired." She put her sewing back into the wicker basket and gave a resigned sigh as she started changing for bed. Rose had been alone all day and had been looking forward to having a "chat" with her wolf. Disappointed that he was so tired, she blew out the tallow candle she had been using and let the remaining firelight guide her to her small bedroom.

Eyes opened to small slits, Wolf watched and waited patiently until all movement inside the other room stopped. Knowing how lonely she really was, he would have preferred to sit by the fire to dry off, listening to Rose recite the events of her day. But, he needed to get back. He would make it up to her next time. When her breathing evened out, he padded into the bedroom to make sure she was down for the night. He then checked that the fire had been properly banked. *Last thing we need is this cabin burning again*, he thought. When he was satisfied that all was well, he left the cabin through his private hatch.

Walking slowly towards the River, Wolf sniffed the sky. The fog was thick now just as he had expected it to be. It was almost time. He could feel the electricity in the air as it caused the thick hair along his spine to stand straight up. He entered the River and swam slowly with the current, waiting. Wolf was almost to the beaver dam when the lightning first streaked across the sky and touched the River, sending up a huge array of sparks. Gritting his teeth, he closed his eyes when it overtook him and swept him into the vortex.

Disneyland – 2007

"**P**addles up! As we round the bend near the Mark Twain, this is the last break you will get. Paddles up!" Walter Davis, or Wals as everyone called him, loudly repeated as he stood in the bow of the Davy Crockett Explorer Canoe facing his fifteen teenage passengers. "Paddles….all right, quit paddling!" he ordered, get exasperated. "Fourth row, that means you too. HEY! Quit splashing the guide in the back…. Guys! Knock it off!"

The fourth row continued to ignore Wals, using their paddles to send cascades of water over their friends in the rows behind them. Wals quickly glanced over his shoulder at the Mark Twain and the huge paddlewheel slowly churning the water behind it. They were not allowed to continue until the Mark Twain had left its berth for its own trip around Tom Sawyer's Island. The bigger the boat, the bigger its right-of-way.

Trey, the guide in the back of the canoe, had resorted to back-paddling to try and maintain their proper distance from the Mark Twain. He threw a desperate look for help to Wals. Some of the other teens had taken up paddling again while others had joined the water fight. None of them were paying any attention to Wals. Strain already showing on his face, Wals knew Trey wouldn't be able to keep up his back-paddling for very much longer.

Coming up with a not-quite-recommended solution to their dilemma, Wals leaned his paddle against the front row seat. Crouching down, he grasped the sides of the canoe and began rocking it violently side to side. With yelps of fright, all the teenagers quit their various actions and grabbed their seats to hold on. Their eyes got big as the edges of the canoe got closer and closer to the greenish water. Even though the teens were all drenched with the river water, they still had no desire to actually fall into the River—into water that they actually thought of as "dirty."

When the desired quiet had finally been attained and all eyes—sullen as they were—were on him, Wals calmly stood back up. "Well, that was refreshing, wasn't it?" he asked with a big grin. Only he and Trey knew two important facts: 1) The River was only about four feet deep at that point, and 2) The stabilizers on the canoes prevented them from actually being tipped over by the action Wals had just used. "Now that I have your attention," he announced with a voice dripping with sarcasm, "I would like to ask you to *please* refrain from paddling until the Mark Twain resumes her journey. Thank you *so much* for your cooperation. Enjoy the lovely scenery."

Trey, wiping the sweat off his face, was trying desperately to hide his amusement. If the kids saw him laughing, they would know it was a ruse and start in again. However, the unknowing teenagers sat stiffly in their seats, afraid to move, waiting until such time as they could get off this horrible ride. The ones near the back spent the time trying to wipe the water off their faces, and, in the case of the girls, trying to fix their dripping hair as best they could and to pull away their tops that were now plastered to their bodies.

Once the stately triple-decked Mark Twain was well on her way and there were no Tom Sawyer's Island Rafts in their path, Wals gave the command for them to resume paddling. The subdued teens applied themselves as they had never done before just so they could get this ride over with as soon as possible. Wals smiled to himself as they sped along. *Any faster and someone could probably water ski behind us!*

After one more bend in the River, Wals told them, "Paddles up! Please keep your hands and feet inside the canoe as we approach the dock. I don't want our freshly-painted dock to get all scratched up." He jumped out as soon as the canoe entered the loading area, picked up the tow rope, and brought the canoe to its proper loading spot on the dock. "Paddles in the bins on the left, please. Thank you so much, and please, please come again," he called after the departing horde of teenagers. Only one of them looked back at Wals' parting remark and casually flipped him off.

Trey came up to him as he and Wals swapped places with the next two canoe guides on the dock. His mustard yellow costume was plastered to his body, his dark hair dripping into his eyes. "Man, I hate Free Friend Day," he muttered so only Wals could hear him.

Wals glanced at his watch—his waterproof watch. He had learned the hard way the first week he worked canoes that he needed a waterproof watch. Happily, he saw it was time to close the ride. After making sure the rope was in place to block the entrance to the canoe dock, he answered his friend, "Yeah, I know. Me, too." He watched as the last canoe of the evening slowly drifted its way past the lower level of the Hungry Bear Restaurant. The front guide, Chloe, standing in the front of the canoe and facing the passengers, was busy explaining the proper way to paddle a canoe and listing the three rules of canoeing. "Rule Number One," she was loudly proclaiming, "Keep paddling at all times. Rule Number Two: Keep paddling at all times. And, Rule Number Three: Remember Rule Number One."

Wals chuckled. He used those lines many times, but he liked the somewhat-threatening inflection Chloe always managed to convey. As the guests began their awkward paddling, oars bumping into each other in the water, Wals turned back to Trey. "Hope Chloe has a better group than we did. She takes it personally when they don't follow her directions."

Trey grinned at that. He had been dating Chloe for a couple of months now. "That is true. Want me to hang around with you until her canoe comes back?" he asked, wringing out his imitation coonskin cap and slapping it against his leg.

Not averse to having a few minutes alone on this peaceful stretch of the River, Wals shook his head. "No need. You go ahead and clock out. It's getting colder. You need to dry off."

Trey nodded his agreement and turned to leave. "Oh, Wals," he turned back. "Are you coming to the party tonight? Maxx is playing at The Club."

Maxx was their favorite local rock band. They proudly proclaimed themselves "The Band of the '80's" who was "so good they didn't need to write their own music." Even though the current year was

2007, Maxx decided to go with a good thing and kept the same repertoire. The only thing that regularly changed was the female lead singer. The band was constantly getting new ones.

"Can't tonight. I'm on the late shift for *Fantasmic!* Say hi to Diane for me."

Trey smiled. "Sorry, Wals, but she's gone. Had a fight with the bass player she was dating and left the group."

Wals shook his head and scowled. She had been really cute. "Figures. Have fun without me."

"I'll try."

Wals watched as his friend walked up the ramp and headed over towards the Briar Patch gift shop across the walkway in Critter Country. There was an access door to the cast members' backstage area that allowed them to get from their assigned ride in that part of Park to the lockers and costume department. This backstage area was designed by Walt Disney himself so a cast member dressed in a Tomorrowland costume could walk freely to another area without spoiling the illusion of a different land, like Fantasyland. And, as *not* designed by Walt, it was also a popular area to meet a girlfriend or boyfriend out of sight of the guests. There was even an unseen grassy nook on top of the Briar Patch that was frequently used as a private picnic area for cast members desiring a little alone-time.

Wals settled against one of the realistic wood-like posts of the ride enclosure to wait for Chloe's canoe to return. He spoke to a few guests who had hoped the ride was still running and had to turn them away. Within ten minutes, Chloe was back and smiling. Either hers had been a good canoe-load of guests, or she was thinking about the fact it was the last canoe-load of guests.

When the last guests had left, Chloe turned to Wals. "I saw something odd on the Island near the Settler's Cabin just as we went through the Rapids. Not sure what it was. Wasn't moving or anything. Just something dark on the edge of the trees that shouldn't be there."

"Do you think it was someone hiding out for the night?" Every now and then, a guest would attempt to hide in various places inside the Park just so they could brag to their friends they outsmarted Security or to get a free day in Disneyland the following morning. They were hardly ever successful. The area Chloe was describing was considered a No Man's Land for guests roaming over Tom Sawyer's Island. Someone would have had to either climb over various fences and gates to get to that particular secluded spot or jump off one of the River boats or canoes.

Not really caring, Chloe tiredly shrugged as she pulled at the collar of her fringed shirt. She was done for the day and wanted to get out of her uncomfortable costume. "I don't know. Should I call it in to Security?"

Wals looked towards the bend in the Frontierland River that hid the cabin from their view. "No, that's okay. Let me check it out first. I have some time before we have to set up for *Fantasmic!*"

Fantasmic! was a water and light spectacular show that was held on the Rivers of America in front of New Orleans Square once or twice a night, depending on the season. Huge fan-shaped sprays of water erupted from the River and the story was projected onto the back of the spray. It was the classic story of Good versus Evil that combined lasers, pyrotechnics, floating rafts with dancing characters, a huge thirty-foot tall fire-breathing dragon, and the Sorcerer's Apprentice himself—Mickey Mouse. It was an extremely popular show. Wals, along with a group of fellow cast members and a few security guards were always on hand when guests came hours early to stake out a spot for the best viewing. Thousands of people would be seated on the walkways and planters watching and applauding, Wals and that small, determined group of cast members would be on hand, attempting to keep the walkways in the back open, keeping the guests seated in the front, and helping the mass of people exit smoothly when the show was over, just about the time for the fireworks to begin over Sleeping Beauty's Castle.

Without a backwards glance, Chloe headed for the same exit as Trey had used. She knew he would be waiting for her at the second bend to the right, hoping to jump out and scare her.

Wals bypassed the thirty-five-foot long canoes used by the guests that were now placidly tied to the quiet dock and walked towards the neighboring building. There were two small eighteen-foot canoes hidden at the far end of that lower level of the Hungry Bear Restaurant. Pulling his ID tag out of his wallet, he slid it through the lock on the concealed door and pushed through to the access ramp. The two canoes bobbed easily in the water. Painted to match the larger canoes used by the guests, most people assumed these were extra canoes to be brought out when needed as the Park filled with more guests and the ride became more popular. However, these were smaller canoes without the stabilizers necessary when twenty inexperienced guests were attempting to paddle around the

Island. Wals untied the first canoe and waved to the kids who had stopped eating their dinner to watch him. With a few powerful strokes, he entered the gentle current of the River.

He enjoyed being out alone like this on the Frontierland River, or Rivers of America as it was also called, so he took his time paddling. He wasn't needed for another hour for the *Fantasmic!* show's crowd control. There would be no other traffic on the River now. Both the huge sailing ship Columbia and the riverboat Mark Twain were stopped out of sight, being readied for their participation in the *Fantasmic!* show. The sky was mellow as dusk settled around him. Wals noticed the temperature had become cooler and he could feel a breeze picking up. The steam train's whistle broke into his reflective mood as it passed the Hungry Bear Restaurant and chugged slowly down the tracks. He could see the flash of a camera as someone tried to take a picture of the Settler's Cabin across the River. *Good luck with that!* he thought with a smile. They were way too far away for a good shot.

He steered his canoe over to the left bank. Standing on a realistic-looking log protruding out over the water, stood an animated shaggy white dog slowly wagging his tail, watching a Native American boy as he leaned down to peer into the dark green water, his eyes following the fishing line tied to his hand. Wals chuckled to himself. Over the years cast members had come out alone after dark—as he now was—and attached something or other to the end of the fishing line. Then it was up to their friends to have to retrieve it. Once the little white dog had sported a pair of Mouse ears for three days before they were removed and a stern warning given to all the wide-eyed, innocent-looking river workers. Wals now wished he had thought to bring something with him. It would have been the perfect opportunity to set it up.

His attention was again diverted as the gentle breeze suddenly became a gusting wind and the temperature started to drop more rapidly. Glancing up at the sky, he was surprised to see fog coming in from the west. He knew it wasn't in the forecast. Wondering if it would affect the 8:30 showing of *Fantasmic!*, he knew there would be a lot of disappointed guests that they would have to pacify if the show was canceled at the last minute. Wals glanced at his watch, having to push the button for the backlight to see what time it was. It still read 5:30, the time he had come in from his last run. The watch must have gotten too drenched this time. Pulling his cell phone out of his pocket, he saw that it, too, read 5:30. *Odd*, he thought as he turned the canoe back towards the Island. If he didn't hurry, it might be too dark to find whatever it was that Chloe had spotted.

The wind was now pushing against him, the usually slow-moving current in the River seemingly reversed. He had to fight the current to keep the canoe aimed towards Tom Sawyer's Island and a neglected dock he knew was on the east side of the Settler's Cabin. He dug in with all his strength to make it into the secluded haven of the mature trees that surrounded the little dock. Climbing out of the canoe, he had to keep a firm hold on the tow rope to fasten it to the metal tie rings. Once this dock had been used to berth the extra Keel Boat at night, but now that ride had been gone for ten years.

Pushing through the overgrown tree branches,

he was assaulted by the full force of the wind. The faux-fur coonskin cap he wore as part of his costume was instantly blown off his head and disappeared into the darkness behind him. The halogen spotlight that was supposed to light the Settler's Cabin at night sputtered on and off, giving the isolated area an eerie strobe-light effect. Years ago, this cabin used to be lit by real flames that burned day and night to go with the storyline told on the Mark Twain and other riverboats as they passed by, but time and use had corroded the gas pipes that fed the flames and they were never replaced. As the spotlight flickered on again for a moment, Wals spotted the dark pile of *something* over near one of trees. It was partially covered with carefully arranged branches and leaves as if it was purposely hidden. He started over to the mound wishing he had brought his *Fantasmic!* crowd control-issued yellow flashlight with him. Just when he reached it and realized it was a pile of clothes, a flash of lightning lit the dark sky. Wals' head jerked in the direction of the wooden Mill that was across the River from the Mark Twain dock and where *Fantasmic!* would be centered. *It couldn't possibly be time for the show.* Another flash tore through the sky. Only, he then realized, the flash had come behind him— in the opposite direction from where *Fantasmic!* would be shown.

Not one to be easily startled, Wals looked back towards the silent cabin, and then to the River. The pile of clothes forgotten, he walked slowly towards the cabin and the fiberglass brown horse standing silently behind the split-rail fence next to it. The fog was now so thick he couldn't even see across to the River to the Native American chief seated on a mustang, raising his hand in greeting to the different boatloads of guests. Wals then realized something else—there was no *BOOM* of thunder after the lightning. Before he could work out that mystery, another jagged bolt of lightning flashed and ripped along the surface of the River, sending green water and an odd shower of pink sparkles flying in every direction.

Shielding his eyes from the brilliant light, he turned away, feeling the hair on his head stand away from his scalp. Then, as suddenly as it came, the lightning stopped, the wind died down, and the last of the sparkles burned themselves out in the River. The fog still swirled around the water's edge as Wals approached the River, wondering what in the world could have caused that phenomenon. He took up the walkie-talkie attached to his belt to report to Security, but only heard static on the multiple frequencies. Replacing it, he looked to the left towards the direction of the Hungry Bear Restaurant and the canoe dock but could see nothing through the fog. Even the screams coming from the huge drop at the end of Splash Mountain were muted, making them sound as if they were coming from the other side of the Park.

What he could hear clearly, though, was a groaning sound that came from the opposite direction. He hurried over to the other edge of the clearing, near the rocks of Keel Boat Rapids. The Rapids was a channel just wide enough for the canoes to go through in their trek around the Island. Using air pipes, the water would be turned in bubbling, frothing "rapids" to make it more exciting for the guests. Across the small channel he saw someone submerged in the water and clinging to one of the rocks.

Plunging into the waist-deep water, Wals rushed over to the prone figure. Another groan was heard and the dark head turned when Wals put a hand on a man's bare shoulder.

Wals gasped. "Mani? Is that you? What are you doing in the River? You hurt?" Wals got an arm under his friend to help him up. "Can you stand?"

Mani moaned and shook his head violently from side to side, sending more water flying over Wals. "Rose?" he whispered hoarsely, looking up towards the cabin, concern etched on his dripping face. He let Wals help him stand and together they waded over to the clearing. Once on land, his legs gave out and he promptly sat, his face lowered onto his arms. Wals hovered nearby, concerned, but unsure of what to do.

"Uh, Mani? Any special reason why you're naked?" Wals ventured to ask when his eyes again adjusted to the low light. "And, who is Rose?"

"Slol wa yea shnee." Mani's breathing evened out and he looked around as if he was getting his bearings. He then looked up at Wals, his eyes clearing. "Ah, you're not Rose," he remarked in English.

"You hit your head on a rock or something?" Wals asked, worried about his friend. "You're talking kinda weird. What language was that?"

Wolf shook his head again. "What did I say?"

"Heck if I know. Sounded like you bit your tongue and sneezed. Did you bang your head on the rocks?" he asked again, becoming more concerned.

"Maybe. Not sure." Mani felt through his thick black hair. "No. I can't feel any lumps."

Wals came and squatted in front of his friend. "How many fingers am I holding up?"

The blue eyes narrowed into slits as he glared at his hovering friend. "Fourteen," he answered through clenched teeth.

Wals relaxed and gave a lopsided smile. "Okay, you're fine. So, what are you doing skinny-dipping in the River in the middle of a lightning storm, Wolf?"

The features on his handsome face evened out. Ignoring a direct question as was his habit, Wolf instead commented, "I am glad to hear you're back to using my nickname. Thought I was going to have to start calling you Walter."

Wals grimaced. He preferred Wals as he knew Mani preferred Wolf, which was short for his last name of Wolford. Once, in a rare moment of disclosure, Wolf had told Wals that his first name came from Sumanitu Taka which meant Wolf in the Lakota tongue. "So your name is actually Wolf Wolford?" he remembered asking at the time and had received a silent glare for his brilliant observation.

Once his concern for his friend's health was pacified, Wals became worried again and looked back towards the River. "What about this Rose you mentioned? Do I need to go look for someone else? Was she swimming with you in the River?"

Wolf got shakily to his feet. At six-feet tall, he was only two inches taller than Wals, but with the way he carried himself, he always seemed taller. Wals eyes strayed to Wolf's muscular chest. There was an odd patch of white hair in the dark mat of hair that covered his upper torso. When Wolf swayed slightly, Wals took a step closer in case Wolf wasn't as steady as he thought he was. "No, there was no one with me. She doesn't care for the River," he answered briefly, shaking his head again to clear it.

Wals waited for more of an explanation that he really knew wasn't coming. Wolf was more of an observer than a talker. He watched his friend head towards the cabin and veer towards the dark pile of clothes he had seen before the weird lightning storm. It was then that Wals realized the clothes were Wolf's Security uniform. As the halogen light flickered again, he could see the blue of the pants and the white of the shirt and hat as Wolf got dressed. He could also see Wolf grimace as he pulled on the shoes.

"Feet hurt?"

Wolf looked up. "No. I just hate shoes."

Wals smiled in the darkness as the light went out again. "You working tonight, Wolf?"

Wolf looked confused and paused in what he was doing. "What day is it?"

This was an interesting development. "Tuesday," Wals answered slowly, amused. *Must have been some party I missed on the Island. Why is it I always hear about the great parties when they are over?* he wondered to himself.

"Tuesday," Wolf repeated quietly, thinking. *Time is moving differently again*, he thought to himself. *I left three days ago, yet it was only one night. They must be waiting for me.* Out loud he answered his friend, "Yes, I am working tonight."

"That's too bad. Maxx is playing at The Club tonight. I heard Julia will be there," he teased. Julia worked on the Pirates of the Caribbean ride and it was obvious she found the dark haired, well-built Wolf fascinating.

Not answering Wals, Wolf strode towards the hidden dock where he correctly assumed Wals would have a canoe tied up. The feisty redhead was equally appealing to him, but…. Wolf let out a small, frustrated sigh unheard by the trailing Wals. There wasn't an opportunity in his life right now for a Julia—or anyone else for that matter. He didn't know if there ever would be.

The intense blue eyes narrowed again. Someday his life would be his own again. Someday he would find *Her*. His lifemate was out there. The gray-tipped hair that fell against his collar an inch over regulation bristled as he strode towards the canoe.

Someday he would be allowed. Someday it would be over. But not today.

He still had work to do.

The Island – 1816

The sixteen-foot tall log walls of Fort Wilderness loomed in front of Rose as her mare carefully picked her way down the rocky path. The mare's steps were slow; Rose's attitude reluctant. Today was Market Day at the Fort. Today was the day food, fabric for clothing, and household items were ferried over from the docks at New Orleans. Today she would stock up on supplies for the coming month. And, today was the day she dreaded more than any other day out of the month.

On either side of the brown mare hung woven baskets holding most of the produce out of Rose's tiny garden in front of her cabin. Those vegetables she would trade for what she needed to round out her food supply. *Hoped* to trade, she reminded herself with a sigh. She never quite knew what to expect from the local women and the soldiers still stationed at the Fort.

One more time, Rose glanced nervously to the side of the path. On one side was the ever-present River lined with low shrubs, reeds, and water flowers. She could hear families of the noisy ducks and mud hens who lived there. On the opposite side was the dense forest that separated her lone cabin from the Last Outpost of Civilization—Fort Wilderness. But, no matter how many times she anxiously looked for him, she knew Wolf wasn't there. He usually went with her on these trips, hidden in the lacy ferns and the covering undergrowth of the forest, watching, protecting. She hadn't seen him for two or three days now. This wasn't necessarily unusual for Wolf, but he seemed to somehow sense when she needed his support during these infrequent trips to the Fort, but now he wasn't there.

Her mind carried her back to when she had first met Wolf. He had proven his loyalty and his protectiveness to her on that fateful day long ago. He had earned her trust, but she, on the other hand, had subsequently earned the scorn of some of the Fort's inhabitants. Leaving the mare at home, she had decided to walk to the Fort that day. It had been a beautiful, peaceful spring day, early enough that the mist was still rising from the ever-moving green water. There hadn't been as much to trade back then. She was still struggling with the lonely lifestyle after the fire in her cabin had gone out and she hadn't yet gotten her garden properly established. She recalled having words with the gambler who had taken over her husband's position. Shocked that no one had stood up for her when he insulted her, she had ducked, shame-faced, into the supply store. Once her trading was done, she hurried out of the stockade gates and turned towards her home. Hearing a commotion behind her, she looked back to see the gambler, backed by half a dozen soldiers, walking slowly after her. She hurried her steps, knowing she could never hope to outrun them, hoping they would tire of the chase and give up. She had stiffened when a rough hand grabbed her by the shoulder, spinning her around. Foul breath assaulted her as the gambler verbally abused her again, calling her every vile name he could think of. Panicked, she looked over his shoulder for help, only to see the soldiers urging him on, a half-empty whiskey bottle in one of the men's unsteady grip. The bright sunlight shone on something below her vision. Looking down, she was terrified to see a knife in the gambler's hand. She remembered then hearing a low rumbling noise getting louder as it was coming from behind her. The vicious look of victory on the gambler's face changed to one of stark terror in a split second. A snapping, snarling black fury leaped past her and caught the gambler in the middle of his chest, flinging him backwards away from her and landing in front of the stunned soldiers. Being unarmed in their hurry to torment the beautiful blond, the men turned and fled back to the Fort, leaving the gambler to face the black demon on his own. The knife had flown out of his grip in the assault and he held his hands in front of his face to protect himself from the biting, clawing animal, his screams for help going unheeded. When he eventually realized the snarling had stopped, he cautiously opened his eyes and wished he hadn't. Intense blue eyes filled with hatred glowed with an unnatural light. The dripping fangs were a mere inch from his exposed neck. There was a low growl coming from the open mouth, deep, penetrating, one that could be felt deep within his own chest. The wolf just stood there, his teeth bared, not moving. The message was obvious—Let Her Be. Still terrified, the gambler tensed when the wolf shifted. Stepping off the man's chest, the wolf stood in front of Rose, his head lowered, feet apart, back legs bunched for another leap. Getting slowly to his feet, blood dripping from cuts on the back of his hands, never taking his eyes off the wolf, the gambler backed slowly all the way back to the Fort. When he was around the corner and out of sight of the black terror, he turned and ran to the cantina and slammed the door. After that day, the gambler was never seen at Fort Wilderness again. Rumor had it he went across the River to New Orleans and caught the riverboat, disappearing. Rose was now safe from the gambler, but it was a different story with some of the soldiers, for they began to treat her with contempt. However, they didn't dare come near her if they thought the wolf might be nearby. Gossip spread—as it always did—about the odd woman who lived alone in a burned-out cabin and called on the animals to help her. Her beauty alone was enough for the local women to shun her. Add a large black wolf to the mix, and she had no chance for friendship, no sense of belonging.

Two sentries were watching her from the lookout towers that stood next to the huge wooden gates that had been swung open for Market Day. She stole a quick glance up at their smirking faces. The gold braid and buttons of their blue Calvary uniforms caught the bright morning sun. Under the pretense of adjusting her reins, she did one final quick search for Wolf hoping to see his blue eyes amongst the greens and browns of the forest. No blue eyes. No Wolf.

Straightening her shoulders and holding her head high, she knew she had to get through this. She nudged the mare forward and entered the dusty parade grounds of the fort. The mare was left at the livery stable with a kind man, Private Smitty. He gave her an encouraging smile and unlatched her baskets for her. As she left the stable, the two woven baskets were reluctantly handed over to the soldier in charge of the bartering. She was rudely pointed over to some half-logs that were used as benches and told to wait. The shingled awning of the stable provided her some shade as she fanned herself and watched the comings and goings of the Fort. On a little pedestal surrounded by river rocks, stood the tall flagpole. The fifteen stars on the U.S. flag were unseen as the flag hung limp in the motionless air. She saw three of the local women laughing and gossiping around the stone-enclosed well in front of the Regimental Headquarters. Rose was aware of their scrutiny, just as she was aware of the fact that they didn't call over a friendly greeting or ask her to join them to share all the latest news. She tried not to notice their new dresses and plumed bonnets. Unconsciously brushing the trail dust off of her white apron, she tried to keep her focus on the displays of deer antlers that were used to decorate the roof of the three-story-tall Headquarters building.

But that didn't help divert her upset mind. The antlers reminded her of the death of the deer—even though the meat was necessary for survival. The death of the deer reminded her of another death—one that was also prominently displayed. On the wall between the supply store and the cantina was nailed a well-preserved skin of a different animal. Rose didn't allow her eyes to stray there, for she knew what it looked like and it made her ill each time she thought about it. It was the silver and brown fur of a wolf. It had been a magnificent animal, though a smaller wolf than hers.

The soldiers who remained at the Fort after the hostiles had left the Island were eager to add another skin to their wall. They wanted her Wolf.

Rose thought about entering the Headquarters and filing another protest with Major General Andrew Jackson. He had been assigned here after the Battle of New Orleans, and she knew him to be a fair, if strict, man. She even got up from her uncomfortable seat and walked over to his open door, her long lavender skirt stirring up dust on the parade ground as she walked. The chattering of the women at the well stilled as Rose walked past them, back straight and eyes straight ahead. She ignored the loud whispering when she reached the open door. However, before she went inside, she first looked in through the glassless window to make sure the Major General was there. She could see him working at his ornate desk, an oil lamp providing meager light in the darkened room. Behind him, a painting of President James Madison was proudly displayed under red, white and blue bunting, and a gold eagle with outspread wings was nailed near the ceiling. Long rifles stood propped against the logs of the wall, easily within reach should they be needed, with powder horns hanging next to them on a wooden dowel. She could see a tall four-drawer chest with a mirror atop off to the side of the room. There were a few chairs in the room, stools mostly, with woven mats as the seats. As she watched, Jackson took a drink from his pewter mug sitting on the desk, amidst spread-out papers of maps and Dispatches.

Seeing the extra chairs were empty, Rose took a deep breath to steady her nerves and was going to enter when she heard a deep man's voice in the office, a different voice than that of the Major General. Surprised, she peeked through the open door and saw a tall man dressed in buckskin with a furry cap on his head. Standing at ease, unaware of her scrutiny, the man gestured calmly as he spoke. There was another man in the room a step behind him. Dressed similarly in the clothes of a hunter, he too held a long rifle in his hands, a powder horn slung across his chest and a knife stuck in his belt. Rose hurried away from the office and resumed her seat in the shade. She had never seen these two Army Scouts before, but she immediately recognized the two men. Why, everybody knew about Davy Crockett and Georgie Russel!

Seeing these two men in the Fort somehow made Rose feel more relaxed. Wolf wasn't outside the gate watching her, but she felt a little more at ease, a little more protected. She knew from their reputations that they were fair men. Fierce fighters, but fair. She even managed a smile for the soldier, Private Daniel Crain, who came and told her it was her turn in the Supply Store. Her smile showed her dimple and her even, white teeth. The soldier mis-read that smile, and taking a step closer, smirking, he began reaching for her. In an instant, her frown returned as she hurried around him, almost running towards the Supply Store. As she left, she could hear him swear at her and spit on the ground just as she reached the door of the single-story, squat store. She could also hear the laugh of the women standing by when the soldier walked over to join them. Slipping his arm around the waist of the curly-headed brunette, he began to loudly tell the other women what a stuck-up biddy she was. Always eager for more stories to tell about the blond, the women clustered closer around Daniel who was clearly relishing the attention.

The clerk behind the counter had offered her less than she thought her vegetables were worth, but she had expected it and took it with stoic silence. *The crazy woman who lived by herself with a wolf wouldn't know any better.* Rose knew any argument on her part would be curtly put down, and she would fare worse the next time. She carefully piled the flour, sugar and tea in one basket and arranged the scant meat and other provisions in the remaining one. Being the last customer they had called in, she knew there was no one waiting to trade behind her, so she took her time packing so as not to damage any of her precious supplies.

Struggling to get the baskets into position so she could carry them both, she was startled to hear a deep voice coming from behind her. "Can I get that for you, ma'am?"

A ready protest died on her lips as Rose swung around when a man's hands easily grabbed up her two baskets. "Davy Crockett!" she managed to say in her surprise. Nobody ever helped her. She even forgot her manners in calling him by his first name even though they had never been properly introduced.

"David," he calmly corrected as he always did. He stood there waiting with a kind smile on his rugged face.

Rose came out of her trance and returned his smile. "Oh, why, thank you, sir! This way please. My mare is in the livery stable."

After securing her baskets to the sides of her horse, Davy ran a knowledgeable hand over the mare. "Beautiful animal, Mrs....."

Rose blushed. "Mrs. Stephens. And thank you for your assistance."

"Mrs. Stephens," he acknowledged with a nod. "I have to admit, ma'am, that I knew who you were before we met. You see, I was hoping to meet your wolf."

Even though his facial expression didn't change from being pleasant, Davy was inwardly surprised at the anger in Rose's expression as it instantly altered her beautiful face.

"That is the last thing I would do, Mr. Crockett!" she fairly spat at him. "For I know who you are, as well. Lead somebody with your skills to Wolf? Never!" she heatedly exclaimed, hurriedly pulling the mare over to a wooden stool so she could mount easier without assistance.

Davy put out a restraining hand, stopping just short of actually touching her. "You misunderstand me, ma'am. I'm not like these here soldiers," he told her in his deep voice, indicating with his chin the men who were lounging outside the stable. "I know the stories. I know *your* story, ma'am. I also know the story of the skin on the wall." He broke off when she paled and cast her eyes down as emotion overtook her. "And I am sorry about men like that. But, there is nothing we can do about them. Sometimes evil natures run deep. I just wanted to see him. That's all. Story is he is a beautiful animal. You say you know who I am. Then you should also know that I am not known to be a liar."

Even though his reputation for tall tales preceded him, Rose knew it was an insult to call a man a liar. She saw she was out of line and blushed, not being used to kindness. "I do know of your honesty and I'm sorry, Mr. Crockett. I didn't mean to snap at you. I can see you are just being kind. And I do appreciate it." Glancing quickly at the half-closed stable door, her voice lowered so he had to lean in to hear her. "Wolf isn't with me today. I…I haven't seen him in a couple of days," she hated to admit. "He will show up…eventually. I just don't want the soldiers to know I came in alone."

Davy Crockett stood back from the mare and nodded his understanding. "Another time then, ma'am." He touched his forehead in a respectful salute and took the reins from her to lead the mare out of the stable. Georgie Russel was waiting in the shade of the Cantina overhang. When Davy came out of the stable, he showed no surprise seeing his friend leading a lovely lady on a horse. Falling into step, he silently joined them on the opposite side of the mare, his long rifle tucked easily in the crook of his arm.

Walking on either side of her out of Fort Wilderness, the two scouts gave a silent warning to those few bad soldiers who were watching. Once on the rocky path, they said their farewells. Rose turned westward to head home to her cabin. Davy Crockett and Georgie Russel turned eastward towards the raft landing that would take them across the River and on to the new assignment that had just been given to them by the Major General.

The soldier who had misread her smile had climbed the rickety wooden stairs to one of the watchtower of the Fort to see what happened with the odd trio once they left the gates. Private Daniel Crain watched the blond as she rode past Injun Joe's Cave and approached Castle Rock, his misdirected anger at her blossoming into a living, breathing hatred. He hadn't missed the subtle message given by the two Army Scouts. Coward that he was, he hadn't made himself known to them, but, he noted with smirking satisfaction, they were heading to regions far across the wide River. And she was going back to her lonely, isolated cabin.

He lifted his rifle to his shoulder and sighted down its long barrel. He took his time aiming. When he was satisfied, he slowly squeezed the trigger. The hammer dropped on the empty chamber. He uttered one word. "Bang."

Unknowing, Rose slowly rode on towards her home.

CHAPTER THREE

Disneyland – 2007

Wolf was tired, exhausted more than likely. Mentally. Physically. Just back from visiting his family, he had finished his shift on Security, taking some time to catch up with his partner Lance Brentwood. Two of the subjects they discussed were the ever-present dilemma of the need for Doctor Houser to remain in the past and the threat of the still-missing blackmailer Tom Bolte. Wolf could add "frustration" to his list of complaints. He had been searching for the missing man ever since that fateful day in the hospital in 1966. *How could it possibly still be unsolved after all this time?* he asked himself yet again.

Using the state-of-the-art technology in the War Room, Wolf had searched every Tom Bolte that came into the databases. He even checked alterations on the spelling of the name, just in case it might have been modified after the heist. Plus, because of all the odd jobs the man had done while working for Disneyland, he could have gone into any number of fields—a lot of which didn't require reporting to the government, like cash-under-the-table construction and handyman jobs. Otherwise it would have been easy to track him through his Social Security number. Not wanting to rely just on printed data, Wolf wasn't satisfied until he had physically followed up on almost every one of the leads to see for himself if that "Tom" he had just found was the one he wanted.

Modesto – 1975

After chasing down what seemed to be his fortieth dead-end lead in the ever-lengthening trail of blackmail suspects, Wolf was now once again deeply involved in following his latest solid lead. This time, in November of 1975, he found himself in the San Joaquin Valley, more specifically, in the central California town of Modesto. Darkness had fallen as he sat in the quiet neighborhood of Sylvan Village. Wolf had been watching a ranch-style house across from the community pool on Fairington Lane for hours. His Mustang was parked just around the corner on Bartley Drive in front of a white stucco house with high curved fences that blocked anyone inside the house from spotting his stake-out position.

Wolf was once again taking his usual cautious approach—not approaching the suspect, but just watching from a safe distance, getting a feel for the man's movements, looking for any suspicious ac-

tivity. Since he had never seen Dr. Houser's pred-
ator face-to-face at Disneyland after he had black-
mailed Walt, he had to be absolutely sure of his
perpetrator before he took action.

This suspect's name was Thomas Boalt, a
part-time janitor at the newly-opened Fred C. Beyer
High School just three blocks away on Sylvan Avenue. With his name phonetically similar to the Tom
Bolte Wolf was looking for, this man owned a fairly
nice home, had a new Harley Davidson motorcycle
in the garage and a recently customized '65
Ranchero parked in his driveway—yet, he worked
part-time at a high school doing custodial work. All
of this combined to make Wolf seriously question
whether a part-time janitor's earnings could support
his standard of living or whether he had had
$100,000 worth of help from Walt Disney. Yet, after
spending several days trailing him, Wolf hadn't yet
seen anything unusual. Once again, it was all starting to feel like this was just another dead lead. That
night it all changed…

Late that evening, Tom slammed shut the front
door to his house and bolted into his Ranchero. It
had almost caught Wolf off guard, but he quickly
started his Mustang to follow. *Why did I have to go
with a red Mustang?* he thought, as he maneuvered
just far enough behind so as not to be spotted tail-
ing the suspect. It was obvious, as Tom headed
right on Sylvan Avenue, that he was going out to
the country. After a rapid turn left onto Claus Road,
he continued north as he wound through Riverbank
and ended up at a small park next to the slow-run-
ning Stanislaus River. There he stopped his truck
and just sat waiting in the darkness. When he saw
Tom rolling to a stop, Wolf killed his headlights and

pulled to an easy stop on the other side of the park. His Mustang, now enveloped in the darkness, was no longer red, but just blended beautifully into the night.

Wolf waited. After a few minutes he realized that he was probably too far away to see Tom and what may be going down, and knew he needed to get nearer to the Ranchero. As he started to inch his way closer, he stopped and questioned the situation. *Maybe Tom spotted me, maybe he recognized the stake-out, and maybe this was a trap!* Just then, a beat-up '56 Ford truck pulled in beside Tom's Ranchero. After nervously glancing around, Tom got out, approached the old Ford truck, and leaned in the open passenger window.

Still too far away, with mist rising from the river to mix with the low-swirling tule fog, Wolf couldn't tell exactly what was exchanged, but the interaction didn't take long. Before he could steal closer, Tom was holding a hand inside his jacket as he hurried back to his Ranchero. Wolf didn't have time to reach his Mustang before both trucks roared out of the park and were quickly out of sight. Not sure where his suspect went, but deciding this was indeed very suspicious activity, all Wolf could do now was return to Tom's house on Fairington, hoping he would return soon.

After observing similar activity on four separate nights, Wolf was now able to follow Tom afterward. He would always return down Patterson Road until he reached Old Oakdale Road, turn back onto Sylvan Avenue the short distance to Shelby Lane, then back to his home on Fairington.

Tiring of just watching and not doing, Wolf wanted to know exactly what was going down in that quiet river park. He decided to arrive earlier than the two men. Parking his Mustang on a nearby unlit neighborhood street, he hiked through the thin fog into the park and crouched down behind one of the massive walnut trees. He didn't have to wait long.

The '56 Ford truck arrived first this time. He just sat there with his engine idling, gray smoke billowing out of the rusty exhaust pipes that mixed eerily with the tule fog. When Tom arrived, the '56 flashed his lights on and off twice. Wolf was close enough this time to see Tom hesitating inside the Ranchero, looking as though he was unsure of what to do. When the driver of the '56 did nothing, Tom shrugged and came up to the driver's window to find out what was wrong. Wolf could hear an argument ensue with the unseen driver doing most of the yelling. Hearing the words "narc" and "followed you, idiot" over and over in the curse-filled tirade, Wolf knew he was the topic being loudly discussed and that he had been spotted. It sounded as though Tom was confused and quickly becoming irritated. As Wolf attempted to come in closer to hear everything that was being said and to finally get a good look at the elusive Tom, he stood from his nearby cover.

And immediately slipped on a cluster of walnuts and twigs hidden by a thick cover of leaves, sending his feet out from under him.

At the sound, easily heard by the two already-nervous men, Tom was roughly pushed out of the way by the driver of the '56 truck as he jerked it into gear and sped off, a spray of rocks and gravel peppering the now-sprawled suspect.

Both men came to their feet at the same time,

eyes locked. Wolf had enough time for a good look at the face before his own eyes dropped to the small handgun in Tom's hand. Diving to the right, the first shot buried itself in the tree Wolf had recently used for cover.

Trying to aim at the moving intruder, Tom yelled at him to "next time, leave your red car at home, narc" and fired again, going wide.

Taking to the trees for concealment, Wolf relied on the training he had received as a boy, focusing on staying behind cover yet always moving as quietly as he could. When he could hear Tom clumsily following him through the thickening trees, Wolf began a circling maneuver.

Tom came to a skidding halt when it became obvious Wolf had gotten away. He could hear no movement through the bushes and undergrowth, no running footsteps, nothing. Turning jerkily this way and that, trying to peer through the misty fog, Tom suddenly had the sinking feeling that he, somehow, had just become the prey. The other man had moved too fast and too easily.

Gun held shakily in front of him, he started backtracking to his Ranchero, hoping he would make it there first. When he rounded one large oak, he came face to face with the dark, silent, angry-looking Wolf. He tried to get off a shot, but found his arm suddenly pinned to the tree by a knife that came out of nowhere. "Who are you? Why are you following me?" he demanded, trying to still the nervousness in his voice.

The threat of the gun now removed, Wolf came in closer and studied the face glaring at him. This man seemed far too young. "Are you Tom Bolte?" he demanded. "And don't even try to lie to me."

"Who wants to know?"

Wolf allowed a growl deep in his chest. The pale eyes staring at him grew wide. "Answer me," Wolf said quietly.

"Yeah, I'm Tom. Who are you? A narc? You going to arrest me?" The wide eyes showed dilated pupils full of fear.

Wolf ignored the questions. "Did you used to work at Disneyland?"

"What? Disneyland? Are you kidding me, man? What is this?"

"Answer me." The tone conveyed threat and warning.

Tom picked up on that and swallowed deeply. "No. Went there for my grad night. Worst eight-hour bus trip of my life.... I never worked there. I...I've lived here most of my life. Why have you been following me?"

Wolf reached down for the gun that had dropped when Tom had been pinned to the tree. He tossed it into the nearby river and reached up to retrieve his knife. Tom flinched. Ignoring that, Wolf merely commented, "Sorry, wrong man." He resheathed his knife and turned to go back to his car.

As expected, as Wolf faded into the fog, he could hear a string of curses revolving around the ruined gun, a ruined contact, a ruined shirt, and a bruised ego that followed him all the way through the park until he was out of sight. Driving back into Modesto, Wolf headed to his motel on McHenry Avenue. Throwing his few clothes into his bag, grumbling to himself, "another dead lead, more wasted time, and another five and a half hour drive out of here," he gassed up the Mustang and headed for the 99 freeway and home.

Disneyland – 2007

Over the decades, as technology advanced, Wolf's search became more refined and extended internationally. And yet, with all that, the man he wanted seemed to have vanished into thin air.

Wolf even began to wonder if perhaps it would be better for him to go back to 1966 and just prevent the theft and the threat in the first place. Then the doctor would not have had to be put into the 1800's. He could have continued his work…. Wolf sighed. If you change one thread in time, what else would have been affected? What would be the advances in science now? Better or worse? There was no easy answer. No, he knew he could not mess with the events that had already happened. It was all too uncertain and potentially dangerous for everyone concerned.

As Wolf continued talking, his security partner Lance tried to be encouraging, but he had been distracted, continually glancing at his watch. He wanted to get home to his wife Kimberly and their firstborn, Peter. Lance's face always lit up when he talked about his son and how Peter keeps asking for "Unka Wolf" to come over and play horsey with him again.

When the two friends parted, Wolf felt an uncustomary twinge of jealousy as Lance walked off with his long stride. Lance had had his problems in the past, but he was doing wonderfully as a family man—and in his newfound position as one of the trustees for Walt Disney. When her father had died, he and Kimberly inherited the Blond-Haired Man's position of keeping their fingers on the pulse of everything relating to Walt and his future prospects. And, he, Wolf, as one of the remaining Guardians, continued to work right along with the couple.

The small feeling of jealousy over Lance's happy family life faded as Wolf continued his reflection on his own Guardianship and all it had entailed over the decades. There were certain aspects of it that still bothered him—even after all these years. Yes, he had been successful in his ability to retrieve the heart pendant and return it to Walt just in time, but his lack of success in finding the blackmailing perpetrator was still a thorn in his side. Before he left for the night, Lance had confirmed what Wolf thought: As long as the man was at large, the doctor's safety was a very real concern. Wolf knew the search had to continue, even though he had little to go on at this point in time. All he basically had now was the man's name, that he was aged thirty-five at the time of the heist, which was now forty-one years in the past. When questioned years ago, Tom's superiors in the Maintenance Department had reported him to be an unimaginative worker who had delusions of grandeur but no backbone to implement them. That was why his supervisors had shuttled him around to different jobs, trying to find something he was good at doing or showed some initiative. By the time Wolf had retrieved the pendant from one of the flowerbeds lining the Casey Jr. Circus Train, the "unimaginative" Tom had fled with Walt's $100,000 and somehow had managed to vanish completely. *Could* he still be out there watching, waiting for the doctor's return?

Wolf paused and wondered if Tom had been someone like himself with the same abilities. As he walked through Critter Country, heading for the Security office to check out for the night, Wolf shook his head. No, that couldn't be. He knew that others existed—the story about the wolf that had bitten his mother was proof of that—but that wasn't what they did with their power. Or, shouldn't do…. He wasn't exactly given an owner's manual when he went through the vortex that first time when he was young and suddenly found his whole life had been turned upside down.

Leaning against the wood-like railing lining the Rivers of America, Wolf stared unseeing at the barely-visible watchtowers of the old Fort Wilderness on Tom Sawyer's Island. Almost all of the lights on the island were out as the crowds had gone for the night. The maintenance workers would be coming into the Park soon to begin their ritual of cleaning and repairs. Swallowing a sigh, Wolf felt he wasn't doing his absolute best for Walt. Tom was still out there, he felt sure of that. He would be in his mid-seventies by now. Would he really still be a threat to Doctor Houser? Wolf, Walt and the Blond-Haired Man had never intended for the doctor to be gone this long. But, as time passed, and absolutely no sign of Mr. Bolte had been found, they had to seriously question the situation. When could they take the chance? When was it safe to bring him back? Kimberly, Lance and Wolf—Walt's remaining Guardians—had been keeping up with the latest discoveries in cryogenics. Encouraging progress was being made, but not enough for their end goal. Would Doctor Houser be able to speed things up? Was this the time to bring him back to continue the work he had already started? Or had things not progressed even further because he had not been there?

Wolf had more questions than he had answers as he rubbed a tired hand over his eyes. He wished Walt was still around to talk to. Even the Blond-Haired Man was gone. His daughter, Kimberly, hadn't even been born yet when all this went down in 1966. She knew, of course, about Doctor Houser from her discussions and learning at the hands of her father. But, it wasn't the same.

He wanted to talk to Walt, even if just for a little while to put things into perspective. It would help clear his head of all the doubts and questions that were continually assailing him.

The "how" of it was easy for Wolf. He could go just about anywhere back in time. But, where should he go? *Well*, he thought, *where did Walt go when he needed to refresh and regroup?* Wolf smiled a very wolfish smile in the darkness. That was easy. Marceline, Missouri, the small town where Walt had lived as a boy and dearly loved. Walt and his brother Roy would take trips—both publicized and private—to Marceline and they would visit the farm where they used to live and see Walt's special Dreaming Tree. Walt and his younger sister Ruth had spent hours under that tree dreaming dreams and enjoying nature.

Okay, now that Wolf had his destination, there was a more important aspect he needed to figure out: When in time would be best? When had Walt been there so Wolf could meet up with him? He knew Walt had been too sick to dedicate the Midget Autopia ride from Disneyland that he had donated to the children of Marceline in 1966. What about a little before that? He would have to do some research.

A growl rumbled deep in Wolf's chest. *I don't want to do any research.* Impatient, he wanted to go now. He knew where the portal for that particular jump would be. *Sometimes you just have to take a chance*, he told himself as he strode purposefully towards Main Street.

Once inside the deserted Main Street Cinema, Wolf paused. Because he hadn't used this specific portal before, he wasn't sure what form he would take on the other side. Going backwards in time, he always seemed to emerge as a wolf. When he returned to his proper time, which, in this case, was the year 2007, he would revert to being a man. There had never been any jumps into the future…. Wolf's head started hurting as he once again tried to figure out the logic of what happened to him when he used a portal. He was a man now simply because he had lived through all the preceding decades since he had first starting traveling, not aging, and relocating as necessary when it became obvious by his unchanging outer appearance that "something" was different about him—he even had had to quit Security at Disneyland for a number of years until he could hire on again with a new group of guards. He only became a wolf when he would portal into the past, such as when he visited his family on The Island.

He smiled ruefully. His father has not seen his face—his real face—since he was teenaged and had left the encampment on his own to "figure things out." When much time had passed and he found the way to go back and visit, he always arrived as a wolf. Well, he was happy that at least he had the ability to talk even though he was a wolf. That had come in handy that first time he arrived and his father and the braves had come at him with clubs and arrows.

Shaking off his futile musing, Wolf figured he had to assume he would come through as a wolf. At least Walt knew that is what happened to him. His boss had never seen it, but...depending on *when* in time he arrived, Walt might not know him yet.... Wolf's head started pounding again. With another growl in his chest, he knew he would just have to play it by ear when he got there.

Realizing that his clothes wouldn't make the change, he would rather they be put in a safe place than just abandoned on the floor. Going behind the red velvet draperies next to the largest screen, Wolf found a small unused cabinet where he neatly stacked his uniform. If all went well, he would be back approximately at the same time of night—give or take a few hours. Any later and the vortex might open with guests viewing the Mickey Mouse cartoons playing in the Cinema. It wouldn't do to have a disoriented, unclothed security guard suddenly falling into their laps....

Smiling as he let that mental picture slide by, Wolf tilted his head back and let out a soft, lingering howl. The Cinema might be empty, but there could be any number of maintenance people working right outside the door on Main Street who might become curious at the strange noise coming from the supposedly closed building. He didn't worry about the brightness that accompanied the vortex spilling out onto Main Street. The Cinema's double-curtained entry system allowed the interior to be in constant darkness as necessary for the six movie screens that circled the room.

Standing calmly near the back of the room, he didn't have to wait long in the darkness. A swirling mass of pink glitter formed on the middle of the polished wooden viewing platform, growing in height and then falling in on itself as lightning flashed from the ceiling. When the sparkling mass formed a tornado-like funnel and moved across the floor towards him, Wolf jumped into the center of the eye as one last bolt of lightning lit the small room. The pink funnel collapsed over him and all faded from sight.

Marceline

A sudden gust of wind blew the paper flyers all over the ornate lobby of the Cater Opera House. The small chandelier overhead rocked back and forth as the wind circled the room and blew out of the entry door and into the dark street outside. Lightning cracked as a wolf struggled into a sitting position just outside the Men's Room door, next to the metal radiator used for heating the lobby.

Groaning, Wolf sat there for a minute, mentally gathering himself. When he realized he was no longer in the Main Street Cinema at Disneyland, his head jerked around to make sure he was alone. He heard no screams, so, so far, so good. Getting his hind legs under him, he forced himself up, shaking his black fur into place. *At least I know where I am*, was his first thought. *Now I just have to figure out the* when *part.*

Eyes adjusting to the darkness, he immediately discovered an important fact: He was *not* in the Uptown Theatre as he had expected. Shaking off the effects of the vortex, he tried to determine where exactly he had landed. Having been to the Uptown Theatre in more recent times, there should have been a candy counter and popcorn machine in the narrow lobby. His stomach growled—a little popcorn would be nice right about now. But, there was no popcorn machine waiting for the next group of movie-goers. There was a glass display case and a wooden countertop, but both were empty. Thick gold ropes hung in front of the two doorways that led to the main part of the Opera House. Curving stairs led to the theater upstairs. In a golden frame was a smallish sign announcing that the traveling company would perform "Peter Pan" starring Maude Adams one last time on Saturday night. Wolf used a claw to pull over one of the papers littered over the cement floor. "Cater's Opera House, W. A. Cater, Prop. And Manager, Marceline, MO." the flourished title read across the top of the pale yellow leaflet. On the left, next to the title, was a purple oval cameo of a woman named Ruth. Below her likeness were advertisements for the visitor proclaiming lucrative features of the town—such as "Four First-Class Hotels" and "Four Great Coal Mines that offer Eight Pay-Days a Month." The center of the leaflet announced the coming speech entitled "The Sin of Sloth" by a local minister. Giving a short, "Hmmph," Wolf couldn't find any reference to the current year.

Still wondering, Wolf padded to the entry door and peered through the glass. There were no lights that he could see in any direction. Since it was still night, he knew he had a little time before he would have to make a run for cover. Finding the doors unlocked, he used his shoulder to push through. He didn't want to leave any tell-tale nose prints on the glass. Walking past the rectangular ticket booth jutting out from the building, he paused to look at the building. It was an impressively large, square brick building on one of the corners of Kansas Avenue. Just past the box office was a flight of stairs. There was another entry door between two tall, narrow plate-glass windows, one of which read Drug Store. Leaving the sidewalk, Wolf stepped onto the dirt road of Kansas Avenue, the main thoroughfare of Marceline. *The road is still dirt? How far back did I come?*

If Kansas Avenue was still a dirt road and not paved, he knew he had to have come back pretty far in time, probably quite a bit farther than he had planned. Thinking about the possible time period, the thought came to him that there would mostly likely be plenty of early rising farmers and shopkeepers. Farmers and shopkeepers always had rifles handy—and, all of them usually did not like wolves.

Loping at a swift pace, glancing over at the newly planted Ripley Park, Wolf ducked behind the stores lining the main street and took to the alleyways, heading north for the almost-two mile trek out to the Disney farm, and hoping all the time that he had not made a jump too far back in time for it to not even be there. A few dogs rashly challenged him as he ran, but, once they got a smell of the wolf, they wisely sank into silence and slunk off back into the darkness of their yards.

The eastern horizon was just starting to pink, heralding the start of a new day. Walt's father, Elias, was a hard worker and would be starting his day early. Wolf melted into the tall weeds and grasses a ways off from the large cottonwood tree Walt would later refer to as his Dreaming Tree. The barn was a ways back further from the road, out of sight from where he waited as the noises of a farm awakening drifted over his secluded hiding spot. If he got too hungry, there was always the apple orchard nearby. And there were pigs and chickens…. Wolf opened his mouth for a silent laugh. *That wouldn't go over very well with Walt's mother, Flora!*

He must have nodded off in the warm sunshine that slanted over his thick black coat. Wolf awakened to the sound of a harness jingling as Elias and Flora rode off in their wagon, apparently heading for town. He heard Elias call back some instructions for the "youngsters to keep out of trouble this time" and that they would "be back presently." Careful not to move too much or make any sudden movements, Wolf slowly lifted his head as the wagon rumbled down the dusty road. The horse must have been aware of the strange animal lurking in the weeds as he shied to the left, his head tossing nervously. Elias had to use a strong hand to bring the horse's head around. Once there was more distance away from the disturbing smell, the horse settled down and the wagon disappeared from sight.

Alert now and interested to see what would happen next, Wolf turned his head towards the direction of the small farmhouse. His ears picked up an animated conversation long before the speakers came skipping into view. Dressed in blue overalls, there was young Walt. He looked like he must be around eight years old. Holding a long stick like a sword, he jumped over an imaginary foe and proclaimed that it was safe for Ruth to come into the meadow. In a tidy pink and white gingham dress, Ruth, who would be around six, gave a curtsey to her noble brother as she skipped over to the cottonwood tree.

"You have the best imagination, Walt! How do you come up with all these things?" she wanted to know, gazing in wonder at her brother.

Walt took a few practice jabs with his sword and then flung it off to the side, barely missing Wolf's ears as it flew past him. "Gosh, I don't know, Ruthie. It's all just there in my head!"

"How long do you think mother and father will be gone? I hope they bring us a sugar stick!"

Walt, still smarting from the lecture he had been given last time, mumbled, "I doubt it. They were pretty mad, still."

Ruth pouted at the thought of not getting the desired treat. "Well, it was your fault. I knew we shouldn't paint a picture on the side of the house with tar. It still hasn't come off."

"It was a good picture, though! They won't stay mad forever," he said, silently adding, *I hope*.

A soft breeze drifted over the fields, stirring the diamond shaped leaves overhead in the cottonwood tree. Cocooned in their cottony protection, seeds started falling from the branches. Walt watched as they floated across the shafts of sunlight streaming through the limbs and leaves. "Oh, look at that, Ruth!" he exclaimed, pointing upwards.

Used to the common sight of leaves and seeds falling, Ruth wasn't sure what her big brother was talking about. She sat down next to him on the grass and looked around. "Look at what, Walt?"

"Remember that play we saw? Peter Pan? These are the fairies! See how the sun lights up their wings as they fall to the ground, twirling around like that? Fairy dust!"

"You mean like pixies in the story books?"

Walt was entranced. "Yes, that's it! Pixie dust!"

Lost in watching the two children, Wolf gave a snort that would have been a laugh if he had been a human. Two young heads spun around at the noise. Knowing he had been seen, Wolf's mouth snapped shut. "Oops," he muttered. Dropping his head, he flattened his ears, trying to look contrite.

Ruth let out a piercing scream and scrambled to get behind the protection of her brother. "It's a wolf! Oh, Walt, I'm afraid of the big, bad wolf!"

Walt looked around quickly and scooped up some rocks that he started throwing at the huge animal. He was surprised when the wolf just easily dodged his stones and sat there, staring at them. "It's okay, Ruthie, I'm not afraid of your big, bad wolf," he gulped, grabbing more rocks.

This could go on all day, Wolf sighed as he avoided the next missiles. Walt had a pretty good arm on him. Deciding to try another tact, Wolf let the next rock hit him. Unfortunately, it was aimed straight at his head. "Ouch!" came out unchecked. When he saw Walt's eyes get big, he changed it to a whine and limped forward two steps and fell heavily at the side of the clearing.

Walt's eyes narrowed. "Why was he limping if I hit him in the head?"

Ruth was still standing behind him, too afraid to move. "Is...is it dead?" she asked hopefully as she peered around.

They could hear the animal whining pitifully. "I think I really hurt him."

Wolf slowly crawled forward, ears down and tail limp. Two steps and then he stopped. The two children just stood there, staring at him, so he let out another pitiful whine. *Gosh, what does it take?!*

He rolled to his side and let his tongue roll out. He gave one last loud whine for good measure. Looking up at young Walt, he nodded his head and held up a paw.

"I don't think he means to eat us, Ruth. It looks like his paw is hurt. I'll bet he's a nice wolf. I also thought I heard him say ouch."

The concern on Ruth's face gave way to smiles. "Oh, Walt. There you go again! You know animals can't talk."

"I'm going to try and pet him."

"You were told to keep out of trouble, Walt! Let's go back to the house," Ruth tried to reason.

"You go ahead. I want to see if he is okay. I'll be fine," he insisted as Ruth hesitated.

Her caution overcame her concern for her brother, and Ruth ran all the way back to the farmhouse. When Walt heard the back door slam, he licked his dry lips and took another couple of steps towards the motionless animal.

"I'm not going to hurt you, fellow," he said softly, still advancing slowly, his hand out in front of him.

Wolf made a decision. "I know, Walt," he replied as quietly as his deep voice allowed.

Eyes as big as saucers, Walt stopped in his tracks. "I knew it! You did speak!"

"Can I come and sit in the shade? It's getting awfully warm out here."

Walt, still surprised, dropped into a sitting position himself. Taking that as a yes, Wolf crawled slowly forward until he was within touching distance.

"You knew my name," Walt muttered. Shaking his head as if in disbelief, he thought to ask, "What's your name?"

"Wolf."

"You're kidding."

The tooth-filled mouth opened in a silent laugh. "Not very original, but it is true."

"Do you live around here?" Walt was hopeful. A talking wolf would make a great pet. That is, if his father allowed him to keep it....

Wolf shook his head. "No, I live far away. In California. You should go there some day," he added. *You never know.*

Disappointed, Walt just said, "Aw, shucks. Can I pet you? I don't have a dog."

Wolf chuckled to himself. "Sure, go ahead." A boy is a boy is a boy.

He let Walt explore the gray-tipped fur on his ears and run his hands over the coarse hair on his back. "Wow," Walt whispered, "I'm touching a wolf! Wait until I tell Roy!"

"No, no, you shouldn't do that, Walt," Wolf admonished.

The hand rubbing his back stilled. "Why not?"

The big head swung around to look at him. "Do you really think he will believe you?"

Walt's mouth opened to answer, and then he suddenly shut it and shook his head.

"Let's just keep this between you and me, okay? Just don't forget your talking wolf. You might need me someday." *More than even you can imagine right now, too.*

"I won't forget! I promise! Hey, where are you

going?" cried Walt, as Wolf stood up and looked towards the seclusion of the orchard.

"I need to go. Your parents are coming back.
Be sure to tell Ruth I was a big doggie. It will make
her feel better."

Walt was looking down the lane. "I don't see
them. Are you sure?"

Wolf nodded. "I can hear them talking and can
smell the horse. Be good, Walt. But, not too good!"
He turned away to go to the orchard to wait it out for
the day, and head back with the covering protection
of darkness.

"Bye, Wolf! I won't forget! Thank you," he
waved as the wolf bounded away.

"No, thank you, Walt."

That night, long after the farmhouse had gone
dark and all the Disneys had fallen asleep, Wolf still
crouched in the orchard, waiting. It had been a
good visit, an interesting one. Silently padding out
into the meadow, he looked over at the barn that
would have a home in California when he went back
to his own time. "I'm glad I came," he said contentedly. "Now I can get back to work."

Not wanting to run the distance back into town
and take his chances with the Cater Opera House,
he decided to try something different. Going under
the Dreaming Tree, he sat and quietly called the
vortex. A nervous neighing and stamping could be
heard coming from the barn. The horse, which had
been skittish when hitched to the wagon earlier,
heard his quiescent howl and knew "something"
was still around—"something" that was different and

deadly.   Hoping the noise of the horse didn't awaken the household, Wolf watched as the fog drifted out of the nearby pond and covered the meadow, the sparkling lights dancing in front of his eyes. Wondering *why is it always pink?* he waited until the right moment and quickly made his escape into the void.

Just he emerged in the back room of the Main Street Cinema and his year again became 2007, one last bolt of lightning illuminated the Cinema. In Marceline, at that the same moment in 2007, a phantom swirl appeared over the exact spot where he had just been sitting—and, unknown to Wolf—a lone blaze of lightning blasted through the branches of the Dreaming Tree, practically splitting it in two.

CHAPTER FOUR

Disneyland – 2007

Rubbing his forehead, Wolf was surprised to find a welt. Apparently Walt's rock yesterday had hit him harder than he had thought. "Great. Now I have to come up with an explanation for this if anyone asks," he muttered to himself. He smiled in spite of his grousing. Walt did have a pretty good arm on him. Wolf's walkie-talkie beeped and interrupted his private thoughts. He saw it was his private channel direct from the War Room—the secret room Walt had built into the Blond-Haired Man's mansion in the Fullerton hills. This was the central base of operations for watching and protecting the Hidden Mickey searches he had set up prior to 1966. Now under the control of Lance and Kimberly Brentwood, the War Room was just as active as it had been in the beginning as Disneyland continued to grow and develop over the years. There were still secrets and more clues that needed to be protected for future discoveries. And, there was still some unfinished business, such as Doctor Houser's protection and well-being.

Walking past the busy entrance of the Blue Bayou Restaurant, Wolf brought the speaker to his mouth and gave a brief, "Just a minute, Boss," as he headed for a more private section so he could talk freely if need be. Knowing the steam train, the *C. K. Holliday*, had just left the New Orleans Square station, he chose the empty exit ramp at the opposite side of the station, far enough away from the nearby French Market Restaurant's outdoor tables and the busy entrance to the Haunted Mansion so he would not be overheard. "Sorry about that," he said when situated.

"Hello, Wolf. Kimberly here. How are you?"

Wolf smiled to himself. It must not be too important if she was going through the pleasantries. "Fine, thank you. And you?" he answered dryly.

He could hear her throaty chuckle. "All right, Wolf, I'll get to the point! We think we have a lead on your, uhm, missing person." She seemed hesitant to reveal more.

"I'm in a secure location, Kimberly. You can talk freely."

"Oh, good. Lance found...Peter! Put that down, honey. That's not a toy. I'm talking to Uncle Wolf...No, not now. This is important, hon...."

"Unca Wolf!" came an excited scream through the earpiece. Wolf had to hold it away from his ear.

"Hau Peter. Híŋháŋni," Wolf smiled. He had been trying to teach the boy a few words of Lakota.

"Mornin', Wolf!" the boy exclaimed back and giggled, excited he had understood what Uncle Wolf had meant. From the other sounds Wolf could hear, it was obvious the boy was also getting adept at eluding his mother.

"Very good, Peter. Let me talk to you mother. Now," he added firmly.

"Okay. It's for you," as the walkie-talkie was immediately handed back to Kimberly.

He could hear the amusement in her voice. "You'll have to teach me how you do that."

"It's the voice."

She lowered her voice to a gravely depth. "Is this better?"

Wolf gave a short laugh. "No, you'd probably scare him. You said something about a missing person?" He wasn't much for chit-chat.

Understanding Wolf's idiosyncrasies, Kimberly got back to business. "Oh, yes. Lance ran across a rundown landscape business way out in the high desert around Apple Valley. From what he could tell, it never appeared very successful, but he thinks it is a viable lead."

"What's it called?"

"T.B. Landscapes."

Wolf gave a low chuckle. "Perhaps the name had something to do with the lack of success."

Kimberly appreciated that and laughed. "Yeah, could be. Anyway, Lance thinks this might be our long-missing Tom Bolte. Do you want to check it out, or do you want Lance to make the run?"

"I'll do it," Wolf answered immediately. "If this T.B. is Tom, Lance might be put in danger, and we can't have that. Besides, if it is Tom…I have some unfinished business with him."

Kimberly felt a shiver go over her arms. "We thought you might say that. I'm sending the address to your navigation system. Have a good drive." She broke off. She was going to add, "Be careful," but didn't want to insult him. "Uhm, over and out," she mumbled instead and ended the connection.

Wolf smiled at the static he suddenly heard on the line. "Roger that," he replied with a grin as he returned the device to his utility belt.

His grin faded as he headed to the Security office to check out and change clothes. Yes, he had unfinished business with Tom and sincerely hoped this was not just another dead lead.

The classic Mustang roared north on the 57 freeway, where it would merge onto the 60 for a short jaunt, before hitting the Interstate-15 for the final leg of the trip. The distance was a total of about eighty-five miles; then he would head for Victorville and on into Apple Valley. Kimberly had added that the landscape business was "out in the country." Wolf gave a dry chuckle as that terminology seemed to define most of the area through which he was traveling.

His portable navigation system directed him to a remote area of the Valley. A weathered sign announced "TB Landscaping. No job is too small." Wolf pulled to a stop in what might have been a parking lot at one time, and the dust cloud that had been following him settled over the bright red paint. The white racing stripes were now a dull gray color. "Great," he grumbled, as the driver's door clicked shut behind him.

There were only a few dozen plants in containers waiting to be sold. A couple of drooping white birch trees seemed to be begging for water as he had driven past them on his way to the main building. Ten pine trees seemed to be in slightly better condition in their huge wooden tubs. Whatever flowers were to be bought had long ago lost their blooms and were indistinguishable from one another. Rows of cactus appeared to be the only healthy options for purchase. Four tall metal windmills could be seen behind the sales building; their silver blades idle in the still air. A trellis near the dripping water faucet had some kind of orange flower hanging onto the faded white wooden slats. Parked near a stack of forty-pound bags of potting soil was a 1970's model Ford flatbed truck with the company's logo still readable on the dented door.

Wolf took all this in as he walked slowly along the dirt path. There had once been pebbles on the pathway, but they had long been pressed into the dirt base. He couldn't see any indications of prosperity—either now, obviously, or of any past grandeur that had faded over the course of time. *Is this what Walt's money had paid for?*

As Wolf approached the wooden building, a skinny man of medium height and sun-bleached hair emerged from the darkness. Dressed in overalls and a threadbare cotton shirt that might have been yellow at one time, the man wiped his forehead with a bright blue bandana. "Hot enough for you?" he asked pleasantly, looking over his prospective customer, his eyes stopping for a moment on the large welt in the middle of the man's forehead.

Wolf couldn't honestly have said if this man was forty-five or seventy-five. The desert sun and his profession had obviously taken its toll on the man's skin. "Are you Tom? Tom Bolte?"

"Yep, that's me. How can I help you? Have some lovely cactus for sale." He swung an arm in the general direction of all the plants laid out on the ground.

Casually putting himself between the man and the truck, Wolf put what he hoped was a friendly expression on his face and asked him, "I knew a Tom in Anaheim years ago. Did you used to work for Disneyland?"

Tom mopped his forehead again. "Nope, I've lived here all my life. Musta been my dad. That your car? Nice! Always loved the Mustangs. Yours could use a wash, though." He silently laughed at his own joke, abruptly stopping when he saw the stranger didn't share the humor.

"Your dad here? I'd like to say hello."

Tom looked away as if deciding what exactly to say. His dad had talked on and on about his time at Disneyland, how he had personally run the Landscaping Department for years. This man in front of him looked too young to have worked for his dad. "Yeah," he finally said, "Dad loved working there. Said he had the Landscaping Department working like a fine-oiled machine. When he had saved enough money, he moved out here and started the family business."

Wolf let the inaccuracies about which department Tom had really worked in slide by. It wasn't up to him to settle that aspect of the matter. "I take it he isn't here? Is he…uhm, still with us?" That was about as delicate as Wolf was capable of being.

Tom turned his head to gaze at the distant hills, shimmering purple in the heat. A wave of emotion crossed his lined face. "No, he isn't. He's been gone for, oh, about ten years now." He glanced back at Wolf's face again, frowning. "You said you thought you knew him?"

Wolf just nodded and remained silent.

Not caring enough to get into the discrepancy of their ages, Tom shrugged. "Dad kinda wandered off one day. As you can probably see," he admitted with a despondent wave around the area, "we aren't exactly what you would call thriving. It always bothered him that he couldn't do as well here as he had done at the Park. During one particular dry spell, he kinda snapped. Started muttering about some red heart-shaped ruby, of all things! Never did figure that one out," Tom muttered, shaking his head at the memory.

"Where did he go?" Wolf prompted when the man remained silent for a few moments.

Indicating the hills again with a tilt of his chin, Tom replied, "That way. Me and my wife found him face down with his hand down an old gopher hole. He was still alive—barely. We poured some water over his face. He was mumbling something about bubbling pots of mud and that he fooled them all. Not sure who he meant by 'them all.' We got him to the hospital in Victorville, but it was too late, he was too far gone." He looked over at Wolf's face, hoping to get some answers to his father's confused ranting. "Any idea what he was talking about? We've never been able to figure any of it out. You're the first person who ever came by who says they knew him back then."

His own questions answered, Wolf hesitated. He saw nothing good that would come from his explaining what had really happened so long ago. There was no need for him to shatter whatever illusions this man held of his father. He now knew the lingering threat hanging over the doctor was over. The money was obviously gone. The secret of the heart pendant still seemed to be safe. "No, I'm sorry. I wish I could help, but I have no idea. I'm sorry for your loss." That was sufficient.

Tom just gave a noncommittal grunt and nodded his thanks. He hadn't really expected to learn anything.

Wolf was about to leave when he heard shrill laughter coming from behind the sales building. "Are those your…" he broke off, not sure whether to say children or grandchildren.

Tom's face broke into a wide smile that transformed his entire face. "Grandkids. We've got three of them. Little devils," he added proudly as they came tearing around the building, mindless of the heat or the dust. Seeing someone with their granddad, they came to a noisy halt, staring at the dark stranger.

Coming to an instant decision, Wolf pulled his wallet out of his back pocket. Opening it, he chose one of the passes he always carried. Handing it to Tom, he explained, "This is a two-day park-hopper pass for up to eight people. Good any day of the week. Just present it at the main gate."

Tom showed it to the three young ones who were pulling his arms down so they could see. When they saw the word Disneyland over the face of the pass, they got all excited. "This is where your great-grandpa used to work!" Tom proudly told the youngsters.

Over the clamor, Wolf added, "Be sure to show them the topiaries over at It's a Small World. I think they will appreciate the workmanship." He just failed to mention that Tom Sr. would have had nothing to do with those beautiful landscaping items.

"Thank you!" was Tom's heartfelt reply after he sent the children off in search of their grandmother with the good news. "This will mean a lot to all of us."

Wolf just nodded as he headed for his dusty car. *You're turning into a regular softie*, he told himself as the Mustang ate up the miles on I-15. *Good thing Mato wasn't here to see that. I'd never hear the end of it…. Lance doesn't need to know, either.*

Disneyland – 2007

Wolf could feel the electricity in the air. His hair felt prickly and he was jumpy, eager. He now knew that it was the right time to go back to the Island. And, this time he also knew he needed help.

The Westside Operations cast member briefing had lasted two hours. General safety and regulations had been discussed as required by law. New cast members were introduced to the Lead on whichever ride they had been assigned in Frontierland, Adventureland, or Critter Country—the area known as the Westside. And, most importantly to Wolf, new rides and attraction changes were discussed, timetables were set, and affected assignments were rearranged. The main focus of the meeting was the coming changes that would affect both New Orleans Square and Tom Sawyer's Island. Pirates were coming, and they were going to take over the Island. The changes would tie in nicely with the alterations that had been implemented within the popular ride Pirates of the Caribbean. Pirates were big now, and they felt it was time to give the fifty-one-year-old Island a facelift.

As the briefing proceeded regarding New Orleans Square, Wolf half-listened impatiently to the changes being outlined, his eyes straying to the aluminum clock high on the wall behind the speaker. The Lead cast member lectured in a continuous monotone. Again Wolf found himself glancing anxiously at the clock, its hands continuing to count down the time in relentless monotony. Tick. Tick. Tick. Tick.

Tugging at the collar of his security uniform, it felt tight against his neck as an unfamiliar, nervous sweat broke out on his forehead. *Why does he keep droning on and on? He's worse than my father. You need to get out of here*, his mind warned him. He had called the fog. It was coming. Soon. He glanced at the clock again. Very soon.

His collar seemed to be closing in on his windpipe. Glancing around at the other cast members idly listening to the speech, no one else seemed to notice the loud ticking of the clock. Wolf slowly raised his hand to his hair, slowly so no one would see his movement and look over. Did his hair seem longer, thicker already? *It is too soon! It shouldn't change yet!*

Heart rate speeding up, Wolf felt a wave of panic. *Not here! This isn't right*.

He lowered his hand and rested it, palm down, on his leg. Eyes closed, Wolf tried to concentrate on his breathing to calm himself. In. Out. In. Out. *There is plenty of time*.

Tick. Tick. Tick.

His eyes flew open as the sound of the clock came to his ears once more. Was his hearing getting sharper? *Who in here had bologna for lunch?* he wondered as his nose picked up the unpleasant scent and his head turned unconsciously towards the guilty person seated a few chairs over.

The claw on his leg curled, digging into his thigh. His blue eyes widened in shock as he looked down. His nails had grown long and curving. There was thick black hair on the back of his hand now, tipped in silver like the hair on his head.

With a startled gasp, he brought his hand protectively to his chest, hiding it as best he could. His eyes quickly darted around the room. Good. No one saw the transformation.

Get out!

The words bounced through his mind over and over. It felt more like an instinct than an actual thought. Still battling the change from human reasoning to animal impulse, he tried to rise slowly from his chair. The power coming into his legs made him awkward as the chair crashed to the floor behind him.

Ignoring the chair, Wolf lunged for the door, grateful for the push bar exit rather than having to try and turn a door knob. Everyone had to be looking. They had to see the hideous change coming over him. They had to see it. His uniform was getting tighter and tighter.

Without a look behind, Wolf ran down the passageway towards the freedom of the outside and the welcome, covering darkness of night. Just as he reached the door, he could see his reflection in the window and came to an instant halt. His paw reached up and touched the tufts of black fur sprouting out of his cheeks. His silver-tipped ears were now pointed and lay down angrily on his head.

Get out!

The sound of a door being pushed open came to his ears at the same instant the instinct came to his mind. Tugging at the buttons threatening to suffocate him, Wolf barreled through the door at a run, swerving to the left to get into the trees and the River.

Senses alert, he forced himself to stay on his hind legs, to run upright as he sought the safety of the River. Perhaps he could cancel the fog and the swirling mass waiting for him…. He had never tried that before.

Head up as he ran, he tilted his face to the sky. As he was going to let out a soul-piercing howl, he saw the full moon directly above him. He snarled at it as he effortlessly climbed the berm, putting more distance between himself and his friends at the meeting.

The silver-tipped fur covered his entire body now. His feet had pushed through the thick leather of his security boots, the claws menacingly protruding out of the front. His hat had already fallen off somewhere behind him, lost in the tangle of the trees surrounding Frontierland.

As he emerged from the trees behind the Hungry Bear Restaurant, he started pulling off the shreds of the white shirt still hanging from his torso. His sharp canine teeth tugged and the buttons popped off onto the walkway, bouncing like gold nuggets in the bright moonlight.

"Wolf? Is that you?" came a feminine voice through the fog of the change within his brain.

His mouth closed with a loud *Snap* as his head

spun towards the unexpected noise.

Julia. The vivacious redhead from Pirates. Her hair gleamed a burnished copper in the glow of the moon. She stood with his security hat in her hands, holding it out like an offering to a god.

His animalistic impulses surged through his body. *She is so beautiful*.

He tried to reach out to her, to take her hand, to draw her close to him for the kiss he had always wanted to taste from her lips. His mouth tried to smile as he took a step closer towards the beauty standing in the moonlight.

Julia saw a claw reach towards her. She saw a mouth suddenly open revealing sharp, dangerous teeth. She saw the huge creature—mouth open, claws extended—coming closer and closer to her.

Her piercing scream echoed back from the tallest spire of Splash Mountain as she crumbled to the walkway in a faint.

Wolf stopped in his tracks, arms still out-stretched for a welcomed hug, as she fell. The sound of her scream—so different than that of the happy guests on the thrill rides—brought the un-wanted attention of other guests who were nearby. Wolf could hear their concerned mutterings as they got closer to his location. The mutterings turned to shouts of warning and fright as they spotted him standing over the fallen woman.

Grabbing up fence posts and breaking off signs, the men came at him armed as best they could. Someone grabbed one of the burning torches on the canoe dock and was gesturing for more men to come help. A knife blade, somehow snuck through Security, flashed in the waning light as the men grouped together and slowly formed an advancing semi-circle to hem him in.

Backing slowly away from Julia, Wolf's eyes darted over the approaching mob. The moon was obscured now, the coming fog a welcome relief for him. As the swirls of mist got thicker, Wolf edged closer and closer to the edge of the River. Soon the lightning would flash and he would be safe.

As the men saw the creature backing away from them, wary, they thought he would break for the trees and they would lose him. With a com-manding shout, the man with the knife yelled, "Let's take him!" The numbers gave them courage and they surged forward as one, sharpened, broken ends of their impromptu spears in front leading the way, chest high.

Seeing the attack, Wolf's eyes widened in fear. He dropped on all fours and turned to the safety of the River.

He heard the whistling sound before the blade ever reached him. Glancing over his shoulder, he saw the knife heading straight between his eyes.

With a start, Wolf awakened and the plastic chair he had tilted back crashed to the floor with a startling bang in the quiet room. All eyes turned to the usually staid security guard who was obviously trying to figure out where he was.

Red-faced, Wolf ignored the few snickers that went around the room as he picked himself up and righted his chair. Eyes half closed, he glanced over at nearby Julia. Unperturbed by his less-than-graceful awakening, she gave him a sly wink and smile.

Ignoring her open invitation, he cleared his throat and resumed his usual outer calm demeanor as he tried to figure out where they were in the lecture. As the memory of the nightmare faded and his heart rate settled back to normal, he still had to force himself to remain seated and not pace the back of the room like a caged wolf. He did, however, reach a hand up and touch his cheek. It was smooth and he let out a pent-up sigh of relief. It was only when the speaker got to the part about Tom Sawyer's Island that he became instantly alert and leaned forward in his chair, the previous embarrassment nearly forgotten. As the coming drastic changes were being listed, Wolf came to realize one fact: He had to go tonight. He could feel it.

He looked around the room at the various cast members in attendance. He knew all of them, of course. It was Security's job to know them. His eyes stayed for a moment on certain men. He was analyzing them, measuring them. Feeling eyes boring into the back of their heads and not knowing why they felt that way, some of them shifted uneasily in their seats. Some looked quickly around the room in confusion. Wolf's eyes kept moving over the seated cast members until he found his eyes kept returning to one man—his friend Wals Davis.

Staring at the back of his friend's head, Wolf made the instant decision that Wals would be the one to go back with him. He was steady and hard working. He was good with people and could take instruction when necessary. And, just as importantly, nobody else here knew the history of the

Park and Tom Sawyer's Island as well as Wals.

Decision made, Wolf settled back in his hard plastic chair, the rest of the briefing washing over him unheard. He knew this would be the best choice for all concerned.

Now all Wolf had to do was convince Wals.

Wolf shook his head. That wasn't going to be easy. Maybe it would just be easier to conk him over the head and dump him in the River at the last minute.

Julia looked over again when she heard Wolf's low chuckle. She was curious as she hadn't heard anything remotely funny since the meeting began. He seemed to be in a better frame of mind since the embarrassing fall out of his chair and he was looking right in her direction. *Maybe he is coming around*, she thought as she gave him another one of her trademark devastating smiles just for good measure. Her smile slowly faded, though, and was replaced with a disappointed pout. Those gorgeous sapphire blue eyes set in his sharply defined, handsome face looked right through her, unseeing, as he folded his arms over his broad chest and laughed to himself once more.

"I need your help with a project, Wals," Wolf started, trying to broach the subject of time shifts, swirling pink vortexes and the fact that sometimes he was also a real wolf. He was having difficulty coming up with the right words to say. *Go figure*.

The two men were seated on the old Keel Boat dock in Frontierland, overlooking the River. Between that dock and the Raft ride was a new, huge sign the Park had put into place announcing the coming of the new and exciting Pirate's Lair to the Island. The sailing ship Columbia was docked at Fowler's Harbor right next to them. The Keel Boat dock was now used as a smoking section for guests, but today was a slow Wednesday at the Park and it was otherwise empty. Wals, on a break from the canoes, sat with one of his moccasin-clad feet propped up on the wood-like railing of the old dock. Wolf leaned his rear against the same railing, facing New Orleans Square and the Haunted Mansion, still on duty as Security. His eyes never stopped moving as he watched the guests as they strolled from one land to another or stopped to take pictures along the River.

Wals' curiosity was piqued. Wolf never asked anybody for anything. Even though they were good friends, he still figured it had to be something big for Wolf to seek out his help. And, knowing Wolf as well as he did, he waited patiently for the explanation. No one hurried Wolf.

Wolf finally ran an exasperated hand through his thick hair. "I have no idea how to get into this," he admitted, shaking his head.

Wals' interest was really piqued now, but, wisely, hid his amused smile. "You in trouble?" he ventured. That would be something. Wolf had the cleanest record of all the cast members. Sometimes he was gone for an odd number of days, but Management didn't seem to mind.

"Depends on how you define trouble," was the answer given with a half-grin. "I need to get two people out of a bad situation, and I need assistance doing it. I was hoping you could help me."

Wals foot came down off the railing and he

leaned forward. This was getting more interesting by the moment. "Is one of them possibly a female friend?" he asked with a grin. "What is it? Do you have an angry boyfriend you want me to take care of?"

Wolf looked momentarily confused. "Boyfriend? No, no, nothing like that." He broke off and looked out over the River. A Raft was making its trip across the narrow River, probably the last raft of the evening as dusk was getting closer and closer. Wolf suddenly felt a change in the air and lifted his head towards it.

"Did you just sniff the air, man?" Wals asked, surprised, his eyebrows up under his brown bangs. "I wouldn't do that with all these ducks floating by."

Not realizing he had slipped back into his other habits, Wolf turned away from the Island and the urgency it was sending him. "Remember that night when you found me in the River?"

"Yeah, I wish I had had a camera with me," Wals chuckled. "I could've sold those pictures of you for a lot of money to some of the gals who work here!"

Wolf ignored Wals humor. "More specifically," he stressed, "do you remember my mentioning the name Rose?"

Wals nodded, silently wondering about his friend's serious demeanor—not that that was too unusual for Wolf. "Yeah, I was hoping to find some cute little gal skinny-dipping with you. If I remember correctly, you then said she didn't like the River. You seemed kinda confused that night."

"That's putting it mildly," Wolf muttered, more to himself than to Wals. Louder, he explained further, "Rose is this friend of mine. She is one of the two people who need my help, but the thing is, neither one of them realize the situation they are in."

"I don't know any Rose who works on the Westside. Where is she? Fantasyland? Main Street? And who is the second person? A cute friend of Rose's who finds canoe guides irresistible?" *Never hurts to ask.*

Ignoring Wals' hopeful romantic encounter, Wolf continued, "Rose lives on an island and I need to bring her back here. She might not want to come with you. Actually, the other person, Doctor Houser, might give you some trouble, too."

Wals slapped his knee. "Oh, you mean they live on Catalina Island! Why didn't you say so? I haven't been over there in years!" He then remembered what else Wolf had said, "What do you mean 'come with *me*'? You're going too, aren't you?"

Taking a deep breath, Wolf looked at his friend. "That's where it gets tricky. I can't help them and neither one of them will know you. But you will still need to convince them to come back with you."

"I don't understand this at all. Won't you be there?" Wals was frowning now, trying to piece it together.

Yes, I will be there. I will be a wolf and you will probably be terrified of me, Wolf sighed to himself. There was nothing he could do about it. "I'll be there too. But you might not recognize me." The hair on the nape of his neck started tingling. Looking westward, he could see the fog starting to gather. Time was running out. He shook his head. He wasn't getting anywhere with Wals. And he knew the absolute truth would not be accepted or even heard. "Look, Wals, I need to ask you to trust me here. Can I rely on your help, come what may, one friend to another?"

"Come what may? I've never heard a guy use that term before...." Wals broke off his kidding when he realized the serious expression on Wolf's face. This was important to Wolf—whatever *it* was—and he was being asked for help. "All right. I'd like some more explanation, but I'll trust you. When do we leave for Catalina? Saturday? I'm off then."

Wolf held himself back from sniffing the air again. It would be sooner than he thought. He could feel the change starting within his body. He needed to get across to the Island now. The fog was beginning to creep across the River. His sharp hearing caught the cast members over on Tom Sawyer's Island trying to herd the guests back to the Rafts early. The darkness was falling quickly.

He had to take charge now and get Wals moving. "We need one of the little canoes. I have to go over to the Island."

Wals was surprised when Wolf started heading towards Critter Country and the secret dock for the canoes, bypassing his canoe dock. "Now? What about Catalina Saturday? I still have a shift to finish and then I am doing crowd control for the Fireworks."

Wolf lifted his walkie-talkie to his mouth. "This is Security Two. I am going offline in three minutes. I will require the assistance of Wals P. Davis, currently working Canoes. Check him out on my say, and consider him offline until further notice." The radio indistinguishably squeaked back at Wolf as he returned it to his belt. Kimberly had now been alerted and knew who was going with him. She would now be making the necessary call to Management in behalf of Wals. "You're finished. You ready?"

Totally confused, Wals pointed at his shirt. "I'm still in my costume. Is that all right?"

"Actually, it is perfect." They had reached the far side of the Hungry Bear and the small, locked gate. "I'll use my security card."

Looking over to the right, Wals could see the deserted canoe dock. Apparently his ride had shut down early, too. He looked worriedly into the sky as the wind picked up. It was supposed to be a clear night. As they pushed the little canoe away from the dock with their oars, Wals, sitting in front, tried to peer through the thickening fog. The farther they got away from the sheltering cove under the restaurant, the choppier the water was getting. Wolf was in the back steering. Wals called back to him, finding he had to yell to be heard over the wind that was now gusting past them. "Wolf! We need to dock this canoe. It's too choppy out here. Don't you remember the other night? It was just like this! These canoes don't have stabilizers, you know. Wolf?"

"Keep paddling," was all he heard.

Grumbling to himself and fighting down a rising panic, Wals bent his head into the wind and did as his friend asked. He fought to help keep the canoe upright.

Lightning suddenly streaked across the sky in front of them. Not easily startled, Wals still let out a yell and started back-paddling. The bolts were coming more frequently and seemed to be aimed right at them. "Keep going!" he heard Wolf call. He then felt the canoe rock violently and heard a loud splash over the sound of the wind. "Wolf? You okay?" When he received no answer, he looked back to see what had happened. He turned pale. The canoe behind him was empty. "Wolf!"

A forked bolt of lightning hit the water in front of him. As it did, it illuminated Wolf's Security hat as it floated by on the water that was now glowing with an eerie pink light. Eyes wide, Wals saw a swirling black hole open up in front of the canoe. Trying to avoid being swept in, he threw himself sideways, hoping to veer the canoe away from the menacing hole. Instead, the canoe was capsized and he fell into the foaming water, losing his grip on the slick paddle. The current grabbed Wals and the canoe and forced them towards the blackness. As he made one complete turn in the swirling water, arms flailing, Wals came face to face with the sharp features of a black wolf struggling to keep its nose above the water.

That was the last thing Wals remembered. The canoe swept past him, turned suddenly and banged him in the back of the head. The darkness overtook him and swept his limp body away.

Just as Wals entered the River and saw the terrible chasm open in front of him, sending a cold vein of fright coursing through his veins, Lance, on patrol in Tomorrowland, received a similar call on his two-way radio.

"Lance, this is Ken. You, uh, have a visitor." He sounded odd, like he was either trying not to laugh or not to scream.

Picking up on his friend's inflection, Lance smiled, "Come on, Ken. You know I'm on duty.

Who is it?"

Ken hesitated. "She is sitting right here," he tried to whisper. Louder, for the sake of his mysterious audience, he added, "She wouldn't say. She said she wants it to be a surprise."

Lance groaned. "I thought these 'surprises' had basically stopped in the past five years." He ran a hand through his hair. "Tell her I'm married and to go away."

Normally Ken would have chuckled at that. It was then that Lance heard a throaty laugh coming from the woman who apparently had heard him through the radio. A very familiar laugh.

"I'll be right there, Ken."

As he turned his steps towards the Security office, Lance could feel his heart rate speed up and his breathing become shallower the closer he got. The images going through his mind would not still. Clenching his hands into fists was the only way to keep them at his side and not wipe the sweat off onto the leg of his uniform. Lance entered the office at the instant Wals and Wolf entered the vortex, lightning blazing across the sky, thunder drowning out any other sounds. He knew he would soon be face to face with the enemy—the enemy so cold, so heartless that fear was struck by the very mention of her name. As the last deadly, ominous flash died, Lance greeted her the only way he knew how:

"Mother."

CHAPTER FIVE

Disneyland – 2007

Amanda Brentwood used the small, lighted vanity mirror to check her hair as Lance's Jaguar navigated the twisting turns leading up to his home in the Fullerton Hills. "You've barely said three words to me, darling." Glancing over, she could see the muscles in his cheek twitching.

"Well, you have to admit this is rather sudden, Mother," he finally said in a deceptively calm voice. "I am rather speechless."

The mirror snapped shut into the visor, the brightness that had illuminated her face faded. Her smile did not fade, however. Amanda seemed to be enjoying her son's discomfort. "Can't a mother want to visit her favorite son?"

"I'm your only son, unless I am mistaken."

He was surprised to feel a light reproving tap on his arm as she chuckled. "You always were incorrigible!" Glancing out of the window at the wonderful view of the valley below, all shimmering lights in the darkness, she added, "Where are we going, dear? It looks like the top of a cliff."

Don't tempt me, he smiled to himself.

Amanda saw the smile before it quickly disappeared and the frown that he had worn since he stepped into the Security Office returned. She gave a silent sigh and folded her hands in her lap.

"Unless you would rather stay at a hotel, I was taking you to my home to meet my family." He glanced over at her when the road allowed it. "You do know I am married, do you not?"

Lance felt an internal pleasure when her eyes narrowed before answering him. "Yes, I do. Not that you invited us," she muttered under her breath. Clearing her throat, Amanda continued, "When the news reached us that you also had a son, I thought I would stop by on my way to Paris."

"Paris!" Lance exclaimed, with a surprised laugh. "I may not have been a whiz at geography, but isn't Paris in the other direction from Boston?"

"Don't be ridiculous, dear. You were a whiz at everything."

Lance gave her a sly look. "Did I hear the tiny sound of pride in there somewhere?" he asked.

Amanda flashed him a sincere, warm smile—one of the few he had seen thus far into the conversation. "We never had any complaints about your schoolwork, Lance. You could do anything to which you applied yourself."

Here it comes…..

"Which is why we were so shocked when you abandoned the family business."

And there it is.

"But," she sniffed. "That is all water under the bridge now."

Easy for you to say.   He didn't take away your *trust fund.*

She patted the leather of the console between them in the Jaguar. "You seem to have done well for yourself, I must say. This is a beautiful car...."

Wait for it....

"Even though it seems to be an older model."

And, zing. "Yes, Mother. It is an '89. But, Jags never go do out of style." *God, I sound just like her.*

"I prefer Mercedes," she commented as they pulled into the circular drive of the mansion. "But, as I said, this is a nice car."

Wincing to himself, not entirely sure whether or not she was referring to his Mercedes that his father had repossessed, Lance had to admit silently, *Oh, you are good, Mother.*

It pleased him immensely to hear her shocked intake of breath as she got out of the car and looked at his house. "This...this is where you live?" She turned to him, clearly confused, her mouth open as if to say something else and unable to.

Lance gave her a crease of a smile. "Your mouth is hanging open, Mother. Yes, this is our home."

Cheeks reddened a little, Amanda turned back to the three-story house. "And you work for Disneyland." She sounded incredulous.

He took her by the elbow and steered her towards the stone entryway. "I got a raise."

The massive oak front door swung open and a small figure flew towards Lance. "Papa! You're home early! Me and mom are playing scouts like Unka Wolf...." Peter broke off his excited prattle when he saw the stranger with his father. His eyes narrowed as he scrutinized her.

"Mom and I are playing," Lance tried correcting, but seeing Peter's attention was now diverted, knew there was no reason to continue. "Peter, this is your...."

"Lance! You're home early! You are just in time to rescue me...," Kimberly came breathlessly to the door, a smile on her pink-cheeked face and her hair half-bound up in some kind of bandana. She, too, came to a halt when she saw Lance was not alone. Her sharp eyes darted from Lance's angled face to the identical cheekbones on the woman standing next to him. "Hello," she smiled, holding out her hand, "You must be Lance's mother. I'm Kimberly. And I think you just met Peter," she grabbed out with her other hand to haul Peter back to her side. "Peter, say hello to your grandmother, Mrs. Brentwood."

Amanda admired the sharpness of this beautiful girl, her eyes going over her disheveled appearance. Before she could respond, the disgusted cry of a child broke the air. It was soon followed by the matching cry of another.

Kimberly dropped the hand she was in the midst of shaking. "Oh, the twins! Peter, we left them tied up in the library! Come on," as she rushed back in the house with her son in tow.

As the two ran back into the house, Amanda slowly turned to her son. "Twins tied up in the library? Are you two doing daycare or something to help pay the bills, dear? Perhaps I came at a good time."

"Babysitting, not daycare, Mother. Alexander and Catie are the children of our friends Adam and Beth Michaels," as he steered her towards the library, shutting the front door firmly behind him.

"They took an anniversary trip to the Hotel Del Coronado in San Diego and asked if we could watch the twins for them."

Amanda's eyes never stopped moving around the house as she was being lead towards the library. She was very impressed by the warm, rich décor. "Indeed," she muttered as if disinterested.

The library was a welcoming room with floor-to-ceiling hardwood bookcases lining three of the walls. The tall windows were closed off to the darkness outside by antique-looking navy blue velvet drapes, a tasseled, thick gold cord scalloped over the valance. The dark walnut desk was cluttered with the usual paraphernalia of children at play. Sitting back to back on the Kashmiri carpet, were two identical brown-headed moppets, angrily complaining about being ignored and forgotten. Three years of age, they were uninterested in the stranger who entered the room as they were both clamoring for Kimberly's attention.

"Now, Alex, you know you could have pulled off the scarves yourself. They were just for show," she crooned as she pulled him into her lap.

"But, you 'n Peter were 'posed to rescue us! Catie was lost in the forest just like Uncle Wolf taught us. She was real scared," Alex was asserting as Catie, laughing, went running out of the room after the departing Peter.

"I'm sorry, Alex," she hugged him, smiling up at Lance. "We will have to finish our game tomorrow. We have company now," she tried to say brightly, indicating Amanda who still standing just inside the doorway, "And it is your bedtime."

"Aww, five more minutes?" Alex pleaded, looking at the door through which the other two had escaped, ignoring the older woman.

Kimberly exchanged a quick look with Lance. He gave a slight indication with his head. "Come on, sweetie," she told Alex. "I'll take you all up to bed."

The sound of whooping and hollering deep in the house stilled and was replaced by three complaining voices going up the stairway.

As the noise faded, Amanda turned to Lance. "Never dull, are they?" as a smile inched across her face.

That wasn't what he had expected. "No, it's never dull around here," he admitted with a large grin. "Come into the family room. We'll be more comfortable there," as he took her elbow to lead his mother to another part of the house.

As they settled across from each other on matching brocade sofas, Peter came running back down the stairs. "I wanted to say good night," he claimed as he hurled himself into his father's arms. Then, as he settled himself beside Lance on the sofa, it was apparent he had no intention of going back upstairs.

Knowing the tricks, Lance allowed it for a moment. "Peter, you were never properly introduced to your grandmother." He was faintly surprised when Peter got off the sofa and went over and extended his hand to Amanda.

"Wíyuškiŋyaŋ waŋčhíŋyaŋke ló"

Amanda's mouth opened to speak again, but froze in place. "I beg your pardon?" She looked to Lance for explanation.

Lance, looking rather proud of his son at that moment, even though he had no idea what the boy had just said. But, anything that made his mother speechless was fine with him. "In English, son."

Without missing a beat, Peter replied, "Pleased to meet you. May I call you Granny?"

Ignoring Lance's stifled laugh, she sniffed, "I'd prefer you didn't. How about Grandmother?"

Peter screwed his handsome little face up as he thought. Amanda's hand unconsciously went to her heart. *He looks just like Lance did at that age.*

"Gramma?" he tried to barter.

Amanda sat back on the sofa and laughed a deep, honest laugh. She impulsively held out her arms to hug the boy. Smiling, he crushed himself into her Chanel suit. "Oh, Lance, he's a pip."

Warmed by the affection she was showing his son, Lance relaxed his instincts. "Yes, he certainly is. His Uncle Wolf is teaching him some phrases in Lakota, his native American tongue," he offered in way of explanation.

The old Amanda surfaced. "Why ever? I should think French would be more productive."

Lance just shrugged. "It's good to know another language. Peter soaks it up like a sponge."

Sensing a change in the mood of the room, Peter slowly edged back towards his father. He didn't want to make too many moves to draw attention to the fact it was past his bedtime. But it was too late; he should have stayed still.

"Bedtime, Peter." Lance grinned to himself when he saw his son's face fall. That trick never worked. "Say goodnight to your grandmother. You two can get to know each other better tomorrow." He looked over the boy's sandy blond hair at his mother as he wondered: *Would she still be here tomorrow?*

She gave a small nod and held her hand out to

Peter. "Yes, I will see you tomorrow, Peter."

Looking chest-fallen that he had to go to bed, Peter glumly shook the proffered hand. "Taŋyáŋ ištíŋma yo," he muttered.

"Peter," Lance warned.

"Good night," he stressed slowly in English. Seeing his father's look, he quickly added, "Sorry."

"Off with you now," Lance went over and took the boy's hand, leading him to the doorway. Giving him a kiss, Lance sent him off with a light swat on his behind.

Amanda could see the love and warmth infused on Lance's face as he watched the boy run up the stairs. Moments later she saw a different warmth and love play over her son's features as his wife came into the room, self-consciously smoothing her tumbled hair into place. She could tell Kimberly was flustered by their unexpected guest, but was graciously trying to cover it. *She would do well in Boston*, Amanda decided with a satisfied smile.

As Kimberly sat next to Lance, grasping his hand between them on the sofa, an uneasy silence descended on the room. None of them seemed willing to speak first, to get to the reason of the visit.

Lance cleared his throat and was rewarded by two pairs of eyes instantly boring into him. He looked quickly from one woman to the other. They weren't going to speak. Kimberly's hand tightened. "Yes, well. Kimberly," he started lamely, "Mother tells me she stopped by on her way to Paris."

Kimberly's eyes got wide. "Paris? Isn't that in the other....?" She coughed, and tried again. "How lovely. Do you go often? I've never been."

They could see the amusement in Amanda's eyes. *How she loves this*, Lance thought to himself.

"Yes, we enjoy the city. We bought a small house five years ago just on the outskirts of the Paris...."

"Five years ago, Mother?" Lance demanded in a clipped voice. The hand gripping Kimberly's was getting tighter. It was only that grip that kept him from leaping to his feet. "Isn't that about the time Father had my Mercedes repossessed?" *And took away my trust fund from Grandfather?*

Amanda inwardly cringed. She hadn't meant to bring that up. Outwardly, she examined her immaculate nails. "Well, yes, I suppose it was around the same time. I hadn't thought of that." She looked from Lance's tight, angry face to the pale countenance of his wife—who surely knew the whole story. Amanda's mouth took on a firm, determined line as her chin raised a few inches higher. "While we are on that subject—which I had hoped to avoid...."

"No kidding," Lance muttered under his breath, but still loud enough for her to hear.

"We might as well get to the reason as to why I am here," Amanda continued as if unaffected by his sarcasm. She reached for the large gold-accented, quilted leather purse next to her.

The couple across from her just watched with curious, wary eyes. *What else can she take away from me*? Lance thought, feeling the comforting stroke of Kimberly's fingers on the palm of his hand. Knowing there was nothing his parents could do to further humiliate him, he felt himself relax. And, with his relaxing, Kimberly gave a small sigh of relief. Not realizing he had transferred his feelings to his wife, he gave her a small smile and raised her hand to his lips for a quick kiss.

Ever aware of what was going on around her, Amanda knew the exact moment when Lance relaxed. She had come knowing he would be angry and resentful. She had not known, however, the circumstances in which she would find him, with the beauty of his wife or the beauty of his house. There was a story there that his mother knew she would probably never learn. Accepting that, she finally found the papers she sought.

Pulling out a small sheaf of papers, she announced with a pleased smile. "I brought you a wedding present."

Lance eyed the papers in her hand. They looked rather official. "Is that a summons, Mother?" He had tried to sound light, but the animosity came through. "Or am I being sued?"

Amanda's eyes narrowed. "At least you remember some of your training from Harvard," she said with a toss of her free hand. At the cold answering stare she received, both the papers and her free hand fell into her lap. "Really, Lance, I feel as if you do not trust me at all."

His eyes mirrored hers. "Now, why would you think that, Mother? Disinheriting me? Disowning me? Disapproving of everything I did that was different?"

A manicured finger shot into the air. "You were never disowned!"

Lance put a hand to his chest and bowed his head. "My mistake," he chided.

He and Kimberly were both surprised when Amanda burst out laughing. "Oh, Lance! Your grandfather used to make that same gesture when he was being sarcastic! Oh, how I miss him."

There were tears in her eyes when her laughing finally stopped. "You look just like him, you know."

Lance, thinking of the grandfather he had truly loved, smiled at the thought. "Yes, I know. I miss him, too, Mother." *He was the only warmth and love I knew*.

Kimberly, unsure of what to say or do in this explosive setting, looked from one to the other. Their faces were so similar with the high cheekbones, strong chin, and clear brown eyes. She, like Peter had done, chose to sit still and not be noticed rather than jumping into the fray.

Amanda seemed to draw herself up to get on with business. "He was a wonderful man. Sometimes I wonder how I turned out like I did. Must have been my mother...." She caught Lance's incredulous look. "Yes, I do know how I am. I was trained to be exactly what I am. And I was trained to marry a man just like your father." She looked over at the silent Kimberly and smiled warmly. "Thank goodness you had the sense to leave Boston, Lance." At the confused look on her son's face, she waved her hand. "And if you tell your father I said that I will categorically deny it. Now," she picked up the papers in her lap again, "before we get off on another tangent...which I know we are well capable of doing...I would like to give you this." She handed the papers across the antique coffee table between them. As her eyes took in the luxury of the room, she mumbled under her breath, "Not that it would be as welcome now as it might have been five years ago...."

Lance leaned over to meet her halfway. He frowned at her words as he sat back next to Kimberly and looked at the proffered papers. He heard

Kimberly take in a sharp breath.

"Oh, Lance!"

He tried to still the thoughts whirling through his mind—thoughts of his beloved grandfather, thoughts of the injustice served on him, thoughts of the inconsistencies and the admissions of his mother. He tried to focus on the papers in his hand. His eyebrows shot up as he read.

Amanda seemed pleased at both their reactions. "Well, I thought it only seemed fair, Lance. I hope you enjoy it and can someday share it with your father and me. If you can, next week would be lovely."

Lance glanced over at his mother at this last remark. In the warm glow of the lamps lighting the room, she looked somewhat fragile to him. She had always been a pillar of strength, right or wrong. Now she looked hopeful and beseeching. Perhaps it was time to bury the hatchet. He saw the pleased look on Kimberly's face, the excitement of the possibilities. She nodded to encourage him to say *something*.

"Well, we can't this coming week, Mother. But, I have heard Paris is lovely in the spring. How about if we talk then?"

Some of Amanda's surrounding wall cracked and fell around her Versace pumps. "Yes, spring would be wonderful." She knew when it was time to withdraw. "Kimberly, would you be a dear and show me to my room? It has been a long, tiring day."

Belatedly recognizing her need to extend hospitality to Amanda, Kimberly interrupted. "Mrs. Brentwood, I am so sorry! I should have offered you something to eat earlier. Lance, I already ate with the children, but how about if I make you and your mother a nice dinner? There's always something to eat around here with Lance. It wouldn't take any time at all."

With a chuckle, Amanda stopped her saying, "Lance always was a good eater. But, no thank you, Kimberly. You are a dear, but I, too, had dinner. Actually I dined at Club 33 in the Park just before meeting up with Lance, so I really am fine and appreciate the offer. I really am tired and would rather just get some rest." She held a hand out to Kimberly and the two women walked arm-in-arm out of the room.

Lance sat back on the sofa, slightly stunned. He would have enjoyed a snack about now. But, other than that, it had been an eventful day. Wolf and Wals were on their way to bring back Doctor Houser. His mother had dropped in after not speaking to him for over seven years. And now this. He looked at the papers again.

In his hand were three open-ended airplane tickets to France and the deed to a house on the outskirts of Paris.

The Island – 1817

Much farther upstream than he usually cared to travel, the wolf awakened in the dim light of morning. Pulling himself up on the muddy riverbank, he found he didn't even have the strength to shake the water off his drenched coat. He must have fallen asleep again as he found the day was more advanced when he awakened a second time. Getting slowly to his feet, head down, he padded silently into the forest, away from the sound of the River.

Hunger. There was no coherent thought. Just a feeling, an instinct that he needed to feed. Gliding through the tall pine trees, the wolf's sharp sense of smell detected something different and, instantly alert, he immediately changed directions. Emerging in a clearing cut out of the forest, he saw a roughly cut green grass lawn spread out in front of him, a large Magnolia tree shading one of the grassy slopes. The wide green lawn led up to an impressive three-story white manor house. Stone paths edged with brick wound over the lawn and led to a small cemetery on the side of the house. Small ornamental evergreen trees and shrubs had been placed in matching brick planters. There were ornate filigree railings painted green that surrounded the balconies on the upper stories that overlooked the wide river. Four huge pillars supported the largest balcony and guarded the front door. The green ironwork also decorated the sweeping front porch that extended around the side of the house and out of sight. A huge hanging basket of greenery hung between the two center pillars, just above the marble steps leading to the entry. On the roof, surrounded by brick chimneys, was a four-sided birdhouse topped by a weathervane. A metal sailing ship turned this way and that as the breeze played with the direction arrow.

Wolf walked cautiously across the lawn, instinctively aware that he was now in full sight of both the house and the nearby river. Ears erect and forward, he was alert for any noise. His muscles were tense, poised for instant flight. The sharp blue eyes caught a movement; his nose caught the smell. A cat. Small. Frightened. *Easy kill.*

In a flash, he turned with a snarl, and bounded after the terrified tabby. Dodging to avoid tree trunks, he easily followed the scent. When the smell suddenly ended, he knew to look up into the tree in front of him. Lips pulled back, he growled deep in his throat. The tabby climbed to a higher branch.

Breathing hard, fangs dripping, Wolf paced back and forth beneath the tree. *The cat had to come down sometime.* And he would be there when it did. A snapping branch on the other side of the tree startled him, catching him unaware of any other presence. The wolf jumped around to face the new danger. Head down, ears flat, the fur on his neck bristled as he snarled in the direction of the noise.

"Hau Misun."

Wolf backed up a step when the brave, Mato, emerged from behind the tree. There was an arrow cocked in his bow, but it was relaxed at his side. "Hau Misun," Mato repeated, squatting down on his heels, calmly looking at the defensive posture of the wolf.

Taking another step back, the animal was confused. He looked up at where the cat was still hidden by the protecting branches, and back at the human in front of him. The instincts within him braced him for a fight. Wolf's muscles bunched, yet the brave didn't appear worried. Not smelling fear off the man, not sensing danger, the wolf was even more confused. Mato slowly extended his hand, palm down, towards the sharp nose of the wolf. Teeth bared, Wolf was ready for…. He couldn't remember what he should be ready for. As the hand got closer, the smell of the man emerged over the tang of the crushed pine needles underneath and the fear of the cat overhead. The black-lipped mouth closed, hiding the rows of sharp teeth. He cautiously sniffed the hand in front of him. The hair on the back of his neck lowered.

"Hello, Little Brother," Wolf repeated back, his voice a hoarse whisper as if he hadn't spoken in a long, long time. "Mato? Did it happen again?" Wolf's head drooped as he sat back on his haunches.

"Do not worry, Sumanitu Taka. I knew you would not harm me." The dark brown eyes regarded Wolf closely. "It took longer to remember who you were this time, didn't it?"

Reluctantly, Wolf nodded. There was no point denying it. "Yes. It gets more difficult each time I go through."

"Maybe you should quit going through."

"You sound like father."

"Perhaps he is right," Mato pointedly told him, as they all did to no avail. It was hard for them to understand Wolf's need to go to the other world so many times. Actually, it was hard for Mato to understand any of it. He watched as Wolf got back on his feet and turned towards the deeper part of the forest. "Tokhiya la hunwo?"

Wolf gave a snort of a laugh. "It should be obvious where I am going. I need to see my father."

"Wašté kte šni," Mato muttered to himself as he turned to follow.

Wolf's sharp hearing caught the words. He gave a sigh. "Yeah, I know. It won't be good."

Mato chuckled. "I keep forgetting you can hear like a wolf," he smiled.

"I am a wolf."

"You are a filthy wolf, actually. You look like you have been rolling around in the mud."

"Actually, the mud rolled around over me. The current was deadly last night."

Mato nodded. "We saw the oskeca. We wondered if that storm would bring you back. It has been a long time."

Thinking about his father, Wolf missed the remark. He veered off towards the river. "I'll meet you back at the village," he called as he loped away.

As his brother ran off, Mato glanced up into the branches, hearing a movement. Seeing the cat's tail nervously switch back and forth, he knew it would not come down for a long time. With a sigh and muttering about "stubborn men," he went to where he had tied up his brown and white pinto. Grasping the horse's mane, he easily swung onto the broad back. Guiding with his knees, he, too, headed for the wicote.

Plunging into the green water, the wolf paddled easily with the current as it took him downstream towards their encampment. He glanced across the wide River as he swam past Rose's cabin. That would be his next stop.

Then he had to find what happened to Wals.

"**O**wákaȟniǧe šni." Wolf remarked, looking at the Shaman, confused. They were seated in front of the deerskin that was stretched across the back of the rocky overhang.

"Which part do you not understand? That we found your odd clothes floating in the River, or that you have been gone over a year?" The Shaman was glad the wolf headdress he wore hid his eyes. The humor in them belied the seriousness of his facial expression—and he wanted Wolf to take this seriously.

One of Wolf's ears turned backwards as he thought. "A year! How could it be a year? I just went back knowing I needed to get my friend's help. It had to be only a few days."

"And yet it is not. Mato said you were chasing a cat up a tree."

"Bear needs to mind his own business," Wolf replied disgustedly.

"Mato is your older brother. It is his business," the Shaman reminded him. "He said you did not know who you were or where you were."

Wolf looked out over the River. "It took longer to remember," he finally admitted.

"One of these times you might not be able to remember at all." The words were spoken softly, but they conveyed the fear his father felt deep inside.

"If we can get Rose and the Doctor safely to their time, perhaps my mission will be over." Wolf was hopeful, but there never seemed to be any explanation or solution. There never had been.

The Shaman just grunted. He didn't know either. "You saw the new white house?" he asked, changing the subject.

"The Mansion?" Wolf nodded. "I knew it would be built, from talk at Fort Wilderness that Rose told me about and from plans in the other world. The story is that there will be a tragedy and eventually nobody will live in it. Yet, it will continue to have many visitors."

The Shaman chuckled. "Now you sound like me! Talking in riddles and mysteries. That is a good sign, my son."

Wolf's lip peeled back in a toothy grin. "So I do. I need to watch myself. Where did you put my clothes, by the way?" he asked, looking around the rocky enclosure. "I will need them when I go back."

His father folded his arms over his chest. "Perhaps if I do not tell you, you will not go back."

One black shoulder raised in a shrug. "I left more clothes here and there in the other world."

"You would."

Wolf came over to lean against the older man. It was his version of a hug. He felt a tug on his left ear. "Have you seen any strange boats recently? It might be good to know before I head over to Rose's cabin. She is probably worried sick about me being gone so long. A year?" he repeated in amazement. He hoped nothing bad had happened to her without his protection.

The Shaman ignored Wolf's concerns over the wiya. He knew she was safe. Mato would sit for a while on his pinto across the River from her clearing, just to see if all was well. But there was no need to tell Wolf this. He would need to find out for himself. "There have been no strange boats. Only the fancy white paddlewheeler with its smelly black smoke stacks. The double-decked little brown boats no longer go by. You called them keel boats."

Wolf just nodded as he listened. So the Keel Boats were gone here too. Only one was left in the future, the Gullywhumper, and it just sat in the water as something to see along the River. "You didn't happen to see a stranger in the River last night, did you? I brought my friend Wals back to help Rose and Doctor Houser."

"No, just your clothes came to our shore. That is how Mato knew to go looking for you. Are you leaving already?" as the wolf got to his feet and stretched.

"Yes, atewaye ki. I will be back," he promised. "Maybe I will bring Wals to visit." He thought he saw his father roll his eyes before turning away.

"Do what you must. Be safe, my son. Doka."

"Yes, see you later."

Sukawaka, Rose's brown mare, touched noses with Wolf. Long accustomed to Wolf's special scent, she was no longer afraid of the huge animal. Sensing no fear or urgency from the horse, Wolf turned to the log cabin. The split-rail fence around the cabin was leaning in a couple of places. The dead tree off to the side now had a huge nest built in the bare branches. The garden looked a little overgrown with weeds, giving an air of neglect to the front. A splash of color came from some blue gingham curtains Rose had added to the two front windows. He recognized them from an old skirt she used to wear. He heard something drop inside and went to stand in the open front door until she spotted him.

The shadow of a wolf fell over the floor where Rose was sweeping up the fragments of a broken mixing bowl.   The straw broom was quickly dropped as she gave a happy cry of recognition.

"Oh, Wolf! You're back!" As he walked in, she threw her arms around his thick neck. Closing his eyes, he leaned into her embrace. She smelled of lilacs and bread dough. "Where have you been all this time? For the longest time I was afraid the soldiers got you." She pulled back, showing the tears in her eyes.

Wolf reached up and caught one of her tears with the tip of his rough tongue. He felt badly that he had worried her. He lay down at her feet and gave a small whimper. *Good thing Mato can't see me*, he thought to himself. He would never hear the end of it.

"There has been so much going on," she exclaimed, happily dropping down on the floor next to him, stroking his head and forgetting the bread she had been attempting to make. He sighed and put his head on the white apron that covered her lavender-colored skirt. "I've missed having you to talk to. Let's see, what's first? Oh, that big white Mansion way across the River was finally finished. It is so far from New Orleans, though, I don't know what they were thinking. I could see it through the trees last time I went to the Mill." She giggled. "Some of the soldiers at the Fort say it is haunted and nobody will live in it. Can you believe something that silly? I can't imagine living in a place that big! They say it has a ballroom for dancing! I'd love to see that. I haven't been dancing in…." She broke off, confused. The hand on Wolf's head stilled. "That's funny. Have I ever been dancing? I can't remember. I've been here so long it's hard to remember ever being someplace else."

That's why I need to get you out of here now, Rose. You don't belong here.

"There's a new man coming and going out of the Fort now," she told him, the quaver in her voice betraying the intense interest she found in him. "His name is Mr. Davis, but his friends call him Wals. Isn't that cute? Wals. I think it is short for Walter." Wolf's head shot up. "What's wrong, Wolf?" she asked, worriedly looking out the door. "Is that despicable Private Crain back? Not again! Go look. Out!" she commanded, pointing outside.

Already knowing there was nobody out there, Wolf still obeyed one of the commands she "taught" him and did a quick run around the house. He was more interested in hearing about Wals. She made it sound like he had already been here for a while.

When he came back inside, Rose stood waiting with her flintlock rifle in her hands. Apparently Daniel Crain had become even more of a problem while he was gone. Wolf certainly did know this coward. It was back in the future year of 2002 when he had kidnapped his own niece, Kimberly, and held her for ransom to get Walt's red diamond pendant from Lance. In his interference, he had threatened Walt and all that the others were trying to preserve. When the chance came, Wolf brought him here— where he could never harm or threaten Walt or Kimberly again. Little did he know that Daniel would become a threat to Rose, and that he would still be a troublemaker for Wolf in this time period. He was also one of the soldiers who were out to add Wolf's hide to the wall next to the other pelt on the wall of the Fort.

Knowing Rose, he knew she would relax only if he was relaxed. Wolf went to his sleeping pallet that was always waiting for him in the kitchen area. He just didn't know how to get her to resume talking about Wals.

Rose replaced the rifle on the hooks over the fireplace and went to sit heavily in her rocker by the fireplace. The fire was low and warming her dinner. She used the edge of her apron to mop her forehead. "Oh, Wolf, that man will not leave me alone! It took a few months, but somehow they seem to have figured out you weren't around. I've had to keep to this cabin most of the time. If not for the mare warning me, I would have walked into their trap more than once. I'm so glad you're back!" she confessed when he silently moved beside the rocker and put his head in her lap. Slowly petting his fur, she calmed down as the stress left her. Brightening, she told him, "Oh, let me finish my story! There's this new man at the Fort. Mr. Davis. I've only had glimpses of him, but he is so handsome. He seems to be quite a ladies' man. My, excuse you, Wolf!" She stopped when Wolf snorted disgustedly, shaking his head. "Anyway, he took over the supply runs on the rafts going back and forth to the mainland, oh, a long time ago. Sometimes he goes by here in a canoe heading downriver. There used to be more trade downriver, but with many of the miners leaving over the last few years, that's all changed. I heard they just abandoned a little yellow mine train engine and coal car on some of the old track. Not sure why they would paint it yellow…."

She kept talking to Wolf, but his mind was churning. *What happened to Wals? How come he was a known figure already? Why wasn't he trying to help Rose? And*, most importantly, *why did he have a job and seemed to be settled in Fort Wilderness?*

The Island – 1816

Groaning at the ache in his head, Wals tried to get his bearings. He was near the wooden Mill, its huge waterwheel slowly turning. Unable to reach the edge of the wooden fishing dock, he slowly pulled himself out of the River and tried to stand up. The world tilted and he fell into the tall water grass at the edge of the mud. "I need to call someone," he moaned, reaching in his side pocket for…. His hand stilled as it patted the empty pocket. What was he trying to find? He couldn't remember. He heard voices approaching him down the dusty walkway. Maybe one of the guests could help him get to First Aid.

He felt strong hands reach under his arms and pull him to his feet. He moaned with the sudden movement. "You all right?" he was asked.

Wals' eyes tried to focus, but he was having difficulty. All he could see was something dark blue and something shiny. "My head," he managed to croak out.

He could feel a hand roughly go over his scalp. "Yep, you got a whopper back there," when he winced in pain. "You the new canoe man?"

Canoes? He remembered canoes. He tried to nod, but it hurt too much. "Yes, canoe."

He felt himself being roughly drug along between two people. "Let's get him to Doc. Not very chatty, is he?"

"Nope," the other blue shirt replied. "Meebe he's simple."

"Could be. Hope not, if'n he's the new man."

It felt as if they drug him for a mile along the dirty path. When his vision finally cleared, Wals made out the tall pointed stakes that made up Fort Wilderness. The huge gate was open and he was pulled along towards the barracks across the parade grounds. "Haven't been in here in years," he whispered more to himself as his eyes tried to make sense of where he was. He became more baffled and tried to pull back, looking around the dusty expanse. "This is in the wrong place. Where are the caves? Thought the fort was further back on the island. This isn't right."

"Thought you were new to the area," one of the voices sounded confused. "Where else would the Fort be? It's protecting the island, dummy. Wouldn't do no good way back in the forest. Hey, Doc, we pulled the new supply man out of the River. He's talking kinda crazy. Must have capsized his canoe somehow and hit his head. Hope he floats a raft better'n that if he wants to keep his job."

Wals was dumped onto an uncomfortable cot and his two rescuers strode out without a backwards glance, mumbling the word "idiot" as they went. The small cot rustled as he moved about on it. Doc Houser moved into his line of vision. He, too, was dressed in a blue uniform. Calvary, if Wals was thinking straight—and there was no reason to think he was—with gold trim on the shoulders and a double row of gold buttons down the front of the tunic. He lifted a candle up close to Wals face, examining his eyes. "What's your name, son?"

"A candle? Did the lights go out?.... Lights?" Wals broke off, his head throbbing, as he tried to looks upwards towards the ceiling that was shrouded in darkness.

Doc looked at his candle. The flame was perfectly visible. *Must be a harder hit than we thought.* "Don't you worry about the candle, son. Do you remember your name?"

"Yeah, I'm Walter Davis. My friends call me Wals." He looked over the man's outfit, trying to think back. "When did they bring the soldiers back to the Fort?"

"Back?" Doc scratched his head and leaned back on his heels. "We've been here for a lotta years now. I myself was sent for, oh, golly, how long ago was it?" he broke off, perplexed, trying to figure out dates and time. Sitting for a moment staring at the tiny flame in his hand, he finally muttered, "Time has a way of being...."

"Vague?" Wals added, feeling somewhat lost himself.

Doctor Houser looked up and grimaced. "I was going to say unimportant, but vague works, too. That is so odd. There was the war...."

"In the Middle East?"

He slowly shook his head side to side. "No, it wasn't east of the city. Mostly along the water and backcountry. There was an emergency here at the Fort, and I was sent for. During the Battle for New Orleans they needed a field doctor."

New Orleans. Wals grasped onto the name he knew. "How long were you assigned in New Orleans?"

"Assigned? I lived in the French Quarter. Right friendly place," he added with a smile that did nothing to hide the confusion in his eyes.

"I never got to work there. I was always on the River. But I thought the Fort was closed."

Doc shrugged. "There's always talk. Most of the soldiers have been transferred to different posts since the hostiles went away, but some are still assigned here. I liked the pace here better'n New Orleans, so I stayed on after the war ended, you see." Shaking off the vague feeling of displacement, he got back to what he knew for sure: doctoring. "Follow the light with your eyes, Mr. Davis."

Wals didn't see. "Hostiles? I don't know what you mean." Falling back on the cot, some of the filler poking him in the back. "What's this bed made out of? Rocks?"

"My, we're a little grumpy, aren't we? You'll feel better once you rest. I don't see any permanent damage. No, its corn husks under you, not rocks." Doc stood back, frowning, as he watched his disturbed patient try and settle into the cot. Wals was still soaking wet, but he could tell his outfit was some type of thin deerskin. It was probably some shade of yellow, fringe hanging off the arms and down the legs, brown moccasins on his feet. It was almost the attire of a hunter, but not quite. Doc couldn't place his finger on what was wrong with it. "I'll let the Major General know you are here. Get some rest, Mr. Davis," Doc said as a parting, blowing out the candle.

"Major General?"

"Andrew Jackson. In the Regimental Headquarters."

"Andrew Jackson," Wals repeated back with a ghost of a smile. "Of course he is," and fell promptly asleep.

In the morning, when he awakened in darkness, Wals stumbled to the log wall near the door. He kept fumbling around, feeling over and over the rough wood about waist high, searching for a switch or something to make the darkness go away. What he did find was a latch that opened the door, allowing the morning light to stream in. As he blinked at the sudden brightness, he forgot whatever it was he had been looking for. Stepping onto the wooden porch, Wals wasn't now as surprised to see more of those blue Calvary uniforms. He made his way across the dusty parade grounds, nodding hello to the calico-dressed ladies as they smiled shyly and some not so shyly in his direction and went about their business inside the Fort. Stopping in the center of the parade grounds, he gazed in all directions trying to figure out why there was so much activity in all these wooden buildings. He even climbed the shaky stairs to one of the lookout towers. Apparently knowing him, the sentry on guard just grunted hello, his rifle mounted on a stand and poking out through a narrow slit in the logs. Wals just looked over the River and the forested land surrounding the Fort. It all felt familiar, as if he had been there many times before.

It was Market Day and there were a lot of people coming and going. Returning to ground level, he went inside the cantina and ordered a drink. Sitting in a wooden chair by the window, he just watched all the activity going on outside. His eyes strayed to an attractive blond-haired woman who had just ridden in on a brown mare. A private had taken her baskets and rudely pointed where she was to wait. His attention drawn to the lovely group of women chatting by the well, he didn't notice that particular woman again until she had gone out the gate with Davy Crockett and Georgie Russel beside her.

Wals looked down at the pewter mug in his hands. A wave of confusion again washed over him. Pewter? Was that right? A vision of a soft white cup entered his mind, twirled around for a moment and vanished like the morning fog on the River. He looked around the dimly lit room. There was some kind of oil lantern burning over the wooden bar, its blackened wick sending curling wisps of smoke to the darkened wooden ceiling. That, and the light coming in through the dirty window next to him, was the only illumination in the room. His fingers tapped on the scarred table top as his mind tried to figure out why he was so confused. His index finger started doodling in the layer of dust coating the table. His finger started drawing an arch, then a straight line that curved about an inch and went back under the first line. He connected that straight line up to meet the arch. A circle was drawn at each end of the bottom straight line. He then added a small standing rectangle inside the arch that touched the bottom line. He stared at the figure he had drawn. His mind painted it blue, the circles were black. Black wheels. Black tires....

A feminine voice distracted him from his thoughts. "Hi there. I'm Yvette. You must be the new supply man. I was hoping you'd come in."

He looked up at the petite redhead dressed in a tightly laced black dress with a red frilly petticoat showing at the hem. The ruffled top was low enough to show her ample charms. And Wals was amply charmed. "You can call me Wals," he smiled. "All my friends do."

"You have a lot of friends?" she asked, bending over to wipe a damp rag over the scarred table, erasing the primitive drawing Wals had made of his Nissan 300ZX.

"I…I think so…." Forgetting all about the car, his mind strayed to names and faces. *Wolf, Chloe, Trey, Diane, Rose.* "Rose?" he muttered aloud, wondering why there was no face to go with that particular name.

Yvette did know that name and the face that went with it. And, she didn't like it. She leaned over a little further and recaptured Wals wandering attention. "I think you need some new friends," she smiled sweetly, her green eyes half closed. "You interested in going on a picnic at Castle Rock this Saturday? It's in a nice secluded place near Injun Joe's Cave. I can introduce you to a few of my friends."

"I would be charmed." *Charmed? Where the heck did that come from?* he wondered.

Yvette flashed him another smile and took his empty mug back to the bar. He watched her swaying hips and gave a satisfied sigh.

The wooden raft dock was built up on pillars that were sunk down deep in the river bottom. Wals unhooked the leather straps from the holding piers and allowed the current to pull the log raft into the River. Using the long paddle attached to the back as a rudder, he expertly steered the raft across the wide River. Even after plying that raft for over a year now, for some reason, it still always surprised him how long it took to get across the River. He felt it should have been two, three minutes top. Yet it always seemed to take over thirty minutes now. The perplexing mystery always receded as quickly as it came. Whistling, he bent to his task, his eyes on the nearing dock.

The riverboat, the Mark Twain, sat waiting in her pristine white beauty with her two black smoke-stacks rising majestically into the air. Passengers strolled each of the three decks. The women were in long elegant dresses with lacy parasols protecting them from the sun. The men were dressed in buff or black frock coats with tan breeches tucked into knee-high boots, tall beaver hats perched on their heads. As soon as the cargo was loaded, the Mark Twain would sound her shrill whistle and the ropes holding her tight against the dock would be loosened from the huge logs. The captain was in the wheelhouse, his black cap pushed back on his head, a black garter holding up the sleeves of his white starched shirt. He was eager to get under-way. This might be a sightseeing trip for his passengers, but he would also carry needed supplies to what was left of the mining community called Rainbow Ridge upriver a ways. The passengers were being served mint juleps on the lower level and a small band was tuning up to entertain them. They were in no hurry. But, the captain was behind schedule and he wanted to get going.

Wals bumped the raft against the waiting dock and a deckhand from the Mark Twain hurriedly secured the raft with the straps. They worked quickly to unload the produce brought over from the Fort onto a waiting cart. Once finished, the deckhand ran the three-wheeled cart back to the waiting ship. The white picket railing was slid shut behind him just as soon as his feet hit the deck. Wals watched as the captain checked the surrounding water for smaller craft and let out a shrill blast from his steam whistle. Turning the huge wheel, the Mark Twain slowly slid away from the dock. The passengers gave a cheer and the band started playing 'Yankee Doodle'. The green water from the River churned white as the paddlewheel turned faster and faster. Some people from the nearby city of New Orleans who were strolling along the River stopped and waved at the passengers. Wals watched until the ship went around that first big bend and was out of sight. The River water was still churning as some mallard ducks rode out the waves from the wake.

Thinking he would like to take a ride on the Mark Twain someday, Wals turned back to unloading the rest of his raft. Someone from New Orleans was supposed to be there to pick up the boxes. He then found the stack of goods marked for Fort Wilderness. With the practiced ease of someone long used to his job, he expertly piled the waiting boxes and crates onto the center of the raft to take them back to the Fort. He knew he had to get back soon. The soldiers had bartered some goods with the native village and they needed him to be back so he could make the trade. He would have to make that run in one of the canoes. The raft would make the trip downriver just fine, but would be impossible to get it back upstream against the current. The Island was so large that a trip around it would take him days on the raft to go all the way around.

Whistling "Yankee Doodle" to himself while he worked, Wals didn't see the sharp blue eyes that were watching him, hidden in the shrubbery around the eerie, white Mansion.

CHAPTER SIX

The Island – 1817

"Hallo the cabin!"

The words, indistinct and faint, sounded as if they were coming from a great distance away or uttered with some unknown difficulty. The voice—it was definitely male. Rose's head shot up from the sewing she had been trying to do by the inadequate firelight, turning quickly towards the front door of her cabin to make sure the beam was in place barring it shut. *It's too late at night for callers*, her panicked mind thought as she hurriedly glanced over at Wolf's pallet and saw it was empty. A little more relieved, she knew he had already gone outside to investigate, the panel of his hidden door still swung slightly from his abrupt exit. Throwing down the black vest she was trying to mend, she rushed over to the fireplace. Reaching over the mantle, the flintlock rifle came easily off of its hooks. Testing the weight in her hands, the cold metal of the barrel felt reassuring. Licking her dry lips, she knew the gun was already loaded.

Louder now, closer to the cabin, she again heard, "Hallo the….Ouch…dang it…"

In the middle of that, Rose heard a distinct *thump* near her little garden. With a smug smile she realized whoever it was had just tripped over that exposed tree root she had refused to dig up. She had known it would come in useful some day. The blue curtains were slowly moved aside as the rifle barrel was pointed out the window. Peering through the gun sight of the weapon, there was a figure lying facedown on the path from the River. She was about to warn him away when she recognized the clothes he was wearing. Expecting to see the dark blue of a Calvary uniform, the full moonlight instead revealed the mustard-yellow color of the shirt and the fringe on the legs of the pants that were splayed out and deathly still.

"Wals!" she whispered to herself, one of her hands unconsciously reaching up to smooth her hair in place. Her heart started pounding. What was he doing here so late at night? Was he alone or was he with that dreadful Private Crain? Was this another attempt at an ambush? Where was Wolf? The questions that were going round and round in her head stilled when she realized Wals hadn't moved since he last called out to her.

Hesitating only a split second, she threw a shawl around her nightclothes. Unbarring her front door, she walked slowly out of the cabin, the rifle easily nestled in the crook of her arm. "Mr. Davis? Are you hurt?" she softly called. Still wary as she approached him, her eyes darted quickly over the edges of the surrounding dark forest. She couldn't see anything or anyone else out there in the gloom, but, would she? Mindful of the distance to her front door and the safety of her cabin, she took another few tentative steps. "Mr. Davis?" Her voice became more anxious as he remained unmoving on her path, the toe of his moccasin still entangled in the protruding root.

At the sound of her voice, Wals lifted his head. He could see her standing there, backlit by the light of the fireplace. She looked beautiful in the glow. Her golden blond hair had been loosened from the tight bun she usually wore. Held back from her forehead with a black ribbon, it cascaded in waves down her back. He gave a ghost of a smile at the lovely vision and tried to push himself upright. He was immediately sorry. Intense pain rushed through his body and he fell back onto the ground, lights twinkling around the dark edges of his vision. "Need some help here. Call 911," he groaned, not sure if she could hear him or even if he had said it out loud.

He heard a shrill whistle and the command, "Go search." Hurting too bad to try and understand what that meant, he then felt the hesitant probing of fingertips on his back and softly moaned.

"Where are you hurt, Mr. Davis? Is anything broken? Can you hear me?" She wasn't sure where it was safe—or proper—to touch him.

"My head," he whispered, imagining he was pointing it out with his good arm, but, in reality, not even moving an inch. "Just now hit my head in the Rapids. Banged up my arm. Fell on it again when I tripped on some dang rock or something….oh, beggin' your pardon, ma'am."

Rose gave a small smile in the darkness, her hand resting on his soggy back. "That's alright, Mr.

Davis. I've called it that myself once or twice. Do you think you can sit up?"

"Thought I was," he mumbled, lifting his head and opening his eyes. Realizing his prone position, he groaned, "Oh. Guess not. I can try."

He felt her arm go around his back for support and, with her help, he managed to get into a sitting position. Water from the River and sweat from the exertion of sitting up was dripping off his hair and his clothes. He was turning the path into a small mud puddle.

She squatted down on her heels next to him. "Is that better, Mr. Davis?" when he seemed stable enough to sit there by himself and not fall over again. She reached out to smooth the hair off of his forehead, but pulled her hand back, blushing.

Seeing the aborted movement, he looked over at the anxious face peering into his. Her lavender shawl had fallen off and was lying forgotten on the path behind her. With the help of the firelight coming through the open door of her cabin, he could see the outline of her body through her thin cotton nightwear. *Gosh, she is so beautiful*, was his first coherent thought. His second thought was that this was neither the time nor place to act on his first thought. He shook his head to clear where his thoughts were running and immediately regretted the movement. Both his head and his arm were killing him. "I hate to impose, ma'am, but could I please dry off by your fire?" He lifted his good arm to show the water running off of the fringe. Not waiting for her to answer, he made a feeble effort to get his feet under him. Failing miserably, he had to admit, "I don't think I can stand up on my own."

Rose, unaware of the sensual scene the firelight was giving Wals, came to her feet. "Of course. You're drenched and it is getting colder." In her concern for him, she reached out to help, pulled her arms back, and then reached for him again. She seemed flustered. "I don't think I can lift you myself. I'll get some help."

Confused, remembering the rumors that she lived alone, Wals looked oddly at her. But, before he could question her, she put her fingers in her mouth and let out another piercing whistle. He winced as the sound bore straight through his ears. Within seconds, a huge black animal bounded out of the darkness and came to stand by her side, his head low and watchful.

Wals eyes got huge. "That's a big doggie you have there, ma'am," he gulped, now wondering if he should have taken his chances and stayed in the River.

"He's not a dog, Mr. Davis," was all the explanation he would get. "You are going to have to lean on him to get up. He won't hurt you. Unless I give him the command," she added with a pointed smile.

Did he really want to ask? "What command is that?"

"Kill."

"Ah." Wals gulped. He didn't know if she was kidding or not. Wolf came and stood calmly next to him, keeping his face averted away from Wals. He didn't want Wals to see his telltale sapphire-blue eyes just yet. There were some answers Wolf needed and hoped he might overhear something tonight if Wals stayed conscious long enough to start talking.

Hearing about a huge wolf and having it standing right next to you are two completely different things. His breathing shallow from both the pain he was in and the nearness of a wolf, Wals put out a tentative hand towards the animal. The wolf seemed to be ignoring him. Assured a little, Wals put his good arm over the wolf's broad shoulder. When the animal moved slightly, Wals suddenly tensed and then realized the wolf only seemed to be bracing himself for his added weight. Wals almost chuckled at his own reaction. Almost. It was still a wolf....

Once he had gotten into an upright position, the wolf was no longer able to assist him. Rose took over for the animal and put Wals' good arm over her shoulder. Dragging the rifle behind her, she helped Wals into the log cabin. As soon as he saw they were safely inside, the wolf disappeared into the darkness. Rose was going to let Wals rest in her rocking chair by the fire, but he resisted, saying the water and mud would ruin it. Thankful for his consideration, she helped him lower onto the handsewn rag rug in front of the waning fire. She put another log on the blaze, sending a bright shower of sparks up the chimney. Watching the display, he muttered, "Fireworks."

"Excuse me?"

He looked from the brightness of the flames to the anxious look on her face, glowing in the golden light of the fire. *She is so lovely*.... The vague thoughts of a pink castle dimmed from his mind. "Uh, nothing."

Seeing he was settled and somewhat more comfortable, she went to the wooden shelves in her tiny kitchen. "May I ask you a question, Mr. Davis?" she asked, rushing back to get some coffee steeping in a small pot set near the glowing embers.

Wals was gently feeling the bruises on his arm. It was going to be a glory of black and blue in a couple of days. "Ask away."

"Why were you in the River tonight? How did you get hurt? It is awfully late for calling." Belatedly realizing her shawl was missing and that she was standing there in her nightclothes, she gave a murmured, startled, "Oh, my!" and hurriedly looked around for something else to make her decent.

Wals was disappointed when she pulled some beaded, crocheted black thing around her shoulders and sat in the rocking chair next to him. "Oh, I wasn't come calling, Mrs. Stephens. No reason for me to do that...." He broke off at the odd look on her face, not realizing he had just hurt the feelings of a very lonely woman. "No," he continued quickly, with a covering, nervous cough, "I was in a canoe race with the Pinewood Indians from the village up-river a spell."

Insult momentarily forgotten, her mouth fell open. "A canoe race? At night?"

Encouraged by her interest in his story, the maleness in Wals took over and he shifted closer towards her. He was instantly rewarded for his efforts by a low, warning growl that came from the back of the little cabin. Properly warned, he immediately moved back into his previous position. Peering into the shadows, he could see the wolf was back in the room and was busily chewing on something. It looked like half of his canoe paddle. Turning back, subdued, he answered Rose with a charming drawl he had picked up somewhere in his jaunts to New Orleans, "Well, it wasn't supposed to be a night race, ma'am, but we got a late start from the paddlewheeler's dock."

"Why, that's miles upriver!" Rose leaned forward in surprise, the crocheted shawl sagging. "Where were you racing to?"

Wals opened his mouth to answer, and then promptly shut it. "Umm, I don't know," he admitted with a laugh. "We never talked about that."

She liked his laugh. "If that was the case, how would you know who won?" she asked with a returning grin, settling back in the rocker.

Surprised at her humor, he threw his head back and gave a hearty laugh. The sharp movement of his head caused a wave of pain to cross his face. Eyes closed against the severe headache, he paled under his deep tan.

"How did you get all wet?" she tried to distract him, not knowing what to do to help his injuries.

He opened one tentative eye and could see she was wavering on getting up and trying to help him in some way or just diverting his attention away from the hurt. Knowing there was nothing she could do right now, he just answered her question. "Well, when I saw I was falling a little behind in the race, I decided to cut through Keel Boat Rapids. Just as soon as I entered the Rapids, I hit the rocks in the dark and must've keeled over." He shook his head in disgust and then winced. "I know that River better'n the back of my hand. Banged my head and my arm on one of the rocks. Not sure what happened to the canoe," he admitted, giving her a charming smile.

"Maybe it kept going and won the race," she suggested with a grin. "Do you think your friends are going to come looking for you?" she asked, looking towards the door.

Misunderstanding the reason for her question,

he tried to assure her, "Oh, no. No, you don't have to worry about the Pinewoods. They've been right friendly to me. They won't bother you none, especially with me here." His head shot over to the corner of the cabin where the wolf was. He would have sworn he heard a muttered, disgusted, "sheesh," come from that part of the room. All he could see were two eyes glowing yellow from the reflection of the firelight. As he looked, the eyes narrowed into two slits. His heart suddenly pounding, Wals turned back to his lovely hostess.

Apparently not having heard anything unusual, Rose had leaned back in her chair and was talking. "Oh, I don't worry about *them*, Mr. Davis," was her hasty assurance, waving an elegant hand in the direction of the west. "Ever since the Hostiles burned this cabin, they all leave me alone. It took quite a while, but once I got the flames put out, they apparently considered the debt paid and they left. It's really the soldiers I have to worry about," she admitted bitterly, frowning as she pulled the shawl closer around her shoulders.

"Wait, back up a minute. I heard about the Hostiles when I first came here. I think it was the Doctor at the Fort who mentioned them…. Anyway, I was told they were camped across the River for the longest time, always a line of them, watching. That's why the Calvary was stationed here in the first place. Then, suddenly, overnight, the Hostiles just left. What is the debt you mentioned?" Wals was confused. This all sounded so very familiar to him, but not the way she was telling it. His mind was picturing a band of hostiles sitting on their horses across the narrow River, war paint and spears in their hands. They sat there, unmoving for years…. No, that isn't right. He never actually saw them here. The River wasn't narrow at that point. So why was the memory so sharp in his mind? He didn't notice those deep sapphire eyes intently watching him from the corner of the room, ears turned toward the couple to catch every word. His confused thoughts were interrupted by her reply to his last, already-forgotten question.

When his eyes refocused on the present, he could see Rose looked embarrassed. She was looking at her lap, her long fingers nervously playing with the fringe of her shawl. "My husband, Jedadiah Stephens, or Jed as we all called him, thought he was an expert card player. He thought being good at cheating made him an expert." She broke off, disturbed and disgusted at the memory, and looked into the fire, her hands falling idle in her lap. "He would play anyone who wanted a game. He used to brag to me that he cheated both the natives as well as the soldiers and for some unknown reason he thought he got away with it."

"But he didn't."

Rose shook her head in the firelight. The tips of her hair caught the wavering flames and glowed a brilliant gold. "No, he didn't. I came back from a swim at Cascade Peak and found him bent backwards over the fence in front of the cabin with an arrow in his chest. The cabin had been set afire and the hostiles were just sitting there across the River watching." She stopped for a moment, but he could see she wasn't finished with her story. "But, the funny thing is, Mr. Davis," she continued, lowering her voice and leaning closer to him as if in confidence, "I don't think they did it."

"Who? The Hostiles? Why do you say that,

Mrs. Stephens?"

She looked away into the darkness of the cabin, thinking back, her delicate brow furrowed in thought. "I can't quite put my finger on it, but it just didn't look right. I'm not an expert, but I don't think that arrow belonged to the tribe across the River."

"Who do you think did it, then?"

Rose looked back at him, and suddenly remembered who he was and where he spent his most of his free time. She became wary. "I'd just as soon not say, Mr. Davis," she told him, her eyes back in her lap as she nervously smoothed the thin material of her nightgown. "Let's just say the cabin burned for the longest time. The logs must have been very green and full of sap. I just couldn't get it out. Then, suddenly, it just seemed to burn itself out. I even tried to whitewash these inside walls to help get rid of that awful burnt smell. Afterwards, when Wolf joined me, a rumor got started that a 'Wolf Spirit' was watching over the cabin now and everyone across the River left me alone. Well," she amended, with a grateful smile, "sometimes the Pinewoods kindly leave me something on the doorstep, like grain or meat. They seem to know just when I need it the most," she drifted off, wondering for the thousandth time how they would possibly know.

Wals turned to look over at the wolf when she mentioned him, and suddenly a wave of familiarity ran through him. "You call him Wolf?" he mumbled more to himself than out loud. He was brought back by Rose's startled gasp. The fleeting image of a familiar blue-eyed face swirled into a vapor and vanished from his mind.

"Your head is bleeding, Mr. Davis!" She hadn't

seen the cut before because of the darkness. Reaching for a clean cloth from her basket, she dipped it in the kettle of hot water that was ever present on the fire. She carefully dabbed the wound. Close up to him again, he could catch the faint aroma of lilacs and wood smoke. She, on the other hand, caught the pungent smell of sweat and river water.

He couldn't help but noticed the grimace on her face, even though she was trying to hide it from him. "Sorry about the smell, Mrs. Stephens. It was awful hot today, and it's a long walk up here from the River. Thought the River water would have washed some of it away, but I guess it didn't," he admitted, giving her his best charming, boyish smile.

Stuck between propriety and kindness, Rose wasn't sure what to do. If he was found in her cabin this late at night and she in her nightclothes no less, her reputation would be ruined. She suddenly gave a bitter laugh at the thought. The people of the Fort already thought she was fairly odd and don't give her the time of day anyway. What did she care what they thought? This was Wals and he needed her help. And, her eyes were going to start watering if they didn't do something about that awful smell right away. Kindness won out over propriety.

"I have a bit of hot water ready, Mr. Davis. Would you like to take a bath? Perhaps the soaking will help your sore arm," she blushed, fully aware of what she was offering.

Happy with this turn of events, Wals readily agreed. The crocheted thing around her shoulders proved to be in her way, so she unconsciously dropped it over the back of the nearest chair. Moving efficiently around the small room, a wooden tub that she used both for bathing and for laundry was readied. She had planned on taking a bath herself that night, but failed to mention that fact to Mr. Davis. It was already embarrassing enough. Who knew what he would think if she mentioned herself bathing. She kept herself busy by locating her small cake of milled soap and a clean wash cloth for him to use. Holding them out to him, Rose was surprised when he made no move to take them.

Wals made an effort to keep his face straight. Pointed to his banged up arm with his chin, he sounded perplexed, "I'm afraid my arm is kinda useless right now. I'm going to need a little help."

The soap and the wash cloth hung as if suspended in midair when she suddenly realized what he meant. Blushing an even deeper shade of red, she audibly swallowed. The wolf silently got to his feet and came to stand beside her, his back to the fire, his eyes half closed as he stared at Wals. Rose put a hand on the wolf's head for reassurance.

Wals wasn't so confident in his scheme when the wolf joined the mix. The wolf wasn't being threatening. He was just *there*. Watching. And, somehow, Wals thought it looked as though the wolf was frowning.

Rose took a deep breath and muttered to herself over and over, "I was married. I can do this. I was married. I can do this. He just needs my help. He just needs my help...*But, it's Wals*," her heart added. *It was the duty of the lady of the castle to bathe visiting knights-errant.... Oh, my... Where did that come from?* she wondered, still standing with her hand out in front of her, clutching the items in a white-knuckled grip.

With a resolute sigh, she set the soap and

washcloth down next to the wooden tub. She couldn't look him in the eye. "If you will hold your arm out as well as you can, Mr. Davis, I will try to help you off with your shirt." With shaking fingers, she managed to undo the odd buttons on his shirt. As she unbuttoned it she couldn't help but notice the buttons had the initials *DL* on them. When he turned away from her, she eased the shirt carefully over his bruised shoulders. Then, so help her, she couldn't help but notice just how wide those shoulders were and how tight the muscles were across his back. *Please don't turn around, please don't turn around,* her mind wordlessly pleaded with him.

Wals turned around. Embarrassed by her admiration of his back, she couldn't meet his amused eyes. That meant her eyes had to drop down to his bare chest—which she immediately saw was covered with a fine mat of soft brown hair. Oh, that wouldn't do. Her eyes whipped up again. Straight-faced, Wals was cradling his sore arm in his good one. He gave a small groan of pain, those soft green eyes staring steadily at her. "Can you help me with my moccasins? It hurts my head too much to bend over," he managed to moan.

She gave a sigh of relief. She expected to be asked to help with something else. "Yes, sure."

Wals had to keep trying. "My hand hurts really bad. Can you help me with my belt?"

Again the dim firelight did nothing to hide her profuse blush. Eyes wide, she stammered, "Absolutely not, Mr. Davis! I...you...No!"

Looking down he hid the grin in his eyes. "Well, then you had better turn around, because my pants are going next."

Amazed at the speed with which she turned,

he silently laughed as he quickly shed himself of the pants and climbed into the hot, steaming water. He gave a heartfelt moan of appreciation as the warmth seeped over his bruised body.

Misreading the meaning of the moan, she turned to him. "Did you hurt yourself, Mr. Davis?" She held herself back from approaching any closer to the tub. When she saw his back was turned towards her, she relaxed. After watching this whole scenario work out, the wolf gave a disgusted snort and returned to his pallet in the darkness.

Not one to miss an opportunity with the ladies, Wals moaned again. "No, no, I'm better. This feels wonderful," he added truthfully. "I, uh, I can't reach the soap unless I get up," pretending he was going to rise from the water.

Rose just about dove for the soap next to the tub and placed it in his outstretched hand. "Here it is. Sorry, but lilac soap and rye are the only two choices I have. The lilac is rather soothing. And the rye would probably rub raw on the sore spots." She stopped talking when she realized she was probably rambling.

He brought the soap to his nose and inhaled. Now he knew where she got her fresh scent. "This is nice. I'll probably be called a sissy by the soldiers when I get back to the Fort, but it is nice!"

Satisfied that she had done all she could for now and that he was covered up as much as possible under the circumstances, Rose settled back in her rocking chair and picked up her sewing. She couldn't concentrate on her stitches and kept pricking her finger. "I don't know what it is about needles, but I keep poking myself with them!" she muttered, more to herself than to her guest. Her ears were attuned to the sounds behind her and her mind was in somewhat of a turmoil over the fact that the fascinating Wals Davis was actually in her cabin. Late at night. And naked. Oh, heavens! Her hand rose to cover her open mouth.

The splashing sounds coming from the tub continued for a while and then died off. Surreptitiously glancing back, she realized that Wals had fallen asleep. With her head turned in that direction, the aroma from his clothes piled behind the chair assaulted her nose again. Picking them up at arm's length and averting her face, she wondered how she could possibly clean them this late at night. Shrugging, she tiptoed over to the tub and dropped them in the sudsy water near his submerged feet. *Better than nothing*, she figured.

Wals made quiet, sleepy sounds as he soaked. His head was tilted and rested on the edge of the wooden tub. Stealing a look at his face, Rose again resisted the urge to reach over and brush that darling tendril of hair that had fallen over his forehead. Going back to her chair again, she gave out a long sigh filled with frustration and longing. Wolf padded over to her and looked expectantly into her eyes. She rubbed his right ear and his eyes closed with pleasure. "Oh, Wolf," she whispered. "What am I going to do? It's Wals! I mean, Mr. Davis…. And he's right here in my cabin…in my tub." She sighed again. "I've listened in to some of the stories he told at the Fort, but I didn't know he was so funny!"

Wolf tilted his head. He hadn't heard anything funny out of Wals tonight. Just some new pick-up lines. Wals was supposed to be figuring out how to get her back to their proper time, not start an affair with her. That is, if Wals even had the slightest remembrance of where he came from…. Wolf looked over into the fire, his eyes frowning. Maybe that's what's wrong. Wals was probably forgetting. The Island did that to people, Wolf knew. It sucked away their memories and lulled them into their new life. The shift might have been too much for Wals. It certainly got more difficult for Wolf each time…. How can he get Wals to remember his other life and want to go back? Wolf decided he needed to go talk to his father again. But, not tonight. This was all too interesting. Irritating, but interesting.

Rose was still whispering on and on. Wolf knew she had been intrigued by the newcomer Wals, but underestimated the extent of her interest. He wondered if the interest she felt for Wals would come in handy later when it was time for all of them to leave. If she had feelings for him, she might be more apt to follow him through the terrifying vortex. "…and those brown eyes of his are simply mesmerizing," she concluded with another soft sigh.

If Wolf could have rolled his eyes, he would have because he knew something Rose didn't. Wals wasn't asleep. He was listening intently to every word she said but Rose didn't realize that. *Darn egotist*, Wolf thought. Before Rose revealed some innermost secret or desire she might regret later, Wolf had to do something. He left the delightful ear-rubbing he was getting and silently padded over to the washtub. With his superior height, he could easily see over the sides of the tall tub. He walked behind the pretending Wals and pressed his cold nose against the back of Wals' neck. With a startled yell, Wals jerked forward and caught himself just before he jumped to his feet.

"Oh, you're awake," Rose exclaimed at the

sudden movement.

She missed the glare exchanged between the man and the wolf. It was then that Wals saw those sapphire-blue eyes for the first time. A thread of remembrance wormed its way through his brain only to be pushed aside by the overriding thought that *this was a wolf, a wolf, Wals!* Seeing the encouraging flicker of recognition suddenly extinguish from Wals' eyes, the disgusted Wolf turned and went back to his pallet and proceeded to chew the rest of the canoe paddle into kindling.

Trying to look contrite, Wals said hesitantly, "I hate to ask again since you have been so nice, Mrs. Stephens, but I really could use some help."

Oh, lord. She slowly approached from behind, looking only at the back of his head over the edge of the tub. *That was safe.* "Yes, Mr. Davis?"

"I can't reach my back."

There was complete silence except for a loud snort from the wolf. "Umm, well, I, well," she finally stammered. "I suppose I could help you." This wasn't what she had expected at all. She didn't know *what* she had expected, but this wasn't it.

"Oh, thank you, Mrs. Stephens. I 'precciate it." He leaned forward away from the tub and helpfully held out the soap and wash cloth out to the side for her.

"I'm going to burn in pits of Hades," she mumbled under her breath. She frowned and looked away. "Where did that come from?" She broke off her musings when Wals managed a pitiful moan again.

"Mrs. Stephens? This position hurts my head. Could you start, please?" She couldn't see his wide grin.

Her lips in a firm line, she squared her shoulders. *He is a guest. He is injured. He needs my help.* "Certainly, Mr. Davis."

He sighed with pleasure as the soapy wash cloth moved tentatively over his broad shoulders. When he felt she had to be in just the right position, he groaned loudly and flung himself back against the tub. His action caused a wave of water to splash out of the tub and over the front of Rose's nightdress, resulting in it being plastered to her body.

Not realizing what he had done to her, Rose was only concerned about his injuries. "Are you all right? Did I hurt you?"

"No, no. I just got a cramp. This water is cooling. I really should get out of the tub." He couldn't wait to turn around and see the outcome of his handiwork.

"Oh no," she muttered aloud without thinking. "Towel! You need a towel. A really, really big towel." *Why hadn't I thought this through before I offered him the tub?* "Wait!" she about shrieked when he started to stand from the tub. She rushed into her small bedroom and flung out a pile of clothes that had been stashed under her bed. She found an old robe of Jed's that had been under there for…for how many years? She paused, confused, as she couldn't remember. She looked at the flannel robe in her hands and couldn't recall anyone ever wearing it. She knew it was a robe, a man's robe, but she had no memory of seeing it before. She stood from her crouched position. Looking slowly around the tiny room, she tried in vain to see some sort of remembrance of that part of her life. Why could she not bring up any memory of the time before she found him bent backwards over the front fence and the cabin set afire? He was a card cheat...that is what everyone had told her over and over again at the Fort...she knew that, right? A wave of panic was starting to come over her. Something wasn't right.... Looking at her left hand, there was no wedding ring. She should be able to remember.... When Wals called to her from the main room, it broke some of her trance.

Walking slowly into the room, she still stared at the robe in her arms. At her unusual silence, Wolf looked up from the splinters of the canoe paddle, concerned. He could see that Rose looked confused and frightened. What had caused the sudden change? He followed her wooden movements as she absentmindedly handed the robe to Wals and then sat heavily in her rocking chair, staring into the blazing fire.

Even self-absorbed Wals noticed the difference. He temporarily forgot his Master Plan, even forgot she was now soaking wet herself. After belting on the long flannel robe, he considerately dropped the crocheted shawl back over her shoulders. Now genuinely worried, he asked, "You okay, ma'am?"

She looked up at him as if she had forgotten he was even there. "Oh, yes, Mr. Davis. I...I guess I am just tired." She sounded far away. "It's been a long day."

He gave a small grin. "I would offer to get out of your hair, but my clothes seem to be in a lump at the bottom of the tub."

Glad to have something to do to occupy her mind that was running in circles, she gratefully rose to her feet again and hurried over to the tub. "I am so sorry, Mr. Davis. Could you help me here?" as she handed him his dripping pants. "I'll have to hang them up here by the fire to dry. Not sure how long that will take. I'm not familiar with this fabric," as she wrung out his shirt. She fingered the material for a lingering moment before hanging it over a rope that had been strung across the room for just that purpose. "At least, I don't think I am familiar with it." She broke off, confused again. "I'm not sure of a lot of things all of a sudden."

As Wals draped his pants over the line, he asked, "Would you please call me by my first name, Mrs. Stephens? All my friends do."

Some of the disturbed cloud cleared from her face. She seemed pleased by his words. "All right, Walter," she said, using his proper first name.

He gave her his boyish grin. "You know better than that. You know it's Wals!"

She pulled the shawl closer around her and sat down next to him by the fire. He had added another log. The dancing flames turned his eyes amber. "Yes, I know it's Wals. Then you should call me Rose," she added shyly.

He wanted to distract her from whatever was troubling her. He preferred her lovely smile to the bewildered expression that had been on her face just moments ago. "Say, did you ever hear how Keel Boat Rapids got its name?" he suddenly asked with a sudden inspiration.

Brightening, she gave a little laugh. "Why, sure. Everyone around here knows that story. It used to be just called The Rapids. Then some idiot Keel Boat pilot was trying to save a little time on his supply run to Rainbow Ridge. He had to get back to New Orleans with the rest of the cargo and tried to cut through the Rapids. He hit the very first rock in the channel and 'keeled' over. All the boxes he was carrying for the ladies of New Orleans got dumped into the River. I heard that the Pinewood women were sporting colorful feathered silk hats and the men were wearing beaver top hats for months after that! I found that black beaded shawl the same way...." She broke off when she saw a look of embarrassment pass over Wals' face. She started laughing when the realization hit her. "Oh, my! *You* are that idiot! It was you, wasn't it?" She tried to stop laughing but just couldn't. She rocked backwards in her amusement, exposing a little more leg than was proper. "Oh, I'm sorry!" she gasped at the hurt look on his face. She managed to bring the laugh down to a snicker and had to hide her mouth behind her hand.

"So, I guess you did hear," he muttered, causing her to break out again in laughter. She looked so cute he had to smile himself. *Well, that certainly didn't work out the way I planned*, he thought to himself. *Oh, well, at least she is smiling again*.

When it got to be even later, it was obvious that Wals wouldn't be able to leave the cabin before the morning. Rose tried to excuse herself to go to bed in her little room.

Wals caught her hand as she attempted to get up from in front of the dying fire. "Please don't go," he begged, looking into her clear blue eyes. "Stay and talk to me. This has been so nice," he told her honestly.

Looking deep in his brown eyes, she could only see sincerity in them. She glanced down at his sun-tanned hand lightly holding her white one. As she looked, his fingers entwined with hers and he gave a little tug. "Please?" he whispered.

She allowed him to draw her back down to the rug on the floor. Fingers still entwined, they stared into the glowing embers, sitting in companionable silence. When they did talk, it was in low tones, necessitating leaning closer to each other to be able to hear. He pulled a rough blanket around their shoulders and they sat together through the rest of the night.

When Rose finally dozed off, leaning against his shoulder, Wals glanced over and noticed the wolf was gone. Figuring the animal had gone into the bedroom to sleep, he turned his mind back to something that was starting to bother him. He knew the story had to be true because it had been told so many times. He had heard it over and over again— usually because he himself had been the one telling it.

But, the thing that bothered him the most was that he could not for the life of himself actually remember ever steering a Keel Boat.

CHAPTER SEVEN

The Island – 1817

Wolf accompanied Rose and the banged-up Wals to the edge of the River. He wanted to make sure Wals was well on his way back to Fort Wilderness and not trying any more of his shenanigans with Rose. He had wanted Wals to help get Rose back to civilization, not get her to fall in love with him and start up a cozy life together in the little log cabin.

They found Wals' canoe was half submerged at the entry of the Keel Boat Rapids. It was wedged in-between two rocks but appeared undamaged. Half amused, half disgusted, Wolf noticed that Wals' arm had made a miraculous recovery during the night and he was able to free the canoe without much problem. The only paddle in the canoe had been snapped in two during Wals' accident. When Wolf found it the night before, he had drug it into the cabin and promptly destroyed what remained of it. Noticing the paddle was missing and then remembering the wolf chewing on something during the night, Wals glanced sharply at the huge animal standing protectively next to Rose. If the wolf had been human, Wals knew the look on Wolf's face would have been described as supremely smug. His eyes strayed to the white patch of fur on the wolf's chest. A hazy memory tugged at the back of his mind—a man he used to know had had a similar white patch of hair on his chest. Then, reminding himself this was just an animal and animals couldn't look smug, Wals shook off the thought and decided to tie up the canoe at Rose's unused dock and walk back to the Fort.

Rose was quiet and thoughtful as Wals waved good-bye and disappeared up the trail towards the Fort, hating to see him leave. She hadn't had such a pleasant visit in a long time. After seeing Wals at the Fort every now and then and hearing so much about him, she had wanted a chance to get to know him. Now she had gotten to know him very well and she was smitten. Giving a sigh, she put a hand on Wolf's head. He looked up expectantly at her. "You coming in, Wolf, or do you have big plans for the day?" she asked with a hopeful smile.

Not needing to look down the trail, Wolf could no longer smell Wals' new lilac scent, and knew his friend was long gone. Wolf allowed himself one wag of his bushy tail before he headed into the forest. Glancing back once, he could see Rose still watching him, a lonely sag in her shoulders. He gave a short apologetic "yip" and vanished into the thick growth.

When he had traveled far enough to be unseen from the cabin, he emerged from the forest and walked to the River's edge. He entered the green slow-moving water for the long swim across to his father's village.

Mato was waiting for him when he emerged from the water. "Théhaŋ waŋčhíŋyaŋke šni," was his greeting.

"It hasn't been that long," Wolf retorted.

Mato, who had been watching his brother from across the River as Wolf interacted with Rose, gave him a cocky grin. It was the kind of grin brothers use when they are going to start pushing each other's buttons. "I wonder if you will be chasing sticks next."

Not bothering to answer, Wolf suddenly shook himself, sending muddy river water flying all over his brother. Calmly walking away to go see their father, it was Wolf's turn to grin. He wondered where Bear had learned those new words he just muttered in disgust.

The Shaman was talking with the gray-haired Cooking Woman who was stirring the huge pot hanging over the community fire. One of her daughters was nearby cleaning a staked-out deer hide. Instead of approaching the elders, Wolf waited patiently and sat near the stacked canoes until his father was finished.

The Shaman took his time walking past Wolf and stood in his position under the rocks in front of the hanging deerskin. Wolf followed and sat across from him. Out of respect, he would let his father speak first. He might have to listen to a long story before he could bring up what he wanted to say but it was the proper thing to do. And, knowing his father, he would probably launch into one of his favorite windy tales just because he knew Wolf would have to sit there and listen.

"Théhaŋ waŋčhíŋyaŋke šni."

Wolf gave a surprised snort. "What is it with this 'long time, no see' business? I just got that from Mato as well."

"It has been two moons. We missed you and we worry. That is all."

Wolf's head tilted to the side, eyes narrowed. "Two months? It didn't seem like that long," he muttered, more to himself than to the Shaman. "Time must be moving differently again."

His father watched one of their canoes go by. Mato was teaching his son, Igmutaka, how to paddle and control the canoe. Once they floated past the beaver dam, Mato had him turn back towards the encampment. "Time passes as it always does."

When it became obvious the Shaman was not going to launch into one of his tales, Wolf decided it was all right to bring up the reason for his visit. "Things are getting overly complicated," he began. If he had had hands, he would have run them through his hair. Since he couldn't show his frustration that way, he began pacing the rocky ground in front of his father, his ears laid back on his head. "I don't know where the doctor has gone. He isn't in the French Quarter of New Orleans any longer. My friend Wals isn't remembering his other life at all. He seems content and happy here with his new life and his new job."

The wolf headdress turned to face him. The unseeing, glassy eyes always bothered Wolf. "Did you ever think that perhaps they both belong here in this time? That they should stay? Also?" he couldn't help throwing in.

"You know as well as I that Wals does not belong here," Wolf stressed, tearing his eyes away from the headdress. "I thought he would be able to help me with Rose and Doctor Houser, but she seems ready to worship the ground he walks on. He, in turn, is starting to lust after her. Even worse, the women at the Fort are falling all over him. The soldiers seem to think that he is their long-lost buddy. Even my brothers here welcome him and are now including him in their canoe races! And what if Doctor Houser decided to jump on the paddlewheeler in New Orleans and move away? How in the world am I supposed to find him then!?" Wolf broke off, flustered, and looked to his father for some kind of wisdom or guidance.

The black eyes regarding him twinkled under the mask. "Perhaps you did not think it through well enough when you were in the other world. Did you not prepare your friend?"

Wolf resumed pacing, his tail switching angrily from side to side. "I tried. There wasn't enough time! After I called it, the fog came quicker than I expected. Then he banged his head pretty bad in the whirlpool."

"I hear a lot of excuses as to why everything is going wrong. I hear nothing as to how you will make it right."

Wolf held himself back from actually growling. "I. Am. Working. On. It." At the dark look on the Shaman's face, he took a deep breath and began again in a more respectful tone. "The power of the Island is strong. It seems to be working on Wals, draining him of his past memories. Since nothing here will make him remember, I think I need to go back to our time. Maybe I need to bring something back, something that may help to jog his memory."

He was met with stony silence, as he had expected. He knew his father would not like the idea of him going through the fog again so soon and would offer no encouragement or advice.

"So," Wolf tried to lighten the mood, "where did you hide my clothes this time?"

"In my tipi." The words were quiet, resigned. There was no point arguing. Before, they had made something of a game of hiding Wolf's clothes. Once he had found them stuffed in the blackened chimney of Rose's cabin. It had been difficult explaining that mess to the Costume Department. "Mato told me something you should know. He would have told *you* if you had been here." When Wolf refused to be baited, he continued, "There is a new doctor at the Fort."

Wolf's ears perked up and turned towards his father. "There is? How old is he? Did Bear get his name? How long….?"

The dark eyes stared at Wolf until he stopped asking questions. Pulling the wolf skin tighter across his shoulders, the Shaman turned just in time to see his grandson ram the canoe into the beaver dam. The chapa watching from the safety of the pool slapped his tail angrily on the water. "All he said was that the pejuta wica sa was a kind man with hair the color of tree bark."

Knowing that was all the information he would get from either his father or his brother, he wondered how he could get into Fort Wilderness to check out this new man. He couldn't simply walk through the gates, stick his head in the Infirmary, and ask if his name was Doctor Claude Houser. His father looked over when he heard the wolf chuckle. Wolf remembered that Dr. Houser had brown hair when he brought him to New Orleans, but a lot of years had passed in the other world. Wouldn't he have gray hair by now? He gave a sigh and shook his head. The amusement quickly faded. His father didn't have a handy calendar pinned up in his tipi to check the current year, so Wolf could only go by the appearances of the Island and the Fort to determine *when* in time he was. Would the doctor age here like he would have in his proper place in time? Or, did Wolf come farther back in time than he thought so that the intervening years would not come into play? More questions and no answers. Well, he was grateful for the new information, at least. "Philámayaye," he told his father respectfully.

"You are welcome, my son. When do you go back?"

"I hope tonight, atewaye ki."

His father turned towards the River again, watching Mato's son trying to master stroking against the current. At that moment, Wolf knew he was dismissed.

Disneyland – 2007

A huge, three-masted sailing ship floated majestically past, all sails furled. The calmness of its passage was belied by the frenzied activity on its deck as a rowdy sword fight was in progress. A young girl wearing a blue nightdress was tied to the tall central mast. She was mostly ignored by all of the pirates as they swarmed over the deck, some up in the rigging, all of them waving swords and shouting. Their captain, dressed in flamboyant red with a large feather sticking out of his hat, was engaged in a one-on-one sword fight with a young boy dressed all in green. The boy, holding a small dagger, kept taunting him and calling him a 'codfish,' jumped nimbly out of reach of the longer sword that was repeatedly jabbed at him. Suddenly losing his balance, the captain caught a dangling rope and, calling for help from his first officer, swung way out over the green water of the River and then back onto the ship again. He seemed terrified because a huge ticking crocodile was slowly chasing the sailing ship.

Wolf sunk deeper in the reeds on the water's edge, trying to remain hidden as the Columbia went past his submerged body. He knew the Mark Twain would follow in a few minutes with all the costumed cast members waving brightly colored flags to the watching crowd as part of the grand finale of the show, *Fantasmic!* Spinning pinwheel fireworks lit the all-white ship as it, too, sailed slowly past his hiding place.

Wolf waited patiently in the water while his mind cleared and the ships were far enough away on the other side of Tom Sawyer's Island. He had come out of the vortex close to the entry of the canoe dock. Disoriented from the turmoil of the storm, he had gotten his directions wrong and almost swam straight into the middle of the ongoing show.

He knew the canoe dock would definitely be empty of people this long after sunset and he could get past there easily enough. But, it was the Hungry Bear Restaurant that gave him worry. Two levels of people having a late dinner of hamburgers and hotdogs would probably notice a naked man swimming by.

Near the loop the Splash Mountain boats made into the River, he carefully crossed underwater to give himself distance—distance from both the people and the flocks of ducks and mud hens that congregated around the Restaurant hoping to get fed on French fries and hamburger buns. The last thing he wanted was to have to swim through that mess. Once across the River in relative darkness, he swam past the silent Settler's Cabin and then through the rapids. When he was far enough from any prying eyes, he crossed the River once more.

Hidden by the tall, thick marsh grass, Wolf had to wait at the water's edge for the steam train to make its journey past the Friendly Village. The Village was now lit in various places that strategically highlighted the peaceful scene. From where he waited, he listened to the recorded voice of the Shaman telling the story of how the flute came to their people.

When the last car of the train had disappeared into the tunnel that took it to Fantasyland, he made his way to the backmost tipi in the clearing, ducking inside so that he would not be seen by the next train. The flaps were open at the top to allow the smoke to escape. Only, there was no smoke rising tonight. His family was not there. This was where he found his Security uniform just as his father had told him it would be. He sat in the middle of the round dwelling as he got dressed. It was an odd feeling. He had just been here hours earlier discussing his problems with his father. Now the likeness of his father wearing the same headdress was standing under the same rocky overhang. He had just walked past the Cooking Woman stirring the pot. It was a little trippy for him—even after all the times he had made the transition.

Using the train tracks that circled the Park, he made his way back to the trestle in Critter Country. Walking across the trestle, he came to the exit of a tunnel. If he had kept walking, that tunnel would go past the Splash Mountain viewing window that allowed passengers on the steam train to see a glimpse inside the ride. This was the riverboat scene that was close to the final fifty-two-foot screaming drop. He also knew that it was in this very tunnel that Lance's friend, Adam, five years earlier, had rappelled into one of the colorful caverns and retrieved a clue capsule left decades ago by Walt Disney. When Adam's rope had been discovered near the yellow cavern after he had to literally run out of the tunnel in front of an approaching train, Wolf had been one of the security guards called in to investigate. When it became obvious that nothing was damaged and the perpetrator had long vanished, it was easy for Wolf to dismiss the case as too unimportant to waste more time in an investigation. As the security force walked out of the tunnel, Wolf had smiled in the darkness, wishing he could have seen the look on Adam's face as the light of the train bore down on his back.

Nobody in the queue for Splash Mountain or walking through Critter Country seemed overly concerned or surprised to see a security officer walk across the trestle and then stride down the cast member-only steps near the line. Had they looked closely, they might have wondered why his hair was wet and he was not wearing any socks. As he had swum across the River, Wolf hadn't noticed that his socks were now hanging from the mouth of the shaggy white dog standing on the log that reached out over the green water.

Wolf moved silently behind the scenes at Disneyland. The area was called 'backstage' by the cast members. He hoped to avoid talking to anyone until he could determine exactly *when* in time he had come back. Heading for the lockers where the employees would change out of their costumes and then go home for the night, he knew there would be a calendar on the wall.

Stifling a groan, Wolf nodded a curt greeting to two determined Haunted Mansion women. They recognized the handsome Security guard and were intent on getting him to attend a private party in the Stretching Room of the Haunted Mansion after Disneyland closed in a couple of hours. It would be a coup for them. None of the women in the Park had been able to get the mysterious Wolf to join them in any of those private little rendezvous. They were again disappointed when he barely answered them and kept walking.

Wolf stared at the calendar tacked up on the wall in the locker room. Each day was carefully crossed out. It was tradition. No one messed with the calendar. *Thursday. Good, it was only one day has passed since Wals and I went through the vortex together, but how can that be? We've been gone two months.*

As Wolf considered the situation, he kept coming back to the same conclusion that he could no longer properly gauge the time difference. Whatever he had to do, he had to do it soon. Events on Rose's Island were moving along much faster than he had previously thought.

Surreptitiously glancing around, he saw he was alone in the locker room. He found Wals locker and inserted his own master key into the lock. He swung the door open and stared at the jumbled contents. Clothes, shoes, CDs of music, a paperback novel, deodorant, after shave, a mirror, extra cast member nametags, the latest edition of *Disneyland Line*—the cast members' own newsletter that held all the news of what was going on at the Park, a paper sack that held the remains of some forgotten lunch, a stack of phone numbers, a handbill advertising the band Maxx, a brochure for a pizza parlor, a broken canoe paddle he hadn't smuggled out of the Park yet. Usual stuff in the usual locker.

The CD wouldn't work unless Wolf took back a player that would withstand the energy and water of the swirling vortex…. Okay, he decided, nothing that actually had to *work* once it went through…. Paper products would be ruined in the water. Clothes? Shoes? No, it had to be something a wolf could easily carry, possibly tied around his neck. Wolf's eyes kept going back to the nametags on the upper shelf. Wals had quite a collection that he had swiped from his friends when their backs were turned as they changed clothes. Wolf picked up Wals current Dream tag that had the blue castle in the clouds at the top and the gold stars around the edges. *This may work just fine*, he smiled to himself. Now all he had to do was find some kind of thin rope or thick thread and perhaps a small bag to hang from it.

But, what about the Doctor? Wolf paused in front of Wals' locker. Since he hadn't seen the doctor personally yet, he had to assume, by both Wals' and Rose's behavior, that the doctor would be in the same mental state of not being able to recall his other life. Wolf knew he had to be prepared for that contingency. He would need something that would jog the doctor's memory and make him recall his former life. Even if Wals remembered, that was only half of the problem. Doctor Houser had now been gone forty-one years—well, forty-one years in today's time frame, he reminded himself. It was impossible to gauge how much time had actually passed for the doctor. What would possibly be relevant to the doctor that Wolf would be able to access? He had only met the man once in Walt's apartment. It was at that moment that he recognized the importance of what his father had said, "Perhaps you did not think it through well enough when you were in the other world...." Perhaps he had been in too much of a rush when he had taken the doctor into the River that night. *Slow down, think... follow the trail.* Leaving Wals' locker, he remembered following the simplistic trail the maintenance man had left. Wolf's eyes narrowed as he thought back. *The overcoat and hat.* He then recalled had worn Dr. Houser's coat and hat when he had made the switch with the money bag. Not knowing what to do with them, he had taken the clothing back to Walt's apartment, stashing them in the little closet. Well, there was only one way to find out if they were still there.

Wolf headed back into the Park and entered

the little side gate next to the Fire Station on Main Street. Again using his master key, he let himself into the silent, waiting apartment. The only illumination was the nostalgic light left burning in the front window for Walt. Opening the small closet, he felt a wave of sadness and loss wash over him as he thought about his boss. Because of his superior eyesight, Wolf didn't need to turn on an interior light that might alert someone either on Main Street or walking behinds the scenes of his presence in the supposedly secured and empty rooms. Pushed way in the back was the doctor's overcoat. Some-one probably assumed it was Walt's and had left it. *Good, something is finally going right.*

Not having gone through the pockets before in his rush to finish the switch, Wolf didn't know what he might find. The outer right-hand pocket still held the crumpled ransom note. The left pocket was empty. Wolf's spirit flagged a little. He had hoped this coat would hold something he could use.

He was just about to put the coat back on the hangar when he remembered some of his own jack-ets had an inner pocket. Sliding his hand inside the silk lining, his fingers closed on something cool and metallic. He pulled out an old Zippo lighter, silver in color, with engraving all over the front. Hope return-ing, Wolf strode over to the light burning in the win-dow, careful to stay off to the side, out of sight. Turning the lighter back and forth in the light, he could make out the engraved words "To Doctor Houser. Into whatsoever house I shall enter…. Our thanks. 1962." In the center, surrounded by the words that formed an enclosing arch, were a mor-tal and pestle and the rod of Asclepius—the medical symbol of a staff entwined by a snake.

Wolf smiled in the darkness. He didn't know what the doctor had done to earn this special thanks, but it had to have been important enough for a non-smoking man to carry a cigarette lighter. If anything could make the doctor remember, this should.

After one final look around the carefully preserved apartment, he carefully locked the door. With a determined step, Wolf headed for Costuming where the cast members got their outfits. He figured he could talk to the Sewing Department there and get what he needed.

The Island – 1817

Rose looked around frantically one last time for her wolf. He was nowhere to be seen and Private Crain was gaining on her. She knew she wouldn't make it back to the safety of her cabin before he caught her. Without a thought to the possible danger inside, she ducked into the dark opening of Injun Joe's Cave. Only the bravest of the Islanders ever ventured alone into the winding, confusing labyrinth of tunnels. Some of them had never come out again.

The underground tunnels wove around for miles in a jumbled maze. Some of the paths led to dead-ends. One led to some beautifully colored phosphorous pools. One skirted the edge of the dangerous Bottomless Pit. At least one tunnel led to the other side of the Island and surfaced across from the old mining town. It was in a remote part of the Island, far from what should have been the safety of the Fort. It wasn't safe for Rose. That remote section was where she was headed. If she made it through fast enough, there would be plenty of places to hide until Crain gave up the chase. Wolf had led her through the tunnels many times, teaching her, she now realized, how to navigate the twisting turns.

She could barely distinguish what sounded like swearing as Daniel Crain had plunged into the musty darkness after her. Unlike Rose, he was unaware of the low-hanging rock formation just past the entrance. It caught him right square in the middle of his sweating forehead. Trying not to make any noise as she hurried along, she smugly smiled in the growing darkness when his cry of pain reached her. The path she was following dropped at a gentle slope, just as she knew it should. She placed a guiding hand on the wall of the tunnel as she kept moving; it was getting darker and darker as she moved further from the light of the entryway. One more turn, and then the ground should start to rise again.

She stopped short, a little confused. The tunnel abruptly ended. Frantically feeling her hands all over the rocky wall, she just knew she had been on the right path. *Who filled in this tunnel!?* She hadn't realized she let out a sharp gasp until Daniel called out to her, "Ha! I heard that. I know where you are now, stuck-up female! You are trapped."

Not wasting time replying, she quickly backtracked until she found the forked trail. One path led back to the main entrance and the other went past the Bottomless Pit. Beyond that, if she could find it, was one other route to the outside.

She could hear the labored breathing of Private Crain echoing through the tunnels. Unused to any physical demands and secretly frightened of the growing darkness, he was fighting for control. If he did succeed in catching her, she knew she would not survive the outcome. Suddenly she tripped on a rock in the pathway. Quickly bending down, she picked it up in her hand. Her fingers closed over the rock, making a solid fist. Her blue eyes narrowed in the darkness. If he did catch up to her, at least she would go down fighting.

Hesitating for only a moment, eyes closed, she mentally thought through the alternate route. Choosing the wrong tunnel at this point could prove to be fatal for her. She lifted the hem of her skirt so it wouldn't drag on the ground, possibly alerting Daniel which way she fled. With the sounds of him stumbling after her filling her ears, she hurried into the tunnel on the right, praying she remembered correctly.

The wolf picked up the pieces of his uniform that were stuck in some low-flung branches at the edge of the River. He was careful not to bite down too hard and leave holes in them. The Costume department hadn't been too happy the first time he had returned the shirt for repairs. It had been difficult to get them to fix it without an explanation as to why and where a dog had bit him while on duty. He made as neat a pile as he could behind Rose's cabin and drug some fallen branches over them for cover.

It only took a moment for him to realize Rose

was not at home. He wondered why she would leave without the mare when he saw that Sukawaka was placidly nibbling on some weeds growing near her fence. Debating on whether Rose would have gone swimming at the Beaver Dam or would have walked to Fort Wilderness, he decided to check the Fort first. Nose up to catch any warning scents, he loped easily down the winding path along the River.

Hiding in the thick undergrowth across from the open stockade gate, Wolf watched all the activity going on inside the Fort. There seemed to be fewer soldiers now, he noted. He could see that the Regimental Headquarters building had been closed and there were now upright bars blocking the doorway and window. While he was hoping to catch a glimpse of the new doctor, he could hear voices coming down the pathway he had just used. He backed further into the covering brush and remained still.

Private Crain was coming into view first, holding a dirty yellow handkerchief up to his bleeding forehead, his soiled white Calvary hat had been pushed back off of his scarred face. His uniform was all dusty and reeked of sweat. "I almost had my hands on that crazy woman, Billy. I almost had her," he was telling his friend. "Then she just disappeared inside the cave. It was like the earth swallowed her up."

Billy spat into the bushes, unimpressed. "Hmph. More'n likely you were too scared to go in very far after her. You always were afraid of the dark, Danny!" he taunted. He could have added thunderstorms and lightning to the list of Crain's fears, but he would save that one for another time.

"The heck I am," Daniel muttered, trying to

save face. "I hope she fell into the Bottomless Pit! Serve that uppity female right."

"Don't know why you even bother wastin' yer time with her. Don't know how many times you need to get your face slapped…. That Yvette in the Cantina seems to think you're all right. For some reason," he added in a snickering undertone.

Daniel didn't like the way the conversation had turned. He had a score to settle with that blond. He blamed her for everything that went wrong in his misguided life—even though his problems were of his own making. Unknowingly, he had transferred all the animosity, all the hatred he had towards his long-forgotten niece Kimberly onto Rose. When he managed to catch her alone, he would finish with his knife on Rose what he had started in the escape tunnel of the Fort with Kimberly…. Lost in his own thoughts, he was barely listening to Billy. He knew Yvette couldn't stand his touch either. She had told him so time and time again. She only pretended to like him when she served him his drinks because it was her job to entertain all the soldiers, and she hoped some day he would actually pay her. He just saw no need to relay that information to his smirking friend. "I heard tell the Cantina is closing soon. Don't know where we'll get our liquor then. Yvette said she was going to get a job as a dancer in that fancy Golden Horseshoe Saloon way across the River." *Good riddance*, he told himself, absentmindedly rubbing the scars on his face with his other hand.

Over the years, he had tried to remember how he got those scars—and the ones on the back of his hands—especially during the sporadic times he bothered shaving. The straightedge razor would stop midair as a lone piece of memory would dart across his mind. He remembered something big and black with wheels that went at a great speed…. It had to have been a wagon or a carriage of some sort. *Was it the horse that had been black? Had he named it Cadillac?* Then the memory would again fade as it always did and he would finish shaving his face, no wiser to the mystery.

The rest of the conversation was lost to Wolf as the two men went into the Fort and headed for their barracks. He didn't care about them right now anyway. He just knew he had to find Rose in the tunnels. He thought he had taught her well enough, but it did get confusing even in the best of circumstances. And, if Crain had been chasing her…. His eyes narrowed. Well, he would have to deal with the Private later.

Making sure no one was nearby to see him, Wolf left his hiding place and ran back to the entrance of the cave. Nose to the ground, he easily followed Rose's scent until it, too, led to the new dead-end. *They are already changing the Island*, he knew instantly. *I need to move more quickly.*

Nose down again, Wolf followed her trail. He could see well enough in the darkness, but knew she would have had to move somewhat slowly— especially when she discovered the blocked path. It still took him over twenty minutes to emerge into the daylight. Wolf knew that it must have taken her hours to come that far. Breathing in the clean air, he was glad to be out of the damp, dark tunnels as he pushed through the vines that had grown over the exit. Not seeing her in either direction, he again relied on his superior sense of smell to find his missing friend.

When the trail ended, he knew to look up. Just as the cat at the Mansion had done, Rose had gone up a tree. There was an old treehouse built up in that huge oak, some wooden planks were nailed to the massive trunk of the tree to use as stairs. He couldn't see her, but knew she would be tucked back into the farthest corner. Never having tried it as a wolf, he was pretty sure he could manage to climb the rickety stairs, but didn't think he needed to. He let out a very low yip and a howl since they were located about a mile away from the Fort. Wolf didn't think any of the soldiers would be close by, but didn't want to take a chance of being heard by anyone but Rose. Almost instantly Wolf spotted her face cautiously peering over the edge. Her face broke into a beautiful smile when she saw him and she let out a glad cry.

"Wolf, it's you! I'm so glad it was you who found me!" She nimbly climbed down the stairs and dropped down next to him, hugging his neck. "I just knew you would come."

He pulled slowly away from her, not wanting her to accidentally find what was tied around his neck. That was for Wals and the doctor. Not wanting to loiter around the treehouse, he walked to the edge of a small ravine. Below was the little stream that cut through part of the Island and dumped into the larger River. It was obvious that they needed to go. Now. He whined and looked back at her.

"All right. All right. I get it. Can't a girl be glad to see you?" she teased. She balked, though, when she saw where he was heading. There was a suspension bridge that would take them across the ravine and a mile closer to her cabin. She was afraid of heights. "Uh, Wolf, can't we go back the other way? What about the barrel bridge? Or, we could go back through the caves," she added hopefully.

He ignored her plea and started across the long wooden-planked bridge. He didn't have the benefit of hanging onto the thick cables of rope on either side of the bridge, but with the agility and balance of his four legs, he didn't really need them. He walked the first thirty feet and looked expectantly back. Rose was still frozen in place, pale, and for some reason had a rock gripped in her hand. Wolf made sure his feet were all on solid boards and then he lay down to show her there was nothing to be afraid of. When that didn't work, he rolled on his back then got up again. He gave a short yip.

"Okay, you don't have to shout! I'm coming, I'm coming," she muttered. Breaking out in a sweat, Rose put a tentative slippered foot on the first plank. She reached up to grab the rope and found she was still holding the rock she had found in the cave. Turning, she gave it a mighty heave in the direction of the Fort. Hearing it crash into the forest, she smiled a little, picturing it hitting Private Crain smack in the face. When she heard another yip, she turned to the bridge again, her tormentor forgotten in the face of this new terror. "Yes, Wolf, I know," she whispered as her fingers closed in a death-grip on the stout ropes that were chest-high on both sides of the bridge. When the plank didn't break beneath her weight, she carefully moved to the next board.

Wolf just sat there impatiently waiting for her to trust that it was going to be all right. With her going only one plank at a time, he could tell this was going to take a while. He had been hoping they would get back to the cabin before dark. Now he wasn't sure.

To cover her nervousness, she started talking to Wolf like she always did. "I really did miss you, Wolf. I haven't had any visitors lately. That nice Mr. Davis, well, he never came back. I, oh!" as her foot slipped sideways on some debris of rotten leaves. She still hadn't gotten to Wolf yet and was already breathless. "I...I was saying, I thought he might come calling as we seemed to get along all right. But, no, he never came back. It's only been a couple of months. Maybe he's busy. Did you know that awful Private Crain tried to come after me again? I know I should have taken the mare to the Fort, but it was such a beautiful day that I decided to walk. I wanted to do some baking tomorrow and knew I would need some more flour from the miller. I didn't know the Mill had closed. It was all locked up!" She stopped in her rambling discourse and looked up from her feet to Wolf. She was dismayed at how far away he still was. "Gosh, how long is this stupid bridge anyway!? Oh, dear. I'd better hurry a little."

Wolf had decided to show his support by moving besides her. The bridge tilted with his extra weight. She gave a little scream of fear. "Don't rock it! Don't rock it!"

With an exaggerated sigh, he moved in front of her another thirty feet. She watched how easily he did it and managed to step board to board a little quicker. He glanced at the sun and groaned. It was definitely going to be dark before they made it back to her cabin. Now he wouldn't be able to look for Wals until tomorrow to try and find out what has been going on. Or, according to Rose, what has *not* been going on.

As soon as it was light the next morning, Wolf left the little cabin and again headed towards the Fort. He had to find Wals and get things in motion.

The stockade gate was still open. The few remaining soldiers seemed to find no reason to go to the trouble of barring it every night. The Major General was long gone to another assignment and the soldiers were more or less doing what they pleased. And it pleased them to do very little. There was an abundance of debris littered over the parade grounds.

Wolf ran quickly past the open gate and headed for the raft landing. If Wals was at work, he would be there. The Mark Twain paddlewheeler was in her berth. The canoes Wals used were all there. One of the rafts was still tied to the dock. It was quiet all along both sides of the River and the wharf.

Not wasting any more time, Wolf turned and ran the mile distance back to the Fort.

Hiding again in the thick bushes, he watched and waited as the remaining horses were exercised in the yard and returned to the livery stable. Smoke started rising from the cook shack. One of the soldiers got some water from the well. He didn't see the doctor or Wals. Not giving up just yet, he settled back further in the bushes, watching.

A squeal of feminine laughter came from one of the lookout towers above him. Two of the Fort women ran lightly down the wooden stairs, one of them carrying a tarnished silver serving platter. Heads together, they were laughing with each other as they headed for the dining room across the compound.

Wals' head appeared in the larger window of the tower. Looking down, he was buttoning his worn yellow shirt. As his arms moved, it was apparent some of the fringe was now missing. Glancing quickly into the open gate and seeing no one, Wolf stepped out into the open and let out a yip to get Wals' attention.

At the same moment, two Privates had come out of their barracks when they heard the noise of the laughter, and they watched the women close the Cantina door with a bang. Smirking and nudging each other, they headed for the tower's stairs. Daniel Crain yelled up, "Hey, Wals, that you up there?"

"Maybe," came the familiar voice. "Can't a man enjoy his breakfast in peace?"

The three humans all heard the wolf yip at the same time. "Oh, crap." Eyes wide, Wolf dove back into the cover of the bushes. Wals headed for the stairs. Private Crain ran for his rifle. And Private Billy ran for his life.

Daniel was jamming a ball into his gun as he emerged from the barracks. "I've got you now, you filthy wolf."

Wals hesitated in the entry of the Fort. He again had seen the white patch of fur on the wolf's chest before it disappeared from view. That, combined with those startling blue eyes, was pulling at his memory again. Daniel tried to push past him.

"Out of the way, Wals. I've got me a wolf to kill," as he tossed aside the ramming rod.

His mind still trying to grasp the fleeting images, Wals attempted to stop him. "Wait a second,

Daniel, you can't...."

"No, no waiting. I've been waiting for that son of a gun to show his ugly face for years now. He's going to join his brethren on that there wall. And I'm going to put him there!" He raised the rifle to his shoulder and aimed into the bushes where he had last seen the wolf. He pulled the trigger before Wals could stop him.

There was a flash and a puff of smoke emerged from the rifle barrel. Leaves flew up where the ball had passed. There was no other movement or sound. With a shout of triumph, Daniel headed towards the bush. Crouching down, he tried to peer through the thicket. A loud, menacing growl greeted him. Wolf's face slowly emerged out of the greenery, teeth bared, eyes a slit.

"You got any more shot there, Daniel?" Wals asked, backing up slowly. The wolf didn't seem to notice him, but was staring straight into the Private's terrified eyes.

Daniel turned a ghastly shade of white. "Thought I would only need one," he whispered. "Give me your knife!" he hissed at Wals, holding his hand out behind him.

"Don't have one. Looks like you'll have to take him with your bare hands." Wals was enjoying this. He knew he was safe. Well, at least he thought he was safe. The wolf knew him. But, then again, the wolf might be injured and could turn on anyone. *Maybe I should rethink this* safe *part*, he thought, backing up a step.

With a girlish shriek, Daniel jumped to his feet and ran all the way back into the Fort, slamming the barracks door behind him.

Not knowing if the Private would eventually

come out with another loaded rifle, Wolf emerged from the bushes and tried to run towards the forest. Wals could see the blood running down his leg. The ball seemed to be embedded in his back leg and the intense pain prevented the wolf from being able to run. With a last, pleading look towards Wals, he limped as fast as he could down the path in the direction of Rose's cabin.

Wals heard the commotion coming from the barracks and knew Daniel was fortifying himself with a drink for another go at the wolf. With that white patch of fur in his mind's eye, he turned and ran after the injured animal.

Wolf glanced back, hoping it was Wals coming after him so he that wouldn't have to make a fighting stand. He might be able to protect himself against a knife, but not another rifle. In a haze of pain, he waited to let his friend catch up, his leg throbbing and bleeding.

Wals held his hands palms out to the wolf. *Probably showing me he was unarmed*? Wolf wondered, swaying from the shock. Wolf took a step towards Wals and let himself collapse at Wals' feet. *If that doesn't do it, nothing will*, he figured.

Wals knew time was running out, but he also knew he wouldn't be able to carry the huge animal all the way to Rose's cabin without being caught by the soldiers. His canoes were almost a mile in the other direction, plus they would have to go past the entrance to the Fort to get there. It wouldn't do to try and hide in the caves because he hadn't been inside them since he started his job there and didn't know his way. He was about out of options when he spotted a native canoe coming towards him from the direction of the village. He picked up Wolf and gasped at the sheer weight of him. "Good thing I've been hefting crates for a few years," he grunted as he tried to jog towards the canoe.

Always watchful of the goings-on of the cabin and the Fort, Mato had seen what had happened to Wolf and was angling his canoe to meet Wals. The soldiers hadn't emerged from the Fort yet. They were probably waiting for blood loss to help even their odds.

"Hau kola," Mato greeted Wals as he braced the canoe for the extra weight.

"Hello, friend," Wals quickly repeated back, setting the wolf on the floor of the canoe and climbing in after him. He hoped to get to the pleasantries later when Wolf was safe. He tried to duck down out of sight as best he could so it would look like the canoe was occupied only by Mato. He didn't know if that would work as Mato calmly paddled the canoe out into the current and headed back downriver. They seemed to be moving awfully slow. When he heard shouts coming from the direction of the Fort, Wals resisted the urge to raise his head. From the amount of noise, the men apparently had regained their courage and were spreading out en masse to find the injured animal. They didn't seem to give Mato a second look.

When the canoe rounded the big bend of the river, and they were shielded by the density of the forest, Wals lifted his head to the edge of the canoe and looked back. He could see no one from the Fort. Sitting up, he ran a hand over the wolf to try and determine the extent of his injury. Wolf's eyes were closed, and he felt hot to Wals' touch. Considering how little Wals knew about wolves, he *thought* the animal felt hot. That could have been normal for that thick coat of fur.

Looking up, Wals realized Mato was going to pass up Rose's cabin. He pointed at her clearing when it came into view, indicating that was where he wanted to go. Mato shook his head and pointed downriver. He was heading for his village. Wals didn't necessarily fear going to the village; he just wanted Rose to know what had happened and allow her to tend to her wolf.

As they got closer to the cabin, they could see Rose was out working in her garden. Her long rifle was nearby, propped up on one of the rails. Wals quietly called out to her. He knew how far sound could travel in the still air, so he hesitated saying too much and telling her about the wolf. Wolf raised his head and whined at Mato. The two brothers locked eyes. Mato said something unpleasant under his breath and brought the canoe around.

Rose met them at the water's edge and gave a little cry when she saw the blood all over Wolf.

"I think it is just a flesh wound, but I haven't had time to really check," Wals explained to her as the canoe got closer.

Mato beached the canoe and carried the wolf into the little cabin. He seemed to be muttering to the wolf in his language all the way up from the River. He received an answering growl when Wolf was placed on his pallet. Once his brother was settled as comfortably as possible, Mato looked around the little cabin with interest. He had never been inside before. Resisting the urge to pick up little knickknacks and examine them, he instead headed for the door.

Wals practiced a word he was learning: "Philámayaye."

Mato nodded once to him and silently left. He needed to report to the Shaman what had happened to his brother. He didn't figure it would be taken well.

"What did you say to him?" Rose wanted to know when Mato left.

"I think it was thank you. At least I hope it was thank you. If it wasn't, they might come back and burn your cabin down again!"

Paling, her eyes widened in fright until she realized he was just teasing her. She lightly slapped his arm and turned back to her injured wolf. "Wals?" she shyly said as she started tending to Wolf's needs, "It's good to see you again. I…I missed you…I mean, I missed talking to you."

He looked into her lovely eyes and wondered to himself why in the world he had stayed away and wasted all that time with the women at the Fort. He gave her a smile. "Thank you. I missed talking to you too," he admitted.

Brightening a little, Rose got some clean rags out of her basket and tore them into strips. She wet them in the warm water hanging over the fire. Kneeling down next to Wolf, her smile faded as she gently dabbed at the seeping blood on his right hind leg. His eyes were closed, and he was breathing heavily. It hurt like the dickens.

When she touched the entry point of the shot, he couldn't help wincing. "Here it is," Rose told the hovering Wals. "Sorry, Wolf, but this is going to hurt a lot. I need to see if the ball is still in there."

As she prodded, the wolf shook with the pain, but remained stoically quiet. Wals squatted down near Wolf's head, hoping silently to himself that the animal didn't snap out in his misery. Somehow, though, Wals knew he wouldn't. As he found him-self again staring at the unusual white fur on the wolf's black chest again, he reached out to touch it when the wolf's eyes suddenly popped open. Those eerie blue eyes stared back at him. Wals looked from the white fur to the blue eyes.

Not sure why it looked so familiar, Wals ran a comforting hand down the wolf's neck. "You'll be okay, Wolf."

Finding that the ball had passed right through his leg, with concern etched on her face, Rose was concentrating on cleaning and bandaging the wound and was unable to pay any attention to what Wals was doing.

As he tried to comfort the injured animal, Wals' hand suddenly came across what felt like some kind of twine tied around the wolf's neck. Curious, he lifted it away from the fur and looked at the tight knot. The wolf was watching him closely. He thought he saw the wolf nod to him as if telling him it was all right and to continue. *That couldn't be*, he thought, mentally chastising himself for such a fool-ish notion. Still, he slowly followed the cord until it disappeared under the thick fur on his neck. Not getting any resistance from the animal, he kept feel-ing along the twine.

His fingers finally met some kind of pouch hanging off the cord. Feeling through the satiny material, he could feel two items inside. Pricking his finger on one of the things inside, he found it might be easier to remove the twine. As the pouch loosened from the twine and fell into his hand, he pulled open the black silk. He recognized the first item as a cigarette lighter, not even thinking about the incongruity. Reading the face, he silently mumbled, "This must belong to Doc Houser," his lips moving as he read. "Hmm. Wonder what the numbers one, nine, six and two mean?" Confused and frowning, wondering what a wolf was doing with the doctor's lighter, he set the silver Zippo aside on the floor and felt inside the bag again to locate that first item that had pricked him. It was smooth and cool to the touch. As he pulled it out, his fingers could feel some deep indents on the surface of the oval item.

The pain-shrouded blue eyes were unblinking, staring right at Wals as he brought the object out into the light of the cabin.

His mouth slowly dropped open as he let the twine and pouch that had been around the wolf's neck fall unnoticed on the floor of the cabin. Wals couldn't take his eyes off of his find as his heart started pounding in his chest.

He now just stared open-mouthed at what inexplicably appeared to be an oval nametag from Disneyland that cast members wear on their costumes. It had a drawing of the tell-tale Disneyland castle at the top, and it had the name *Wals* engraved in deep blue letters.

CHAPTER EIGHT

Disneyland – 2007

Working under the cover of darkness, long after the Park had closed and the guests were fast asleep inside their hotel rooms, hardhat-wearing, competent-looking workers invaded Tom Sawyer's Island. Referring to the large, crisp roll of blueprints, his men armed with jackhammers, dynamite, back-hoes, shovels and hammers, the foreman, John Lafferty, had already directed the closing up of a portion of Injun Joe's Cave. At the same time, an-other part of his crew was busy altering what was left of the inner tunnels and caverns.

Huge halogen lights were raised on the back-side of the Island to illuminate it in the darkness. A walkway had been constructed to tote the heavy construction materials onto the Island. An army of rafts had been borrowed to ferry over the goods that had been stacked on the dock on the other side of the Frontierland River near the Mark Twain. New sea chest props were brought in, existing caves were reinforced with heavy-looking barred doors, and some of the existing mining equipment was taken away. All traces of the peaceful fishing spot had been removed. The old treehouse behind the Fort had been discussed and left untouched as unimportant. Holes were bored into the ceiling of the caverns to wire for light fixtures that would glow eerily on the grisly scenes below. Skeletons, dressed in ragged costumes, were shackled to the walls of the newly-constructed dungeon. Pieces of treasure were placed into glowing inlets—inlets that were wired to grab at the hand of a greedy visitor hoping to claim more souvenirs for himself. A protective walkway and railing was constructed around the Bottomless Pit to insure that one of the guests didn't accidentally fall in while stumbling past it in the darkness. Just out of reach, dull tin swords were stacked in the Hidden Alcove, realistic pistols and shot, even a few kegs stenciled 'gunpowder' were nearby as if ready at hand lest they be needed in a hurry to ward off invaders.

Outside, John had some of his workmen construct a huge round cage, seemingly made out of rotting bones, which would hang over the side of a cliff. The opening was large enough to allow guests to climb in and look around and wave at the people way below them. A newly constructed ship's wheel was rigged with ropes and pulleys so that visitors could turn it, but when they did, what looked like a rotting skeleton, still desperately holding a sea chest, would rise from the water in an attempt to scare the guests. Further down the hiking trail to the east, the peaceful picnic area, that for many happy years had overlooked a beautiful straight stretch of the River, was now overhung with new ship's canvas sails and a new black pirate flag, that was used for background and was also used for shade. Stacks of brightly painted loot, sea chests and plundered goods replaced the benches and tables that had been used for seating. These goods would be left for the visitors for photo opportunities once the Grand Re-Opening was successful.

The foreman had his men continue working throughout the night. The Grand Reopening was only a few weeks away, and there was still a lot of work to do. Glancing at his watch and then at the sky in the east, he could see the pink of dawn slowly advancing over the canopy of trees. He knew their time was up for this night. Pulling an air-horn out of the tool box, he blew a blast into the air to signal his men to return to the dock and prepare to quit work. They had to be out of sight before the first guests of the Park would arrive to greet a new day at the Magic Kingdom. The props that hadn't been placed yet were stashed out of sight and would have to wait until another night. The most elaborate pieces John would set in place himself.

He watched as his men wearily climbed aboard the rafts. There were no unnecessary words, no playful jesting. After a long night of manual labor, the workers were tired and wanted to get to their cars and go home for some much-needed rest. The needs of the Park came first, and the rafts needed to get back to their proper places on the other side of the River. The decks were unnaturally quiet as the rafts slipped their holding ropes and motored into the pink, misty dawn. Looking over his progress sheets, the foreman looked through the remaining tasks. He smiled contentedly as he stood next to the steering rudder of the raft. It was going well. The Grand Reopening would happen on schedule as planned. *Yes*, he thought, *it is going very well, men.*

Inside the Fort, in the parade grounds, the fifteen-star flag had been lowered for the last time. Another flag, a black one, had been raised in its place. With respect for the past and for the history of the Island, the last cast members had been reassigned to other positions, the useable props had been sent to other areas of the Park, and finally, the stockade gate of Fort Wilderness—The Last Outpost of Civilization—was closed and barred for the last time.

The Island – 1817

Working under the cover of darkness, long after the few remaining residents of the Island were fast asleep in their beds, strangely-dressed, savage-looking men invaded The Island. Referring to a dusty rolled sheet of parchment, his men armed with pickaxes, gunpowder, chisels, shovels and mallets, the Captain, Jean Lafitte, had already directed the closing up of an escape route through Injun Joe's Cave. At the same time, another part of his crew was busy digging out new hiding places in what was left of the inner tunnels and caverns.

Brightly burning torches were blazing on the backside of the Island to illuminate it in the darkness. A gangplank from the ship had been lowered to tote the heavy construction materials onto the Island. An army of rafts had been confiscated to ferry over items that had been hidden for months along the dock on the other side of the River near the Mark Twain.   Tightly-sealed sea chests were brought in, a few of the natural caverns were covered with heavy metal barred doors, and some remaining mining equipment was taken away. All traces of the peaceful community had been removed. The old treehouse behind the Fort had been explored and dismissed as unimportant. Holes to the outside were chiseled into the ceiling of the cavern to cast an eerie light on the grisly scenes below. Traitorous shipmates, dressed in rags, were shackled to the walls of the newly-dug dungeon. Pieces of treasure were placed in carved inlets— inlets that were booby-trapped to cut off the hand of a greedy crewman hoping to claim more of the treasure for himself. A protective walkway and railing was placed around the Bottomless Pit to insure that one of their own didn't accidentally fall in while stumbling past it in the darkness.   Sharp steel swords were stacked in a hidden alcove, a few pistols and shot, and some kegs of gunpowder were ready at hand lest they be needed in a hurry to ward off attackers.

Outside, Captain Jean had some of his men construct a huge round cage made of rotting bones which would hang over the side of a cliff. The opening was large enough to only allow prisoners to be thrown in to rot and be able to look longingly at the people way below them. An old ship's wheel was rigged with ropes and pulleys so the crewmember could turn it, but when they did, a rotting skeleton still desperately holding a sea chest would rise from the water in an attempt to warn the crew of what happens to disloyal, greedy crewmembers. Further down the riding trail to the east, the peaceful fishing dock, that for many happy years had overlooked a strategic straight stretch of the River, was now over-hung with unused ship's canvas sails and a new black pirate flag that served as a warning and was also used for privacy. Stacks of crates of loot, sea chests and plundered goods replaced the empty barrels that had been used for seating. These goods would be divided amongst the crewmembers once the planned take-over was successful.

Captain Jean Lafitte had his men continue working throughout the night. The planned invasion was only a few weeks away and there was still a lot of work to do. Glancing towards sky in the east, he could see the pink of dawn slowly advancing over the canopy of trees. He knew their time was up for this night. Pulling a pistol out of his belt, he fired a shot in the air to signal his men to return to the ship and prepare to set sail. They had to be out of sight before the inhabitants of the Fort awakened to greet the new day. The treasure that hadn't been buried yet was hidden and would have to wait until another night. The most valuable pieces Jean would bury himself.

He watched as his men wearily climbed the gangplank. There were no unnecessary words, no crude jesting. After a long night of manual labor, the pirates were tired and wanted to seek their ham-mocks below deck for some much-needed rest. But, the needs of the ship came first, and it needed to get out of sight in one of the hidden coves near the Island. The deck was eerily quiet as the huge sailing ship slipped its moor and sailed into the pink, misty dawn. In his mind, the Captain ran through the remaining tasks. He smiled smugly as he stood behind the pilot at the huge ship's wheel. It was going well. The invasion would happen on schedule as planned. *Yes*, he thought, *it is going very well, mates.*

Inside the Fort, in the parade grounds, the fifteen-star flag had been lowered for the last time. Another flag, a black one, had been raised in its place. Thinking nothing of the needs of inhabitants of the Island, with no respect for the history of the Island, the gates of Fort Wilderness had been breeched, the few remaining soldiers either run off or pressed into service, the Fort looted of anything valuable, and finally the stockade gate of Fort Wilderness—the Last Outpost of Civilization—was closed and barred for the last time.

CHAPTER NINE

Disneyland – 1959

Walt pointed at the poster for his 1953 Academy Award-winning documentary *The Living Desert*. The left half of the poster showed a bobcat sitting on top of a saguaro cactus. "See? This is what we want. Maybe surround the cactus with wild pigs. Make it funny and interesting."

One of the designers looked questioningly at the others. He could tell they were going to leave it up to him. He tapped his pencil for a moment and then spoke up. "You remember, Walt, when the documentaries were first shown? We were criticized for putting humor into the real scenes of desert life. You sure you don't want to play it straight?"

They thought back to the other *True-Life Adventures* that had been filmed. *In Beaver Valley* had won the 1950 Academy Award for Best Short Subject. *Bear Country*, *The Vanishing Prairie*, *The African Lion*, *Nature's Half Acre* and the others, all of them shot over a twelve-year period of time, had been loved by the public. And now, with the expansion of the popular Mine Train ride in Frontierland to become the Mine Train Thru Nature's Wonderland, it seemed natural to include the same elements that made the *Adventures* so popular.

Walt looked back at the bright pink, red and orange poster. The other half of the poster advertised *The Vanishing Prairie* with a herd of buffalo apparently fleeing a burning wildfire. He smiled and nodded. "We are not trying to entertain the critics. I'll take my chances with the public. Besides, playing it straight isn't any fun. Look at what we did at the end of the Submarine Voyage. What do you think people are going to talk about? The natural-looking fish or the sea serpent and the mermaids?"

That brought a chuckle from the designers. Their boss knew what he was doing.

Walt got back to his previous line of thought. "The Beaver Dam is fine just as it is with the one beaver swimming in a circle and another one chewing on the white birch tree, but I want more showcase animals this time. We have plenty of motionless ones. Let's get more big movement going on to capture the people's attention." He walked over to the storyboard covered with drawings. "I'm sure you are all familiar with Marc's drawings and this map of the new track route. For the Bear Country section, as the train goes over this trestle," he pointed, "I want the water filled with bears! I like this old guy scratching his back up on the bank. I like the jumping fish. Let's get them moving!" He moved over to a somewhat crude mock-up of one scene. "Come on up here, Wathel," he invited, "and let's show them what we want."

The two men each took hold of one of the fully articulated plywood silhouettes of antlered elk. With the wooden heads facing down and antlers pointing outward, they did a mock battle to show possible movements of the two male elk who will be battling for the female's attention. Walt was clearly enjoying himself.

Once the men got the idea he was conveying, Walt moved on to the next portion of his meeting. "As you know, we are not just *shooting* for the May twenty-eighth reopening date. It *will be* May twenty-eight," he stressed. Seeing only reactions of agreement, he nodded and looked towards the back of the room. "Now I'd like you to listen to something I had recorded. It isn't the finished deal just yet, but it will let you all know how I want it played out. Could you start the tape, please?"

All in the room looked over in anticipation. Their boss's enthusiasm for the expansion was a viable, palpable thing and this enthusiasm, as it always did, was rubbing off on them. The tape began rolling and static briefly filled the room. Then they all listened closely as the narration began. It was a gravelly voice that sounded like it had been in the sun too long, slightly parched, but still awfully glad to see you. "Howdy, folks!" the narrator drawled, "Welcome to the tiny minin' town by the name of Rainbow Ridge, what we call in these-here parts the gateway to Nature's Wonderland. As our little train gets to rockin', please stay seated at all times and keep yer hands inside the train. Since we don't want no forest fires, there's no smokin' please! Keep a sharp hunter's eye 'cause you never know what kinda wildlife yer gonna see!"

Walt motioned for the tape to stop. There was

a murmur of voices as the men started taking more notes. Walt grinned to himself. He liked seeing that. "You might know Dallas. We're working with him on the full narration for the Mine Train. I think you can tell it is going to work out very well. Whether the train engineers use the taped version or do their own spiel, we will include all the new elements of the ride."

He walked back to the storyboard wall and picked up his pointer. "Here," he slapped some single item drawings. "These are still going to be part of the Living Desert. As you already know, they are the giant saguaro cactus. We're going to have Dallas mention the hot desert sun playing tricks on your mind and the cactus taking on strange shapes, like animals," as the pointer moved across the sheets of drawings, "and even people." One of the drawings, a barrel cactus, looked like a very short person with long stringy hair and a lei of flowers around his neck. Walt went to a taller drawing that looked very similar to the poster from *The Living Desert* he had shown them earlier. "And this section of the ride will be a good place to insert old Mr. Bobcat here, chased up the cactus. Once through the cactus forest, we will enter Geyser Country. The bubbling pots of mud, or Devil's Paint Pots, as they are also called, will be a good lead-in for geysers blowing into the air. Should be a good way to cool people down on hot days, too. No, I don't want them to get drenched," he added as he caught the smiles of some of the men. "Make sure they go off before the train gets there and only the mist is left to drive the train through." Pointing at the largest geyser, Walt continued, "This one is going to be called Old Unfaithful. Dallas will mention that you never know when she will blow and the train will slowly go past her after coming to a complete stop for the first eruption. Make sure the water actually goes over the track here. Then, once the train starts up, have it start bubbling again, threatening. That way we can add some danger for the last cars of the train."

When there was a lengthy pause, the men looked at each other. Their boss was just standing there smiling, staring at the large map of the new layout. Used to this, they still wondered how long they should wait or who should interrupt him. One of the older animators cleared his throat. When that didn't work, he gave a shrug and piped up, "Say, Walt, how many animals and such do you think you want?"

Walt broke off from his thoughts. He was mentally walking each foot of the track in his mind, picturing each one of the geysers erupting and the balancing rocks that would start rolling towards the slow-moving train. Then, disappearing into the dark cavern, the train would come upon glowing pools of fluorescent-dyed water in every color of the rainbow that came to life under the blacklighting. Bridal Veil Falls. Witch's Cauldron. Geyser Grotto. The music was not quite haunting, but mysterious and heavenly…. "Hmm? What? Animals, you say?" Walt momentarily frowned as the vision of winding pools of color faded from his mind. Instantly back on their track, he clarified for them, "Lots! I think, between the mammals, reptiles and birds, we can get at least one hundred and fifty. Maybe two hundred if you all are clever enough!" he kidded. "And I want to hear them, too. I want to hear the elk snorting and the coyotes howling and the rattlesnakes…well, rattling."

Those taking notes wrote "200" and underlined it.

"Let me tell you now about Cascade Peak. It's going to be beautiful!"

Disneyland – 1964

In bright red letters, the words The Order of the Red Handkerchief stood out on the seven-by-ten-inch paper certificate that was just handed to Tony as he finished his shift on the Mine Train. Inside the ornate green border were the fancy letters R.M.R.R. for Rainbow Mountain Railroad on one side, and N.W.R.R. for Nature's Wonderland Railroad on the other side of a brightly colored oval rendering of the yellow Mine Train emerging from a cave and going over the trestle. Two smaller engines, one colored green and the other yellow, framed Tony's name and mentioned he "is a stockholder in good standing" in the Order of the men who worked on the Mine Train and wore the trademark red handkerchief. At the bottom of the "100 Shares" certificate, was a bright blue drawing of the Sleeping Beauty Castle and the dates of the Rainbow Caverns Mine Train of 1956 to 1959 and the Mine Train thru Nature's Wonderland established 1960.

At Tony's pleased grin, he was told, "Congratulations, you were approved. Our next meeting is at the Hilton's ballroom. I was told Walt will be there, too. Bring your I.D. card. You're buying the first round!"

The Island – 1817

Wals stared at the oval piece of plastic in his shaking hands. He slowly stood from where he was crouched next to the injured wolf. Those disconcerting blue eyes were still intently watching his every move. Wals' breathing suddenly became labored as if the walls of the cabin were closing in on him. Closing his fist, the pin puncturing the palm of his hand, he hurried out of the open door, gulping in the fresh air as he tried to calm his erratically-beating heart.

His mind still not quite able to believe what he was thinking, he slowly turned to face the small log cabin and backed up one step at a time until he could really look at it. Small rectangular in shape. One door in the middle. A small, square window on each side of the door. The chimney on the right side of the building. The split-rail fence was four rails high, zigging and zagging unevenly around the little garden plot. The tree that was recently struck by lightning was off to the right side of the yard, a large eagle's nest newly constructed at the very top of the empty boughs. The brown mare, Sukawaka, was standing placidly in her favorite place by the fence facing the River. A few barrels were scattered around the clearing. The now-empty clothesline strung between two leaning posts.

Spinning around and stumbling all the way down to the River's edge, Wals looked to the right.

There, farther away than he thought it should be, was Keel Boat Rapids, lined with smoothed, round boulders, the River's current causing white water to churn and foam around the huge rocks. Raising his eyes from the Rapids, he tried to see the Pinewood Village, but it was too far away, a faint rising tendril of smoke the only indicator it was there at all. Where were the little native girl and her shaggy dog standing on the log? He could barely see the empty log protruding out over the River. *I should be able to see them*, he told himself. *Why is the River so wide?*

His mind now raced to Fort Wilderness. *It's in the wrong place*, his head claimed. Out of everything here, it alone was in the wrong location. It should be on this side of the caves, not on the other side, closer to the raft landing. What had the solider told him? "Where else should it be? It's protecting the island, dummy." He then pictured the interior of the Fort. *Why is it so familiar? Because you have lived there for over a year. No, it was familiar before that*, his mind warred with itself.

The familiar sound of a steam whistle came to his ears and interrupted the mental sparring he was going through. As he watched the Mark Twain move slowly downstream, he noted there were no passengers on this trip. Crates and barrels were stacked haphazardly over the white deck. The pilot saw Wals and gave a friendly tilt of his black hat from the wheelhouse four decks above the water level. *There should be passengers—no, guests— onboard,* he thought. *Where are the guests?* He watched a long time before the ship made a slow, sweeping turn to the right and headed towards what was left of Rainbow Ridge. *It will take hours for the ship to make the run. No, that's not right. It should only take...it should only take 12 minutes....* A canoe followed in the choppy wake of the ship, slowly paddled by some members of the village and friends of Mato. They raised a hand in greeting to Wals as they went by and angled over toward the direction of their village way downstream.

Wals sat heavily on the ground, his mind reeling. The nametag was still clutched in his fist, his engraved name now leaving grooves in his palm. He opened his hand and stared at the white piece of plastic. *Is this place what I think it is? It all looks so familiar, but it just isn't right. This isn't a place to play; these people are really living and working here. What happened to me?*

Rose came out of the cabin and sat down next to Wals. "Well, Wolf fell asleep. I think his leg will be all right if it doesn't fester...." She broke off, noticing the confused look on Wals' face. When he didn't answer her, she became concerned. "Wals, are you all right?" she asked.

He just stared at her as if he had never seen her before.

Rose was alarmed now. "Wals? What's wrong?"

He reached out a tentative hand and ran in slowly over her sculpted cheek. Surprised and yet pleased by his touch, Rose just silently sat there, hoping he would explain himself and ease her anxiety. "You shouldn't be here," he managed to whisper after confirming to himself that she actually was a real, living, breathing person.

When his hand dropped back to his side, Rose let out an exasperated sigh and looked down at her worn slippers. "You, too, Wals?" She was deflated.

Out of all the people she had met here, she had thought Wals would be different, that he would understand her strength and ability to cope by herself. "Everybody tells me that. I think I've proven I can live by myself pretty well," she insisted, defending herself.

Wals rubbed the spot between his eyes that was starting to throb. "No, that's not what I meant."

"Then what do you mean?" eyes narrowed, she asked, trying to fight down the irritation his remark had caused.

He looked down at the nametag again before speaking. After staring at it for a full minute, he finally held it out for her to see. "Does this mean anything to you?"

She took the oval badge from him and gazed at it for a long time. She ran her fingertips lightly over the imprinted letters. "That's your name," she said with a smile, looking up at him. "It's beautiful! That castle…." She stopped talking as a frown crossed her beautiful face. "I remember that castle…but I'm not sure where…or why…." She stopped talking, her mind now whirling. *Why would a castle look familiar to me? There's no castle around here. I can't remember my husband's face or our wedding or anything about our life together, but I can remember a castle? There were blue and gold banners flying in the breeze over the drawbridge….*

Wals interrupted her thoughts. "How long have you been here?" he quietly asked, hoping she could shed some light on this dilemma, that, by the look on her face, she was feeling as well.

Rose handed him back the badge. "Oh, gosh," she said, looking up at the darkening sky. "I don't know. Seems like forever."

That's exactly how he felt. "Where did you come from before you lived here?"

"Back east," Rose replied automatically. She stopped again and thought back. She spoke slowly now as if trying out the words, "That's what I have always said when anyone asked me—back east. But, I'm not sure where exactly." She was getting confused again.

Wals' fingers ran around and around the nametag. It seemed to be his touchstone right now. He somehow knew that if he let go of it everything would vanish from his mind again. "But you don't remember exactly, do you?" At the slow, negative shake of her head, he asked, "What is your earliest memory?"

Rose watched his fingers move systematically around the white oval. "Of here or before?" At his shrug, she continued. "Well, I remember swimming," she stated with a fond smile. "I loved the water when I was little." She looked out over the River, and her face clouded over and the smile faded. "It wasn't like this huge River, though. It was smaller. That's probably why I used to like to go to Cascade Peak. I could go behind the waterfalls of Cascade Peak when I knew the mine trains weren't coming and swim or bathe there. Then, after the waterfalls dried up, I had to go to the beaver dam."

Wals heart started pounding again. "What did you say happened to the waterfalls at Cascade Peak?" he managed to ask even though his mouth had gone dry.

She slowly shook her head as she thought back. "I've never seen the like before," Rose murmured in an awed whisper. It had scared her at the time. It had scared everyone. "They just dried up one night. The River dried up too, just about the same time. Had all of us worried sick. I mean, what were we going to do? The River is our life force. Thankfully, the rains in the mountains must have come again because the River filled back up. But, for some reason, those waterfalls at the Peak never flowed again. Then the Peak itself just started eroding over time. It's a pity, too. It was such a beautiful waterfall. It's mostly gone now. That was probably about the same time business at Rainbow Ridge started to decline."

Heart still pounding, Wals thought back. "You ever hear of Catfish Cove?"

"Oh, yes! It was way on the other side of the Island, though. I heard it was the best fishing spot on the Island."

"What happened to it?"

Rose shrugged. "I don't know. Guess the bears from the wilderness—you know where I mean? Bear Country? They must have cleaned it out before they were all chased away. We used to have more elk around here too. Now, just a few moose and deer are left. And the beavers, of course. I hope the hunters don't get them as well." She broke off, her eyes distracted and sad. "I suppose you were here when the earthquake hit, or at least heard about it?"

"Which earthquake? There's always earthquakes in…in…," he stopped. *Was California even settled yet? Of course it….* He looked back at the nametag in his palm, the images in his head swirling around and threatening to vanish again. "Tell me about the earthquake," he rasped out.

Playing with the hem of her white apron as she

thought back, a frown created a line in her forehead. "Well," she finally started, "at least I *think* it was an earthquake. What else could have caused that much destruction?"

"Destruction of what?"

"Why, the whole Painted Desert! Now, I was never able to go there personally and see it, of course, but I heard plenty of talk about it at the Fort. It was too far away for me to visit and I couldn't afford the stagecoach fare before that stopped coming, too. I suppose I could have paid to go with the burro supply train once, but I never did."

He stared at her with an open mouth. "Old Unfaithful Geyser and the bubbling pots of mud? Rainbow Caverns?" he could barely speak the words. *How did she know about them?*

The blond head nodded as she silently wondered about the expression of astonishment on his face. Everyone knew about the Painted Desert. It was…it was just there. And then it wasn't. "So, you did hear about it."

His head moved up and down and then side to side. "Tell me what you heard."

"They said it was like the ground opened up and just swallowed the whole area! Nothing was left but a couple of the taller arches. You would think something that tall would have gone first in an earthquake, but, no, they somehow survived. It was everything else that was just gone. It had to have been an earthquake, wouldn't it?" She was hoping Wals could shed some light on the then-terrifying occurrence.

"The Mine Train," Wals whispered, he thought to himself.

"You probably saw the wrecked engine across

the River on the other side of the Island." Rose nodded as she let out a sad sigh, drawing her knees up to hug them with her arms. "So much has changed over the years. I thought this little Island was so far from civilization that it would never change! I was kinda hoping to see Mr. Crockett again some time. He seemed awfully nice."

"You saw Davy Crockett? Where? In the Fort? When was that?"

She slowly nodded, thinking back. "Yes, I guess it must have been a short time before you came. I'm not sure. He and Mr. Russel were usually seen deep in discussion with the Major General in his office. But, they left one day and never came back. It was too bad, too. Mr. Crockett was the nicest man. So kind to me," she smiled warmly at the memory. "I guess their assignment took them elsewhere across the River."

Wals didn't mention he had seen her that same day when the two scouts escorted her safely out of the Fort. He didn't want to detract from his line of thought. "What else has changed? Anything?"

"I don't know if you heard, but that nasty Private Crain tried to waylay me again yesterday. I swear I don't know why he hates me so." She tried not to start shivering as she remembered her experience. "But I ducked into the caves. I know my way around them pretty well. But, something was wrong. I came to a dead-end where there was supposed to be a short-cut to the other side of the Island. It was all filled in. Wolf had taken me through those caves many times. Actually, now that I think about it, he was teaching me how to get through them without getting lost in the maze, so I know that part of the cave should have been open. Luckily I knew another route. Private Crain didn't," she added with a smug smile. "I don't know what happened to him. I hope he fell down the Bottomless Pit!"

Wals sat real still. *So that was what Daniel was grousing about. It was Rose he had gone after! I'm going to kill him!* "Don't worry overmuch about him. He hates everyone. Are you the one that hit him in the forehead?" he asked, hoping his voice wasn't shaking with the anger he was feeling.

Rose gave a nervous laugh. He could tell she was still upset by the encounter. "No, but I wish I had. He probably hadn't been in the caves before and didn't know about that low rock right in the entrance."

The caves that were built with shorter children in mind, Wals reminded himself. "What else is different?"

"You came. That was nice," she added shyly, looking out across the River and not meeting his eyes. On a huge flat rock, Mato sat watching on his pinto again. He raised an arm in greeting to them. "I do miss seeing your Keel Boats. They were such funny shaped little boats. What happened to them?"

"One of them actually keeled over and dumped the guests...I mean, passengers," he hastily corrected, "into the water. Somebody got hurt. The...the owners sold one of the boats."

"That's too bad," Rose sighed. "I heard the other one was being lived in, like a house, if you can believe it! The soldiers said it was pretty beat up and looked like it was slowly sinking."

"Yeah, I heard that, too," Wals answered, drifting off. This was too much for him. He needed to think it out alone. He had to ask her one more time, "So, you really can't remember where you lived before you came here?"

She thought back again and started to look perplexed. "No, I really can't. Isn't that odd? All I can remember is a lovely pool of water and a beautiful castle like the one on your brooch."

"My what?" He had no idea what she meant.

Rose pointed at his hand. "Your white and blue brooch. Well, that is what I call it. What do you call it?"

"My nametag." *I wear it when I work the canoes at Disneyland so guests will know my first name. I pin it to this mustard-yellow fringed shirt. There's even a reinforced patch of fabric in the exact spot where it goes.* He was starting hyperventilate so he abruptly stood up before Rose could see how bewildered he was. Concerned for him, Rose started to rise also, but Wals told her to just stay outside and enjoy the lovely evening. He said he needed to check on the wolf to see how he was doing.

Wals entered the darkened cabin and went to where he knew Rose kept her small stock of candles. Lighting one of the soft yellow beeswax candles in the ever-present burning fire, he took the wavering flame over to where the wolf was stretched out on the floor.

Squatting down, Wals held the light out to shine over the sleeping animal. His attention was focused on that odd white patch of fur on the wolf's broad black chest. The wolf's blue eyes suddenly opened. Unable to get into a sitting position, Wolf fell back in pain. Panting slightly, he stared back at Wals.

Wals reached out a hand and touched the wolf's outstretched front paw. The claws bent back at his touch and relaxed again. Wals shook his head as if he didn't believe what he was about to do. "Well, Rose talks to you all the time. I guess you are a good listener, huh, Wolf?" He gave a nervous laugh. "They say everyone has a twin. If a twin can be another species, I think I know your twin." He broke off when he thought he heard the wolf groan in disgust. "You hurting, boy? I'm sorry, but I don't know anything that will help. I thought Mato might come back to check on you." Again the wolf seemed irritated. "I am totally confused, Wolf. I don't know how to explain it except that I seem to be somehow in the wrong place, or the wrong time, or both." Wals got up from in front of the wolf and paced back and forth in the tiny room. "I am in the right place, sort of, but none of this should be real." He swung his arms around to indicate everything around him. "The only things that are *wrong*, that shouldn't be here, are you and Rose and me. Everything else belongs on the Island, but not as living….breathing….people!" Exasperated, he dropped into Rose's rocker and stared into the fire. "And I am talking to a wolf!"

Rose came back in and heard Wals' last statement. "Oh, I do that all the time! Wolf is a great listener." First giving a quick glance at Wolf to make sure he seemed all right, she then went over to the rocker. "Are you all right, Wals? You seemed so:…so…I don't know…confused?" She put a worried hand lightly on his arm.

His hand covered hers. He could feel the warmth of her skin. He could smell the soft scent of lilacs coming from her clothes. Looking up into her clear blue eyes, he gave a small tug on her hand and brought her around to sit in his lap. Her breathing became shallow as his mouth neared hers. His cool lips closed over her warm mouth. She was real. She was just as real as he was. He could feel her heart that was now pounding against his chest. It was she who broke the contact with his pleasant lips and snuggled her head against his shoulder. His arms came protectively around her in a caressing hug as they sat quietly in the firelight.

"Oh, Wals, you seem so lost," she sighed and then added in a whisper, "Just like I am."

As good as it felt to relax with a beautiful woman in his arms, Wals couldn't stop his mind from spinning around and around his situation. He stroked her back while he stared into the flickering flames. In the safety of his arms, with the warmth of the fire and his comforting hands on her back, Rose fell into a peaceful sleep—the first she had had in many a night.

Listening to her steady breathing, Wals rested his chin on the top of her head while he mentally tried to work it all out. Every change she had mentioned, every instance, he knew had happened to his Island in his…his time? *Was that it?* Frowning, he looked away from the fire into the darkness of the room. Was he out of step with time? How could that have happened? Was it even possible? And, if it was possible, when did it happen to him?

He tried thinking back, but the memories were confused. The reality of his former life was too entwined with this current life. They were so similar that they were difficult to separate. Was it the same for Rose? How could she not have any memory before coming to this Island? He, at least, knew there were two islands. Or was it the same island at a different time? He thought he knew everything about this Island. He knew when it was built and opened in May of 1956. But he was now living way before 1956. If he knew his history, Davy Crockett lived around the time of early 1800-and-something. Wasn't he involved in the war of 1812? That was about the time period in which Fort Wilderness had been set. He knew all the changes that had been made to the Island and the surrounding Frontier-land area over the years.

And each and every change had been mentioned by Rose. She had either seen them or heard about them at the Fort.

Is that the conundrum? That there is an alternate reality for the Island? That everything that happened in Rose's time ended up happening to the Island he knew?   Like history repeating itself?

Wals had another disturbing thought and gave a startled gasp. Rose's descriptions were of things that had happened in recent history, not decades ago. So, if that was accurate, to make it even worse, what if the converse was true? What if everything that happened to Tom Sawyer's Island in his time affected this Island and its inhabitants in this time period? Perhaps it wasn't that everything in the present affects the future. *Perhaps it was that everything that happens in the present affects the past!*

If that is true, what is going to happen next in this reality? What will be the next big change to the Island that was all the latest talk at the Park? How could it affect the people living here on this Island?

The fuzziness that had settled over him since he arrived fought against the reasoning and the reality he had to remember. He had to pace. He couldn't just sit still. This was way too disturbing. Wals tried to sit up, but the weight of the forgotten Rose in his lap held him back. She stirred at his sudden movement, but settled back into sleep when he murmured soft nothings into her ear. Unconsciously, as if he did it every day, he gave Rose a light kiss on her forehead as she drifted off again. Trying not to jostle her too much, he easily stood with her in his arms. After settling Rose comfortably back in the rocking chair, he pulled her beaded black shawl off of a peg driven into the log wall to tuck it around her shoulders.

Wals fingered the oval nametag he had stashed in his pants pocket. He had to keep touching it, to feel its comforting reality. *The Zippo lighter.* His head suddenly shot up. He had forgotten all about that. Where was the lighter that had been in the same pouch as his nametag? It didn't belong here in this time period either.

Looking frantically around, Wals ultimately found himself turning complete circles and accomplishing nothing. *Think, man. Where were you? With the wolf.* He went to the pallet on the floor and, ignoring the blue eyes that were still intently watching him, felt around on the rough wooden planks that made up the floor. *It had to be here.*

Behind the leg of the crude table, his fingers closed over cool metallic smoothness. Grabbing it, turning it back and forth to catch the firelight, he reread the words of praise for Dr. Houser engraved on the face. *I'm such an idiot!* he told himself. *The numbers are a year. It is 1962. But, my time is 2007. How could Dr. Houser's lighter dated 1962 be here? That's a forty-five year difference. He's not that old.* Wals' reckoning abruptly stopped as the reality of what he was saying seeped into his consciousness. *If what I am thinking is true, then Dr. Houser doesn't belong here either. When did he get here? He was here when I arrived. How did he get here? How did I….*

With his mind starting to go in unanswerable circles, Wals realized he needed to concentrate on only one perplexing problem at a time. Maybe if he thought about how he got here the rest would fall into place. *What is my last memory of my real time? I was in a canoe. I was paddling down the River. I was making a supply run to Rainbow Ridge…. No, that's not right. That was what I did* after *I got here. Think back, Wals. Think!*

Wals closed his eyes and pictured the scene. He was in a canoe. He was paddling down the Frontierland River. It was night. He was alone on his supply run… No, there was no supply run. And, he wasn't alone that night. His friend was with him. It was Mato…. No, it wasn't Mato. But, he was dark like Mato, though. They had been friends for years. Mani. That was his name. Sumanitu Taka was how he had pronounced his full name. Mani for short. Or…Wals whispered into the night, "Not Mani. Wolf. It was Wolf. I was with Wolf in the canoe that night. There was a sudden, freaky storm that night and we paddled right into it."

He kept his remembrance going, talking out loud to himself as he passed to and fro in the small room. "The sky lit up with lightning and there was a black whirlpool in the water. Wolf had to have fallen out of the canoe. I looked back. He was gone. The canoe tipped over and we were caught in the whirlpool." He unconsciously rubbed the back of his head where the canoe had smashed into him. "I never saw Wolf again," he stopped and frowned. "I never even thought about Wolf again until now. But I remember…I remember there was something else in the water with me…." Eyes narrowed, he took up the remaining stub of the candle and walked over to the pallet on the floor. Wolf was still reclining on his rug, his bandaged leg stretched out behind him, his ears pointed directly at Wals, eagerly listening to every word. The deep blue eyes regarded Wals steadily. "It was a wolf. I saw the face. It was your face! The black fur on the ears and the mask of gray around the face." He stooped down and shone the wavering light in Wolf's face, studying the sharp features and the hopeful eyes. "It was you, wasn't it? You were pulled into that inferno with me, weren't you, boy? But what in the world was Rose's wolf doing in the River at Disneyland? Did you get lost too, like I did? Dang! It must have been terrifying for you."

Wals got up and went back to the fire to lean against the river-stone that made up the fireplace. "I need to go to the Fort to talk to Dr. Houser," he decided as he pocketed the Zippo. Falling silent, deep in thought with his mind whirling through the scenes of both of his lives, he didn't see Wolf slowly shake his head side to side in disbelief at what he had just heard nor did he hear the wolf mumble to himself, "Unbelievable!"

CHAPTER TEN

The Island – 1817

It was too late at night for Wals to go back to Fort Wilderness to speak to Dr. Houser. He also now had some unfinished business with Private Daniel Crain—regarding both Rose and the wolf. He didn't anticipate the meeting with Crain would go very well. Most of the soldiers were decent, hard-working men. The private did not fall into that category. Daniel Crain was a loud-mouthed bully, a coward. But, Wals reminded himself, Crain had a lot of friends—friends Crain knew would protect his back if push came to shove. Wals knew he would have to go to the Fort prepared for anything.

Turning his head from the fireplace, he looked over at Rose. A small, desire-filled smile filtered across his face. Noticing the awkward position in which he had left her, Wals realized she would have a stiff neck if she slept in the rocker all night. He carefully lifted the sleeping beauty to carry her into her tiny bedroom. She made a small sleepy sound and put her arms around his neck. He breathed in the lilac scent in her hair as she settled into his arms. Eyes closed, he stood still in front of the flickering fire, enjoying the warmth of her body nestled into his. Knowing he couldn't stand there all night holding her, he slowly walked to the bedroom and gently laid her on the bed. With the silver moonlight streaming in through the curtainless window, she looked so beautiful, her wavy golden hair spread out to frame her face. He touched one of the glimmering curls, feeling the silkiness roll between his fingers. He then saw her lips part in a breathless sigh. Going against every primal urge flowing through him to bend down and kiss those lips, Wals gave a resigned moan and, instead, tucked a worn quilt around her shoulders. Making a contented noise, she snuggled deeper into the quilt and turned onto her side, one arm outstretched as if reaching for him. With a deep groan, he quickly spun around and left the room.

Wals returned to the fireplace and stretched out on the wood floor in front of the dying fire, the memory of her face playing through his mind over and over. *Even this hard floor is better than sleeping alone in my canoe*, he smiled to himself, hands clasped behind his head. His smile slowly faded as he realized what he had just thought. He had to stop thinking of this time period as Home. The disorientation was threatening to overtake him again. It had to be the Island working against him, working against his memories. *Think of your apartment in Huntington Beach. Think of your 300ZX. Think of your friends Trey and Chloe and Wolf. They are your reality.* He touched the nametag he had decided to pin on his shirt to help keep his mind focused.... *No, his costume*, he reminded himself. *This is just a costume. Your clothes, your* real *clothes, are waiting for you in your locker at Disneyland. You need to get back to them.... And you need to take Rose and the Doctor with you when you go, just like....just like...*as he struggled to think...*who was it who had told him that?*

Wals propped himself up on an elbow, frowning at the glowing embers of the fire. A spark jumped out of the remnants of the fire and landed on the rough plank floor. Absentmindedly, he reached over to pat it out. Watching his finger go round and round the small burn spot, he knew he wouldn't sleep that night. His memories were getting all confused again.

Wolf, hoping his friend was drawing close to putting it all together, pushed through the pain and hobbled over to where Wals was sitting to lie down next to him. Wals could see the animal was favoring his bandaged, injured leg and a small whine of pain escaped his lips when it hit the hard floor. He placed a comforting hand on the wolf's wide, silver-tipped back.

"Sorry you got shot, Wolf. Don't know what you were doing outside the Fort though, but you should have run instead of just standing there. Seemed like you were staring up at me. Were you looking for me? Did Rose send you to find me?" Wals gave a little self-conscious laugh. "I keep expecting you to answer me. Silly, huh?" He rubbed the wolf roughly on the head between his ears and received a low, warning growl. Quickly jerking his hand back, he apologized. "Umm, sorry, boy. My Dalmatian used to love that." He heard a disgusted snort from the wolf. "Darn, but it seems like you can understand everything I say. Probably Rose thinks the same thing, too." He gave a deep sigh and shook his head slowly side to side, again placing his hand on the warm fur. "I'm just trying to work all this weirdness out. Wish you could talk back. You might know something that could help," he chuckled at his little joke.

Wolf turned his massive head to look at directly at Wals, his eyes half closed. If the wolf could have spoken, Wals was absolutely sure he would have heard the word, "Duh."

Rose was only able to fix a light breakfast for the three of them as her supplies were running low again. Wals promised to stop in at the Supply Store inside the Fort for her while he was there.

The wolf hobbled outside with him when Wals was getting ready to leave. Thinking Wolf was going to try to come with him, he crouched down in front of the animal. Palms out towards Wolf, Wals talked really slow, "Wolf, I want you to stay here. Stay, Wolf. Stay with Rose. Okay, boy? Stay!"

He didn't know what to think when Wolf tilted his head to the side and let out an exasperated breath of air like 'humph'. Wolf lifted his face to the sky like a petition, shook his head once, and, turning his back on Wals, limped back into the cabin. Using his nose, he managed to slam the door shut.

Wals stared after him, dumbfounded. "How the heck did I just insult a wolf!?"

Thinking he might need a faster get-away from

Fort Wilderness if things with Crain got out of hand, Wals, with Rose's practiced help, put a bridle and reins on the mare who had been watching from the edge of her little rail corral. *She is always waiting there*, Wals thought. *Now and then. Amazing,* he smiled.

The ride along the riverbank in the early morning mist was quiet and peaceful. Way across the wide River, Wals could barely see the little native girl who was checking her fishing line from on top the log that had fallen out over the water. Having better eyesight and hearing than his mistress, her shaggy white dog looked over when he heard Sukawaka and gave a friendly bark. Wals gave a wave back when the little girl looked up. Now recognizing the familiarity of that scene, he reached for his nametag. This got Wals thinking again about the two Islands and the differences he was now noticing. Like this ride to the Fort, for instance. In his time, well, there was no path all the way to the Settler's Cabin. It was located in No Man's Land, fenced off so the guests wouldn't wander around the backside of the Island. The actual dusty path was only a few hundred feet long, winding along the River as he was now doing and ended at the old Fort. But he knew that here Rose's cabin was close to a mile away from the Fort. And then there was the River itself. From being overturned in his canoe more times than he would like to admit—both in this time period and the other one—Wals knew the River here was fifteen to twenty feet deep. More than deep enough for the paddlewheeler Mark Twain to have safe passage. There was no guiding rail under the green water here. The pilot actually had to safely steer the large white ship, avoiding sand bars, rocks and submerged trees.

Knowledge like that made his current situation all the more confusing. Everything here was so much *bigger*. Bigger and very, very real. Was he really in the same physical location? Or did the vortex take him to an alternate reality in a different location? He now wished he had paid more attention to the science fiction shows he used to watch on television.

The mare's ears perked forward and she turned her head and whinnied as they passed the entrance to Injun Joe's Cave. Looking at the dark opening, Wals remembered he hadn't been in the caverns since he was a kid. He used to have so much fun running over the Island, whooping and hollering with the other kids, playing hide and seek, and trying to ditch his parents. Lost in his memory and not knowing enough about horses, he didn't take the warning message from the mare. He simply tugged her head back to the path and nudged her with the heels of his moccasins.

As he kept riding towards the stockade gate, his mind drifted back to Rose and the beautiful picture she had made while she was sleeping last night. How could he have not seen her beauty when he had first spotted her in the Fort? He was literally dumped right at her doorstep during the canoe race, yet he passed up a golden opportunity to keep the budding relationship going. Why hadn't he kissed her then? Why had he wasted so much time with the Fort women and never gone back to see her? Well, he was going to make sure he did things right this time....

Wals musings stopped when the mare stopped her rambling walk. Before he could wonder why

Sukawaka had come to a halt on the dusty path, he instantly knew something was wrong. The stockade gate was closed. He glanced at his wrist to see what time it was. *No watch, moron*, he told himself, shaking his head, *it probably fell off in the whirlpool.* He checked the sun. It was late enough in the morning that there should have been soldiers on duty and river people coming and going from the docks.

"Hallo the Fort!" he called, looking up at the watchtowers. No familiar face peered down at him. No rifles pointed out of the small slits or the larger windows. There was no answering call within the Fort. Sukawaka shifted uneasily beneath him, ears flat, eager to be moving. Reining her in, he tried again, louder this time. "Hallo the Fort!"

Again there was no answer. The logs of the structure were too close together for Wals to be able to see between them. Trying to think of the other ways in, he knew the Escape Tunnel he had used as a boy had been filled in and closed years ago. The only other entrance was a man door on the back side of the Island. But, it would take him a couple of hours to work his way around back there.

The Mark Twain let out a shrill blast of its whistle as it approached the entry of the Fort, as per custom. There were a few passengers seated on chairs that were painted white to match the pristine ship. The ladies, shaded under parasols and fanning themselves with colorful embroidered silk, properly ignored the River worker while the friendlier of the gentlemen lifted their tall beaver hats to him as they slowly sailed by. Riding to the water's edge, Wals yelled up to the pilot if he knew what happened to the Fort, but couldn't be heard over the great distance or over the noise of the engine and the huge paddlewheel churning in the back. The pilot, thinking Wals was just saying hello, gave a friendly wave and returned his attention to the River.

Riding back up the small hill to the Fort's entrance, Wals mentally added up his height and how tall he thought the mare was. He was wondering if he would be able to reach the top of one of the shorter pointed logs that made up the Fort's gate and then pull himself over. While the logs that made up the outer walls of the Fort were sixteen-feet tall, the logs of the gate were only about twelve-feet tall. Sidling the mare next to the gate, Wals picked out the shortest of the logs. Hoping the mare would stand quietly—she did it often enough in her little corral—he slowly brought his feet up on the back of the horse in an attempt to stand. Not getting any kind of reaction from the mare, he even more slowly came to a standing position, arms out for balance. Making a leap for the top of the gate, he hoped he didn't impale his hand on one of the sharp points. Hitting his mark, and slamming hard into the upright wood, he held still for a moment to catch his breath. Then, using his feet and the strength in his arms, he pulled himself up so he could peer over the gate and into the parade grounds.

All the while, the mare, seeing some lush River grass, calmly walked away and began nibbling at the tender green shoots.

Wals didn't notice that the mare had left him hanging. He was too busy staring open-mouthed into the empty, deserted Fort. The only movements he could see were some leaves blowing across the dirt. Pulling himself higher and carefully bending between the two sharp points, he leaned over far enough to see that the stockade gate had been nailed shut with two huge crossbeams. Most of the doors to the different buildings within the compound, however, were hanging open, some with damaged hinges. There was some broken furniture half in and half out of the barracks. The bucket that had been used inside the stone well had been smashed to pieces, its rope cut in two. Some of the wooden stairs leading up to the four guard towers were missing.

Wals stared at the desolation, not comprehending how it could have happened so quickly. He had just been there. *It was just yesterday! It was yesterday, wasn't it?* Wals frowned as he hung there. He was again beginning to have a difficult time thinking back, trying to figure out the actual passage of time. He remembered back to his breakfast the day before and the women who brought it up to him. The wolf had shown himself just outside this gate and then had gotten shot by Daniel Crain…. It seemed so recent, but this…this wreckage laid out in front of him. *How could this happen overnight?* Where were the soldiers? Where was Doctor Houser? Looking over, he could see that the Infirmary had obviously been ransacked. Where were the women? What happened to Yvette? Looking over to the left, he saw that the cantina's door was completely missing. The rubble he could see thrown about inside had to have been made from the tables and chairs where he used to sit.

Head slowly shaking in disbelief, he looked

around the parade grounds again. His eyes came to rest on the flagpole. The fifteen-star flag had been taken down. The rope and pulleys that had been used by the soldiers were still there. Only now there was some kind of black flag hanging limp in the air that had gone still. He couldn't make out what kind of flag it was or what those white markings were that showed in its folds.

Dismayed and confused, Wals knew there would be no more answers here. There was no Supply Store to get Rose her needed foodstuffs. There was no Doctor Houser to show the Zippo lighter to see what light he could shed on matters. There was no reason to linger any longer. Ready to drop, he looked down towards his feet. He now saw that Sukawaka was no longer below him. Instead, the mare was still calmly nibbling on the juicy grasses several yards away. "Great. Now you move," he groused out loud. She ignored his attempts to call her. When he whistled for her, she swished her tail and moved even farther towards the River away from him.

Stifling a curse, he knew he had to either let go or wait for someone to come by and help him get down. Not knowing who was left on the Island, the last option of waiting for someone might either take a long while or might not be particularly advantageous. He knew the Mark Twain would now be gone for hours. He hadn't seen a canoe all day. The Island rafts were too far away.

He was left with the 'let go' option. "This is going to hurt," he mumbled, letting himself down as far as his arms could reach. When he was hanging on by just his fingertips, he took a deep breath and dropped. Remembering to tuck his legs and roll, he hit the hard, well-packed dirt and rolled down the small incline. He came to rest face down in the dust. "Oww," he groaned, catching his breath. Feeling hot breath on the back of his neck, he looked up as the mare nudged him in the shoulder with her nose. "Great. Now you come," he told her, slowly rolling onto his back. Making a grab at the dragging reins, he tried to use them to pull to his feet. But every time he tugged, the mare lowered her head and he wound up in the same position flat on the ground. Pretty soon, her nose was almost touching the ground and Wals was still laying there on his back. "Bad horse," he scolded, being glad, for once, that his friends at the Fort couldn't see him. With a toss of her head, she backed up a few steps, dragging Wals with her. Now within reach of a stump of a tree, he used that to get to his feet.

Finding nothing broken, he pulled himself onto the now-docile Sukawaka's back and headed her towards the wharf. His left ankle started to throb as he rode. With each painful motion of the horse, he began to realize that it should have taken him all of two minutes on horseback to reach the raft docks from the gates of Fort Wilderness. Instead, he rode for almost another mile. This helped him get a grip on the differences between the two places again. He had been daydreaming and was starting to imagine sharing a certain log cabin with a certain beautiful blond.

When he finally reached the docks, Wals found the Mill had been surrounded by a new, restricting wooden fence. It was obviously closed for business. The rafts were across the River, secured to the dock by their rope cables. He could see none of his old friends around. A lone deckhand lounged in the shade of the paddlewheeler's ticket booth, too far away even to holler a question. A few people from New Orleans strolled along the dirt path along the River, but the general air was that of desolation, neglect. *Or*, Wals suddenly thought, *or was it the air of change? Is that what I am seeing?*

"What was coming next?" he said out loud, trying to remember. "Everything had been closed down while they were....darn it, what were they doing? I wish Wolf was here. He paid more attention at those meetings than I did."

As he headed the mare back to Rose's cabin, he again thought about his lost friend, Wolf. *Did Wolf get out of the path of that spooky whirlpool that caught me? Maybe he never got sent here like I did. Surely I would have seen or heard about him by now. Did he see what happened to me or did he think I drowned in the River?* He had a sharp intake of breath. *Or did Wolf himself drown in the River?*

With more questions to ask and no answers to be found, Wals rode silently back along the dusty trail. This time he did notice the mare's ears turning towards the Cave as he rode past. The horse seemed way too interested in the opening of the cave. Reining her to a stop, he began to carefully slide off her back, trying not to land on his sore ankle. The mare, seeing something fascinating to eat, started moving before Wals was safely on the ground. His inexperience with horses caused him to panic and jump away from her, landing firmly on his sore foot. "What is it with you and food?" he yelled at the unconcerned horse, cradling his foot as he leaned against the rock wall. "I liked you better when you were made of plastic!"

Realizing he was yelling at an animal and re-membering why he had stopped in the first place, Wals clamped his mouth shut and hobbled over to the entrance of the unfamiliar cave. He was recall-ing the times he had run all over Tom Sawyer's Is-land when he was young, but his experience in this time period told him this wouldn't be the same cave. And from what Rose told him, it wasn't even the cave she knew either. It had already changed.

As he started his slow entry into the darkness, Wals thought he heard voices or noises of some kind. Thinking, hoping, it was just the wind playing tricks through the rock formations, he was even more cautious as he proceeded forward. Not know-ing the true passageway through the cavern, he nervously told himself to keep to the left at every fork. He hoped by doing that he would be able to find his way back to the entrance easily should he need to make a hasty retreat for any reason.

The noises he thought he had heard seemingly ceased except for the sounds coming from his own movements. Just then, he painfully banged his leg against some object in the dark. Off to the side, he could see a faint light filtering in through a hole in the roof of the cave. From the smoky dust circling eerily through that beam of light, he figured it was either a new hole or someone had been there re-cently. For his own well-being, he chose to dwell on the "new hole" theory. Bending down, he found the object he had run into was actually a chest made out of rough wood. There were two bands of metal, probably steel, bent over the domed top. He decided he would drag the chest over into that tiny pinpoint of light to get a better look. Finding the chest extremely heavy, he put his back to it and managed to push it, grunting and straining, until he finally got it close enough.

Once his eyes became adjusted to the feeble light, Wals saw an old lock hanging from the lid of the chest. Curiosity piquing, he wondered why the chest was there, and he just had to know what was inside. Not having a skeleton key handy, and still not being able to see very well, he felt around for a rock. When his hand found an abundance of loose dirt and rocks, he left the chest to investigate. Crawling over on his hands and knees, he found the beginnings of a rather large hole in the side of the cavern. Feeling upwards, it seemed like this was new, like someone was digging out another cave. Wondering if this new hole being dug was intended to be a hiding spot for the chest he had just found, he found a good fist-sized rock, and went back to the chest with even more interest. Bringing the rock down on the lock with as much force as he could, he was dismayed to hear the metallic *BANG* echoing through the cavern.

Heart pounding now at his thoughtlessness, he eased out of the light, waiting until the echo died, anxious to hear if there was any answering noise. If the sounds he had heard earlier were voices, they might come racing back to investigate. *That probably wouldn't be a good thing*, he decided, breaking out in a cold sweat.

After waiting for a good five minutes, Wals could now relax a little, recognizing he was probably the only person in the caves at that moment. He returned to the chest and the lock. Taking off his shirt, he used his shirt to help muffle the noise he now knew was going to resonate from his efforts to get that old lock open. It took another four direct hits before the lock fell open. Wals quickly pulled his shirt back on in the chill of the still air. With shaking, excited hands, Wals set the lock aside and lifted the lid to the chest.

Clothes. "Clothes?" he said aloud, not believing it. "How could it be so heavy with just clothes? Why would someone want to hide a trunk full of old clothes?"

Careful not to disturb the garments too much, Wals lifted the first layer of fine silk. It was a pink brocade dress from an era Wals didn't recognize. Too many flounces and laces for his taste. Under that was something stiff made of pure white satin. He thought it might be a corset from the lacings up the front and wondered what Rose would look like dressed in that…. When he found himself fingering the material and daydreaming again, he gave a little laugh and snapped out of it. His fingers next found a heavy velvet-covered box. "This is more like it," he whispered, carefully folding the dress and corset back out of the way. He didn't want to pull the box out of its nestled place inside the chest. Finding a metal latch on the front of the box, he flicked it upwards. He heard a gasp and realized it had been him.

Catching every millimeter of light filtering in from that tiny hole in the ceiling, a large gem-encrusted goblet glowed and sparkled as it nestled in its white silk cocoon inside the box. As Wals moved the box this way and that, myriads of sparkles were flung at his dazzled eyes. He saw the gold of the goblet was etched with intricate patterns, weaving around what looked like brilliant purple amethysts and green emeralds and yellow citrines and red rubies set in the metal. The base of the cup proved to be flat, unadorned.

He looked quickly around him. There was no one there to see him. The light coming from the hole above him seemed to be shifting. It must have been getting late. He had to go. Should he take it with him? Whose was it? Did it belong to the owner of the dress? Was it stolen? Was that why it was being buried in a cave?

All these questions bumped against each other in Wals' mind. Without another thought, he gave a resigned, "No," and reluctantly closed the lid of the box. As he was setting it back in place, his finger-tips brushed against another piece of clothing, but under that was something hard and cold. Curiosity overcoming the necessity to leave, he moved aside the clothes—a blue velvet riding jacket, if he had cared to look. Under the jacket was something else bright and cold. His fingers traced the metal and found it was another, plainer goblet made out of sil-ver. Slightly lifting it, he could tell it, too, was very heavy. Emboldened, he felt deeper in the chest. He found loose coins lining the entire bottom of the chest, probably twenty or thirty pieces deep. He pulled out a handful of the coins and quickly stuffed them in his pants pocket next to the forgotten lighter.

Now he knew why this chest was being buried and why it was so heavy. With shaking hands, he carefully rearranged the clothes, smoothing them out as best he could. When he thought it looked just like it did when he first opened the chest, he took up the broken lock. "Oops," he muttered. This he couldn't smooth out. The rock had dented the metal when it sprang open. He worked the lock through the two locking loops and closed it up as best as he could. He decided not to move the chest back to its original place as it would leave even more ruts in the dirt floor of the cavern. Wals just hoped whoever came for it would not notice it had been moved in the first place. He tried to smooth the dirt tracks but thought that made it look even more tampered. *Just get out!* he told himself.

He counted the turns he made as he went back. Four turns to the right on the way to the entrance. Breathing hard, he stumbled out into the waning light and found Sukawaka with her reins tangled in some brush. With a worried glance towards the deserted Fort, he quickly climbed back on the horse and trotted her back to Rose's cabin. With each bounce, he could feel the coins and the lighter rubbing against each other in his pocket.

This had been an interesting day so far, he decided.

"**W**hat am I going to do for food?" Rose looked worried when Wals filled her in on what he had found at the Fort. "I...I can grow my own vegetables, but that's not enough!" Her blues eyes looked beseechingly at Wals. He didn't know what to tell her.

"Maybe it is time you moved back to civilization," he suggested quietly.

Rose blushed and turned away. "I don't fit in there. I can't explain it well, but I'm just not the same as the other women," she whispered, embarrassed. "They don't want me."

"I want you," Wals muttered, not realizing he said it out loud. The words surprised him, enough that he momentarily forgot which 'civilization' he had meant.

"You don't know anything about me," she claimed, fussing with some carrots she was putting into a stew.

"I know you are brave, well, except for your fear of heights, and you are strong. You have a way with animals," he counted off. "That's a lot."

"What's my full name," she asked with a coy smile, one that dimpled her cheek and sent a shiver down his spine.

"Rose Stephens."

"Yes, but what's my middle name?"

Wals stopped short. "I don't think you ever told me. Want me to guess? Bertha Mae? Fanny?"

He was rewarded with a light laugh. "Oh, those are awful. It's Aurora! I used to use it, but the women at the Fort made fun of me, so I went back to Rose."

"Why, that's a beautiful name. It goes with your blond hair."

"Why do you say that, Mr. Walter P. Davis?"

"Oh, you know—Princess Aurora, the Sleeping Beauty?"

"A princess? Oh, I like that! Maybe that is why I remember the castle on your brooch."

"Nametag," he corrected automatically, not really paying attention. "Men don't wear brooches."

Her response was lost on Wals. His mind was besieged by a disturbing thought. Disneyland had Sleeping Beauty's Castle. That was the castle depicted on his nametag. Sleeping Beauty herself was a tall, beautiful blond with high regal cheekbones and lovely blue eyes. When she had been hiding in the forest for her first sixteen years, she was known as Briar Rose. But that had been a woodcutter's cottage and she had three companions—three fairies who lived as mortals with her for those sixteen years.... But, what was she doing in Frontierland with a wolf for a companion if this is an alternate reality? That was Fantasyland stuff. He stole a glance at Rose. Her hair was held back from her face with a black ribbon. The dingy white apron she had on covered the black bodice of her old floor-length lavender dress.

So, who is she? A cast member who portrays Sleeping Beauty in the shows in Disneyland? If that were the case, then why didn't she recognize the nametag? She only recognized the castle. Her only other recollection was that of swimming in a pond.

No, it can't be the other option. The age of castles and princesses was even further back in history than he now was. Anyway, wasn't that just a story? A fairy tale?

Or, could it possibly be that she ended up here like he, and, apparently, Doctor Houser did?

"Wals? Are you all right? You look like you've seen a ghost."

Rose was peering anxiously at him. So was the wolf. She looked confused. The wolf looked hopeful.

"I...I'm fine. Just lost in my thoughts," he stammered. *How do you ask someone if they are from hundreds or thousands of years in the past? Women generally didn't like it if you were off on their age by two or three years....* He figured it would help if he could recall what was going to happen next to the Island.

"Rose, tell me something. You mentioned the tunnels through the cave had changed. Are you sure?"

Rose put a hand on Wolf's head. He was standing next to her, favoring his hind leg; it was obvious his leg was starting to feel better already. "Yes, I am positive. Wolf showed me over and over how to get through the tunnels quickly and safely. I *know* the tunnel I was in used to go all the way through," she asserted.

Wals hadn't told her he had been inside part of the cave. He wanted to know it from her perspective. "Could you take me there? Could we see if anything else has changed?" he wanted to know. *And, hopefully jog my lousy memory.*

"Of course. But, I don't know if Wolf should go or not…. He seems to be doing a little better," she wavered.

Wolf himself ended that discussion by leading the way out of the cabin and heading towards the cave. He still limped a little and wasn't quite as quick as he normally would be, but he gave no doubt that he was going with them.

Wals linked Rose's arm in his as they followed. "I guess that answers our question!" he kidded.

When they arrived at the entrance to the tunnels, Wolf stopped and sniffed the air. The fur on the back of his neck rose. It was obvious to him that the cave was not deserted this time. He just couldn't tell who it was or where exactly they were inside the darkness.

Wolf blocked the entrance with his body. He looked expectantly back at Wals, hitting Wals with his bushy silver-tipped tail.

Giving a confused look at Rose, he knew the wolf apparently expected him to do something, but he had no idea what. "What does he want? I don't understand."

Rose looked over Wals shoulder. "Oh, he wants you to grab hold of his tail. He is going to lead us through the caves. That's what he did with me. Just don't pull," she advised. "He doesn't like that.... And look out for that first low-hanging rock in the entrance." She had a smug, private smile on her face when she remembered the effect that it had had on Daniel Crain.

Wolf led them silently through the twisting corridors. It got darker and darker the farther they got away from the entrance. Wals felt himself becoming angry again when he thought of Rose being pursued through here in the dark by Private Crain—who had conveniently disappeared before Wals could beat the crap out of him.

Unlike his two companions, Wolf had no trouble seeing in the darkness. Superior eye sight and a superior sense of smell along with his keen knowledge of the tunnels helped him lead them directly to the blocked-off wall. Wals felt around on the barricade and could tell where it didn't exactly meet the roof of the tunnel. It felt like rocks, boulders and fresh dirt to him.

Wolf led them down a different path now, moving cautiously. Neither of the humans wanted to speak out loud in the darkness. "A new railing had been put around the Bottomless Pit," Rose did manage to whisper to Wals as they inched past it on the narrow wooden walkway. Wolf abruptly stopped and emitted a low growl. Wals felt in front of him and came into contact with the wooden chest again. It was still where he had left it when he was there last. Apparently no one had come back yet to either retrieve it or to finish burying it. The old broken lock still hung loosely in the front, keeping it closed, if not exactly secure. "This feels like a sea chest," Wals whispered to Rose. He couldn't see Wolf eyeing him closely. Wolf could smell Wals' scent all over the cavern and especially all over that chest. Wolf knew Wals' trail ended here and had doubled back to the entry. What he couldn't figure out is what Wals had been doing in the caves that he had said he knew nothing about and also why he hadn't mentioned it to Rose.

Knowing he would be getting no answers, Wolf grumbled to himself and continued, moving even more slowly through the twists and turns. He stopped at one inlet that had been sealed with a barred door. They paused momentarily as another new hole in the roof was noticed, allowing a pinpoint of light. As their eyes adjusted, Wals thought it looked like a jail cell and felt sorry for anyone who would be locked in there and forgotten. Propped up next to the cell was a sword. He lifted it and was surprised by the sheer weight of it. This was no prop. This was a real steel sword. Even with the insufficient light he could tell that the straight steel blade was tarnished, as was the elaborate grip that felt perfect for his hand.

"Oh crap!" Wals suddenly hissed, smacking himself in the forehead with his free hand. "I remember now. It was pirates! Pirates were coming to the Island! I am such an idiot. How could I have forgotten that?"

Before Rose could question him, Wolf gave a low warning growl and tugged Wals forward. Dropping the sword back in its place, the trio continued their trek through the pitch black cave. Soon, they could see the darkness was easing a bit. They could feel they were approaching the end of the tunnels on the backside of the Island. Wolf's keen ears suddenly picked up the sound of men talking long before the two humans were able to hear it. He pressed against the side of the cavern and cautiously peered out into the daylight. He could feel Wals pressing against him as he, too, tried to look around the corner of the exit.

There they could see a tall three-masted sailing ship tied up to one of the old fishing docks. Wals and Wolf both recognized the ship as the Columbia, the huge ship that had eventually joined the Mark Twain in carrying guests around Tom Sawyer's Island. Now, as in the finale of the show *Fantasmic!*, the Columbia had been taken over by pirates. The crewmen that could be seen had their heads down and were working steadily on the ship. Some men had just gone up the gangplank after depositing a load of goods onto the dirt path near the pontoon bridge. From the looks of all the cargo both on the deck of the ship and already on the ground, it was obvious they were planning on staying for a long time.

In the moments he had stared at the fierce-looking pirates, Wals thought he had seen a blue tunic or two, the kind a Calvary man would be wearing as his uniform. *Had some of the soldiers been pressed into service? What about the doctor? Become pirates or be killed? Was that the choice they were given?* He could easily imagine Daniel Crain adapting to that kind of a lifestyle. And he could also imagine Crain coming after Rose again—this time with his cowardly back now covered by several sword-waving shipmates. His heart suddenly pounding, Wals flung himself back into the darkness of the cave.

Hearing all of the commotion but not knowing what was going on outside, Rose leaned past the stunned Wals to take a peek. "Raiders!" she gasped, before Wals could stop her or pull back out of sight.

The feminine voice carried in the still air and was heard by the men working closest to the cave. Glancing over in the direction of the sound, her blond hair shone like a beacon before she was pulled back away from the opening. One of the pirates dropped the crate he was carrying to take up his sword. "Captain Lafitte! We've been seen! It's a woman! I call her!" he yelled up to the man dressed in a tight-fitting, brocaded black jacket that reached the tops of his cuffed black boots.

When more crates and boxes were dropped and swords were drawn, Wals pulled on the wolf's tail. "Come on, Wolf! We've got to get out of here!" he loudly whispered in a panicked voice.

Not waiting to see or hear the response of the Captain, Wolf agreed and immediately turned, melting into the darkness, Wals grabbing onto his tail, and Rose holding onto the back of Wals' shirt.

They tried to make quicker time returning. Wolf felt the throbbing pain from his wounded leg. He knew the wound had reopened because he could feel the warmth of the blood oozing down his fur. When yells and shouts could be heard coming behind them, he ignored the pain and broke into a loping run. Nose down, he concentrated on the twists and turns that would lead them to safety.

The noise from the pirates was getting louder. Wals didn't know how many men took up the chase. He didn't even know if he or the wolf had been seen. The pirates might think they were just chasing a woman. He suddenly heard a loud *bang* that echoed through the corridors. Dirt from the wall in front of him suddenly exploded and flew into their faces. The pirates were getting closer and must have heard them to take a shot in the dark like that.

"Hurry, Wolf!" Wals whispered.

The wolf took a series of turns that Wals didn't remember on the way in. He guessed Wolf must be trying to confuse and lose their trackers. When they reached the newly-dug dungeon, Wals grabbed up the sword as they passed the cell. *You never know*, he told himself, all the time hoping he would never need to try and use it to defend anyone. But, he knew they were otherwise unarmed. Even though the grip molded to his hand, it still felt awkward. As he shifted it to his right hand, he sincerely hoped he would not hurt himself with it.

The sounds of the pursuit were getting less pronounced the farther they fled. Either the pirates were lost or they were starting to give up the chase. Wals thought it might be possible they weren't that familiar with the caves yet. The three friends arrived at the newly-fenced Bottomless Pit. "Wolf, hold up," Wals whispered, tugging on the wolf's tail and getting a low, menacing growl in return. "Sorry, fella, but I have an idea. In my time," he hurriedly explained to Wolf, "the Bottomless Pit was just a name to scare the kids. It might be different now. It might actually *be* a bottomless pit. I don't know. But, the pirates fenced it off for some reason. If we break the fence, and have Rose scream, they might think she fell in." He broke off, suddenly remembering that the wolf wouldn't answer him.

Rose was breathing hard from fear and from

the fast pace they had been keeping. "I think that is a wonderful idea, Wals! I think some of them are still coming. Hurry and break the fence."

Wals pulled off one of the rough boards. To his dismay, it barely made a creaking sound. He quickly broke it over his knee, producing a sharp, snapping break. He nodded to Rose who turned away from them and let out a piercing scream, letting it fade away as she pretended to fall deeper in the pit.

Wals grinned in the darkness. "That was pretty good," he whispered to her. Wolf gave a short yip and started moving towards the entrance again. They could hear running feet coming from deeper in the caves. Grabbing the wolf's tail again, Wals and Rose hurried after the silent black animal.

After they rounded a few more corners, they heard some of the pirates reaching the Pit. They seemed to be arguing with each other on whose fault it was that the woman got away. The one man who had claimed her for his prize was the loudest and angriest. Wals then could hear a familiar voice telling his companions that the blond-headed wench was a tricky one and they needed to go report to the Captain.

The rest of the on-going argument from those pirates became fainter and fainter as the trio reached the welcome entry to the cavern. Wals figured the pirates took Daniel Crain's suggestion and returned to the Columbia, but he inwardly felt their reprieve would be a short one.

Glad to be out of the darkness and now in the sunlight, they hurried down the path to Rose's cabin. Not having a scabbard and being in a hurry, Wals came close to badly cutting himself in his clumsy attempt to carry the sword next to him. He finally figured a way to work his fingers safely inside the curved, elaborate grip. It settled comfortably inside his palm—as if it had been made just for him.

Once they had reached the cabin and the door was barred for the moment, Wals took a moment to examine the weapon he had taken from the cave. Though not entirely clear to see in the semi-darkness of the log cabin, there was some elaborate etching towards the top of the tarnished blade near the cross-guard. As he gave the curlicues a cursory look, he almost dropped the sword. He saw the initials W. P. D. engraved within an elaborate circle of leaves. With a catch in his breath and a pounding heart, he examined the rest of the metalwork. The cross-guard itself had an intricate maze of scrollwork that curved around the hand while protecting it. The hilt felt like twining cords of metal, twisting all the way from the cross-guard to the engraved pommel with indentations that fit his hand exactly. Not knowing anything about weaponry, he couldn't begin to guess at the age of this sword. He just knew that it would have to be old—very old. *Are those really my initials or just some other odd, confusing coincidence?* he thought to himself. That, combined with the gold coins and the gem-encrusted goblet he had seen in the sea chest, he wondered just what it was that they had just stumbled across. He was silent for a long time as he stared at the length of tarnished metal.

"No more argument, Rose, we need to get you out of here and we need to do it now. The island is no longer safe for a woman living alone," Wals stressed. To add to his reasoning, he added, "Plus, they've seen you. We both know that was Private Crain we heard at the Bottomless Pit. He knows where your cabin is and I doubt he really believed you fell to your death."

Rose looked around her little home. She was blinking back tears. "I don't know where to go," she whispered. "Can we go back to my castle? I...I miss my mother," she asked, turning a beseeching face to Wals.

"Your mother? Are you remembering something else?" Two pairs of eyes were now staring at her. Wolf, who had been standing guard at the door, turned his head to listen.

She stopped throwing clothes and worthless dishes into a worn-out carpetbag. "Well, while we were running, I started remembering the sight of my mother standing on the rampart of the beautiful stone walls of a castle with colorful pendants blowing in the breeze. There was a tall tower reaching up into the sky. And I saw the lovely moat out front. People were coming and going over the drawbridge. There were horses, too. Does that mean something?" she looked hopeful.

Wals sighed and took her into his arms for a quick reassuring hug. "I don't know," he told her honestly. "It could. I'll do my best to get you back there, Rose. I promise," he added in a whisper, wondering how in the world he would ever be able to keep that promise. He looked past the wolf to the green water of the peaceful River, remembering the maelstrom that brought him here so long ago. *If that is what I think it was,* he thought to himself, *and we ever get to see it again...please don't let her go another direction in time!*

CHAPTER ELEVEN

The Island – 1817

Wolf knew he needed to take matters into his own hands—paws. Wals finally understood the impending danger to Rose and the necessity to get her off the Island, but he didn't have any idea how he could accomplish it. From the last cast member briefing they had attended, Wolf remembered that the Settler's Cabin would be more or less left alone during the major changes being made to Tom Sawyer's Island. But, things were different here. If Wals was correct about some of the soldiers joining the pirates—especially if one of the soldiers was Daniel Crain—then Crain would probably still raid the cabin and that meant Rose would be in terrible danger.

Leaving the couple inside the log cabin to see to Rose's packing, Wolf limped to the edge of the riverbed and raised his head. He gave a loud, lingering howl followed by a shorter one.

Hearing the noise, Wals came out of the cabin

to investigate. Following the direction the wolf was looking, he could see something moving on the water and became instantly alert. Thinking only of the pirates and the impending danger, he was alarmed when he saw that a canoe was approaching their clearing. Not noticing the relaxed stance of the wolf, Wals was ready to race back to the cabin for his newfound sword. As he took one last glance at the River before running off, he noticed the wake trailing behind the canoe. He then realized it had to have come from the encampment on the far side of the River, not from the direction of the Fort. Only then did Wals notice the wolf fully at ease. Seeing that, he could then allow himself relax. Shading his eyes from the glare of the sun off the River, he recognized the brave Mato effortlessly paddling towards him. He wondered what prompted this visit, but was nevertheless happy to see his friend. Thinking about the comings and goings of the tribe during all his time here, he hadn't noticed any of the natives going anywhere on the Island except to the Fort—and even that was an unusual event. They preferred to remain on the other side of the River. Wals had heard Wolf's howl, but hadn't pieced the two together.

After what looked like a brief greeting between the man and the animal, Mato and Wolf headed for the cabin, ignoring the fact that Wals was even standing there. Much to Wals' continued, confused amusement, Mato also seemed to be deep in an argument with the wolf as they walked the lengthy distance up from the water. The two of them disappeared into the cabin and within moments reemerged. Mato was carrying Rose's over-stuffed carpetbag in one hand and the sword Wals had stolen from the cave in his other. His teeth clamped firmly onto Rose's apron, Wolf was dragging her towards the canoe. Rose was used to odd behavior from the wolf, but she wasn't taking this well. She was ineffectively trying to free her apron from Wolf's tenacious grip while voicing her many objections as to why she hadn't yet finished packing and why she wasn't ready to go. Wals could only shrug his shoulders at the questioning look she threw at him as she was drug past him to the waiting canoe.

It was obvious that both Mato and the wolf wanted the two of them in the canoe and they wanted it done right now. All the time wondering how Mato could possibly even be aware of the imminent danger and how man and beast seemed to be working in unison, Wals just gave in and trusted his friend Mato. Wals quickly and silently climbed to the front of the canoe and picked up an extra paddle to help get them across the wide River. The disconcerted Rose and her wolf settled into the middle of the small craft, Wolf still firmly holding onto her apron in case she tried to break free. As they glided away from the clearing, had any of them thought to look, they would have seen that Rose's knuckles were white as she gripped the sides of the little boat. The men hadn't thought to realize that she had never been over to the Village before. Even though she had been pretty sure who had set the fire, the vision of her burning cabin was still playing over and over in her memory, infusing doubt into her troubled mind. She paled all the more and grew even quieter the closer they got to the tipi encampment. Not wanting the men to see her fear, she raised her chin and set her mouth in a firm, even line, looking more like a proud Cleopatra being fer-

ried across the Nile by her slaves than someone trying to escape an attack by a band of pirates.

They were met at the water's edge by the
Shaman. His first greeting was to his two sons,
then to Wals, and then he tried to welcome the
silent, wide-eyed Rose. As she could not speak
their language, she could only be guided by the
friendly gestures that she was indeed welcome
there. Casting a quick glance over to Wals, she
could see he was completely at ease. She recalled
that he had visited here before and was on friendly
terms with the inhabitants, so she too began to
relax. Rose watched with curiosity the many
women who were working at different tasks around
the camp, even breaking into a lovely smile when
she realized that they, too, were stealing glances at
her.

Her attempts to look around the camp was cut
short when Wolf again grabbed Rose's apron and
drug her to the third tipi, back by the edge of the
deep forest. His concern was to get her out of sight
in case the pirates came faster than he anticipated
they would. Wals followed them into the dwelling
and, when Wolf left, they began talking quietly about
their situation and how best to proceed.

"When you said you wanted to get the wiya off
the Island, I did not realize you meant to bring her
here," the Shaman told his son when they were
seated far enough away from the tipi to talk freely.
The opening of the tipi given to Rose and Wals purposely faced in a different direction than the rocky
overhang and the view of the River. Aside from the
safety issue, Wolf didn't think the visiting couple
needed to see him deep in conversation with the
Shaman.

Wolf bared his teeth in a wolfish grin. "I am glad you are not angry with me. I was hoping you would welcome them temporarily."

The Shaman had been irritated when Mato reported Wolf had been shot and did not come home to his own people for help. Worried, of course, but more irritated. He was pleased now that at least Wolf realized his family could offer protection for his friends. "Anyone is welcome here as long as they do no harm." A small smile creased his face. "I saw your friend dragging a sword out of the canoe, but I am not sure he knows how to use it. He might cut off something he will need later."

Wolf chuckled a little. "Let's hope not. It might be difficult to explain a hacked-off limb when he gets home." Wolf let himself picture Wals going to First Aid and trying to describe some kind of event where a sword cutting into him would have been involved. When the silence of his waiting father became obvious, Wolf cleared his throat and got back to the needs at hand. "Wals has finally remembered his other world and former life. All of it, I think, from what he has been saying. It is the woman Rose we are not sure about. It doesn't sound like she is from our time either. Nothing Wals has been speaking to her about seems familiar to her. It would help if I could talk directly with Wals. Do you think now after all that has occurred he would accept me as a talking wolf?"

"Does he realize you are his friend in your other world?"

Wolf shook his head, still wavering between being amused and disgusted at Wals' inability to put two and two together after all this time. "No, he hasn't figured that part out yet. I know at times he sees the similarities, but doesn't seem to be able to get his mind around that fact. It is difficult enough for me to understand sometimes and yet I have lived with it all my life. He has never even heard of such a thing."

"What about the wiya?"

"What about her? If you mean would she accept the fact that I can talk, probably the answer would be yes—more so than Wals. I've always had the distinct impression that she's been quite disappointed I never have talked back to her. But, if it got out at the wrong time that I could talk...," he broke off, shuddering, thinking of cages and laboratories.

The Shaman looked out over the River, thinking. "No. I meant something else. You have said all along that the wiya does not belong here in this time. And now you say she might not belong in your other time. How do you know?"

Glad to get his mind off the thoughts of probes and dissection, Wolf thought about his father's question. He shook his head before answering. "Just a feeling I get every time I am around her. I know that a woman does not live in the cabin in the other time. But there is more to it than that."

The dark eyes were looking at him now, intent and searching. "Explain."

One of Wolf's shoulders moved in a brief shrug. He shifted to take the weight off his injured leg. "All I can say is this: Being around her gives me the same feeling I have when I am in the other world. I belong, yet I don't belong. I am the same as everyone else, yet I am very different. She gives off that same aura. She even mentioned the same feeling as I have."

"What about the doctor you mentioned before? Does he feel the same?"

Wolf groaned. "He is missing. Again. The Fort is now closed and he has disappeared again. I'm hoping he wasn't taken by the pirates. It would be very difficult to get him back if he was." Wolf stifled a curse knowing his father would not appreciate it. Things seemed to be getting worse, not better. "Did I mention that Wals thinks Private Crain has joined the pirates? If he is right, Crain will probably do well with them."

Ignoring the unimportant Private, Wolf's father asked, "Did you consider that the doctor may have left before the invaders came?"

Wolf couldn't help but notice the sly look in the dark eyes staring at him. "What do you know?"

"Mato...." he started, breaking off when Wolf gave a disgusted snort at the mention of his brother—his good brother, the one that had stayed home and raised a family instead of leaving like he did. The Shaman would not let Wolf's childish burst of sibling rivalry pass. There was pride for Mato and anger at Wolf mixed in his voice as he pointedly told his younger son, "Mato keeps his eyes out for the safety of this village. He is concerned for the family. And, he watches out for *you*. His eyes are not so personally focused."

The huge black head dropped an inch and his ears flattened. "I'm sorry. I know Bear is doing his duty and doing it well. I was out of line. What did he hear?" he added, properly chastised.

The black eyes still stared into his blue ones. After a long moment of silence, the wolf headdress turned to face the long stretch of the River. "Mato believes the doctor is now at Rainbow Ridge. You might begin looking there."

"How in the world did he get to Rainbow Ridge?" Wolf growled, shaking his head. "Great, now I need to get Wals to go up there. But, how do I convey that? I still don't think it is a good idea to be known as a talking wolf, even among friends."

The Shaman grunted and said nothing. He would let his son figure it out. "Did you call the next oskeca?"

Wolf looked up at the waning light, his eyes narrowed as he sniffed the air. This night would be clear. "Yes, whenever that will happen. It usually comes immediately, but, for some reason, I know it will not be tonight. For once I am glad it is delayed. I have much still to do."

The wolf headdress nodded once in agreement. "All is not in readiness. Until it is, we must all be watchful until the time is right. My son," he called when Wolf had turned to leave, "when you do go back through the next storm, you must be prepared for any eventuality. It will not be what you expect."

Pausing, the wolf waited. When nothing more was said, Wolf gave a respectful bow to his father. He knew he would be given no more explanation than that.

Across the River from the cabin, concealed by a thick growth of lacy ferns, Wolf kept watch on Rose's home. It surprised him that it took only one more day before he spotted a small band of pirates approaching the cabin. There were five of them in various styles of clothing that had apparently been taken off of captured men. They were all carrying swords and some had pistols. Wolf's attention was drawn to a dark blue jacket with only a few gold buttons left on the front. Wals had been right. It was Private Crain who led the raiders. His Calvary hat had been replaced by a dirty red bandana wrapped around his head. He limped, probably from some initiation rite of passage pressed on him by his new shipmates. The cowardly air that usually hung around him like a waving flag was gone. His attitude was now one of leadership and confidence— a confidence that came with the knowledge that he was backed by a band of cutthroats and nobody would dare defy him. He was finally going to get that woman who had scorned and embarrassed him all those years. And, when he was finished with her, what was left was promised to the four men who had come along with him—the first of whom was the pirate who had boldly claimed her that first day when she had been spotted inside the entrance of their cave.

They had not seen or heard the woman's protecting wolf ever since Daniel had shot him. Crain, figuring he had finally taken the animal down with a fatal shot, brazenly approached the cabin from the front in the bright early light of the new day. Emboldened by his crew standing behind him, the preening Crain himself would lead the attack.

When they were in a semi-circle facing the cabin, they all let out a blood-curdling yell and drew their swords and pistols. One of the pirates fired a shot into the cabin. Expecting to hear the woman screaming in fear, they were now astonished to receive no response at all. "She's hiding inside! I'll get that biddy!" Crain yelled as he awkwardly put his sword back in its scabbard and stalked up to the closed front door. After throwing a smirking grin back at the watching pirates, he used his foot to smash open the unlocked door. With the hollering encouragement from his four cohorts, he ran inside, letting out his own loud, victorious yell. Within moments he was back outside, some of his bravado evaporating when he found there was no easy prey inside. There was no prey at all. At his direction, the men spread out and searched the grounds around the small cabin and a short distance back in the forest. They ignored the mare that just stood there and watching curiously from her little corral.

Wolf, still undercover in the brush on the other side of the river, watched in amusement as they regrouped and huddled in a circle, yelling and arms waving, arguing about what they should do next. Crain had assured the pirates of the easy capture of a beautiful woman. Now there was no woman and no idea of where she had gone. Crain pointed in the direction of the Fort, suggesting she might have run there for help. Or she could be hiding in the old Mill building. The pirates had taken control of the rafts going to and from the Island, so they knew she couldn't have gotten off the Island by that route. The only explanation they did not explore was the encampment out of sight across the River. Crain knew he himself would never have the courage to go across the River and couldn't imagine that the timid female would possibly go over there either.

After a few more minutes of arguing, one of the larger pirates—the one who had claimed her—became disgusted and cuffed Crain in the head with the hilt of his drawn sword. The group of five turned to head back towards the Fort, the deflated Crain now bringing up the rear in the position of shame, holding his bleeding head where he had been struck.

Giving a silent laugh, Wolf turned and trotted back to his village.

Forgoing the use of one of the canoes, Mato decided it would be best if he and Wals went overland through the wilderness. It would be easier to conceal themselves in the forest if the pirates appeared on the River looking for the missing woman. With only a basic knowledge of their language, and Mato's ability to say "Rainbow" in heavily-accented English, Wals got the idea of where they were going in search of the missing doctor. He had shown the men the doctor's lighter and how it worked. With the limited amount of fuel left in the lighter after so many years of sitting idle, it quickly emptied and was considered worthless by the Shaman and his men. Still, Wals knew it would be as important to show Doctor Houser as his nametag had been to himself. And, hopefully, if his reasoning proved to be correct, it would have the same effect on the doctor.

Before they left, Wals had been presented with different options with which he could arm himself for protection—a fact that again made him realize all the more the seriousness of where he was and that the danger they were in was very, very real. He wasn't in Frontierland any more. This was truly the wild frontier. The braves had held out bow and arrows, an extremely sharp hunting knife, the musket that had been retrieved from Rose's cabin, the sword he had found in the cave, and a handful of rocks that he hoped was just a joke and not an indication of their confidence in his ability to defend either himself or anyone else. At the half amused, half irritated look on Wals' face when shown the last option, one of the men produced a leather sling and proceeded to knock in quick succession a row of branches off a far-distant tree. Mollified, Wals chose the hunting knife and was given a clever sheath that attached to the belt of his canoe costume. As he carefully slid the deadly weapon inside, he silently hoped he was never called upon to use it.

Mato, armed as if going on his own private war, carried everything except the clumsy, one-shot musket.

His injured leg still bothering him, Wolf knew he would just slow his brother down and chose to remain behind to protect Rose as well as to keep her company. With Wals gone, she would have been relatively alone because of the language barrier. Plus, he didn't want her to do anything foolish like trying to go back to her cabin for some useless trinket or to check on the mare. He knew the trip for the mare would be unnecessary since he had taught the intelligent Sukawaka how to open her gate to get to the new grasses in the spring.

Not having to worry about hiding their tracks, Mato set a good pace as he led Wals on the journey north to what was left of the mining town of Rainbow Ridge. The trip was exciting to Wals who had only seen this part of the territory from either on one of his rafts or in a canoe on the River.

Mato didn't cross the River, but stayed on the same side as their encampment. They soon saw the Beaver Dam and its residents quickly slipping beneath the water at their approaching sounds. Thinking back about the River in his time, Wals remembered different animals that had been hidden along the banks of the Rivers of America in Frontierland. Knowing he was in a living, breathing version of that area, he hoped that Rose's descriptions of the changes were true here in the backwoods as well. If not, they would be passing through territory claimed by a huge black bear and a screaming panther.

Their path took them past a lone, lightning-struck tree, its trunk scarred and stripped of bark. The ground around the tree was churned up, and Wals recognized it as the black bear's scratching tree. As Mato didn't slow up or seem at all concerned, Wals focused on keeping up with the fleet-footed brave. As the ground rose and became rockier, their pace slowed. Scrambling down the other side of the gravely slope, they approached the large, mossy pool of inviting cool water called Bear Country. Here Mato took their first break, and, squatting down at the water's edge, took a long drink while Wals watched the surrounding forest.

As they wound through the wilderness, the trees became more sparse, the terrain rougher. Seeing the River bending away from them on their right, Wals knew they must be approaching the area that—in his time—used to be known as Nature's Wonderland. The hills took on the coloration of the beautiful canyons of Utah—dull red veins layered in rock of muted yellow. Only a few remaining wind-blown spires reached upwards and they passed one large red-colored arch and a flat-topped butte. With a catch in his breath, Wals remembered that those two monuments were the last vestiges of the beauty of Nature's Wonderland. He knew the arch would go nowhere now. It used to be a gateway. Still, he just had to see it for himself.

With a call to Mato who had not realized Wals had stopped, Wals started scrambling up the rocky side of the butte. Reaching high, he cautiously felt for any handholds in the deceptively smooth side of the tall rock. Finding one sufficient hold after another, he pushed up with his legs, straining to secure himself. Ignoring the warning calls from the irritated Mato below, Wals inched slowly upwards. A few scraggly bushes hung on tenaciously to the face of the butte, only to be roughly grabbed by the intruder and used for leverage.

Thinking his footing was secure, Wals reached for the top of the rock, only to have his moccasin slip out from under him, sending a shower of rocks down on the watching, scowling Mato. For a tense moment, he swung free with only his hands keeping him from plummeting back to where he had started. Sweat pouring down the sides of his face, Wals calmed the panic in his mind and willed his body to become still, his legs to stop their frantic churning. Finding a small ledge for his toes, he pulled himself upwards, getting his right elbow over the top of the butte. Once there, the strength of his arms brought him the rest of the way to the top.

Rolling on his back, gasping for breath, Wals ran his costumed arm over his damp forehead. With a self-conscious laugh at his narrow escape, he got to his feet to survey the surrounding country.

He wished he hadn't.

What should have been a beautiful area of geysers, colored sandstone and vivid pots of bubbling mud looked as if it had been wiped clean with a scratchy rag. Flat. Empty. Barren. A few new trees had begun their slow growth and a few cacti poked up forlornly in the distance. Instead of the howl of a coyote, he only heard the howl of the wind as it blew up dust devils around and far below him.

Upset at the extent of this desolation, he turned and looked over the edge of the butte to signal to the impatient Mato that he was going to start downwards. Mato looked up from where he was resting in the shade, a scowl still on his face. He didn't appreciate this delay. He had wanted to get to Rainbow Ridge in plenty of time before darkness fell.

Wals figured he was going to get chewed out in Lakota when he got to the bottom. But before he could throw a leg over and start down, he caught sight of Mato jumping to his feet and waving his arms, yelling up, "Sinte hla!"

"Yeah, I'm coming, I'm coming," Wals muttered, not understanding.

As he turned backwards to start easing down, Mato yelled at him again, "Sinte hla!"

Looking back over the edge at Mato, Wals was shocked to see him now aiming a drawn arrow right at his face. "Hey, I said I was sorry!" he yelled down, immediately throwing himself back when he saw Mato's fingers release the arrow.

Wals heard the arrow strike the cliff just inches below where he was standing. The other sound he heard did not make sense to him at all. When there was no more yelling coming from Mato, he tentatively looked over the edge once more. About a foot below his position, just above where he would have placed his right foot, was an arrow protruding through the head of a five-foot long rattlesnake, pinning it to the side of the cliff.

Eyes wide, Wals saw Mato nonchalantly motioning him to come on back down now.

When Wals reached his friend, Mato pointed upwards. He then held up two fingers and bent them like fangs and struck them at Wals, calmly repeating, "Sinte hla."

Looking back at the dead rattler, the pale Wals muttered, "Why didn't you say so in the first place?"

At Mato's amused chuckle at his expense, Wals gave an exaggerated gesture for him to take the lead and said in French, "S'il vous plaît."

To his utter amazement, Mato trod past him and slyly grinned. "Merci."

Wals walked a long ways in complete silence.

In time, as the day quickly progressed, they came upon a stretch of abandoned train track and the remnants of a small, weathered engine, the letters N.W.R.R. barely visible on the side of the yellow cab. There were two ore cars full of rocks still attached to the engine, one of them half off the track. A marmot popped it head up in the second car, whistling at the two men before dropping back to the safety of the broken, ragged rocks.

Mato said something to Wals, pointing at the train and then to the east. Mato was indicating that following the track would be the easiest way to reach their destination. Still shook from the near miss with the rattlesnake and the devastation of Nature's Wonderland, Wals merely nodded to his companion.

Now knowing exactly where he was, Wals took the lead for the rest of the distance to the mining

community. Silent with his own thoughts, he was-
n't sure at all what he would find when they reached
the end of their journey.

Not the boom town it had been in its heyday,
Rainbow Ridge was still a fairly active community.
As the two men walked into town, the streets were
almost empty, but there was plenty of noise coming
out of the various buildings lining the main street.
A couple of burros, not needed for the supply train,
were tied to the hitching post in front of the Big
Thunder Saloon whose sign, though somewhat
weather-beaten, still proudly advertised "Poker, Bil-
liards, Entertainment & Dancing." They could hear
the sounds of a honky-tonk piano pounding out a
lively tune amongst the yells of the patrons inside.

After a small side alley, they walked past the
General Store, a one-story adobe building, its porch
covered with goods for sale including a large, black
pot-bellied stove and various traps. The proprietor,
dressed like the miner he used to be in a faded red
shirt, buff trousers tucked into calf-high dusty black
boots and a floppy brown hat pushed back on his
head, was busy sweeping the never-ending dust off
the wooden boardwalk out front. Stopping his activity to nod hello to the newcomers, he took the opportunity to wipe his face with the red handkerchief
tied around his neck. "Howdy, folks!" he called over
in a right friendly way.

Right next door was the town's newspaper, the
Rainbow Ridge Clarion. A pair of bleached antlers
hung crookedly over the sign that told they also offered "Notary Public, Letters Written, and Ornamen-

tal Writing". Wals could hear the sound of the print-ing press clanking in the back of the storefront as they passed by. A wanted poster tacked to the side of the entry door offered $10,000 for the capture of a card shark, his many aliases listed below.

The necessary Assay Office was neighbor to the *Clarion*, its windows were covered with fancy lettering proclaiming "Chemical Analysis of Every Description Made With Accuracy and Dispatch." If you had a mining claim, here you could record it, buy it, or sell it.

Perched up in the hills behind the main street were more buildings, most showing signs of neg-lect or abandonment. Here and there were signs of habitation, like a clothesline with faded shirts hanging limp in the still air.

Near the far end of the street was another di-lapidated, empty building. It had been a pristine white at one time. The three double entry doors to the Opera House, beneath the arched balcony, were still painted blue. Faded posters of the last leading lady hung drunkenly on two of the balcony's posts. A faded red, white and blue bunting had been hung on the blue balcony many years ago; be-hind the bunting, a wooden chair had fallen beside a small round table.

Not to be outdone by the Big Thunder Saloon, Pat Casey's Last Chance Saloon was painted a bright pink, its white swinging batwing doors still moving from the last patron who entered. The sound of a glass breaking and a hearty yell could be heard inside as Wals approached.

Wals was about to look over the swinging doors to see if the doctor might be inside when he heard the familiar high pitched "Toot Toot" whistle of the mine train. It seemed to be coming from the direction of the Opera House, but there were no tracks that they could see. The ground beneath them shook as a large dust cloud suddenly formed and swept down the center of the dirt street, blowing past them and disappearing just after the Big Thunder Saloon.

The ground stilled as suddenly as it had started. "What was that?" Wals asked Mato, who was now staring at the Opera House. They now could barely hear the strains of a singer practicing her scales coming from that direction.

Mato raised a hand to finger the medicine bag tied around his neck. "Wana gi hemani." *Ghost train*.

Standing still a moment, the two men waited. However, when the phenomenon did not repeat itself, they looked at each other and motioned that they needed to keep moving. Wals decided to go to the next building. Before they could check out the two-story El Dorado Hotel that offered "nice beds $1.00" and "sheets 50 cents extra," Wals spotted something on the second story of the saloon. He stopped so abruptly that Mato slammed into his back. As Wals pointed upwards, Mato could see a huge gold colored tooth hanging from a metal pipe protruding out of the only window. He didn't know what the word "Dentist" stenciled on the window meant. Wals pulled the Zippo lighter out of his pocket and showed it to the confused brave and, smiling, pointed upstairs. "Doctor Houser!" he said hopefully as he headed for the stairs on the side of the pink building.

Curious, Mato followed Wals up the stairs. He had never been this far into this town before, so he figured he might as well take advantage of every opportunity to explore how these people lived.

Raising his hand to knock, Wals saw a small sign leaning inside the glass of the door that read: "No Appointment Necessary. Come On In."

A small bell over the door tinkled brightly as the two men entered the small room. A padded metal chair stood near the only window, more than likely to help the doctor see in the darkness of the room. Various vicious-looking medical instruments—none of which Wals would have wanted in his mouth— were near at hand on a small table. Boxes of powders and tins of ointments, a modern-looking stethoscope, and a lot of cotton batting sat on top of a crude pine bookcase.

Before Wals could examine the few books piled on the wobbly bookcase, the door to the only other room opened and Doctor Houser emerged, wiping a knife off onto a white piece of linen. He was dressed almost exactly like the owner of the store, even with a red handkerchief tied around his neck. "Can I help.... Well, well, well, if it isn't Wals!" he exclaimed when he recognized the supply man from the Fort. He seemed very pleased and extended his hand to Wals while casting a curious glance at the silent Mato who still stood near the door. "It's good to see a familiar face, let me tell you! How long has it been?" He broke off as if confused by his own question, his eyes getting a worried slant. He shook it off. "Too long, I am sure. And, who is your friend?"

Wals stepped back and motioned for Mato to come forward. He chose not to. "This is Mato, from the Pinewood Village."

Claude Houser smiled at the silent brave.

"Hmm, long ways from home. Nice to meet you, Mato. My, this is a pleasant surprise. What brings you two all the way to Rainbow Ridge? With the mine closing, there isn't too much left here. What is the news from the Fort?"

Now it was Wals' turn to be surprised. "You didn't hear? I thought maybe that is why you left."

Claude looked from one man to the other. He turned back to Wals. "Hear what?"

"The Fort closed. The Island has been taken over by a band of pirates and some of the soldiers apparently were pressed into service."

Claude sank into the exam chair. "Oh, my, that's awful. What of the ladies? And, what about that lovely young woman who was in the Burning Cabin, as we all still called it? The one with the pet wolf?"

"I can only answer for the gal in the cabin, Rose Stephens, and she is safe in Mato's village," Wals answered him. "I'm not sure about the women from the Fort. I suppose some of them might have gotten taken by the pirates.... I can only hope the others got over to New Orleans in time."

"Which has its own inherent dangers," the doctor mumbled more to himself than to Wals. "Well, what brings you two here? Looking to relocate?" he asked with a small grin.

Wals let out a breath. "Well, I am hoping to relocate, but it might not be what you think."

At the curious look on the doctor's face, Wals reached into his pocket and brought out the lighter. "Doc, does this mean anything to you?"

Dr. Houser took the lighter, and with practiced ease, flipped it open and flicked the wheel to make it ignite. "Hmm, must be out of lighter fluid," he murmured. Then, apparently realizing what he had just done and said, his eyes grew wide and flew back to Wals' face. Snapping the Zippo shut, he brought the front of the lighter up to his eyes, turning it in the dim light so he could read the words engraved on the face. "1962…1962…." He seemed frozen as his mind wrapped around the date and compared it to everything around him at that moment. "This is my lighter. It was a gift from the Medical Society for some charity work I did. There was a huge banquet…in the ballroom of the Regency Hotel…in…," he broke off, unwilling to voice the rest of the scene that had suddenly flooded back into his memory. "My word! Where am I? Really?" His eyes shot back to Wals. "How did you get this?"

Wals took the only other chair in the room, a wooden ladder back with a small woven seat. Mato was busy examining one of the medical books on the shelving, seemingly ignoring the other two men. From what his brother had told him, he knew exactly what was being discussed. And, from the doctor's response right now, he knew just about where they were in that discussion. "I know what you are going through, Doc," Wals was saying. "I went through exactly the same process…with this." He brought his name badge out of the same pocket and held it out to the confused doctor.

Taking the oval piece of plastic, Claude read the words "Where Dreams Come True" and, more importantly, the dark blue words that read "Disneyland" above Wals' name. "Disneyland!" he exclaimed in recognition. "Walt! I was with Walt that last night. Were you there, too? I don't remember you being there."

Wals sat back in the chair and took a deep

breath, licking his dry lips. "Well, here is where it gets really tricky," he paused, wondering how exactly to word this. "Walt had passed away before I came along."

The doctor's face fell. "The last time I saw him was in 1966. I knew he was getting sicker." He shook his head sadly side to side. "Even when you know it is coming, it is still hard to hear. How long has he been gone?"

Wals looked perplexed. "Well, gosh, I need to think about that. Hmm, Walt was gone in December of 1966, and the last date I remember is 2007, so, what does that make it? I guess, at the time I left, he had been gone around forty-one years."

The expected stunned silence greeted his reply. Doing the math himself, his eyes wide, Claude gasped. "Did you just say it's 2007? How can that be? They just cleaned up from the War of 1812 here!"

Wals knew the doctor had to work this all out for himself and remained silent.

"If what you say is true," Claude continued, "if it is 2007, then, according to your calculations, I should be sixty-nine years old. I…I'm not… Am I?" as he reached up to touch his unlined face.

Ignoring that for now, Wals wanted to know, "How did you get here? What is the last thing you remember?"

The doctor thought back, still clutching the lighter and the nametag. "I was living in New Orleans, at Madam Annette's…. No, that's where I moved in. Where was I…. Gosh, why is this so hard to remember?"

"I think it is the Island," Wals told him, still trying to work it out himself. "It seems to drain us of our memories…our *real* memories. How long do you think you have been here?"

"Hmm…maybe just three or four years. I lived in New Orleans for a while, and then I moved to Fort Wilderness during the Battle for New Orleans. The soldiers needed a doctor and I liked it there, so I stayed on. You came along not too long after the hostilities ceased. I remember you had a nasty bump on your head and you were talking oddly…like you didn't know where you were. Like you didn't belong," he concluded, thinking back. Looking out at the growing darkness falling over the town, he went on softly, "Much like I felt. I remember seeing the Mark Twain tied up at the dock and I thought…I thought I hadn't made it through, that I was still in Disneyland."

Wals nodded. It all sounded familiar. "Who brought you?"

"There were two men on the dock…. No, that isn't right. They just took me into New Orleans. It was a man, though. I remember I didn't know him, but Walt did and asked me to trust him. This man had some wild tale about needing to protect me."

This part of the story was not familiar to Wals. "Protect you from what?"

Before he could answer, Mato, bored, indicated he was going to find them something to eat and left before either man could reply. "Hope he comes back," Wals muttered, "We're a long ways from home."

Dr. Houser wasn't concerned about Mato right now. All the strange feelings he had had over the years—the sense of not belonging but fitting in just fine, medical knowledge he had but shouldn't at this period of time—all flooded through his mind. He looked at the lighter one more time. Not being able to read in the darkness, he got up to light the glass-chimney oil lamp on the pine desk in the corner. Returning to the more comfortable exam chair, he tried to pick up the threads of his memories again. "Protection. That's what it was. There was a man who stole something from Walt and then threatened to kill me. Because of a...a project I was working on with Walt, they felt I needed to go somewhere safe. What about you? Why did you come here?"

Wals remembered his friend Wolf who had asked him for help. "I was needed to help a friend rescue two people on an Island," he said slowly as Wolf's wording came back to him. He hadn't remembered that much before. He looked up sharply at the doctor. "He asked me to help him bring back someone named Rose and someone named Doctor Houser."

"And who was it who asked for your help if Walt was gone?"

"A good friend of mine. He is one of the main security guards at Disneyland. His name is Mani Wolford. But we just call him...."

"Wolf," the doctor finished for him, stunned, as memories kept flowing into him like the returning sensations after his foot had fallen asleep. "How old is this friend of yours? He was, oh, maybe about thirty when he brought me here."

Wals just nodded his head slowly. "Yes," was all he could say.

"How could I be forgotten for over forty years? How could...but I *couldn't* have been here that long...I think it has been only about three years or so...hasn't it?" He rubbed at the ache growing behind his forehead.

Wals saw the gesture and nodded in understanding. "Yeah, that's what it does to me, too, when I try to figure it out."

"I think we both need to talk to this Mister Wolf. The sooner, the better." The animosity towards this mysterious man was returning along with his memories.

Wals pursed his lips and reached out his hand for his nametag. He still felt he needed to keep it close to him. "Well, that's where it gets tricky again. I haven't seen Wolf since I got here…however long that has been."

"Do you remember thunder and lightning and a bright pink light?"

Wals continued nodding. He was beginning to feel like one of those toy bobbleheads in the back window of a car. He made a conscious effort to still his head. "That was the last time I saw Wolf. Either he didn't make it through whatever it was, or he drowned in the River…or we did," he finished lamely, trying to make a joke, but neither of them laughed.

"What about that young lady you told me about? Rose Stephens? What does she remember?"

"That's the odd part…. Well, *one* of the odd parts," he gave a small smile as the doctor agreed. "She doesn't seem to remember Disneyland at all—like you and I both do. I showed Rose my nametag, but that didn't mean anything to her. Just the castle on it seemed familiar. She remembers a moat and banners flying over some castle."

"I'd like to talk to her anyway. Where is she? Is she safe, you said?"

"She's waiting for me back at Mato's village. I

have to ask.... Now that you remember your real place, do any of these surroundings look 'familiar' to you? Like you have seen them before, but not quite as...real?"

Dr. Houser chuckled, but it was a dry, humorless sound. "I should be able to say that I have no idea what you mean. But...I do." He looked out the darkened glass again, the noise of the saloon drifting in through the open window. When he began talking again, his voice was quiet. "When I was first pulled out of the River, I thought I was still in Disneyland. But, the Mark Twain I saw was a real paddlewheeler. It made real trips with real customers. I didn't live in New Orleans Square, but in New Orleans, the French Quarter. Fort Wilderness. Your supply rafts. I had seen them all before, but they weren't *real*." He looked over at Wals for verification when he finished talking.

"Yeah, that's what I saw. Only, I could see it one step further than you," Wals explained. "Since it looks like I am from a later period in time than you...somehow...a lot had changed at Disneyland over the years. Lately, more specifically, to Tom Sawyer's Island. And, *each* of those changes at Disneyland appears to have happened here as well—after the fact. That's why Wolf and I...at least I thought it was going to be Wolf and I...anyway, he wanted me to bring you and Rose back to the current time. I remember him telling me it wasn't safe here any longer. And now that I see the pirates taking over the Island, I think he was absolutely right."

"So, how do we get back? How do we pick up our former lives? You never did say how long you have been here."

Wals opened his mouth to answer, and then

shut it. "I was going to say I've been here years and years, but, honestly? I don't know. It's too confusing. It feels like I've been here all my life, that this is where I belong."

Dr. Houser nodded in agreement. "Do we wait here for this man Wolf to show up?" He didn't look like he favored that prospect. The animosity towards Wolf that had begun so long ago now seemed to have been founded on fact.

"Well, since Rose is waiting at the Pinewood village, I think we should go back there," Wals suggested and then added, "Since the three of us are somehow linked together in all of this…whatever it is…I think we should all stay together and wait for Wolf in the village. Mato's family is there…well, at least, I think they are his family. I haven't learned enough Lakota to figure it all out," he gave a charming half-smile in his self-deprecating way. "It's too late tonight, so what say we get an early start in the morning?"

The doctor looked around his small office. He felt at home here, settled. He felt needed. If this preposterous story was true…and he felt, deep down, somehow, that it was…then he was way out of touch with his former life. *If Walt was gone, had any of their far-reaching plans been set in motion? Was all that research and preparation done for nothing? What about my true field of cryogenics? Was that still feasible?*

With a small sigh, he pushed himself out of the chair and looked at the lighter one more time. "Well," he said quietly, "Like Walt always said: 'The way to get started is to quit talking and begin doing'…. I need to pack.".

Nodding in understanding at what the doctor

was feeling, Wals stood. "We'll come back for you at first light."

When Wals left the doctor's office, he stopped by the Rainbow Ridge Clarion and bought a newspaper, curious to see if there was any news of Fort Wilderness or whatever else might be newsworthy in the area. He settled into a chair in a relatively quiet corner of the Big Thunder Saloon and ordered a whiskey from the hovering serving girl, Louise. Soon realizing she was being ignored for the most part, she flounced off to get his drink.

Squinting to see the small print of the closely printed newspaper, Wals wondered if it was the printing or if he needed glasses. He read much lamenting on the closing of different mines, naming each one of them as they closed, the possibility of the Opera House reopening if everyone chipped in to help, and advertisements from the General Store. Smiling to himself, Wals decided small-town newspapers were the same—no matter where or *when* you were! He was about to set the paper aside when a headline caught his eye: "Confessions of a Gold Miner." Recognizing the byline from a small town in Northern California, his interest peaked.

"The weather is turning colder now. Fall has always been my favorite time of the year with the trees changing colors and all. But when my stream starts showing a little ice around its banks —well, fall isn't fall any more. It's quickly becoming winter. I don't like winter so much. I can't work my claim because of the freezing water and the difficulty getting through

the snow. Oh, I still mine gold during the winter, but it's a different kind of mining. And I have always had two ways of mining.

My claim had always been a consistent little thing. Kinda like me. I won't tell you where it is, though. Not that you'd find it on any map of Calveras County. I acquired the claim from a man I called Uncle Joe. Never learned his last name. He was proud of his claim. Even made a deal with the Mi Wuk Indians to leave him alone on it. A deal they have kept with me—even though I know I amuse them greatly. Uncle Joe was pretty lonely when he came here. Just about everyone is lonely. Family and friends are all "back East"—wherever that means. You have to pick your friends carefully up here in the Sierras. Especially in the gold towns like this one. I picked Uncle Joe. I seemed to fill a spot he had and he more or less adopted me. Too bad he insisted on "teaching" me how to play poker. I felt kind of bad to win the claim and his cabin from him. And I felt a little worse when he left here shamefaced.

The water feels freezing cold this morning as I plunge my beat-up pan into the bottom gravel. The only sounds I can hear is the soft rush of the water, an irritating, moaning breeze that has kicked up, and a few birds here and there. The breeze irritates me because I know what is coming behind it. Still, I have to smile at the flakes that appear regular as rain in the bottom of my pan as I sluice it around in the water. Uncle Joe knew what he was doing when he picked this spot. It will never be the

Mother Lode. We both knew that. Just sure and steady like the mule I let Uncle Joe keep when he left. But, sure and steady is good. It all works towards my goal.

What's my goal, you ask? I know you're curious by now. Don't laugh, but I want a respectable life in a big city like San Francisco. And that takes money. I figure two more years and I'll have enough. The closest big city here is Sonora, but that doesn't count. I never go there. No need. But San Francisco! Just saying it sounds elegant. No, I haven't been there yet. But I've heard about it. I know how to listen in the camp town—especially in the one respectable place there. Hotel Dorado. I'm a good listener and I know what I want. I just don't want to keep having to dip my hands into the freezing water any longer than necessary. It's not so bad in the summer when the temperature rises to the nineties. But now? No, it's almost time to bring my stash into camp town and start my winter mining. The last Wells Fargo coach of the season will pass through next week. I have a deal with one of the drivers.

I'm almost ready to go the Hotel Dorado for the evening. My hands irritate me—both figuratively and literally. They're still all red and chapped from my last days at my stream. Oh, well. That's what gloves are for. And these white, open weave gloves seem to be a hit with the burly miners. Of course, the more educated ones know it's too late in the year to be wearing white, but they get their share of attention, too. And I get some of their share of gold.

Yes, the rumor you heard about the gold camps are true. There is a major shortage of women up here. There are a few girls in the saloon tent, but I don't have anything to do with them. Don't need to. And then there are the wives in Sonora. I don't know them, either. They would turn their Eastern noses up at my skirts that I keep two inches short of respectable. Plus, I gave up on wearing corsets. Not much to push up, so why keep pushing?! My friends here don't complain when I might bump against them during a dance they paid for. I have all my teeth and a moderately pretty face. Plus, like I told you earlier, I know how to listen. That's basically all I need.

I've learned never to rest on my laurels. Since I wasn't endowed with too many laurels, I have had to be creative. I learned to know each miner by name and where he came from. Sometimes all they want is a little female attention, someone who thinks what they say is important. Then, drop a hint that you are out of sugar or soap and, voila, you have groceries for the next two weeks. Or find a good family man who misses his wife and kids. You don't need to even touch him on the arm, let alone dance with him. A tear in the eye when he mentions Little Susie getting bigger without him can get you enough dust for "rent" for a month.

It's never boring in this camp town. I was at my claim when a celebrity came through. All anyone could talk about was Mr. Clemens this *and Mr. Clemens that. I didn't do well those evenings when I came in to the El Dorado. That was all forgotten, though, when Big Ted hit a rich vein. I could never do much with Big Ted. He liked the tent girls. Too bad. He could have knocked a year off my stay here. Well, I guess there's no accounting for taste.*

I haven't had any trouble yet. I say 'yet' because there are always new miners coming in and my old friends leaving when their stake runs dry. I guess my air of respectability helps. It's pretty clear I don't go upstairs. And I keep a close account of what I get from whom. Mustn't tap the well too often.

Still, it's not all fun and games as you might be thinking by now. Some of the miners are pretty decent folk. I do well with them. Then there are the others. They're pretty rough characters. They don't take to bathing very kindly, their breath could down a horse, and their beards are downright itchy. It might take me an hour to get a good sized nugget out of them.

Sometimes it's not easy being a gold digger."

Wals put the paper down with a chuckle. He was surprised someone wasn't standing behind him saying, "Gotcha!" The article had mentioned Samuel Clemens, or, Mark Twain as he was more commonly known. As Wals tucked the paper under his arm to leave, he wondered if Clemens could have penned the article himself. Hey, nothing beats a little self-promotion, he acknowledged with a grin.

His chuckling stopped when he began humming the "Darling Clementine" song. It mentioned the miners of 1849—a year after gold was found at Sutter's Mill in Northern California and the start of the California Gold Rush. Frowning as he thought back, he tried to remember something about the Fort. He didn't know the exact date for sure, but Fort Wilderness was supposed to be set around the year 1815 or so. How could this newspaper be mentioning an event that wouldn't happen for another thirty years or so?

Before he could work out the discrepancy, the ground beneath him began to rumble again, just as it had done when he and Mato first came into town. No one else in the saloon seemed to give it any attention, as if it were a common occurrence to them. Jumping to his feet, he rushed through the saloon doors to see the same phantom dust cloud go roaring past him as if a runaway train had just gone screaming through the center of town.

Whispering, "Big Thunder," he stared wide-eyed at the newspaper and wondered what was happening to Time.

CHAPTER TWELVE

The Island – 1817

Doctor Houser fit in as easily at the busy encampment as he had in New Orleans, the Fort and at Rainbow Ridge. Naturally amiable and gregarious, he made friends easily. His looks also made him popular with some of the women who made sure he had plenty to eat and a variety of choices of where to sleep. In an attempt to avoid complications while waiting for the missing security guard to show up, he opted to stay with the Shaman in his tipi and was given a comfortable fur-covered pallet by the fire.

He wondered how they knew he was a medical man when they started coming to him right away with various cuts and ailments. Not knowing the wolf had told the leader his entire story, it was yet another mystery to him.

One more growing mystery was the wolf he had found in camp when Mato and Wals brought him back. He had, of course, heard about the black wolf that guarded the woman in the cabin. Having never personally seen the animal for himself, he hadn't put too much weight in what the soldiers in Fort Wilderness had said about it. At first, the huge animal had terrified him, but he soon saw that everyone else accepted it as if it were a member of the tribe. He could never see any signs of aggression or any activity that would indicate this wolf would have been considered to be a dangerous animal. In fact, he never saw any signs at all of what he thought would be normal wolf behavior.

The longer he observed this wolf, the more baffling it became. Wolf, as he was told was its name, would spend a lot of time with the leader, whom Wals referred to as the Shaman. Off by themselves, he would see them at the rocky overhang with the Shaman appearing to be in deep conversation with the wolf, even stopping as if he was being answered in return. Then, when the doctor would join them, the wolf would get up and quietly leave or just sit back out of the way. He also began to notice the same odd behavior occur with Mato. The man and the wolf would walk off into the forest together, Mato talking and gesturing to the wolf, and then apparently waiting for a response. One day, the doctor attempted to follow them, hoping to unravel this mystery. He hadn't anticipated Wolf's keen hearing. Noisily bumbling after them, the two brothers quickly sensed his attempts to shadow them and they lost him almost immediately in the dense forest.

Looking for an opportunity to have a private moment with Wals and Rose, Claude finally asked them, "Have you noticed anything odd about that wolf? Everyone seems to talk to him. And it always looks as if they expect an answer."

Wals and Rose both just shrugged. "We do that all the time," Rose explained brightly with a grin. "He just seems to be so intelligent and such a good listener. I think he kept me from going mad all alone in that cabin of mine when I had no one to talk to. I wish he could have answered me," she giggled. "That would have been nice—silly as it sounds!"

Not satisfied, Claude just nodded. With all the strange occurrences he had witnessed and had been told about, a talking wolf now seemed to be the least of their worries. Choosing not to pursue the issue right then, he went over to the community fire when he saw one of the braves come limping into camp.

Glad to have someone else to talk to, Wals spent a lot of time in the doctor's company. When he felt like he could trust the man, he asked Claude something that had been bothering him about Rose. "Have you noticed anything particular about Rose's looks?" he asked to broach the subject.

Claude smiled. "You mean other than her stunningly beautiful appearance?"

"Is she?" Wals began, all innocent, and then grinned. "Yeah, besides that…," he broke off, looking self-conscious. "This is going to sound lame, but, does she look at all familiar to you? Like you might have seen her before in a movie…or in a cartoon?"

Claude's eyebrows went up. He wasn't expecting that. "Cartoon? Do you mean does she look like a cartoon character or an actress?"

"Yes. No. I don't know," Wals stammered, running a hand through his messy hair. He let out a gush of air and plunged in. "I had this feeling a while back, looking at her," he broke off at the look on the doctor's face. "Not those kinds of feelings," he protested, and then quickly added, "…well, I did, but that isn't what I mean!" Wals was getting flustered.

"I'm sorry. Go on," Claude said, trying to sound scholarly to put Wals at ease.

"She reminds me of Aurora," Wals dropped his voice. "You know, the Sleeping Beauty princess from the cartoon? With some of the different things she has said and remembered…I've been thinking…it all kinda fits. I showed her my nametag, like I told you, but she didn't recognize it at all. She can't be from Disneyland like I am, but it is also obvious she isn't from here either. All she has talked about in her recollections are moats and castles and drawbridges and a little about seeing her mother who, strangely enough, lived in a castle. Am I nuts?"

"My field is…was…is cryogenics, so I can't tell if you *are* nuts," he answered, keeping his face straight. At the exasperated look on Wals' face, he held up a placating hand. "Sorry, I don't know what to tell you. The animated movie *Sleeping Beauty* came out in the year 1959, just a few years before I came here, so I did see it. Walt was all enthused by the movie, I remember." He broke off and looked away, momentarily saddened as he thought about his boss. Coming back to the present, he asked, "Do you think she could have been the model the animators used to draw the princess?"

Wals thought on that for a moment. He slowly shook his head. "Well, maybe, but I think she might be the real deal, you know, the real princess. But I can't put my finger on it, because she hasn't remembered anything like you or I did in remembering our real lives."

Doctor Houser just stared at him for a moment. "I was going to say, 'How can that be?' However, we have seen a lot of discrepancies in logic lately, haven't we? I honestly don't know." He looked over and saw Rose trying to frolic with the wolf. The wolf was having none of it. Rose put her hands on her hips as if she simply couldn't understand why Wolf didn't want to play. It was obvious to all of them that he would have done so in another place and time. "Look over there, Wals. That just doesn't look too regal to me," he observed with a smile. The little "princess" was clearly upset with the wolf when he turned his back on her and walked away.

Wals watched the same scene with some amusement. "But remember that Briar Rose, as she was known in the forest, did get along with the animals."

"Have you asked her to sing?"

"Okay, now you're mocking me."

Claude laughed. "Well, I didn't mean to, but I guess it did sound like it." He shrugged in a very unscholarly way. "I have no idea, Wals. You said you came here from the year 2007. I do recall that I came here from the year 1966. We were both brought here by a security guard named Wolf who…well, no one has seen since. 'Here' seems to be a replica of Frontierland back at Disneyland. Is she the real Sleeping Beauty? Well, if *any* of this is possible, well, perhaps that also may be. What if she is?"

Wals opened his mouth and left it open, as if not sure what should come out of it. *What if she is?* The words bounced around in his brain. What would happen? Would he lose her when Wolf finally did arrive and take them all back to Disneyland? Did Wolf bring her here in the first place? Was it possible that Wolf drowned in that maelstrom that brought him here?

"More questions than answers," he finally said, and closed his mouth.

When the doctor nodded in agreement, Wals looked over at her again. She had given up on trying to play with Wolf. When she walked back into her tipi, Wals unconsciously muttered the same plea he had said earlier: *Please don't let her go another direction in time!*

Remembering back to some of his lessons in botany, Claude utilized part of his time looking for plants that might come in useful around the camp. The Cooking Woman and the Medicine Woman were already well versed in herbology, but there was always more to learn. Hidden behind the rocky overhang, he was examining the bark of a tree, wondering if it could be used for toothaches when he suddenly heard whom he thought was the Shaman as he began to speak. Another voice, one he had not heard before, answered him in the same language the doctor had made no progress in learning.

One thing Claude had recently learned from his new friends was how to move stealthily in the stick-filled forest. Using this newly-acquired training, he attempted to approach a little closer, keeping behind the rocks that hid him from their view. Listening intently to the two voices as they continued their animated conversation, he heard the Shaman at times sounding somewhat irritated. Peering cautiously around the edge of the rocks, he was stunned to see the Shaman was sitting alone— except for that wolf! Their backs were to his hidden location. The older man continued his speech, the wolf just sitting in attendance silent.

Then, when one of the wolf's ears suddenly cocked backwards, the Shaman quit talking. The wolf's blue eyes looked up at him, shifted slightly, and his father understood that they were not alone. They weren't sure who was listening, but they knew it was not one of their own. To cover what might have been heard, the Shaman changed his voice to a lower register and waved his arms as if describing a fascinating story to the wolf. Then he switched to his own voice again and sent the wolf away with a grand sweep of his hand. Wolf just sat there and let his father walk away himself, pulling his wolf skin tighter around his shoulders to keep them from shaking with laughter. Surreptitiously sniffing the air, Wolf immediately recognized the scent to be that of Doctor Houser who was hiding behind the rocks. He just didn't know why.

Wolf found out soon enough when he left to go watch Rose's cabin again to see if the pirates had returned. He once again could hear Doctor Houser crashing through the brush in an attempt to follow him and wondered who it was that had given him the stealth training he had tried to use when eavesdropping.

Just then the doctor suddenly realized he was alone deep in the forest with a wild animal. Having never been in that possibly precarious situation before, his heart immediately started racing. Trying to regain his composure, Claude began to rethink his master plan. What if the animal didn't recognize him as a friend? What if it could smell fear? He stopped in his tracks when the odd blue eyes swung around to look at him. A tug of memory flitted through his brain of another pair of blue eyes just like those, but vanished before he could put a reassuring hand on the Zippo lighter in his pocket.

Palms out, he advanced slowly towards the wolf. "Hey, there, big fella. Nice wolf. I won't hurt you. Easy there. Don't tear me into tiny pieces," he muttered as he kept walking to the small clearing where Wolf was sitting.

Wolf gave a loud snort as he tried to keep from laughing. He wondered what the doctor had in mind.

When the man reached not-quite-touching distance from the wolf, he squatted down and tried to make himself seem even more non-threatening. He kept up his steam of meaningless words that did more to convey his own nerves than be soothing to the wolf. When the wolf's large head tilted to the side, watching him, his words suddenly stopped. Claude shook his head. "If I ever saw anything that obviously asked 'What?' without a word being spoken, the expression on your face would be it." He laughed nervously and shook his head again. "All right, wolf," he started, licking his dry lips, "I have seen everyone else talk to you, so I might as well do it, too."

Those blue eyes narrowed, and, once again, struck a memory in the doctor. "I know I have seen those eyes before…. Listen, wolf, I need to know what's going on around here. Wals is not the font of information I had hoped he would be. We all seem to be waiting for someone. Someone named…as odd as it may sound…Wolf."

The blue eyes blinked as he lifted his head another inch or so.

"This is stupid," Claude muttered to himself. "This can't be right. And I should still be in 1966," he declared, and decided to go on with what he had planned to say. Forging ahead, he continued, "I want to see if you understand me, to see if you are as intelligent as everyone says you are, all right?" He waited nervously, and then snorted, amazed at himself and what he was doing. "And yet again I await an answer!" He wiped his sweaty palms on the buff-colored miner's pants he still wore. "All right," he started again and spoke real slowly, "Wolf, if you can understand me, make a mark in the dirt with your paw."

The eyes just stared at him until his head swung away, ears flat on his head.

After waiting another moment, Claude softly swore to himself. "Of course not. Of course you won't make a mark for me."

As the doctor was starting to get up, Wolf's head swung back. "Actually, I don't want to get my claws dirty, if you don't mind. They're a real bear to get clean."

Eyes widening and mouth open, the shocked Claude fell back onto his rear in the dirt.

Wolf's mouth opened in a silent laugh. "Sorry, but you did seem to expect it."

"I…I did, but I didn't. How is this possible?"

One silver-tipped shoulder raised in a shrug. "Well, if you ever find out, let me know."

"Wals? And Rose? They don't know?" He hadn't thought to rise from his less-than-dignified position in the dirt yet.

Wolf shook his head. "Too dangerous in this time period. But, when we get back, it won't be a problem then."

"You're going back, too? Why won't it be a problem?"

"I'm hoping you remember the time I told you, that since you were a man of science, you should think of all this as an adventure."

"We met before?" his startled eyes narrowed as he thought back. "I don't remember any wolf… Just…," he broke off with a startled gasp.

"Yeah," was all Wolf replied.

"Did Walt know?" he asked, thinking back to that last night they were all together.

Wolf nodded. "He never saw me like this, but he knew 'something' happened to me when I would make these jumps." Wolf gave a little chuckle. "Walt always wanted to go with me on one of my trips. I'd never let him."

Talking about his boss seemed to settle the doctor. He smiled at the remembrance of Walt's eagerness to try something new and exciting. "Why not? He would have loved it."

"No, never. The disorientation. The possible danger. I would never take that chance with Walt."

Claude thought about his own reaction to the displacement in time—the confusion and the memory loss. "You're probably right. Is he really gone?" he added softly after a moment.

Wolf just nodded.

"I was hoping Wals was wrong," was the sighed response.

"When we get back, I'll take you to see him," the wolf promised, thinking of the chamber below the Pirates ride.

Claude's eyes got big and hopeful. "Really? You can do that?"

Realizing the doctor meant something different, Wolf was about to say no. But, when he thought about his abilities and his own needs, Wolf told him, "Remind me once we are back and you are settled again. You will have a lot of catching up to do. Then I'll see what I can do."

"What else do you know about Walt's…Walt's condition?" He wasn't sure how much Walt had told this mysterious man, if he had been in the inner circle.

"Everything," Wolf assured him. "Wals does not, however, and we need to keep it that way, please. Rose, well, actually I'm still trying to figure her out. I don't know exactly where she fits in with all of this. My father won't tell me what he knows," he added with a disgusted snort. "I just know I was assigned to be her Protector, just as I was with you."

"Your father? Who is your father?"

"The Shaman."

"Of course he is," the doctor muttered, glad he was already sitting down.

Wolf gave his silent laugh. "Like I was saying, once I can get you out of here, Lance, Kimberly, and I will debrief you when we get back."

"Who?"

Wolf got up from his watch of the cabin. The pirates didn't show. He knew they had to be planning something big. "Please try and not worry about it right now. There is a lot you are going to have to deal with." To change the subject, Wolf asked, "Do you remember how we got here? Do you remember the lightning?"

The doctor paled. "Yes."

Starting his way back to the village, Wolf said over his shoulder, "That is what we are waiting for."

"I was afraid you were going to say that."

Practicing the archery skills that he had learned in high school gym class—and hadn't used since—Wals lost yet another arrow behind the rocks where the Shaman told his stories. As the sun got lower in the west, he pushed the bushes this way and that looking for Mato's arrow. Finally finding it, with a shout of victory, Wals turned to go back to the practice ground. The sun was hitting the rocks just right, causing the crystal flakes imbedded in the rock to shimmer like diamonds in the light. He touched the warm surface and was surprised when the solid-looking rock started to move slightly under his fingers. Crouching down, he could barely see the dark outline that forms when dirt or mortar is removed from a setting. Using the tip of the arrow in a way Mato would never approve, he felt around the rock in question. It was tightly wedged and would only move side to side. Somehow knowing there was more to it than that, Wals examined the other rocks nearby. Finding another one higher up that also moved, he found he could pry it out with the arrow. When the new rock fell to the ground, he started to reach inside the small hole. Rising on his tiptoes, his hand kept moving inwards and down. Trying not to think about rattlesnakes or spiders, he concentrated on reaching the first stone in question. When it moved, he exerted more pressure and it, too, popped out of its place. Pulling his arm out, he quickly glanced at it and mentally counted his fingers. Laughing at himself, he now inserted his hand in the new hole. He found that area dropped, too. When his fingers came to a rough cloth with something hard inside, he firmly took hold of the small bundle. His fist was now too large to draw it out of the hole. So, releasing the bundle to just dangle from the tips of his fingers, he was able to pull it out into the waning light. Not sure what he had found, and not sure who else might be nearby, he stuffed it down his shirt and quickly returned the two rocks to their former positions. They settled back into place and he was again unable to wiggle them out of their spots. "Fascinating!" he mumbled and headed for the tipi he was sharing with the unmarried men.

Relieved to find it empty since the others were now around the communal dinner fire, he reached a hand down his shirt and retrieved the bag. The material was similar to that worn by the people in camp and was tied shut with a small piece of twine. Inside, he found a long, heavy metal chain. Pulling it out, he was shocked to find a large heart-shaped red-colored stone in the middle of three familiar-looking gold circles. "Mickey? I found a Hidden Mickey?" He was dumbfounded as he recognized the shape that held the stone in place.

The sun was sending its last rays of light

through the trees before it set for the night. Wals held the pendant into the light that streamed into the tent. He was dazzled by the flashes of color that exploded from the beautiful stone. "Wow. I thought only diamonds did that...." He stopped and held the chain closer to his face to really look at the stone. "This could be a diamond," he reasoned, but such a big one? *Is there even such a thing as a red diamond?*

Not knowing anything about gemstones, he decided this would look splendid around a certain fair neck and smiled in anticipation of her happiness to receive it. With a happy smile, he reached out with his other hand to grab the stone and put it back in the bag.

As soon as his fingers closed over the diamond, his sight clouded and he had the feeling he was somewhere else. The clouds in his mind parted as he saw himself, dressed in some kind of costume at Disneyland. He looked like a prince, dressed in royal blue with a red cape over his shoulders. There was even a feather in his flat hat. The vision pushed him forward, and he was walking into a swirling maelstrom holding some kind of white bird. The swirling continued until a dragon emerged, opening its mouth and coming right at him....

The stone fell onto the dust of the ground as Wals jerked back in fright. The vision immediately stopped and his mind cleared. His heavy breathing continued, though, as he tried to figure out what had just happened to him. Seeing the beautiful heart-shaped stone in the dirt, he swore and bent to pick it up.

Again, his fingers brushed the stone and now

he was dancing…no…he was waltzing with a beautiful blond woman elegantly dressed….

Opening his hand, the pendant fell swaying at the end of the chain still in his grip. "Where did that come from? It seems to be coming from the pendant. That's the only thing different here," he gasped. "It has to be the pendant." He tentatively touched the gold circles that made up Mickey's outline. Nothing happened. He moved the tip of one finger to the cold stone and could immediately feel his mind slipping. Pulling back his finger, breathing hard, Wals slipped the pendant into the protective cloth bag and pulled the twine tight.

"Okay, now what do I do?" he thought, wondering what to do with the now-powerful necklace.

Wals used the quiet days at camp to get to know Rose better. It was obvious to everyone, even to Wals, that she was quite taken with his boyish good looks. Her beauty always captured his attention and would leave him almost speechless.

When none of their apparent skills proved useful around the camp, Wals and Rose had been assigned the low task of helping collect firewood for the ever-burning cooking fire. Working their way inland, away from the River, they found it took longer and longer to return to the encampment. Talking, joking, touching, the time flew by. They eventually found a secluded meadow filled with yellow flowers. After filling her apron with the fragrant blooms, they sat in the shade of a towering pine tree while Rose wove the flowers into garlands. The first would be for her own fair hair. After much protesting, the second would be set on Wals' brown head. She told him it looked "regal." Recalling his thoughts of the Princess Aurora, he kept a mental tally of instances—such as this—that might explain if he was correct in his assumption about her real identity. Besides that, how could he resist any request from such a beautiful woman?

Hand in hand, they finally wandered back towards camp, remembering the wood only when they were almost back and empty-handed. The women of the camp, seeing the looks on the couple's faces, would smile to themselves as they worked. They knew the magic of the woods.

One day while they were out, supposedly looking for more wood, farther north than they usually traipsed, Wals couldn't help but notice that the day had turned particularly warm. He saw Rose as she looked longingly over at the spot where Cascade Peak used to tumble noisily over the rocks. There were still train tracks from the old mine running past the ruins of those falls. Hand in hand, they followed the trail through the trees until it suddenly opened up on a secluded pool of water. The trail ended abruptly and it was obvious there used to be a trestle over that stretch of water. They could still see the tunnel carved into the rocks high above them. Wals hadn't noticed the empty tunnel before when he had taken this same trail with Mato, back when they were searching for the doctor. "This is Bear Country, isn't it?" he asked.

Rose looked around a little sadly. "Yes, it is. We wouldn't have dared come here just a few years ago. There were always bears here either fishing or swimming. That is, when they weren't sleeping. It's such a shame they're all gone now. But it used to be nice." Just then a fish was seen jumping.

He indicated the cool water of the pool with the tilt of his chin. "We're not bears, but do you want to go swimming?"

Rose's eyes lit up. She hadn't been swimming in ages and would love to wash her hair. "Can we?"

Wals surveyed the surrounding area. The pool itself was down inside a small grassy meadow. The ever-present River was a few hundred yards away from them. Once they were down at the lake, there was no chance they would be seen from the far side of the riverbank. They would have complete privacy and security. He started pulling off his worn shirt. Not sure what else he would take off, Rose modestly dropped her eyes until he had entered the cool water. "Come on in!" he called, swimming backwards, wondering what she would really do.

Looking quickly around, she saw no one, not even the pair of sharp blue eyes that were keeping watch from the edge of the forest. She removed her apron and outer dress, leaving on her white chemise. She added her slippers to the neatly folded pile, and then untied the black ribbon holding her hair back from her face.

Wals had expected her to dip a tentative toe in the cool water. He was impressed when she dove straight into the water and swam over to where he was treading water.

"Oh, this feels wonderful!" she exclaimed when she reached him, all smiles, her arm automatically going around his neck to help keep herself afloat.

"When did you learn to swim like that?" he asked, smiling as her legs entwined with his.

A frown quickly crossed her face and was gone. "I don't know. I've always known how to swim, I guess. Do you want to race to the far side?"

He smiled at the eager look in her lovely blue eyes. He was enjoying having her press up against him. He could feel the warmth of her body mixed with the coolness of the glassy water. "No, this is good."

She gave a tinkling laugh and pushed away from him, swimming on her back with slow, lazy strokes, her hair fanning out around her.

He gave a sharp intake of breath at the lovely picture she was forming. Knowing he couldn't keep staring at her like that and keep his sanity, he gulped in some air, dropped underwater and swam until he was right beneath her. Pushing up off the rocky bottom, he surfaced right next to her, grabbing her in his arms.

With a happy shriek, she threw her arms around his neck as he carried her to the grassy bank. The sunlight hit every drop of water beading her face, making her look like she was encrusted with diamonds. Dropping down next to her, Wals started kissing the drops nearest her eyes. She gave a contented purr as his lips continued down her sculpted cheekbones and towards her smiling mouth.

Her hand rested on his arm, strong from his work on the docks. As he pulled closer to Rose, her arm went around him, feeling the hard muscles playing across his damp back. She pulled away from his questing mouth. At his curious look, she asked simply, "Do you mean it?"

Knowing what she was asking and knowing she was serious, he sat up, pulling her up with him. "With all my heart," he whispered. "I can't think of anyone but you. I have something for you. I…I wasn't sure when it would be right to give it to you, but this feels very right."

She watched as he got up and went over to his pile of clothes. He pulled his fringed pants back on over the longjohns he had worn swimming. Picking up all their clothes, he brought them back to Rose. Overcome by déjà vu as he reached inside his shirt and pulled out the cloth satchel that held the red diamond pendant, Wals had a succinct feeling of fate—like he was supposed to follow this grand act of love. Carefully hanging it off of his finger by its gold chain, the pendant slowly turned in the sunlight, red fire shooting out over them. It was brilliant in the bright light.

Rose gasped. "I can't wear that! It's too precious!"

He smiled. Her lips said she couldn't take it, but her eyes were flashing with delight. "You must wear it," he told her. "Think of this Hidden Mickey as my heart that you already possess."

Rose dimpled. "What's a Hidden Mickey?"

He showed her the three iconic circles that made up the back of the pendant. He could tell she didn't recognize the outline of Mickey Mouse. Wals kissed her neck. "Take my gift. It's a powerful heart," he suddenly told her, wondering in the back of his mind if he should really give it to her with its special, mysterious ability. He laughed at her skeptical look. "It's true!" he exclaimed. "I'll bet it's from Merlin's own treasure."

Rose reached out to touch the turning heart. "Powerful, huh? What does it do?"

Pulling it away from her reaching fingertips, and still wondering about the visions he had had, he told her, "It shows you things. Are you sure you want to see it?"

Her beautiful lips smiled. "What do you mean? Like my future? If I can see you in it, then, yes, I do!"

Wals settled the golden chain around her neck. Before she had a chance to touch the gemstone, before Wals could kiss her again, a black blur suddenly came between them. Wolf roughly pushed Wals out of the way. He stared at the diamond, its color stark against the white of her chemise. He looked back at Wals who was irritated at the interruption, even if it was just the wolf.

When the wolf looked back at the pendant and then at Wals again, it was obvious he was demanding an explanation. "Alright, alright, nosey. I found it in a hidden cave behind the rocks where the Shaman tells his stories." At that, both Rose and the wolf looked at him with a demanding, inquisitive look and Wals knew he had better continue with the explanation. "I was retrieving an arrow and saw something that didn't look quite right. Moving some of the stones away, I found this. I'm not sure why it looks like Mickey," he mumbled more to himself, "but the pendant looked as if it had been hidden there for a long time. I left some of the gold I found in the cave in its place. Rose, why am I explaining myself to a wolf?" he asked as he turned from Wolf's inquisitive face to Rose's.

"Oh, I do that all the time. I still think he should answer me," she replied with her own smile. "What gold did you find in the caves? You've never mentioned finding gold in there," Rose asked, momentarily forgetting the priceless diamond hanging around her neck.

Again the wolf turned to him, silently demanding him to continue. Wondering about the odd look on the wolf's face, Wals continued his explanation. "It was after I found Fort Wilderness was closed. As I was riding back to your cabin, the mare seemed too interested in the cave. When I went in to investigate the noises I heard, I ran into—literally," he grinned over at her, "a large chest. I got it opened and found a bunch of old clothes, two goblets—one was gold and the other was silver—the gold one covered with all different color gems, and then below that I saw layers and layers of gold coins. I grabbed up a handful of the coins and left everything else. When we all went back later, the chest was right where I had last seen it." He shrugged when he finished talking. The wolf looked as if he was processing the information. Rose was fingering the heavy gold chain, her attention back on the jewelry. She wasn't interested in anything that had to do with the pirates that forced her from her home.

"Tell me, Wals, how do you know this pendant is from Merlin's treasure?" asked Rose, her curiosity piqued. "Did you hear the rumor?"

Now it was Wals' turn to be confused. "What rumor? You've heard of this? I thought...." He broke off. He didn't want to admit that he was just making it up as he went along to impress her.

Rose didn't seem to notice his unfinished sentence. She lifted the diamond by its chain off of her breast, holding it out and staring at it as the facets flashed colors of the rainbow in every direction. She seemed mesmerized. "I heard a long time ago that Merlin had made a mysterious pendant for Nimue, the woman he loved. She learned all his tricks from him and then refused his love. The fable was that she entombed him in a tree for all eternity.

The pendant was said to have vanished."

"How do you know this?"

Coming out of her daze, Rose looked away, unsure. "I…I don't know. It all seems familiar some how. Even your beautiful words. They seemed familiar to me, as well."

Wolf shook his head. *It can't be. It hasn't happened yet. Has it?*

Wals put his hand gently up to the side of her face. She leaned into the warmth. "Well, wherever the pendant came from, however it came to be in the rocks, it belongs to you now. I did mean my words. Wherever they came from," he added with a smile. "You will always have my heart." He pulled her close for a long, lingering kiss to seal his promise.

When she finally, reluctantly, broke the embrace, she asked if she should touch the red diamond to see if its power worked on her. It was obvious she didn't believe the tale—Merlin or not. Wolf came to stand next to her, wishing he could take it from her and spare her whatever it might show.

"If you want to," Wals replied. He didn't tell her what he had seen in his own mind. He was still trying to figure out the meaning of it. "I'm right here. Go ahead."

"Do I have to hold it or do something special?"

"Yeah, you have to hold out your right arm, turn in three circles, say 'Miska, Mooska, Mouska'…," he broke off and started laughing. "Sorry, couldn't help myself," when he saw her right arm extend. "No, no, no, you don't really have to do that. I was just kidding," he exclaimed when the wolf growled low in his throat. "You just have to touch the gemstone itself. That's all I did."

Wolf moved over closer to Rose again. Somehow, some way, if she seemed disturbed, he would knock the diamond from her grasp. It seemed to him that Wals figured this was nothing more than a cute parlor trick.

Rose again picked up the pendant, but this time by the circles in the back. She let out a short scream and dropped it.

At Wals' startled look, she smiled coyly. "My turn!" She laughed at the expression on his face and waved him off. "You deserved it!"

Settling back on the grass, she put a tentative finger on the bright red faceted surface. She was instantly transported…but where? She saw herself swimming in a moat, her feet webbed and orange, a mask of black across her face. In another instant, she was dressed in a blue ball gown. No, it was pink, and waltzing with a red-caped prince. He was very handsome and looked a lot like Wals! The ballroom faded into a cloud of angry smoke and a huge black dragon screamed at her, blowing fire….

Her hand dropped from the stone on its own. The smoke vanished from her mind and Wals' intent face was close by, anxious. "Did you see that?" she muttered, shook by the specter.

"Are you all right? You went pale," he told her, gently touching her face.

Glancing around at the two anxious faces in front of her, she gave a weak smile. "Yes, I am fine. Whoever heard of a fire-breathing dragon! What a funny trick," but she didn't look very amused. Before Wals could question her further, she stated that she really needed to get back to the camp. The sun was getting lower and Wals could now see that she was starting to shiver. She just wasn't sure if it was from the change in temperature or from the vision.

Seeing Rose was acting more like her usual self, Wals relaxed. Then, as he noticed her shivering, he offered, "I can keep you warm," with a sly grin as she pulled on her worn lavender skirt over her chemise that had already dried.

She turned away from his eyes to lace up the black bodice of her vest. Her heart pounded. But not from the pendant this time. She knew what he was offering. "Do you promise?" she whispered breathlessly, almost too low for him to hear.

"Yes," he whispered back.

"Tonight?" she asked, shyly, her back still turned.

Wals heart started its own pounding. When she turned around, her face averted, her cheeks were tinted a delicate shade of pink. He gently lifted her chin with his fingertips so he could see her lovely eyes to see if she really meant it. "Yes," he whispered, touching his forehead to hers.

Arm in arm, the happy couple walked slowly along the trail on their way back to the Pinewood's encampment. Wolf trotted ahead of them deep in thought. He knew the Shaman thought the pendant was still in a safe hiding place, but the now the missing pendant had been found. He also needed to tell his father about the treasure Wals had left behind in the cave.

"**W**e have no need of gold or trinkets," the Shaman had told him stiffly. "Others lust and kill for those things. They are of no value to us."

"I know that," Wolf nodded. "But life is more complicated in the other places. That gold and those trinkets are thought to make life easier."

"Easy enough to kill for?" The dark eyes regarded his son closely. Wolf had tried to describe his other life, but things such as cars, television, and even Disneyland had no meaning and certainly no interest here. These people proudly lived off the land. Everything they needed was right here. And sometimes the land offered them special items like the feathered hats and fancy wear that had washed ashore from time to time. Even then, the odd items had been shared. No one would dream of harming another for such things.

Wolf sighed. He, on the other hand, understood having to work for a living in his other time. There was no land to live off of in the middle of a sprawling city. "No," he finally replied, "it is for a certainty not worth killing for. I just wanted you to be aware of what was in the cave and where it was located. If the pirates find some of the coins and a sword missing, they will come looking for them."

The Shaman snorted. "They should understand the gesture. Someone stole what they themselves had stolen."

The wolf opened his mouth to grin. "I doubt they will see it that way."

"It matters not what they think. Things have a way of getting back to their rightful owners, like the red gem around the wiya's neck."

Wolf looked closely at him. "Will you explain that, or are you getting all mysterious on me again?"

His father's face broke into a wide grin. "I am the Shaman. I am supposed to be mysterious."

With that, he turned his back to the wolf and

strode majestically back into the camp, his face again a mask of seriousness. Wolf looked after him, amused. His father never failed to amaze him.

Rose had balked at staying hidden in the tipi for days on end, only being allowed to venture out at night or on wood-gathering expeditions deep into the forest with the entranced Wals. With her lavender shawl covering her tell-tale blond hair, Rose attempted to help the Cooking Woman at the community fire. It wasn't very successful, but the amused Cooking Woman appreciated both her efforts and the opportunity to get to know the mysterious wiya from across the River who was being protected by Wolf. The efforts to communicate were getting nowhere, but they had still formed an easy friendship.

As the days slowly progressed, the four companions were getting edgy. Only Wolf and the doctor knew exactly what they were waiting for. Not being able to communicate very well with the Pinewoods, Wals and the doctor continued to do what they could to help around camp, not wanting to venture too far away from Rose. Both men now had a vivid memory of the whirlpool that had brought them here and sincerely hoped that it was not their only option. If Rose had any memory of her arrival here in this time, she never spoke of it. She just knew they were waiting for "something" and that Claude was *really* not looking forward to it.

On the fifth day, Wolf got the familiar tingling along his spine. Wals was next to him when he lifted his head and sniffed the air.

"I wouldn't do that with all those ducks floating by!" Wals kidded. As soon as the words left his mouth, he got the strangest sense of déjà vu. Frowning, he looked at Wolf and remembered saying that same expression to a different Wolf in a different time. He shivered in the growing cold. "Wolf?" he questioned under his breath.

Wolf turned and looked expectantly at him, tilting his head.

"I never did ask how you came to have my nametag and the doctor's lighter tied around your neck, did I?" His eyes were growing a little wide.

Wolf looked back at the coming fog. It was going to be tonight. *Finally.* Wolf whined softly and lifted his head towards the storm that was rapidly approaching.

Wals broke out of his confusing thoughts and saw the coming fog bank. It looked just like it had at Disneyland that night. "Is this it? Is this what we are waiting for?"

Wolf walked over to the stack of canoes and put his paw on one of them.

"Oh crap," Wals muttered. "I was afraid you would say that. We need to talk, buddy."

Wolf's sharp hearing picked up something else. Though it was muffled by the fog, he could distinctly hear a couple of boats approaching from the direction of the Fort, their oars splashing noisily the water. He knew the boats were not theirs. He gave a low short bark and howl. He was immediately joined by Mato and his father. They looked over in the direction the wolf indicated, listening intently. Wals still hadn't heard the noise and was confused by the sudden interest in the foggy River.

After a brief conference in which the wolf

seemed to play a large part, the two men took a canoe off the stack and placed it securely on the River's edge. Wolf ran to the back of the camp and returned dragging a protesting Rose with him. When he released her, Rose just stood there next to Wals, anxiously clutching his hand. Doctor Houser heard the ruckus and came in from the forest to join the others. Giving a shrug at her questioning look, he too wondered what was going on. They could only silently watch as three more canoes were placed in the water that became more and more agitated as the time quickly passed. Mato and his men, armed with spears and bows and arrows, quickly jumped into their canoes and started paddling towards the sounds of the approaching boats that now even Wals was beginning to hear.

"It's the pirates!" Wals unnecessarily yelled over the noise, immediately wishing he hadn't when he saw the fear jump into Rose's eyes. He tried to give her a reassuring squeeze of the hand.

Mato was going to try and head off the pirates in order to allow Wolf and the others the time they needed to get away safely. The Shaman hurried to the back tipi, briefly disappearing inside, emerging again with Wals' elaborate sword from the cave and the doctor's black medicine bag.

Wolf now pushed Rose to the only remaining canoe, Wals and Claude following. "Can you paddle?" Wals asked her, handing her an oar. She gave a fearful glance at the departing braves' canoes that were now being swallowed up in the fog. The pirates could barely see Mato and the other braves coming towards them, knowing there was no longer any need for secrecy and quiet. Just then, they let out blood-curdling yells and curses as all the vessels neared each other at far too fast a pace.

Nodding in response to Wals' question, the frightened, yet determined Rose muttered, "Yes, but I would rather have my musket," and climbed unsteadily to the front seat with Doctor Houser right behind her. Wolf jumped in the middle of the wobbling canoe as the Shaman gave some parting words to his son and handed the tarnished sword and the medical bag to Wals with a curt nod, saying, "Doka."

When they were shoved far enough out into the water, Wals dug in deeply with his oar, paddling as hard and as fast as he could. With growing trepidation, he steered the canoe directly towards the densest part of the fog that was now starting to swirl over the green water, away from the conflict on the river behind them. Over the roar of the wind that just as suddenly sprang up, they could hear shots being fired as a first bolt of lightning lit up the sky. When Wals turned to look back at the battle, Wolf yelled at him, "Paddle, Wals, paddle like you did before! Go!"

With a look of panic and recognition, Wals' head jerked back around to stare at the wolf for a long moment and then he applied himself to his job. He aimed straight for the black water and could see the odd pink sparkles starting to fall from the heaving sky.

Trying to paddle, sweeping more water into the canoe and onto Wolf, Rose let out a terrified scream as a jagged streak of lightning hit the water and came straight at them.

Daniel Crain, in the middle of the lead boat, was waving his sword and urging the pirates to row even faster. Ignoring him, the men did what pirates were supposed to do and pulled out their own swords and knives when the yells of the braves got louder and closer.

When the first arrow flew past his head, Daniel gave a frightened yell and dropped to the bottom of the boat. His shipmates, on seeing that he had deserted his post, started cursing him, shouting at him to get up and fight like a man. As he attempted to regain his composure, they called him a coward and one of them angrily cuffed him in the head.

"Yeah, but I'm a living coward," he muttered under his breath just as another arrow found its target and lodged in the neck of the one who had hit him.

Knowing it was not going as well as he had promised the men it would, he realized he would probably be the next target if he stayed in the boat. Daniel moved to the edge of his boat and was just about to throw himself into the water. With wide eyes, he saw it as it was flying through the air—just like in that nightmare he had had on Tom Sawyer's Island…. With sudden mental clarity, his previous life came rushing to his jumbled mind. That conniving niece of his, Kimberly, she had been the cause of all his problems! And that playboy Lance. He should have hit him harder with that rock…. All this swept through his mind as that flaming arrow arched over the bow of the little boat and headed right at him. Jerking to the side, the arrow just missed its target and lodged into the bottom of the boat, setting it on fire. Flinging himself over the side, the water immediately engulfed him. Not caring about the screams coming from his shipmates dealing with their burning transport, Daniel saw, way up in front of him on the River, the swirling nightmare that he now remembered as the maelstrom that had brought him here to this wretched place.

Ignoring the calls and curses from his mates who were in a pitched battle with the braves, he swam as fast as he could. That had to be the way home! He could now clearly see a canoe heading directly into that whirlpool and the blond head in front, paddling for her life.

"Kimberly!" he spat out. Using hatred to propel him, he was struggling but kept swimming in the choppy water. He was getting closer and closer, spitting out water as he went under, but never losing sight of that canoe.

Just then, the lightning struck the water and he saw the canoe disappear. With a loud, "No!" he continued his frantic push towards the bright light with all his remaining strength. The canoe vanished, but the lightning didn't stop. It seemed to turn and bend and, suddenly, it struck right in front of him. Now terrified, Daniel rethought his actions and tried, just as frantically, to turn back, to get away from the yawning bowels of Hades.

Still fighting the current, he managed to turn around, his arms flailing as he tried to get to the shore of the Island. His eyes wide with fright, Daniel saw the bow of a canoe come out of the smoke and fog. Hoping it was his friends coming to rescue him, he yelled. "Over here! Help!" The words died on his lips when he realized it was Mato's face that materialized out of the mist. Daniel saw the arrow notched in Mato's bow and knew it was pointed straight at his heart. He then saw the fingers holding the notched shaft of the arrow release.

That was his last observation when the lightning hit him with a direct, blinding flash.

CHAPTER THIRTEEN

Disneyland – 2008

A small canoe was half submerged under the low-hanging branches reaching out over the slow-moving Rivers of America in Frontierland. One broken paddle bobbed quietly in the mist-shrouded green water. Wals had once again awakened near the rocks of Keel Boat Rapids and managed to pull himself up onto the clearing in front of Rose's cabin. Clutching the other paddle in a white-knuckled death grip, Wals struggled to regain his equilibrium and tried get to his feet. Head swirling, he dropped back to the ground and could only lie there, staring at the familiar scene. The split-rail fence zig-zagged over the yard. The brown mare stood in her paddock. A few barrels were standing next to the open front door. Some laundry was pinned to the sagging clothesline. The body of Uncle Jed was bent backwards over the fence, an arrow piercing his heart. But there was no smoke rising from the chimney on the side of the little log cabin. It all looked so *small* to him. "Rose?" he tried to call out, only able to squeeze a croak out of his dry throat. He remembered hearing screams and wondered if had been him. He stared at the horse. Sukawaka hadn't moved all the time he had laid there. He closed his eyes again, trying to stop the spinning in his mind. *It's not real,* his mind told him, his heart suddenly pounding in his chest. *It's supposed to be real!*

"Wals? Wake up. Are you all right, man?"

At the familiar voice, Wals opened his eyes a slit. *Had he fallen asleep?* His eyes first saw the tarnished sword besides him. He weakly reached out and touched the engraving. *Why are my initials on it?* He couldn't remember. He then realized Dr. Houser was bending over him, an anxious look on his dripping face. The doctor's wide eyes betrayed how shook he himself was, but he was still trying to help his friend who had been unconscious. The black medical bag was over to the right, apparently forgotten in the confusion they had just experienced. Neither man knew what to tell the other. Were they all right? At this point they couldn't have said.

A loud groan broke the uneasy silence. Wolf was sitting next to them on the grassy clearing. A naked Mani Wolford whose right thigh was wrapped in a soaked bandage.

"Why are you always naked on Tom Sawyer's Island?" Wals managed to ask in a voice that was finally starting to clear. His eyes drifted to the odd white hair in the middle of Wolf's muscular chest. Not wanting to put the obvious two and two together, he shut his eyes again. Maybe there would be clarity in the darkness. "Where is Rose? Did she make it through that inferno? And what happened to the wolf? Where did he go?"

Wolf was kneading his aching leg. "I can't find Rose," Wolf admitted. "I've gone over as much of the River as I could. I'm not sure where she went."

Dr. Houser stood on shaky legs and walked over to the edge of the River. His first thought was how small it all seemed. He noticed a lump of what might have been a lavender dress submerged near the rocks. In a panic, thinking it may have been Rose trapped under the water, he splashed out to help, only to find it was just the dress along with her white chemise. Dazed, he could only stare at the clothes, unsure what to do or say to the others.

Wals, not yet noticing what Claude had found, struggled into a sitting position, his eyes wide. Momentarily forgetting the necessity to locate Rose, he stared at his friend Mani. "The wolf," he muttered. "You didn't mention finding the wolf." His heart started pounding again as he stared at Wolf's intense blue eyes. "Your leg is hurt...that white hair...." He was starting to get freaked out. His head shook side to side. "No, this can't be. This kinda stuff doesn't happen in real life." He wanted to back away, but didn't have the strength to even stand up. Unconsciously, his fingers closed around the hilt of the sword. "Tell me it isn't what I think it is."

Looking down at his leg, Wolf could see some blood seeping through the dirty, soaked bandage. *How am I going to explain this to First Aid?* He had hoped Wals would have figured it all out before they came back like the doctor did and they wouldn't have to go through this now. No such luck. He looked in the direction of the Friendly Village, unseen through the dense trees. He didn't want to lose his best friend. He gave a silent sigh. *What happens happens.* He kept his eyes on his leg. "Yeah, I'm afraid it is what you think," he answered quietly. "I am a wolf in that alternate time."

"Dang," Wals exclaimed more to himself. "How…when…how is that possible?"

At the sound of their voices, the doctor dropped the dress in a wet pile near his medical bag. His eyes went to Wolf when he heard the admission. Seeing the blood seeping through the dirty bandage, he silently went over to check the wound. Knowing the mental confusion Wals was going through right now, he remained quiet and just examined the bullet hole. Other than reopening somehow in the whirlpool, it looked like it was healing well enough. There were no red streaks indicating infection. He nodded to Wolf when he was done and sat back on the ground, his head resting on his folded arms.

"I have never fully understood it fully myself," Wolf admitted. "My father the Shaman…."

Wals' eyes got even bigger. "The Shaman?" he interrupted, "from the Pinewood encampment? That's your father?" Wals pointed in the direction of the Village. "The one that's standing right over there? How could…I don't understand any of this."

Wolf got up and was hurt that Wals leaned away from him and, whether unconsciously or in real fear, brought the sword closer to his body. He silently limped over to his hidden security uniform and reluctantly started dressing. He preferred the freedom from clothes that being a wolf provided.

When he came back to where Wals was still sitting in stunned silence, Wolf could tell Wals had relaxed a little once he was in his familiar uniform. He sat back down on the grass of the clearing a little further away from Wals and waited. Wolf's eyes were still searching the far riverbank for signs of Rose.

Wals broke the silence. He was trying to work his head around the fact that his best friend was also a wolf. "So, does this mean you have some kind of super powers or something?"

Wolf managed to grin a little at that. "You mean like being able to jump over buildings with a single bound?"

"Well, you obviously aren't faster than a speeding bullet," the doctor was able to kid.

Wolf rubbed his leg again. "No kidding. No, I am just your ordinary run-of-the-mill wolf who can talk. I seem to be affected more in this form with better eyesight and hearing. And a sense of smell that usually drives me nuts."

"Wait, wait a minute," Wals broke in, holding up a hand. "You could talk? Then that wasn't just my imagination when the canoe hit the wall? Why the heck didn't you just talk to me and tell me what the heck was going on??"

"Oops," Claude muttered, sheepishly looking away.

"You knew!?" Wals turned on him, stunned. "You were only there, like, what? Four hours.... Okay, it was a couple of days.... At least I think it was a couple of days...," he broke off, getting confused again trying to figure out the real passage of time.

Breaking into Wals' ranting, Wolf looked at him steadily. "Do you really think you could have handled it with all the other stuff you were dealing with?

The Island in that time period has the habit of sapping memories. Even I am affected and I have made the transition more times than I care to remember. How do you think you would have reacted to a talking wolf who told you he was your best friend?"

Wals opened his mouth to answer and then shut it. How would he have reacted? He had been so immersed in that life it was as if it were his own, where he was supposed to be. He had forgotten everything and everyone he had ever known. "I don't know. Probably not well," he finally admitted.

Wolf nodded his agreement. "That's what I figured, and why I remained silent." With a one-shoulder shrug Wals remembered the wolf giving him more than once, Wolf added, "We did all right the way it was. Rose never knew either. I only told the doctor here because he specifically asked, and it was the right time for him to know."

Wals got shakily to his feet and went to the River's edge. It was very early in the morning, obviously before Disneyland opened from the lack of human noise. They could hear the peaceful birdsong coming from the trees. If he hadn't figured out the brown mare wasn't real, he would have thought he was still in the other time…or reality…or universe…. He put a hand on his forehead. "So, this isn't Rose's cabin, but it's the old Settler's Cabin, right?" He was getting a throbbing headache trying to figure it all out. "So, where is she? We need to find Rose, Wolf. She has to be here, right? The four of us came through that…that…whatever it was together this time. Rose!" he called again. Remembering his thoughts that she might have come from a different reality than theirs made him panic again. When he saw her dress in a heap next to Claude's medical bag, his heart began pounding. *Where did Rose go?*

Just as he called her name again, they all heard a soft whistling sound coming from the direction of the little dock. A mallard duck and a white swan came swimming out of the reeds and marsh grass growing on the riverbank. The duck appeared to be startled and was trying to get away from the swan. Finally the mallard took to flight and disappeared over the trees behind the log cabin. The huge white swan started flapping her wings as if she was trying to follow, but had to settle back in the water.

Turning from the swan and the duck that was long gone, Wals recalled that there were two swans that swam around the moat in front of the Castle in Fantasyland and just figured it had somehow gotten out of its pen backstage. And ducks...well, they lived all over Disneyland near the numerous waterways.

This time, however, when he called Rose's name again, the swan let out an angry hiss and came charging up the clearing right at Wals. Wolf's eyes narrowed, wondering if what he was thinking could really be. Wals, on the other hand, knowing the nasty temperament of the swans at the Castle, backed away from it, keeping a wary eye on the advancing bird.

"Should we swim out to the other riverbank? Maybe she is out there and hurt? This river seems so much narrower than the other...."

Wolf didn't comment on Wals' suggestion. On the alert now, he was intently watching this swan in front of them. "Just call her name again, Wals. See what happens."

Wals cupped his hands around his mouth and hollered, "Rose! Can you hear me?"

The swan ran up to Wals and nipped him on the leg, flapping her wings full width and hissing.

Not understanding and letting out a loud, "Ouch!" Wals angrily tried to shoo her away. The eighty-inch wingspan slowly lowered as her tall head sagged. With a dejected, hurt air, the swan waddled over to Wolf, who had now bent down to the swan's eye-level. "Rose?" he whispered, reaching out to the beautiful face masked in black. He gently lifted the face to his eye level. "It's Wolf, Rose. I'm Wolf."

Looking deep into his blue eyes, the swan shivered in excitement, allowing his hand to caress her. Dazed and confused, she had been swimming around all morning with the ducks trying to communicate with the stupid creatures. When she had finally heard Wals' voice calling her and swam right up to him, she couldn't understand why he didn't know it was her. But Wolf! This was her wolf! She didn't know why he was a man now, but she knew this was her Wolf.

Claude and Wals just stared open-mouthed at the two of them. Their eyes went from one to the other and back again. Wals sat down heavily on the ground when he heard Wolf mutter to the swan, "Now I understand her aura." Wolf looked over at Wals' pale face, his hand still cradling Rose's small head. "My father had assigned me to protect her. Now I know why. She was never meant for that time. She must have accidentally been swimming in this part of the River when I called a storm. Apparently she is like me!" Smiling, he looked at Wals as if that explained everything. Well, it did—for him.

"Is that possible, Wolf?" asked the doctor, getting more and more amazed as this incredible adventure of his continued.

Wals was still stunned. "Rose?" he questioned.

The swan turned from Wolf and looked at Wals at hearing her name. She seemed reluctant to leave Wolf's side.

"Can she talk?" Wals asked Wolf.

Rose answered by shaking her head and giving a loud grunt.

"Apparently not," Wolf smiled. "She seems to know what is going on, though."

Wals wasn't too sure. "How can you tell?"

"Can't you see that she is communicating with us the same way I did with you?"

"But you could talk. You told me," Wals pointed out.

On hearing that, the swan turned back to Wolf and angrily shook her wings at him, hissing and grunting again.

"Sorry," Wolf told her, with a half smile, "it was better that I wasn't known as a talking wolf at that period in time." The amusement left his eyes. "You remember what happened to the other wolf at the Fort," he reminded her quietly.

Rose closed her eyes and leaned her elegant neck towards Wolf, resting her face against his leg. She shuddered, remembering all too clearly the hide viciously tacked to the wall of Fort Wilderness.

As Wals watched the white head of the swan lean into Wolf, he couldn't help but remember the beautiful blond-headed Rose leaning against his chest. At first it was for comfort. Then later, it was for love. How could she not be human? It had all been so real. Their feelings had been real. He had begun to imagine a future with her by his side. And now, here she is a swan and their companion who had been a wolf was a man now. And the doctor was…well, he was still a doctor apparently. Wals just stopped talking as his head dropped into his hands. This was all too much to take in.

Wolf saw the gesture and thought he understood. He had always wondered if Rose had been meant for him since he was to be her Protector. But now, with him in human form and she a swan, he knew they would never be. He could see that Wals, too, was struggling with these same emotions. He, Wolf, hadn't been prepared for this outcome. His father tried to warn him. He could see that now. But, Wals…Wals wasn't prepared for *any* of this.

"Wals, remember when Rose saw your cast member nametag? All she recognized was the Castle."

Wals' head came up. The emotion in his eyes slowly cleared as he looked at his friend and gave thought to what at one time had been the love of his life. "Yes? Is this the reason why?" he sadly indicated the beautiful white swan. "Because she was supposed to be swimming in Swan Lake all day in front of Sleeping Beauty's Castle? Is that why she came up with the name Aurora?"

They were both surprised when Rose started flapping her wings at them, making hissing and grunting noises. She was obviously telling them both off. Wals fell back, stunned at her outburst.

"Oooh, I don't think she liked that," Claude muttered, backing away from the fury of the wings.

Wolf put a calming hand on her back once her

wings came to rest. She looked up at him with her blue eyes. "Well, that is partially true, Wals. I think, and I hope she will tell me if I am right, is that there has to be another portal. Rose Aurora, as we knew her before, must have been caught in a vortex at some point in time and transferred to the moat in Fantasyland as we see her now. Maybe that portal brought her from another castle in another time. One that is very familiar to her and probably looks an awful lot like the one we know in the middle of the Park."

Wolf was interrupted by a flurry of movement from Rose. She was excited and shivering all over. Wings outstretched, she dipped her head up and down and started running towards the water.

Wolf stopped her before she could swim in the direction of Fantasyland. "Rose, I take it that means 'Yes'?"

Rose calmed down, but still shivered. She nodded again.

Wals sat in silence as he watched the two of them attempting to work it out. Neither he nor the doctor could come up with anything to add to their conversation. They could only watch.

Wolf smiled at her. "All right, Rose. I understand. Do you know exactly where that portal was? Do you remember where you emerged from the exit point when you came here?"

Her beak began to open and then closed as her head sank in dejection. She couldn't remember. It was too long ago.

"Ok, don't worry. We will continue to work on it until we figure it all out." Wolf said after putting a calming hand on her. Looking over at the silent Wals, he added, "Wals, I think Disneyland is going to open to the public soon. We need to find out what day it is and how much time has passed for us here. We also need to get Rose back to the moat. And," he added with a nod to Dr. Houser, "We need to get you settled and up-to-date."

Now that they were all more calm and thinking rationally again, Claude spoke up. "I want to see…." He broke off, quickly glancing at Wals. He had almost said "Walt." "I need to check on something before I leave the Park," he amended to Wolf.

When Rose began protesting the plan of her going back to the moat, Wolf once again tried to calm her. "Just a minute, Rose." He answered the doctor first, "Yes, I remember, Doctor. And, Rose, it won't be forever. I promise. Wals and I need time to figure this all out and plan what to do next. You just need to do what you did before. You know— just try to act normally as a swan. We will come and visit you every day and let you know what is going on. Deal?"

They could tell she didn't like it, but reluctantly agreed. She looked at Wals and hissed.

He looked confused and shrugged at Wolf.

Wolf smiled at him. "She wants your promise, Wals. She hasn't forgotten the Island either," he added quietly.

When Rose waddled over to him, Wals held out his hand to her. She nipped him lightly on his fingertips. "I promise," he told her. His heart started pounding again. "I believe it is my destiny." He gave a ghost of a smile. "You never asked me my middle name, Rose. Remember Walter P. Davis?"

She nodded once, tilting her head.

"The P stands for Phillip."

"Well, that would explain a lot," Wolf frowned,

muttering to himself.

He was about to turn to Dr. Houser to take him backstage when he heard a startled gasp from Wals. "What is it? Is there something else wrong?" even though he couldn't imagine what else could possibly go wrong. Everything already had.

He was wrong.

"Wolf, is this still 2007?" Wals, wide-eyed, wanted to know.

"Without checking the calendar, I can't know for sure, but I think it is. Or pretty close. The cabin looks just like it did when we left. The eagle's nest was a recent addition."

"Why do you ask, Wals?" Claude asked. "You look like you've seen a ghost—which would be par for the course with all that's been going on," he added in an undertone.

"Wolf," he went on, ignoring the doctor's sarcasm, "didn't they take Uncle Jed away from the cabin years ago, even before the flames were put out? If we came back around the same time as we left, why is he back in position on the fence?"

Wolf's head jerked towards the figure bent backwards over the rail. For years and years "Uncle Jed" had been part of the Burning Cabin scene. The story was that he had been shot with an arrow by the same ones who had set his cabin on fire. Some of the Keel Boat pilots made him a regular part of their spiel: "I need to stop by a little cabin just around this bend to say howdy to my Uncle Jed. Oh, no! Seems someone gave him a house-warming party. That's Uncle Jed there on the fence in his pierced Arrow shirt and his Levi Bend-Over jeans!" Then, as the years passed, the decorations of the set changed and it wasn't politically correct to have a murdered man entertaining the guests. Uncle Jed was quietly removed and remained only in memories and a few old postcards.

All of Wolf's senses came alert. So, that's what that was. He knew it was a scent that didn't belong, but he just couldn't place the smell of Death. Before he had discovered what had happened to her, he had been afraid it was Rose. But, she was...well, not fine, but alive. He motioned the doctor to grab his bag. "You might need that," he murmured as he strode over to the fence. "Rose, stay back," he commanded.

Even before they reached the figure, they knew who it was. They all muttered almost in unison, "Daniel Crain."

The doctor felt the carotid artery in Daniel's neck, checking for a pulse. "I don't think I am going to need my bag. And that arrow is going to be difficult to explain to the coroner," he muttered as if it was an afterthought as the three men stared at the remains of Crain.

Wals looked over at his friend. "How in the world could he have gotten here? Last I saw, he was fighting alongside the other pirates. I thought I saw the whirlpool close in on us as soon as our canoe went in."

Wolf shook his head. "I thought so, too, but, I wasn't really paying attention to Crain since we were all a little occupied at the time. What I do know is that's my brother Mato's arrow. Look there at the markings on the shaft...and look at the feathers." He shook his head as he looked at the body. "The only explanation I can think of is that Crain saw us leaving, got his own memory back, and then got stuck in the vortex. My brother must have seen him. Mato's good…real good. He must have taken a shot just as Crain was closing in on us. Mato never misses."

"Well, I can certainly attest to that. Mato saved my hide once…. Too bad your brother isn't here to clean up his mess," Wals stated, glaring at Crain with his hands on his hips. "What do we do with him now? I can picture a lot of unpleasant questions in an unpleasant place."

"Can you take him back?" The question from Doctor Houser made them all stare at him. "Well, it would certainly solve a huge problem for us, wouldn't it?" he hurriedly explained, waving his arm in the general direction of the still figure of Daniel Crain. "From what you told me about him, this man has been gone from this time period for a long time. Whatever had happened to him has probably already been dealt with. Am I right?"

Wolf groaned. *I don't need this right now.* "Yes, I suppose you are right," he admitted reluctantly. "I hate to make the jump again so soon. But, I don't know what else to do." He gave a deep sigh as he thought it all out. "Okay, here's what we are all going to do." He pointed first to his friend. "Wals, you take Rose back to the moat at the Castle and wait for me at the lockers. If anyone asks what you're doing or where you've been, tell them…I don't know what to tell them. Tell them you found the swan tangled in some brush on the Island, or that you went camping, or something…I don't know. You know how to be creative. You'll think of something. Doctor, you need to be on the mainland. Would you mind swimming over? You're already wet. There's a Men's Room under the Hungry Bear Restaurant. Wait for me there, if you don't mind.

Security never checks that area before the Park is opened. Rose," he took her chin in his hand, his voice softening, "I will see you shortly…really…I promise."

When he got affirmations from everyone, he tilted his tired head and called for the portal once again. His three companions watched in fascinated silence as the sky immediately lit and the water became agitated once again. With the arrow still in place and the body of Daniel Crain hefted over his shoulder, the irritated Wolf waded into the River and disappeared in a fury of pink sparkles.

Knowing what had just happened, but still watching in awe and with a common shudder, all three were glad they weren't with Wolf having to make that trip again. Then giving a silent nod to Wals, Claude waited for the very last ripple of water to calm before he set one foot into the green water. After seeing what happened when Private Crain suddenly reappeared, he wasn't taking any chances.

"That was fast," Claude commented as they walked along.

Wolf grumbled a little before he answered. "There's too much to do here to linger. I made sure Mato saw Crain, and I was able to jump back into the vortex before it collapsed." He paused and frowned as he thought. "I've never done that before. Hope I never have to do it again."

The doctor in Doctor Houser came to the fore. "Oh? Any side effects?"

"You mean besides the vertigo, dizziness, disorientation, a blazing headache and being soaking wet? No, nothing unusual."

Claude smiled and kept silent.

Since Wolf was dressed in his Security uniform and the doctor was attired in an outfit similar to the ride operators who worked the Big Thunder attraction, Wolf had seen no need to get the doctor out of sight backstage to get him over to Pirates. They merely walked the main path through Critter Country, taking a little time to show Claude some of the changes the Park had undergone since his time. Splash Mountain was of interest to him, but not as much as the Haunted Mansion. He came to a complete stop once they reached the wrought iron railing around the attraction.

"Master Gracey's house! It's completed. Those four Doric columns in front. I saw them being erected…." He broke off as he thought back. "I met the man while I was living in New Orleans. I…I was a guest at a few of their dinner parties," he told Wolf. "How can his house be here, as well? This is all so confusing."

Wolf just nodded, thinking of his father at the encampment and his brother sitting on a pinto watching the River. "What happens here has a profound effect on what happens back there in the past. And you are one of the very few individuals who have lived to see the truth of that. What do you remember about Master Gracey? I never met him."

Choosing not to comment on the dubious honor Wolf just mentioned, the doctor glanced at his companion for a moment, remembering him in the shape of a wolf. *Does he mean knowing Master Gracey in this time period or in the past?* his mind asked, but didn't voice. Claude just shrugged as he looked back at the beautiful, finished mansion. "I know Edward was a retired sea captain. Opinionated, of course, like most wealthy men of his time. I didn't see him again after the war once I went to live in the Fort. I heard rumors," he shrugged again. "But, the soldiers were known for exaggeration. They said something about him being murdered by his wife and she took another husband to live in the house—with a similar ending, if you can believe that! He was rather strong in some of his views of religion and politics, I recall, but was very hospitable. I was sorry I lost track of him."

"If you like, we can go in the house. I would be interested to see if any of the interiors are the same as you knew."

"Is there a reason it is called the 'Haunted' Mansion? It looks so handsome on the outside."

Wolf gave him a small smile. "Shall we go see?" he offered.

Claude looked at the white hearse sitting on the front lawn. The rigging for the horse was in place—only there was no horse. A row of small gravestones lined the winding pathway. He shook his head. "Perhaps another time. I'd rather go see Walt."

"As you wish."

Deep under the Treasure Room in the Pirates of the Caribbean attraction, Doctor Houser stared at the refrigerator-like box in front of him. He had built the contraption himself and had gone over it time after time. Now, forty-two years later, here it was, hissing vapor into the still air of the cavern, humming and flashing lights. *It worked*, he excitedly exclaimed to himself, his heart pounding in his chest. *It worked!* He had forgotten all about his silent companion in the room. Wolf, knowing what the doctor was feeling, hung back in the darkness and gave Claude the time he needed.

We did it! Claude slowly walked around the chamber, his eyes examining every fitting, every tube. He went over to the canisters leaning against the wall and began some mental calculations.

"Perhaps he knows too much," a wavering, ghostly voice filled the cavern. "He's seen the cursed treasure. He knows where it be hidden…." The eerie voice trailed off into silence as the startled doctor looked wide-eyed around the darkened room. A booming, resonating voice suddenly sounded all around them, "Dead men tell no…."

"Lance, you're doing it all wrong," an amused feminine voice broke in.

"No, I'm not," was the argument back. "Listen to this: No fear of evil curses have you?"

"Wolf," the woman called into the room from a hidden speaker up above somewhere in the darkness, "Tell him he's doing it wrong."

With an amused chuckle, Wolf spoke up, "Lance, you're doing it wrong."

As the doctor turned sharply to Wolf for an explanation, the first voice came back and leisurely asked, "So, how was your trip?"

"Lance, we didn't go to Bermuda."

"Bermuda would be nice about now," Doctor Houser muttered, folding his arms stiffly across his chest.

Wolf thought he should make introductions.

"Dr. Houser, meet Lance and Kimberly Brentwood. Lance, this is Dr. Claude Houser."

With a disgusted roll of his eyes, Claude decided to ignore the childish behavior of whoever they were and went over to the viewing window where the dutiful red light was still blinking on and off. He reached over to clear the condensation from the window so he could see inside.

Just as his hand stretched out, he heard a panicked, "Don't touch that!" and jerked back as if scalded.

Kimberly's voice scolded over the sound of Lance's laughter, "Lance, that wasn't nice."

Frowning, Claude reached out again. "Don't touch that! Just kidding!" as his automatic reflex took over and the doctor's hand jerked back again.

"Lance," Wolf broke in when he saw the dark look on the doctor's face, "We need your services here. Could you bring a car?"

Lance became all business. "I'll be there in twenty minutes."

"I have a feeling we won't get along very well," Claude snorted, irritated.

Wolf gave a half smile, difficult to see in the darkness. "Lance is all right. Just his odd sense of humor. He and Kimberly have actually done a wonderful job filling in for her father."

With a small, sad sigh, Dr. Houser turned back to the cryogenic chamber. "I was kind of hoping there would be two chambers here when you told me her father was gone, too."

Wolf nodded in understanding. He had had that same argument himself a few times over the years. "It wasn't what he wanted. Some of his ashes are spread on the Island."

"Hmmm," was all the response Wolf was given. Claude was looking at the familiar face on the other side of the window. A feeling of pride and accomplishment flowed through him, mixing with his feelings of loss and displacement. "Tell me something, Wolf," he started quietly, continuing to stare at the still, familiar face. "How old am I? Realistically, I should be in my late sixties, but I don't look or feel that old. Am I going to see all of this through?"

Wolf knew what the doctor meant by "this." He took a deep breath. It was difficult to figure all this out. "Well, from what you told me, you were on the other Island only about three years. It was 1814 when I took you to New Orleans. From the condition of the Fort and what was going on in the surrounding areas, it had to have been around 1817 when I came back for you and Rose. Since I was going backwards through time, I could have landed at any point in history, at any given year." Wolf stopped and could tell the doctor was keeping up with him, so he continued, "If, for instance, I had come back in 1830, you would have been there for sixteen years and you would have been forty-seven years old. Since you are aware of only three actual years passing, physically you are only three years older than you were when you left in 1966."

Dr. Houser just stared at him. "Even though forty-two years have passed in this real time?"

Wolf nodded and let it sink in for a few moments. "For us, it was forty-two years. Not for you. You are around thirty-one years old. Time also passes differently back there, as we can now see from what Wals brought with him from Rainbow Ridge. I actually never know what to expect," he admitted. "But you, you look exactly as you did that first night I met you in Walt's apartment. Well, except for the clothes," he grinned, indicating the beat-up miner's outfit the doctor was still wearing since his time at Rainbow Ridge.

Claude looked down and smiled. He had finally dried out completely, but the outfit was still pretty messy.

Wolf indicated the chamber with a tilt of his chin. "You have a lot of work to do. Depending on what you discover when you get back to work, I think you just might see this through. You're young enough," he smiled.

"Amazing," was all the doctor could mutter, slowly shaking his head.

"And, if my super hearing powers are correct, Lance is here. Let's get you to the mansion in Fullerton."

At the name of the familiar city, Claude relaxed. Maybe he could go home again. As Lance entered and greeted his security partner, the doctor said a silent good-bye to his boss and followed the two friends out of the hidden chamber.

As soon as he stepped into the familiar mansion, Claude heard a different woman's voice from the one he had heard in the cavern. Oddly enough, she yelled out, "Stick!"

Lance got a big grin on his face and called back, "Shrew!"

"Slacker."

"Fish-wife."

"Rounder."

"Harpie."

Claude saw a pretty, petite brunette come out of the library and laugh as she gave Lance a hug.

Lance, all smiles, ignored his guest and hugged her back. "When did you get here, Beth?"

"Must have been right after you left. I finished my shift at the Park and it was time to pick up the twins, not that they want to go home. Peter has been teaching them more Lakota," she explained, looking pointedly over at Wolf. "Not that he is telling me what the words mean."

"I'll find out for you," Wolf promised, wisely hiding his feeling of pride in Peter's learning ability. The boy absorbed like a sponge. Wolf would have liked to take Peter back to meet his father, but doubted Kimberly would ever allow it.

Beth glanced at her watch. "I've got to go. Adam is going to be back from his business trip any minute and I'd like for all of us to be there when he gets home. He's finishing up the blueprints for that low-income housing development we told you about and he had some final meetings with the other investors." She gave a friendly smile to the doctor, running a quick eye over his unusual attire. "Hi, I'm Beth Michaels. Friend of the family. Lance here has forgotten whatever manners he once might have had."

Lance, unabashed, finished the introductions. "This is Doctor Claude Houser. He was a good friend of Kimberly's father and is here for a visit," he told her, going with their prearranged story.

Beth looked at the smooth complexion of the doctor and politely said nothing about what must have been a vast disparity between the ages of the two men. "Well, it is nice to meet you, Doctor. I hope you have a nice visit. Oh, Kimberly, there you are. Have you seen Alexander? I think he's hiding from me."

Claude looked over at the stunning blond who just entered and gave Lance a light hug. He could immediately see the resemblance to her father in her coloring and high cheekbones. Feeling a tug of emotion steal over him, he said nothing as he watched the family scene work itself out.

Kimberly flashed the doctor a wide smile of apology as she left with Beth to round up the missing children.

As the women left the room, Wolf told Doctor Houser in a low voice, "Beth doesn't know about your work or the chamber under Pirates."

Nodding in understanding, Claude followed Lance and Wolf when they motioned him into Lance's private study to allow him some needed time to sort through his feelings of loss and displacement. As Claude looked around, he knew the study used to be Kimberly's father's room. The familiarity of the room settled into Claude and helped him. Not much had been altered since he had been there last. *At least these two have respect for the past*, he thought. *That's good.*

Kimberly joined them after seeing Beth off. "Sorry," she said lightly as she came into the room. "It's a little premature since we just found out, but Beth wants to throw me a baby shower in about four or five months." Resting a light hand on her stomach, she smiled over at Claude, a little of the joy radiating out of her fading. "I wish my father could have known his grandsons."

Lance took her hand in his and patted it. "Maybe someday we can all go back with Wolf and introduce them."

At the look of fright that briefly crossed her eyes, Wolf stepped in and changed the subject of the conversation. They needed to get into the serious discussion of what to do with the doctor.

As his name was mentioned, Claude could feel Kimberly turn and scrutinize his face. He knew he looked about the same age as she. It had to be as trippy for her as it was for him. She hadn't even been born yet when he had worked with her father. He also felt he needed to take some control of the discussion. It was his life after all. After forty years, it was time to take it back. "You might not realize it, but I did have a life beyond Disneyland and cryogenics. I have, had...," he broke off, momentarily confused by the time incongruity. "I had a house on South Woods here in Fullerton, not too many miles away from here. It wasn't huge, but sufficient for my needs. I don't suppose it would still be in my name. The State probably took it for failure to pay my taxes all these years." He gave a small sigh. He had been awfully proud of his first home. "If I remember correctly, I paid $18,000 for it. Sometimes it was difficult to make my $170 mortgage payment with what little research money I took in, but when Walt hired me on...." He abruptly stopped when Kimberly suddenly stood.

"Oh, how can I be so stupid!" she interrupted, smiling. "Doctor Claude Houser! You are Doctor Claude Houser! Oh, for crying out loud. I'll be right back!" as she hurried from the room, leaving the men to look at one another for an explanation. The majority of the looks fell on Lance, who merely shrugged. He had no idea what she meant.

"Should we wait?" Claude asked, still confused. "I was simply stating that I had left some property behind and wondered what might have happened to it. I had a car, too…can't imagine that it would still be in running order." He gave a ghost of a smile as he thought about the car that had seen him through medical school. "It was a 1952 MGTF. Bought it used from an older gentleman who wanted to get a more sedate sedan. I think it cost me around $600, if you can believe paying that much for a used car! But, it was in great shape. Loved that little car." He chuckled at the memory, not seeing the amused looks being exchanged by the other two men.

Kimberly then breezed back into the room, waving a thick, faded manila envelope in her hand. "Found it!" she exclaimed, setting it down in front of the flustered doctor. "I had to dig it out of Father's private safe. Forgot all about it with all the excitement of meeting you."

"What is this?" Claude asked, staring at his name written neatly across the top of the envelope in his friend's familiar handwriting.

Kimberly smiled kindly at him. "Just some things my father wanted you to have when you came back. Go ahead. Open it."

Not comprehending the doctor's wish for some privacy at this poignant moment, the other three eagerly leaned in towards the envelope sitting on the coffee table in front of him. Lowering his head, he took a moment anyway and let the emotions run through him. *He always did think of everything. No wonder he and Walt worked so well together.*

When he was ready, Claude pulled out the time-yellowed documents inside. It was obvious from their condition that they had not been touched since their placement. The first document was the deed to his house. He saw that his mortgage had been paid off in 1970. There was also a Non-Op Certificate from DMV for his car that had been filed around the same time. His medical license and certificates were also enclosed. The last time he had seen them they had been hanging on the wall of his office. Social Security card. Driver's license. Money. Bank book. Photos. Everything that had been in his wallet before he had left. His entire life was preserved in that envelope.

When he looked up from the paperwork not knowing what to say, Lance stepped in to explain, "Your house is still waiting for you. There has been a gardening service that has come by twice a month ever since you left. Covers were put over your furniture to protect it all. And, I think you will like what you find in the garage," he smiled. "All you will have to do is get the registration up-to-date with DMV."

"My car is still there? After all this time? It would have to be worthless by now."

Kimberly exchanged a knowing smile with Lance. "Oh, I don't think it is worthless. My friend Beth who just left? She has a '57 T-Bird that is almost as old as your MG. But, believe it or not, those cool-looking cars are collector items. She keeps her car in as original a condition as possible, and takes her Bird to car shows. In fact, I took her over to your house last year when I was checking on a minor landscaping problem that was reported. Not only did she say your car is indeed a collector car now, but she added that since it was as original as it is, with such low mileage, she said she'd love to buy it for somewhere around $35,000."

The doctor was stunned. "What? Do you mean to tell me that my car is worth more than my house?"

Lance leaned forward clearly enjoying himself. "Well," he drawled, "Real estates values have also changed a little since you were gone. I think, with a little remodeling of the kitchen and bathrooms, your house might bring in around $600,000."

Looking at the man's face, Wolf knew the doctor had had enough for one day. He took the set of keys Kimberly had put on the table near the envelope. "Let me take you home, Doctor. I think you need to have some familiar things around you right now."

"Home?" Kimberly echoed, surprised. "I thought he would stay with us a few days until we get this all sorted out."

Grateful for Wolf's intervention, Claude quickly stood and picked up the papers that were his life. "I agree with Wolf. I would like to go home. Not that I don't appreciate your offer, Kimberly," he smiled to her. "But, I would like to sleep in my own bed tonight. It's been a long time," he murmured in an undertone.

"But, you have to eat," she stammered, not wanting this link to her father to leave just yet.

"I'll work something out," he told her, looking to Wolf to back him again.

Wolf understood and started for the door. "My car in the garage, Lance?"

Lance gave him a cocky grin. "Yeah, I was giving Peter a driving lesson with it. Hope you don't mind."

"You can drive at five years old now?!" Claude was shocked. "Things really have changed."

Lance clapped him on the shoulder. "No, it isn't that bad yet! I was just kidding. You go ahead

and take off. Kimberly and I will bring some groceries over later."

Nodding mutely, he waited for Wolf to come out
of the huge garage. A wide smile crossed his face
when Wolf roared to the entryway. He recognized
the bright red Mustang.

Maybe things won't be that bad after all.

Wolf drove slower than usual through the
streets of Fullerton. He could tell Claude recognized certain parts of the city. Every once and a
while the doctor would blurt out the name of a store,
and how things had changed since he last went
down that street. As the two drove closer to his old
neighborhood on South Woods, Wolf could see the
doctor was relaxing more and more until they
reached his house. Pulling up next to the curb, he
left the engine idling as the doctor got out of the car.

Standing on the trimmed grass lawn, Claude
grinned as he looked at that little flat-topped house
that had been his home for six years. Looking at it
as if for the first time, a wide smile crossed his face
as he thought about the day when he had signed
the papers for it. This was his first major purchase
while he was still in med school and he had been
unabashedly proud of this little house. It felt like he
had just been here a few days ago. But here he
was, nearly half a century later, looking at a house
that was just like him—unchanged in time. *It's like
time stood still*, he pondered.

His mind now turned to his buddies. *I wonder
what happened to Roger....* Roger had lived across
the alley and, good friends like they were, helped

him with several building projects in the six years he lived there. He remembered that thick ivy that had covered the back patio cover they had torn down. What fun that had been, and so different from his field of medicine. Then he thought about the two of them building that nice patio with the built-in lighting inside the skylights, the renovation of that beautiful flagstone patio floor, and the rebuild of that huge brick barbecue. All of it was on the patio next to the garage.... The doctor then recalled hosting many parties back there. With that thought his smile faded a bit.... All those parties...all his medical school friends who had come—like Roger—where would they be now? How old were they now?

Shaking off the feeling of displacement again, the doctor jingled the set of keys in his hand and strode forward.

Wolf grinned as he watched Claude bypass the house and head straight for the garage nestled in the back by the alley.

Yes, he was going to be all right, Wolf decided as he revved his engine and sped back to Disneyland. He still had a baffled Wals and an angry Rose waiting for him.

Three weeks later, Wolf was surprised to get a phone call. "Is everything all right, Doctor?" he asked. He hadn't seen Doctor Houser since he had dropped him off at his home. Lance and Kimberly were keeping an eye on him as he caught up on the missing four decades of his life and started work at a new laboratory.

"Yes, yes, it is going well. Kimberly has been a dear. Her father would be proud of her."

"Yes, he was," Wolf told him.

"Ah, I keep forgetting you worked with both Walt and her father," Claude said. "Since my MG is still in the shop getting its scheduled forty-year-maintenance, tune-up and new tires, Kimberly took me shopping over at the Orangefair Mall. Amazing that it's still there."

"Some things never change. Like women and shopping. Is there something I can help you with, Doctor?" Wolf asked, never really liking chitchat.

Claude smiled into his now old-fashioned rotary phone. He could sense Wolf wanted to get on with it. "Yes, you can. I was hoping you would be willing to keep your promise."

I always keep my promises, Wolf frowned to himself. "What do you mean?" He didn't try to disguise the irritant in his voice.

"Your promise to take me to see Walt."

I was hoping once you saw the chamber below Pirates you would forget. No such luck. Wolf paused. He had made so many jumps in a row lately and was feeling the strain.

The doctor let the silence grow. He felt no need to explain his strong desire to touch base with his old friend and boss. It was extremely personal to him. He needed to talk to him one more time. There was no solid idea of what he would say. He just wanted to see Walt.

Wolf knew he was expected to talk next. "All right," he finally told the waiting doctor. "I have to warn you, though—there is a possibility the timing will be off and we might arrive when Walt doesn't know you. Will you be prepared for that?"

There was another pause. "I hadn't expected that. You seemed so sure when you took me to New Orleans."

"I knew *where* I was taking you. I was not sure of the exact time frame until we arrived. It happened that we hit it just right."

"Do you think we could go back to Walt's apartment?"

Wolf didn't even consider that option. "No, the risk to the room is too severe. I don't know of any portal that would open there, and don't want to try the room itself. There are far too many variables and it is difficult to explain. I will come up with some options and get back to you. All right?"

"I suppose it has to be. Let me know."

The phone clicked in his ear as the doctor hung up. Wolf groaned. He was starting to feel like a transportation service, but, he did promise.

The two men stood on the train track, staring into the first tunnel after the Main Street Station. The sounds from the animals of the Jungle Cruise next to them had been shut off for the night. The sky was dark with a scattering of stars showing dimly through the encroaching lights of the Esplanade off to their left. The sky was dark, but not as dark as the tunnel that would emerge into New Orleans Square and Frontierland.

"You sure this will work?" the doctor asked, pensive.

"No," was Wolf's short answer.

Not caring for the answer, the doctor looked over at him. "Well, will we be able to return here at this point in time?"

"Maybe."

Dressed in ageless black slacks and a thin white pullover sweater, the unseen frown was obvious in the doctor's voice. "Then why are we using this tunnel?"

Wolf tried to keep his voice even. "Because I don't have a map of every portal and every exit, I have to take some risks—besides the obvious risk and side effects of the jump itself. Which, I assume, you do remember."

Claude kept himself from shuddering. "Yes, I remember…. Where do you *think* this will come out?"

"The Marceline, Missouri, train station. Or, hopefully, Disneyland's station five decades ago. It seemed a reasonable possibility." Wolf didn't add a third possibility: New Orleans of the 1800's since the current tunnel exited there. He didn't figure that option would go over too well with the doctor. He had had enough of the Old West.

The doctor looked over as Wolf started removing his clothes. He hadn't expected that, either. "Do you think you will emerge as a wolf? How will that go over in either situation?"

Wolf stashed his uniform behind the bricks that formed the entry to the tunnel. Thanks to Lance and Kimberly's assistance, he knew there would be no maintenance crews working on this part of Disneyland. "I can only go by what has happened in every jump into the past. I have always emerged as a wolf."

Wolf then handed Claude something that had been hidden in the bricks. "What is this? It feels like a leather collar and a chain."

"It is," Wolf said sourly. "If any of my predictions are correct, you will have to pass me off as…your dog," he grumbled, glad he couldn't see the smirk he knew was crossing the doctor's face.

Once the picture had left his mind, Claude was able to reply in a steady voice devoid of any amusement. He didn't want to humiliate a proud man who was his only chance of coming back to the current time—one that he had quickly gotten used to and was enjoying immensely with all its modern conveniences. "Let's play that by ear, then," he told Wolf as he nervously jingled the chain in his hand. "Are you ready?"

Wolf could hear the anxiousness in his voice and ignored the noise of the chain. "Yes, as ready as I ever am. Stick right behind me and head for the middle of the vortex. When it is on land like this, we have to actually jump into it."

There was no reply, only a loud swallow. Wolf felt a hand settle on his shoulder as he called for the lightning. The dark tunnel began to glow ahead of them, the light fading and then stretching forward towards the two men. A distant boom echoed through the darkness and a glimmer of pink swirled to life.

"Run!" Wolf barked as he sprinted forward. He could feel the change surging through him and exalted in the feeling of freedom it gave him. He could hear the doctor stumbling on the railroad ties as he struggled to keep up. "Faster! We have to make it to that column of light! Now…jump!"

Holmby Hills

"Is there a tunnel at the Marceline train station? I've never been there." The doctor's voice was weak, but, as it echoed through the darkness, was still overloud to the sensitive ears of the wolf sitting next to him.

The silver-tipped ears turned away from the noise. They were trying to pick up clues as to where they were. "No, there isn't. Are you all right?"

"Well, at least I am not soaked to the skin this time," was the dry response. "But, yes, I think so. If we aren't in Marceline, then, where are we?"

Wolf could hear the sounds of the man struggling to get into a sitting position.

"Why is this tunnel so short, Wolf? I can feel the roof."

Wolf padded to the exit of the ninety-foot-long tunnel and sniffed the air. "Well, we aren't in Disneyland any more. This isn't even the tunnel to the Casey Jr. Circus Train. Besides, the track gauge is too narrow." He could hear the doctor crawling towards the exit. Wolf had no trouble standing upright in the small tunnel, but the taller man did. "I can smell a garden, a dog or two, and the definite smells of humanity."

Claude stuck his head out of the tunnel and looked around in the darkness, suddenly smiling. "Or you could say we are in Walt's backyard. You mean to tell me you've never been here?"

Wolf padded out and sat down next to the train track that wound into the distance. "No, I haven't. We usually meet at the Park or at the mansion. This is private."

"This is his house on Carolwood Way. Walt built it in 1950, so I guess this could be any time since then. With the looks of the mature trees, I think the house has been here a while."

Wolf could hear the eagerness in the doctor's voice. He hoped, for the doctor's sake, that he was right. It would crush his spirit if he arrived too late after 1966. Glancing at the dark sky, Wolf could tell morning was still a few hours off. "Where are you going?" as the doctor suddenly started striding over the lawn.

"I was going to knock on the patio door and see if I can awaken him."

"Wait a minute, Doctor," Wolf called. "You don't know who is at home. Are you known by the entire family? Do they know what you do?"

The doctor paused in his tracks. Wolf could see his shoulders sag a little. "No, I'm not." He gave an uneasy sigh. "What do you suggest?"

"There's a hammock over there. Why don't you wait out the morning and I'll go back to the tunnel. I shouldn't be seen yet. Until we know who is here."

Claude watched as the dark shape moved silently back to where they had emerged. He didn't like waiting, but could see the wolf's point. He settled into the hammock and fell instantly asleep.

"You get kicked out of that house of yours,

Claude?"

The doctor came instantly awake as the hand continued to shake his shoulder. "Walt! It's really you!"

The familiar eyes twinkled. "Now, who else would I be in my own backyard? What are you doing here? Want to come in for some breakfast? The family is off on a visit. I'm all by my lonesome."

"I…I came to see you, Walt," the doctor stammered, not sure of how much to say. He wasn't sure what happened to the wolf.

"I think the doorbell still works out front," Walt kidded with him. "Even though this hammock is pretty comfortable, if I do say so myself."

Claude looked over towards the train layout. He could see the dark nose just barely sticking out of the entrance of the tunnel. "This may sound very odd, Walt, but, what year is this?"

Walt's expression of amusement turned to one of concern. "You hit your head, Claude? Maybe you should come in and lie down."

"No, I'm fine. Just humor me for a minute, please."

"All right. All right. It's 1963. Does that help?"

"1963," he repeated, suddenly smiling. "Yes, that helps a lot. We needed to know."

"We? Since I already know the date, who is included in 'we?'" Walt asked, curious, turning his head to look in the direction the doctor had just turned.

The doctor had gotten out of the hammock and was standing on the grass. He called over towards the tunnel that traveled under the garden. "Wolf, it's all right."

"Wolf? What's Wolf doing hiding out there? He

knows he's welcome here." Walt broke off as the huge, black figure of a wolf slowly emerged from the train tunnel and stood warily in the early morning light. "Well, I'll be...."

Walt went out to meet Wolf halfway. Wolf came within touching distance and sat on the lawn. He could see that his boss was trying to work it out in his mind and remained quiet. "I've seen you before," Walt almost whispered. "A long time ago. So long ago that I thought it was just a dream or my imagination at work. Isn't that right?"

The sapphire blue eyes swung up to meet Walt's. "Yeah, that was me, boss. You hit me in the head with a rock. I wondered if you ever remembered."

The surprise of a talking wolf caused Walt to stumble backwards. The doctor caught him before he could go all the way down. "Amazing, isn't it?" Claude asked.

Walt shook himself out of Claude's hands and went back to Wolf, peering closely at him. "So this is what happens to you. I've always wondered. You never said much."

One black shoulder shrugged. "Without actually seeing it, it is kind of hard to grasp."

Walt's sharp eyes swung back to Claude. "And you knew? I didn't even think you two knew each other."

"We don't. Or didn't...." He ran an exasperated hand through his hair. "It's complicated, Walt. Let's just leave it at: things happen. A lot's happened to me lately and I, well...I just wanted to talk to you, and Wolf here brought me."

Walt folded his arms over his chest and gave a dry laugh. "Well, all you had to do was come to the

Park or give me a call! This seems like an awful lot of trouble. What did you want to talk to me about?"

The doctor opened his mouth and then shut it again. He looked perplexed. "I don't actually know, Walt. I just wanted to touch base with something…someone familiar."

Walt looked from the wolf to the doctor and back again. He was starting to get the picture that things weren't as they seemed. Then he recalled that the "something" that happened to Wolf only happened when he did that odd transference he mentioned. *When he transferred to the past.* Walt felt his heart start pounding in his chest. "I don't suppose you would tell me the truth even if I asked, would you?" he asked shakily.

"It's best not at this point, Walt," Wolf told him. "We each have our little secrets."

Walt knew Wolf was referring to the mysterious pendant hidden safely in his apartment over the Fire Station at Disneyland. He figured the doctor must now be included somehow in all of that. "Time will tell, I am sure." Knowing he would get no further explanation, he rubbed his hands together and changed the subject. "So, can I fix you two some breakfast? I make some mean eggs!"

"I don't know if your poodle would be too happy to see me, Walt," Wolf gave a silent, open-mouthed laugh. "Maybe it would be best if I stayed out here. You and Claude go on inside and have a chat. We can't leave until tonight anyway."

Walt laughed at that. "Yeah, my ladies get a little protective of me. Wouldn't have it any other way, though. Okay, okay, Wolf, you know what's best, I'm sure. Come on in, Claude. I want to show you my drawings for the World's Fair! You do know about It's a Small World, don't you?"

With a pleased look on his face and a relaxed slope to his shoulders, Claude followed his boss into the sprawling two-story house.

CHAPTER FOURTEEN

Disneyland – 2008

Once Wolf got back to Disneyland, Wals was not waiting for him in the cast members' locker room like he had asked of him. He took the second small canoe hidden near the Hungry Bear Restaurant and paddled out into the River. Somewhat irritated, he found both Wals and Rose were still in front of the Settler's Cabin on Tom Sawyer's Island. "I thought you were going to have Rose back in the moat by now. The Park is open, Wals. The Mark Twain is going to be starting her first run within minutes. This is no time to be messing around!"

"She refuses to get into the canoe! I can't paddle and hold her at the same time. She's being very stubborn!" Wals was exasperated—both by Rose's refusal to cooperate as well as her transformation into a swan. He wasn't sure what to do, so, rather than make a scene traipsing through the park with a hissing swan, he thought it would be best to just stay put until Wolf arrived—which he hoped would be sooner rather than later.

They all heard the blast of the stream whistle signaling that the Mark Twain was pulling away from the dock. The ship and all her passengers would be floating by their location within minutes.

Wolf turned to the angry blue eyes peering out of the black mask. "Rose, please trust us. I know you don't want to go back to the moat, but it is our only option right now."

She hissed at him and backed closer to the little cabin. After all, this had been her "home" for quite a few years and she didn't want to leave it— whether it was real or not.

Wolf glanced over at Wals and signaled him to jump into the fray and help. He could see the look of loss in Wals' eyes and didn't have time to deal with that, too. "Wals, just talk to her. She trusts you."

It was still very difficult for Wals to relate to the swan as he had done with the warm, loving woman. But, he knew Wolf was right. They were running out of time. Squatting down and holding out his arms, he looked directly into the swan's eyes. "Rose," was all he had to say.

Hearing the Mark Twain's spiel getting louder, Rose knew she had to trust them. She rushed into Wals' open arms and closed her eyes as his arms embraced her, listening to the comforting beat of his heart. "It will be all right," he whispered to her. "I love you, Rose...and I will keep my promises."

When Wals picked up Rose to carry her to waiting canoe and the impatient Wolf, his fingers brushed against the gold chain that was still around her slender neck. The pendant itself was buried in the white plumage of her breast. She squawked angrily when he took the gemstone from her, almost beating him with her strong wings.

"I'm sorry, Rose, but I have to keep it for now. It might slip off in Swan Lake, or the handler might see it." He looked into her accusing eyes and felt contrite. "I'm sorry," he repeated sincerely. "I will give it back to you. That, too, is a promise." She stared steadily into his eyes. "I promise! Just as soon as we figure out what to do to get you back to where you rightly belong. Okay?"

She tilted her head and those small blue eyes swept over to Wolf, who was guiding the canoe as close to the shoreline as he could to try and remain unseen by the passengers of the Mark Twain. He was thinking he could stop at the Mark Twain dock, quickly pull the canoe out of the water, and then stash it behind the Columbia's rolling gangplank. Both he and Wals were in costume, so, if questioned, he would just tell inquisitive guests that they were returning the swan to the Castle. He wasn't sure what he would tell them if they questioned Wals' tarnished sword. A security guard and a canoe guide shouldn't be toting around a sword.... Wolf growled low in his throat and then realized Rose was still staring at him. She seemed to be either asking his opinion or telling him to make Wals give it back.

Once he remembered what Wals had just said, he replied, "Don't worry, Rose. If he doesn't do as he says, I'll bite him."

Turning her black-masked face back to Wals, she settled in the middle of his lap. He now saw that she wasn't going to jump out of the canoe and appeared content and willing to cooperate—well, as content and cooperative as any swan could be.

Grabbing up the second paddle, he gave Wolf some much-needed assistance in getting them quickly around the Island. Between strokes, Rose would gently peck his arm.

"Yeah, I heard him," Wals sighed. He just hoped Wolf had been kidding. He wasn't entirely sure at this point.

Once Rose was finally swimming peacefully, if not contentedly, in the moat around Sleeping Beauty's Castle, the two men finally headed for the cast member changing room and their lockers. When Wolf and Wals were out of sight, Disneyland's Animal Handler, Merri, appeared on the side of Swan Lake. On seeing her, Rose gave a happy whistle and almost ran across the water to greet her.

Merri leaned down and gave Rose a hug. "Oh, my darling girl is back! You've been gone for such a long time. Are you all right?" she asked, holding Rose's head and looking deep into her eyes.

She shivered all over, her eyes shining with emotion, and excitedly tried to tell Merri what had been going on all this time. Disheartened when her words came out as whistles and grunts, she looked up at Merri, as if she were pleading with her.

"There, there, child. It's all right. You can tell Merriweather all about it later," Merri crooned, stroking the elegant white head as it leaned against her comforting bosom. "We'll have a lot to talk about once we get back. I'm sure your mother is very anxious about now."

Rose gave a sigh and nestled against her

dearest friend.

Merri settled onto the grass next to Rose. "I see the wolf was limping. You are all right, aren't you, dearie?" On feeling the elegant head dip with an answering, 'yes', she continued, "That's good. He must have been taking his job as your Protector very seriously." Merri's tone took on an amused scolding tone, "You always did like to run off, even as a youngster! Why, the three of us girls never could keep track of you! And even after you ended up here, why, it was the same thing! It took me quite a while to realize you had wandered into Frontierland that night and got caught in the River when the wolf left." She looked away and shook her head. "Three long years it has been. Before when you ran off, I would usually find you swimming in the Storybook Land Canal. You always seemed fascinated by the little Cinderella's Castle up on that hill. You know why now, don't you?"

Rose nodded once and looked up at the pink elegance of Sleeping Beauty's Castle above her.

"Yes, that's right." Merriweather gave a contented sigh. "And it looks like we will finally be going home! Well, we will once those two men get it figured out." Merri threw a look in the direction Wals and Wolf had gone. "Wish I could help them, but I can't. We'll just have to hope they do it soon. I sure hope the wolf picked a good friend to assist him."

The swan gave a wistful sigh and looked off longingly in the same direction, trying to get one last glimpse of Wals. Merri's sharp eyes looked closer at Rose. "Ah, so that's how it is," she murmured. "Well, well, time will tell, my dear, time will tell."

Wals couldn't wait to change out of his clothes. His old canoe costume had been sorely abused in the two years he figured he had been gone. Half of the fringe was missing from the legs, there were more rips and tears than he liked to remember, and he didn't even want to contemplate how it smelled.

Wolf had just come back from stashing the sword in Wals' locker. Wals' mind was so cluttered that he didn't even seem to remember the sword, let alone getting it out of sight in case some other cast members came in early for work. Fresh clothes were forgotten, however, as he and Wolf stared speechlessly at the calendar on the wall.

"How can that be!?" Wals wanted to know, breaking the silence that was growing between them. "I was there for two years!" He turned to face Wolf, again confused. "Wasn't I?"

Wolf shook his head. He, too, was stunned as he thought back, trying to figure out the conundrum. "It is hard to explain. You and I went back to different years. Even though we went through the vortex at the same time, you seemed to be there for a year longer than I was…." He broke off at the perplexed looked on Wals' face. "It is different with each passage. Time must have speeded up back there. According to this calendar, we have only been gone for two weeks."

They were alone in the cast member lounge area. Different cast members had been coming and going as their shifts started. Outside of a few greetings, most of the men were unknown to Wals. And the rest were used to the idiosyncrasies of the silent security guard. "Do we still have our jobs?" Wals wanted to know. "I had some vacation time coming, but I hadn't scheduled it."

Wolf nodded. "I made arrangements with Management when I came back for your nametag. I told them that we went on an extended camping trip. Seemed appropriate," he explained with an amused grin, seeing no reason to mention Lance and Kimberly—whom Wals did not know. "You won't get any more time off for a while, but you are good for now."

Wals didn't even seem to hear him. He looked a million miles away.

"What are you thinking?" Wolf wanted to know, curious as to where Wals' mind was taking him.

"What?" Wals head snapped over to face Wolf. "Oh. I was just thinking about Rose. You know— the way I knew her on the Island. If we figure out how to take her back to wherever she came from, will she be human again as we think Aurora is supposed to be? Could she possibly be an actual princess? Do you think that if you can get her back to where she belongs, she and I can pick up where we left off? I...She and I...I mean, well, we were...." Wals broke off, frustrated, not wanting to voice his deep feelings for the woman.

Ah, so that is what this is about, Wolf hid a smile and lowered his eyelids so Wals wouldn't see the amusement in his eyes. He knew he probably shouldn't do this to Wals, but he couldn't resist. "I wouldn't count on it too highly, Wals. Since Rose was human when you saw her on the Island, she will be human in her right place in time, but I don't know about you. You've made the jump twice now...."

Wals' face went pale, his heart suddenly started pounding. "What do you mean!? I didn't change before. I'm still me! How do you know?"

"There are ways we can tell," he muttered mysteriously. Wolf took his thumb and first two fingers and stretched them out as far as he could side to side. He placed his middle finger on the side of Wals' eye, his index finger near the ear, and his thumb on the vein in Wals' neck. Closing his eyes, he frowned as if in deep concentration, and then he grunted and nodded wisely.

Not recognizing the Vulcan Mind Meld gesture from the *Star Trek* television series, Wals started to hyperventilate, his eyes wide.

Wolf dropped his hand. He smiled and said, "Just kidding."

"Not funny, man! Seriously not funny!"

Wolf held himself back from chuckling out loud. "Sorry."

On a break from the canoes, Wals went in search of Wolf. He found his friend, dressed in a freshly-pressed security uniform, staring out over the Frontierland River. Although it was unseen from their current location, Wals knew the Friendly Village was the focus of Wolf's stare.

"Thinking about home?" Wals asked, sitting on one of the half-log benches of the empty Tom Sawyer's Island Raft dock. The name of the dock had been changed to Pirate's Lair on Tom Sawyer's Island, but Wals never could seem to remember the change.

The intense blue eyes swung around at the

sudden interruption and narrowed. He had been so lost in his thoughts that he hadn't heard Wals' approach. "Home?" Wolf repeated, momentarily confused. He gave a shake of his head to clear his mind. "Not sure where 'home' really is," he admitted with a frown. "Here? There? It gets a little confusing sometimes."

Wals brought up the reason for his interruption. "I have a question about all of this," he began with a general wave of his hand in Wolf's direction.

The serious expression on Wolf's face was broken by a quick smile. "Only one?"

"Well, okay, I have a lot of questions," Wals admitted, returning the grin. He looked around to make sure they were alone and wouldn't be overheard. There were families and couples walking in every direction, but only a couple of women gave the handsome men a passing, second glance. Wals cleared his throat. He seemed unsure of how to word his question.

Wolf's eyes half closed as he waited for whatever it was Wals wanted to ask. Wals saw the gesture and wondered, once again, how he could not have known the wolf had really been his friend. The similarities were so obvious to him now. And the realization that they were one and the same helped him to relax and frame his thoughts. "Okay," he started again. He leaned forward as he began talking, his eagerness coming through. "I wondered about, you know, your transformation," he lowered his voice, looking around again.

Wolf smiled to himself. He had wondered how long it would take Wals to start on this.

Not seeing the amusement in his friend's eyes, Wals kept talking. "How does it feel? Do you know when it is coming? You seemed to know when that whirlpool-thingy was going to open. Do you have a tail or something sometimes? Does it bother you when, like, the moon is full?" He broke off at the odd expression on Wolf's face. He remembered insulting him somehow when he was a wolf. Did he just do it again? He was just curious after all.

Torn between being amused and irritated, Wolf narrowed his eyes and allowed himself to growl deep in his chest. He was inwardly pleased to see the eager expression on Wals' face fade a little.

Wals cleared his throat to cover his sudden nervousness. Perhaps his curiosity wasn't such a good idea.

Wolf let him stew for a minute and then let him partially off the hook. "Considering you have seen me come back through the vortex a couple of times and have seen me arrive without any clothes on, did you *see* any tail?" he allowed himself to snap. He didn't want Wals to feel free enough to continually question his transformation any time he felt like it. One question asked around the wrong person at the wrong time could be disastrous for them all.

"Uh, no," Wals admitted sheepishly, holding up a restraining hand. "Sorry if I seem nosey, Wolf, but you have to agree that this is all pretty spectacular. You were a wolf and Rose is a swan. Anyone else we know? What about Trey? Is he a gazelle or something?"

Wolf let out a hearty laugh at that. "No, Trey is just Trey. A gazelle!" he chuckled at the thought. Trey wasn't exactly fleet of foot as they had found out during the employees' annual softball games.

Wals took the laugh as a good sign that he wasn't going to get chewed out, literally. "Well, I just can't get my head around the fact that Rose might really be Princess Aurora, you know, the real Sleeping Beauty. I mean, that's only supposed to be a fairy tale, right? How can she possibly be a real person?"

Wolf gave his one-shoulder shrug. "Why not? Can't you think of any other literary figure who was based on a real person? What about Count Dracula?"

Wals visibly paled, his eyes widened. "You know him?" he asked, his voice a shaky whisper.

"We were college roommates," Wolf shot back. He rolled his eyes at the look of horror that crossed Wals face. "Oh, for crying out loud, Wals! No, of course not! It was just an example...."

"A pretty dang lousy example, if you ask me," Wals muttered, embarrassed he had just exposed a deep-seated childhood fear.

Wolf continued, "Dracula was said to be based on Prince Vlad the Impaler of Romania—which may or may not be totally true. His reputation of atrocities against his enemies became a fable, a legend, that was said to be taken and later turned into Count Dracula in works of *fiction*," he stressed the word fiction as he could tell Wals still hadn't recovered yet. "How can we say that the Sleeping Beauty *wasn't* based on a real princess, whether or not all the circumstances revolving around her were real or imaginary?"

"I cannot believe you put Aurora and Count Dracula in the same category!"

Wolf shook his head and groaned. "I didn't put them in the same category. It was just an example, but do you understand my point?" he asked slowly as if to a small child.

"Yeah," Wals nodded, still a little irritated and not completely mollified. "I do. I guess we'll just have to wait and see. And," he added as a peace offering, "I will try and hold off any more personal questions until you decide to tell me something more. I just wondered if there were any others like you out there."

"Deal." The mysterious Wolf came instantly back as he turned to go back to work. "But, Wals," he muttered quietly, "there are *always* others." Before Wals could panic and interrupt again, he raised a silencing finger and added, "First and foremost, we need to figure out how to help Rose and get her back to her own rightful time." His eyes narrowed. "Have you visited her today?"

Wals dropped his glance from Wolf's accusing stare. He found it increasingly difficult to relate to the swan as he had done to the human. "No, I haven't," he admitted reluctantly.

Wolf wasn't going to let him off easily. "Don't forget your promise! She is still Rose—whatever form she is in. And she still needs our help. Swans mate for life, in case you didn't know. If she has fallen for you—as you have obviously fallen for her—if you let her down now, she could die."

There was no need for Wals to answer. He knew Wolf was right. Checking his watch, he had to get back to the canoe dock. He would go see Rose after his shift. He knew Wolf would be there too.

Wolf had arranged with Disneyland's Animal Manager, Merri, to allow them access to the moat around Sleeping Beauty's Castle. It was easier to accomplish than he had thought. With the exception of the huge horses that pulled the Main Street Trolleys, the general public was never allowed access to the Park's animals. Unbeknownst to Wolf, Merri knew why the female swan was so attached to the two men. Plus, she knew any kind of diversion was good for the well-being of the animals. It helped prevent them in general from getting bored and Rose in particular from getting despondent over how long it seemed to be taking the men to figure things out.

Wals and Wolf always visited Rose towards the back of the moat called Swan Lake, near the west side exit of the Castle. A lot of the Park's guests didn't use that quiet walkway as it ended at the little-used Plaza Gardens and Bandstand. Most didn't know that if they kept walking on the path, they could go into the side entrance of Frontierland and not have to go on the busier Main Street at all.

After Rose had excitedly greeted them and chased away her confused swimming companion, she settled onto the grass next to Wals. He had brought her some French bread from New Orleans Square that she was quietly nibbling as she listened to the two men as they tried to work things out.

"We have some news for you, Rose," Wolf was telling her. "You might not like it."

Rose looked over at him, the bread forgotten. She tilted her head, telling him to continue.

"We found out through the cast member newsletter, *The Disneyland Line*, that there is a major change coming to Sleeping Beauty's Castle. If your previous time period reacts like my previous time period did, this might affect you. Remember when we found out that Tom Sawyer's Island here would be taken over by pirates?"

The elegant white head dipped once.

"Well, we knew my Island would be altered as well and that you and the Doctor would be in danger. I have no way of knowing for sure, but I think we need to assume your previous time period will be altered as well from the coming changes."

Wals broke in, his hand resting on the pure white plumage on her back as Rose nestled next to his side. "We found out that Disneyland is going to open the Sleeping Beauty Castle Walk-Through again. It had originally opened in 1957 and was then redesigned in 1977 as technology got better and they could put more movement in the displays. It has been closed since 2001."

The swan's head tilted sideways and she looked at Wolf, not understanding the significance.

He told her, "After being closed and quiet for all that time, Maleficent will now be back, free again to roam the hallways of the Castle."

Maleficent—the evil fairy. Maleficent—the conjuror of all things bad. Rose started shivering, looking wildly from one man to the other. She had to get back and warn her family.

Wals held her closer. "We have some time, Rose. The Walk-Through isn't scheduled to open until July 17 of this year and we still need to find the correct portal…."

Rose suddenly broke away from him and dove into the water, swimming over to the first decorative tunnel under the drawbridge, the one closest to the Castle. She flapped her wings, half rising from the water. Guests walking by stopped to admire the beautiful bird, some taking pictures of the swan that usually just swam dejectedly around the small moat.

Seeing Wolf gesturing to her, she hurried back to the men. Wals then put a calming hand on her neck. Her plumage settled back down and she relaxed a little, still breathing hard. Wolf looked directly into her eyes and asked, "What are you trying to tell me? Is that the portal? That first tunnel?"

The head dipped once.

"You sure?"

Rose nipped his leg.

Wolf ignored the welt that was already rising. "So, you remembered?"

Rose stood back from him and began shivering all over. She got back in the water, swam over to the first tunnel again and then pointedly turning away from it, she swam through the second tunnel. Coming back the same way, she then returned to the men.

Wals was confused, but Wolf seemed to figure it out. "So, you just have an odd feeling when you approach that tunnel? You don't use it, do you?"

Rose became excited and whistled at them.

Wolf gestured for them to remain where they were when he got silently to his feet. Without any explanation, he walked the little path into the Castle and reemerged through the more common main entrance at the base of the drawbridge. He stopped when he was directly over the first tunnel. As Wolf stood there, they watched him close his eyes and concentrate. To their amazement, the placid water running through the moat began rippling, centered inside of that tunnel. Wolf opened his eyes and looked down into the water, nodding once in confirmation.

When he rejoined them, they both looked expectantly at him. "Did you see it, too?" he asked.

"If you mean seeing the water start to move, then yes, we did. You did it, didn't you?" Wals wanted to know.

Wolf just nodded, thinking. "I wasn't sure where all else it would work," he muttered, more to himself than to them. "I never knew the extent of it. I was a boy when I learned the location of that first vortex on the River. That's where my Father killed the wolf that bit my Mother. All the other locations I have had to figure out—sometimes by trial and error. I never knew about this one." His eyes cleared, coming back to the present. "Now that we know we have another portal here and it may be Rose's doorway to her time, we need to make some plans. Wals, I'm going to arrange for you to transfer to Fantasyland for two reasons. One: so you can be closer to Rose. And, two: so you can keep a better eye on the progress of the Walk-Through. We might have to leave faster than planned."

"And what are you going to do?" Wals asked.

Wolf looked over towards Frontierland. He answered quietly, "I need to go see my family."

Thinking he understood, Wals nodded. "To give you a chance to say good-bye?"

"My people don't say good-bye. We say doka."

"Oh, really? What does that mean? I thought I heard the Shaman say it right before we went into the storm."

Wolf thought for a moment. "The closest meaning would be 'See you later.'"

"Well, tell your father 'pispisza' for me," Wals told him, proud of himself for remembering.

Wolf gave him a half-grin. Wals, knowing his

friend well, saw the grin and figured he had just said something stupid. "What did I just say?" Wals sighed, not sure if he really wanted to know.

"You just called my father a prairie dog."

Wals gave a chuckle. "Hmm, that might not go over well. How do you say thank you?"

"Philamaya." Wolf told him correctly.

"Yeah, that," Wals smiled. "Thought I had it right." Getting back to their original topic, Wals wanted to know, "How long do you think you will be gone?"

Wolf looked to the west. It was coming soon. "I don't know. I shouldn't be gone too long, but this is important. I don't know when I will see them again." *Or, if*, he added silently to himself.

It was well after midnight. Two men and a swan stood quietly together in the darkness on the grassy patch next to Swan Lake. Wolf was holding a package tightly wrapped in a waterproof cloth. At Wals' questioning look, Wolf handed it to him and explained, "Rose's clothes. If this goes like we are hoping it will, she will need something to wear once we get there."

The two men looked at the swan, her white plumage brilliant in the moonlight. They could see a faint pink blush rising around her cheeks before she averted her face.

Wals was dressed in a princely outfit he had swiped from the Costume Department. He had chosen royal blue velour, with a gold-trimmed white blousy shirt and blue riding breeches tucked into tall black boots. The red cloak hung off one shoulder, pinned in place with a large gold medallion. The newly-polished sword he had found on the Island was hanging from a black leather belt around his waist. An oval hat flopped over towards one eye and a jaunty white feather moved in the faint breeze of the night. He hoped it all wouldn't get ruined in the water and the passage. To protect the pendant, he had wrapped it in an extra sock and stuffed it in the toe of his boots that were half a size too large for him.

Wolf had already removed his Security clothes and hidden them behind one of the brick turrets of the Castle. He assumed he would be a wolf when he got wherever they were going. If not, he would be cold, embarrassed, and naked. He took back the package that held Rose's outfit and put the heavy string around his neck. Wals would have enough to do.

Wolf broke his concentration for a moment. He needed to talk to Wals. His blue eyes picked up the moonlight and reflected it back to Wals as he turned to face his friend. He was serious, pensive. "I need you to know that I am not sure what form I will take once we get to Rose's time."

Also worried about that, Wals tried to lighten the tense mood. "Well, just as long as you're not one of Maleficent's flying monkeys!"

Wolf did not return the smile. "I don't know what I will be." He paused, and then added quietly, "We might be on opposite sides, Wals."

Wals was about to joke, "Opposite sides of the moat?" but decided the time for joking was over. He knew what Wolf had meant. He put a steady hand on Rose's head. "I will do what I have to do to protect her."

Wolf gave one nod. "Understood. And I will do what I have to do as well."

Wolf stuck his hand out to Wals. Wals regarded his friend's outstretched palm for a moment. He looked into the familiar sharp eyes. Wals gave him an answering nod and shook. "Understood."

Far above them, standing on the balcony of the tallest spire of the Castle, a plump figure dressed all in blue was intently watching the proceedings below. She gaily clapped her hands and exclaimed, "We finally get to go home!" With the flick of her wrist, a shimmering wand appeared in her hand. "Oh, I've missed you!" she told the seemingly inanimate object, hugging it to her ample breast. "Shall we join them?" With a flourish, the wand made a glitter-filled circle over her head and a shimmering Merriweather was reduced in size to an inch tall. Humming happily, she stepped over the edge of the balcony and dropped towards the moat below.

The time for words was over. All eyes were now focused on the tunnel under the drawbridge. For a moment, they were lost in their own private thoughts. Wolf turned away from them and lifted his handsome face to the night sky. Frowning, his eyes narrowed at the tiny blue sparkle falling from the sky.

So, I see you've finally made yourself known, he threw out his thought towards the glitter of light.

Yes, yes, let's get on with it, wolf. We've a lot

to do.

Ignoring her now, he closed his eyes in concentration. His hands rose to chest height and reached out towards the dark tunnel. The quiet of the night was split by a startling sound that rose from deep within Wolf's chest. It rumbled and climbed through his still body. It chilled Wals to the core and made Rose shiver. A plaintive cry rose on the breeze and dispersed until it was a soft moan drifting on the breeze. Wolf called again and the hairs on the back of Wals' neck tingled.

It was working. Wolf could feel the change beginning within him. Everything was getting sharper, more in focus behind his closed eyes. He felt exhilarated, free.

Wals and Rose watched in scared silence as the fog began creeping over the still water. It seemed to be coming from Snow White's Grotto on the other side of the Castle. The fog kept low on the water and filled in every space. In the center of the tunnel, the one that held their fascinated gaze, a swirl appeared in the water, subtle at first. There was barely a ripple in the moving fog. Then, as they watched, it began to take on more form, more definition. It turned in on itself and grew in height. The sides of the fog rose and fell inward again, turning, ever turning.

When the first streak of lightning touched the water near the topiaries, they all knew it was time. With the quivering Aurora held securely in Wals' arms, the two men entered the shallow water of the moat. They felt a current pick up in what should have been still water all around them. As they strode forward, the force in the water increased, pushing, forcing them forward into the swirling tunnel. They watched wide-eyed as the jagged bolt of lightning hit the water and headed straight towards them.

COMING IN 2012!
READ AN EXCITING EXCERPT
FROM
HIDDEN MICKEY 4 WOLF!
HAPPILY EVER AFTER?

An Island – 1189

A cold fog had rolled in over the coast, dimming a nearly full moon and obscuring the stars that would otherwise be seen in abundance. The sound of the ocean's waves crashing against the rocky shoreline was muted into a pleasant distant roar. Night sounds from the surrounding dense forest were heard only as ghostly whispers through the swirling vapor.

The surrounding blanket of gray and its sound-restricting presence was a welcome cloak to the two people nestled together on that small strip of sand. Standing, facing each other on a lichen-covered boulder, their foreheads touched as they whispered. A crescent strand of black, volcanic rocks formed a natural wall, blocking their view to the south and east. The only approach to the young man and woman was from the north, along the stretch of sand that sloped gradually from a forest of pines and vine-covered shrubs down to the approaching and receding foamy waves of the sea. Unless the hunters who sought the pair could somehow miraculously emerge from the waves crashing upon the rock-strewn beach, the two felt they were safe enough. Should they be wrong, however, he knew they would be able to detect any impending approach in time and be able to melt deeper into the shadows of the fissures that formed between the boulders behind them. If that failed, he had his sword at his side.

They talked in low, earnest whispers—the whispers of those who should not be meeting together, nor as others would righteously insist, should be meeting alone at all. Theirs were quick exchanges of vows and promises, of heartfelt passion and pent-up desire. They used stolen kisses when words failed. Their hands were clasped by the necessity to be always touching. Her blue eyes brimmed with happiness at their time together. Their lips murmured promises while their hearts filled with love.

As if disobeying an unspoken promise of obscurity, the brilliant moonlight momentarily broke through the shroud of covering fog. The silver light of the moon shone down on the two lovers, illuminating them as if they were lone performers on an empty stage. Her unbound waist-length golden blond hair glimmered in that light; the regal golden circlet pressed over her hair shone like a band of fire. His brown shoulder-length hair was tipped by the silver light, his brown eyes lit only by the intense love he felt for the woman held in his arms. Neither paid notice of the play of light being fashioned by the moon. Too intent were they on each other and the gift he had just pressed into her unbelieving hands.

As the moonlight did its magic, the gift glowed and throbbed in the light as if it was a living, breathing thing. She caught the glimmer of this large heart-shaped object, recognizing it to be a beautiful diamond. What else could throw out colors of the rainbow even in the dim light of the moon—expertly cut into a multi-faceted gem? As she held the diamond by its golden setting in her hands, the moonlight caught each facet and flung out reddish blaze like the glowing embers of a well-stoked fire, or the glowing pits of Hades. Surrounding the diamond heart, almost too heavy for its blood-red glow, were circlets of gold. The three golden circles surrounding the diamond had been set by the most cunning of hands. The heart hung from a heavy golden chain that would soon be placed around her fair neck.

Shaking her head, she tried to press the gift back into her lover's hands. "I can't wear that! It's too precious."

But he was insistent. "You must wear it. Think of this gift as my heart that you already possess," he pleaded. "You must remember me until I can come back for you."

"I have no need of jewels to remember you. You are already etched in my heart," was her answer, her eyes flashing the truth of her words.

Smiling at her response, he kissed her fair neck as the moon slid into obscurity once more. "Take my gift. It is a powerful heart," he claimed, smiling at her frowning, dubious look. "'Tis true!" he exclaimed. "'Tis said to come from Merlin's own treasure trove."

"King Arthur's Merlin?" she exclaimed, her eyes still skeptical.

He put a finger against her lips, holding it there. "Shh…Yes, *that* Merlin," he whispered back with a sly smile. He replaced his finger with his lips, issuing an assuring kiss. With a grin on his face, he leaned back as she brought the precious gemstone up by its chain between them, feeling extremely proud of himself.

"What does it do?" she asked, looking at the object in her hand with a curious scrutiny, its fiery radiance now subdued into a blush of red by the gloomy fog.

If rumors are to be believed, he prefaced silently to himself, and then said aloud, "It shows you things. Are you sure you want to see it?"

Her lips smiled and created a little dimple in her cheek. "You mean, like my future? Then the legend must be true because you are my future."

Noticing the dimple, he kissed it. "But we know I cannot stay. Your brothers will kill me until I can prove myself to them."

She gave an unladylike grunt. "My brothers can go…."

Her sharp retort was cut off by the approaching sound of muffled footsteps crunching on the sandy beach in front of them. His fingers again went to her lips to silence her, this time unnecessarily as she was very aware of the footsteps and the clink of armor moving closer and closer to their location. Momentarily using the imminent danger as a distraction, he slipped the golden chain over her head. Knowing their perilous situation, not taking the time to argue, she carefully tucked the diamond into the blue bodice of her dress. The pair pressed back further into the sheltering darkness of the boulders, the shallow niche providing temporary concealment. She slipped the hood of her black cloak over her head, hoping she hadn't been too late in hiding her radiant blond hair.

The intruders were as silent in their approach as they could be on the sand. There was no talking amongst them. They knew where they were going and they knew who was hiding there. They had followed their quarry's tell-tale footsteps in the sand; the two pair of side-by-side depressions that appeared from a path in the dense foliage had betrayed the pair's direction as well as any sign could have done. Beyond the footprints across the beach, just as they had emerged from the forest, the hunters had seen a flash of movement deep within the natural jetty of boulders running from the land out to the sea. Swords already drawn, it was now just a matter of steps. Like a pack of wolves that had trapped their prey, the men picked up their pace, triumphant smiles already on their unshaven faces.

Armed only with his sword pulled silently from its leather sheath, the young man stood resolutely in front of his love. His heart pounded with anticipation. Fear never entered his mind. He would take as many of them as he could before…. He couldn't finish the thought. He would take them all on.

The insulation of the protective fog became their enemy now. They couldn't tell how many were coming or how far away they actually were. He felt her hand on his shoulder, squeezing, encouraging, reassuring, and then, suddenly, the intruders were upon him.

The sword flashed and bit, plunged and parried. The clanging of metal against metal echoed along the rocks. The sounds of the battle were fierce and loud. The sounds from the men, however, were eerily quiet with only a grunt or a moan issuing from their determined mouths. Glints of metal flashed as blade collided on blade and recoiled. A muted blow of one blade evading another and finding flesh, sinking deep; one attacker fell back bleeding at the hip, another eager to take his place in the confines of the boulders. Try as he might, there were too many for him. His sword was straight and true, but it was no match for their many longswords. The woman watched in dread as one skilled attacker, his sword circling in an elaborate flanking move, caught her lover's hand at an awkward angle. His sword was flung to the ground, clanging against the rocks and then silenced in the sand. Disarmed now, the point of an enemy blade aimed at the hollow in his neck, he could only watch in mute fury as his woman was roughly pulled out of the shadow of the boulders behind him. The moon betrayed them and came out of hiding once again as her hood was yanked off of her head. The golden chain, just so recently bestowed on her, glowed and shimmered around her neck, its heavy links parading down the front of her dress. And, at its end, the beautiful diamond heart, framed by the slope of her breasts, radiated its red glow like a crimson beacon. Rough hands followed the chain down the bodice of her dress. With an outraged cry, she bit the hand that was daring to touch her. Her assailant ignored her outburst and the bleeding gash on his hand as he brought out the prize—the encircled red diamond—into the light. He tried to yank it off her neck, but the chain was surprisingly strong. He tried again, but she held her head high and gave no indication of the pain it was causing her.

Sensing his confusion, her quick mind took a chance. "Beware. It is enchanted by Merlin," she whispered. "You cannot harm us."

Within the moonlight, at the sides of her vision, she noticed the point of the blade aimed at her lover's neck wavering with superstition, a sliver of light danced along the blade in its slight tremor. He wisely said nothing, moving a step away from his woman, lest his captor decided to test the theory. Another man standing beyond the group, a bloody hand pressed against his injured hip, forgot his pain as he listened in disbelief and began backing away.

The leader of the assailants looked from the fire of the gemstone to the fire flashing from her blue eyes. There was no fear in those eyes—only hatred and unwavering faith. He had felt his heart suddenly start to pound at her whispered words. Now it was threatening to burst out of his chest as the implication echoed around in his mind. He had heard the rumors, of course, the whispered talk of her brothers in the village. Everyone had heard the rumors. But he had scoffed at their words of warning and had wanted the gem for himself. The brothers had known her lover would give the fabled stone to her; they had been told the stone was in his possession. The leader of this group of marauders had heard of the legend and the power that this stone was said to possess. In his mind, such mystery was a myth. He had only been interested in the wealth the gemstone would bring and the power such wealth would ensure. Now he was not so positive.

In those few moments of hesitation, another sound came to their ears, one that instantly struck fear in all of them. It was a low sound, one they usually heard in the dead of night when they were tucked safe in their beds, covers pulled high to their chins. It filled their ears and rumbled around deep inside their chests causing their hands to shake of their own accord. The growl came again, louder this time, closer. But, closer to which one of them? Who would be the first victim? One by one the assailants slowly turned in full circles where they stood in the sand, swords drawn and ready, aimed low. Another snarl. It seemed to echo around in the swirling fog coming from nowhere and everywhere all at once.

A black blur wove between them faster than their eyes could follow. Ankles were suddenly bleeding; feet were knocked out from under them. Huge paws landed in the middle of the chest of the leader, pushing him; the force knocking him away from the woman and onto his back in the sand. The golden chain broke from around her neck and his fingers tightened around the prize as he fell. As the chain broke, he thought he heard a muttered curse come from the wolf that now stood on top of him, teeth bared, inches away from his unprotected neck, his sword dropped in the suddenness of the attack and out of his reach. As his fingers touched the fiery red surface of the diamond, he forgot the wolf that was hovering over him and the fact that he was now unarmed. His eyes rolled away from the wolf as his mind clouded and whirled, and he could see himself in a different place, inside an opulent castle. The man with him was a king who had raised a sword before him. The sword was held in the position for knighthood. Pride swelled in his chest. But, why was the sword coming so fast?....

Seeing the huge beast pinning their leader, unaware of the vision he was now seeing, his men broke from their defensive positions and ran down the beach towards their frightened horses. In a frenzy of screaming, stamping horses, cursing men and blinding sand, they threw themselves onto the backs of their mounts and plunged away in the opposite direction. Knowing the assailants were now gone and the lovers clasped together with the sword in hand once more, the wolf inexplicably stepped off the leader. His head remained down, teeth bared, front feet wide apart. They recognized the position of attack.

As the vision continued to assail the leader, his hand jerked and the pendant fell into the sand, the gold links of the chain still entwined in his fingers. Once the gemstone broke contact with his hand, his mind instantly cleared and he remembered the black wolf. Shaking his head back and forth he tried to understand what had just happened to him, what he had just seen. Not sure why the animal had let him go, he backed away slowly, the chain still clutched in his white knuckles. He never dropped his eye contact with the wolf. Forgetting his lost sword, he didn't stop backing until he, too, was at his frightened horse. With a curse, he found he had been abandoned by his men. Vaulting into his saddle, he viciously spurred his rearing, snorting horse. Unarmed and knowing how far a wolf that size could jump, he galloped away into the swirling gray of the fog. Only when he was far enough away did his mind begin to function normally again, and he was able to remember those startling blue eyes.

They had been on the golden-haired girl...and, closely matching hers, they were on the black wolf! He tucked the cursed heart into his shirt and rode after his men, all the while his mind still swirling.

As the assailant's departure grew more distant, and his horse's hoof beats faded into the night, the defensive posture of the wolf relaxed. He sat and listened, ears forward, hearing the horse far longer than the two people left behind were able to. Assured the men would not be back, that they had gotten what they had come after, the black wolf turned and faced the couple. Eyes wide with fear, the man and the woman backed away from what had been their savior. Shaking his head slowly side to side, the wolf gave an audible sigh and lay down on the sand, trying to show that they had no reason to fear him. Panting after his exertion, he seemed to be waiting. The couple stopped moving backwards and looked at each other in confusion.

"I don't think he means to harm us," she whispered to the man who still held her protectively in his arms. She noted at the same time the sharp ears of the wolf coming around to her words. "All right," she smiled at the wolf, "I know you can hear me." She crouched down in the sand, her courtly dress settling around her. She waved off the concerned expression on her companion's face. "I think it is all right. Animals always trust me." She held out her elegantly-shaped hand towards the wolf. "I trust you. And I thank you," she told the huge animal.

The wolf got up and walked slowly towards the

outstretched hand. He could see a white line of tension appear around her lips at his movement, but she maintained a level of calm and her hand didn't waver. He could smell mild fear emanate from her, but that was to be expected. He stopped just short of meeting her offered hand and sat again, head up and proud.

Her white front teeth caught her lip as she contemplated her next action. Her hand came cautiously forward and stopped in front of the sharp black nose. When the wolf ignored her movement, she slowly raised it until it was the height of his head. She slowly lowered her hand until it rested on top of the wolf's head between his alert ears. She smiled in delight to be touching a wolf. It was unheard of! She studied the fur she was petting as well as she could in the dim light. The ends of his black hair were tipped in silver. It was coarse on top, but there was a soft under-fur near his skull.

When the wolf had had enough petting and had proven his point, he suddenly stood. His abrupt movement startled the two humans. The man, who had been hovering defenselessly behind her, caught the woman in his arms when she fell back off her heels, his retrieved sword falling to the sand. The wolf ignored them, tilting his head to the sky and letting out a piercing, lingering howl. This was a different sound than before. There was no menace, no warning threat to this sound. It was a haunting, lingering call. The woman was filled with inexplicable sadness as her eyes filled with tears. As the wolf looked pointedly towards the unseen ocean, they turned to look as well. Suddenly a streak of lightning across the sky caught them by surprise. They couldn't help but recall that the day had been fair and there had been no warning of an imminent storm. They realized they could now hear the sound of the roaring sea, no longer was it muffled or stifled from the thick fog that had earlier descended upon them. The ocean now sounded angry, the waves rising, and then almost pausing before thundering down against the shoreline. Expecting to get drenched in the coming rainstorm, the two lovers clung even closer together.

Just then, a bolt of lightning from the sky collided with another flung up from the sea. The blaze of jagged bolts then combined into a bright ball of fire which came hurtling towards them from the epicenter of the explosion.

The wolf stepped down off the boulder jetty onto the fine white sand below, stopping just before the ebb of waves that lapped onto the beach. The orb of shimmering light that had grown out of the sky moved through the air over the water towards them. The bright light ignited the shoreline and then suddenly burst apart, dissipating before them in a dazzling shower of twinkling pink sparks that emanated outward in a widening circle.

"What about the pendant?"

Over the noise of the storm around him, the wolf heard the question. His head suddenly spun towards them as if he had forgotten the gem in the fury of the battle and in the fierceness of the storm. Ears flat, he stared at the pair who was still standing closely together. He then looked in the direction that the leader of the marauders had gone in his flight. His brilliant blue eyes closed as his head shook slowly side to side as if in disbelief.

The couple had confused looks on their face as they watched the wolf hesitate on the edge of the hovering inferno—for it did seem to be waiting. They could see his black lips part and they could clearly hear his disgruntled comment, "Here we go again."

When the last of the sparks died out, the sea was again peaceful and the moon played its silver light across the lapping waves and the sand. It was so lovely it was as if the sea and the moon were apologizing for the moments of terror that had been experienced before. But the couple wasn't looking at the charming scene around them. They stared only at the edge of the lapping waters of the sea.

The mysterious wolf was gone.

The Limited Edition
Red Diamond Heart Hidden Mickey Pendant

Featured in Hidden Mickey novels
IS AVAILABLE AT:
www.HIDDENMICKEYBOOK.com

THANKS AND ACKNOWLEDGEMENTS TO:
KAYE MALINS, CONNIE LANE AND THE REST OF THE
LADIES AT THE WALT DISNEY HOMETOWN MUSEUM
IN MARCELINE, MISSOURI – FOR THEIR
CONTRIBUTIONS TO HISTORICAL RESEARCH
WWW.WALTDISNEYMUSEUM.ORG

AND ALSO TO MY PROOFREADERS AND EDITORS:
JOEY KITZMAN
KARLA GALLAGHER, ENGLISH BA
KIMBERLEE KEELINE, ENGLISH PH.D.
AND JAMES D. KEELINE
WWW.KEELINE.COM

WITH THE POPULARITY OF THE FIRST HIDDEN MICKEY BOOK, "SOMETIMES DEAD MEN DO TELL TALES!" THE HIDDEN MICKEY FAN CLUB WAS FORMED.

FAN CLUB MEMBERS GET A MONTHLY E-MAIL NEWSLETTER CONTAINING BEHIND-THE-SCENES ARTICLES WRITTEN BY VARIOUS PAST AND PRESENT CAST MEMBERS WITHIN THE DISNEY PARKS, AS WELL AS ADVANCE ANNOUNCEMENTS ON FUTURE BOOK SIGNINGS, SPECIAL EVENTS, AND SPECIAL OFFERS. IN ADDITION, FAN CLUB MEMBERS GET SPECIAL PURCHASE OPPORTUNITIES FOR THE NEXT HIDDEN MICKEY SERIES BOOKS AND MERCHANDISE BEFORE THEY ARE RELEASED TO THE PUBLIC.

JOIN THE HIDDEN MICKEY FAN CLUB:
www.HIDDENMICKEYBOOK.COM/fanclub

ALSO AVAILABLE FROM DOUBLE-R BOOKS

FIRST BOOK IN THE HIDDEN MICKEY SERIES
HIDDEN MICKEY: SOMETIMES DEAD MEN DO TELL TALES!
BY NANCY TEMPLE RODRIGUE AND DAVID W. SMITH
IN PAPERBACK AND EBOOK FORMATS

SECOND BOOK IN THE HIDDEN MICKEY SERIES
HIDDEN MICKEY 2: IT ALL STARTED...
BY NANCY TEMPLE RODRIGUE AND DAVID W. SMITH
IN PAPERBACK AND EBOOK FORMATS

COMING SEPTEMBER 2011
HIDDEN MICKEY 5: CHASING NEW FRONTIERS
BY DAVID W. SMITH
READ THE PREVIEW ON THE NEXT PAGE
IN PAPERBACK AND EBOOK FORMATS

COMING IN 2012
BY NANCY TEMPLE RODRIGUE
THE CONTINUATION OF THE STORY OF WOLF!
HIDDEN MICKEY 4 WOLF! HAPPILY EVER AFTER?
IN PAPERBACK AND EBOOK FORMATS